STEFAN HERTMANS

War and Turpentine

Translated from the Dutch by David McKay

VINTAGE

1 3 5 7 9 10 8 6 4 2

Vintage
20 Vauxhall Bridge Road,
London SW1V 2SA

Vintage is part of the Penguin Random House group of companies
whose addresses can be found at global.penguinrandomhouse.com

Penguin
Random House
UK

First published in Vintage in 2017
First published in trade paperback by Harvill Secker in 2016

First published with the title *Oorlog en terpentijn* in
the Netherlands by De Bezige Bij in 2013

www.vintage-books.co.uk

A CIP catalogue record for this book is available from the British Library

ISBN 9780099598046

Published with the support of the Creative
Europe programme of the European Union

The European Commission support for the production of this
publication does not constitute an endorsement of the contents which reflect
the views only of the authors, and the Commission cannot be held responsible
for any use which may be made of the information contained therein

The translation of this book has also been funded by the Flemish Literature
Fund (Vlaams Fonds voor de Letteren – www.flemishliterature.be)

Printed and bound by Clays Ltd, St Ives Plc

Penguin Random House is committed to a sustainable future
for our business, our readers and our planet. This book is made
from Forest Stewardship Council® certified paper.

STEFAN HERTMANS

Stefan Hertmans is the prizewinning author of many literary works, including poetry, novels, essays, plays, short stories and a handbook on the history of art. He has taught at the Royal Academy of Fine Arts in Ghent, at the Sorbonne, the Universities of Vienna, Berlin and Mexico City, at The Library of Congress in Washington, and University College London.

David McKay lives in The Hague and is the proprietor of Open Book Translation. Alongside literary prose and poetry, he also translates writing on art, history, and culture.

For my father

The days are like angels in blue and gold, rising up untouchable above the circle of destruction.

Erich Maria Remarque, *All Quiet on the Western Front*

I

In my most distant memory of my grandfather, he is on the beach at Ostend: a man of sixty-six in a neat midnight-blue suit, he has dug a shallow pit with his grandson's blue shovel and levelled off the heaped sand around it so that he and his wife can sit in relative comfort. He has slightly raised the sandbank behind them for shelter from the August wind, which blows over the receding line of waves and out to sea under high wisps of haze. They have removed their shoes and socks and are gently wiggling their toes as they sit, enjoying the cool damp of the deeper sand – an activity that struck me, at the age of six, as uncharacteristically frivolous for this couple always dressed in grey, dark blue or black. Even on the beach and despite the heat, my grandfather keeps his black fedora on his nearly bald head; he is wearing his spotless white shirt and, as always, a black bow tie, a large one, larger than bow ties normally are, with two ends dangling over his chest, making it look from a distance as though his neck were adorned with the silhouette of a black angel spreading its wings. My mother made his peculiar bow ties according to his instructions, and in all his long life I never saw him without one of those black ties with tails like a dress coat; he must have owned dozens. There's one here somewhere among my books, a relic of a far, forgotten age.

After half an hour, he made up his mind to take off his jacket. Then he removed his gold cufflinks and put them in his left pocket. Next, he went so far as to roll up his shirtsleeves, or rather, he

3

carefully folded them over, twice, to a point just under his elbow, each fold exactly the width of the starched cuff, and now he sits with his neatly folded jacket draped over his arm, its silk lining gleaming in the afternoon light, as if he is posing for an Impressionist portrait. His gaze seems to wander over the distant crowd, losing its way among the shrieking, splashing children, the shouting, laughing day-trippers chasing after each other as if they were children again. What he sees is something like a James Ensor painting set in motion, although he despises the work of that Ostend blasphemer with the English name. Ensor is a 'dauber', and along with 'toss-pot' and 'riff-raff', 'dauber' is the worst accusation he can make. They're all daubers, today's painters; they've completely lost touch with the classical tradition, the subtle, noble craft of the old masters. They muddle along with no respect for the laws of anatomy, don't even know how to glaze, never mix their own paint, use turpentine like water, and are ignorant of the secrets of grinding your own pigments, of fine linseed oil and the blowing of siccatives – no wonder there are no more great painters.

The wind is growing colder now. He retrieves his cufflinks from his pocket, rolls down his sleeves, neatly fastens his cuffs, puts on his jacket, and tenderly drapes his wife's black lace mantilla over her shoulders and over the lustrous knot in her dark grey hair. Come, Gabrielle, he says, and they stand, pick up their shoes, and with some effort begin the ascent to the promenade, he with the legs of his trousers rolled up six inches or so, she with her long black socks stuffed into her shoes. Under their dark forms, I see their four white calves swinging, slow and measured, over the sand. They make their way to the bluestone steps that lead to the promenade, where they will sit down on the nearest bench, brush and pat off the sand until their feet are thoroughly clean, pull their black socks over their alabaster feet, and tie their shoes with what they call drawstrings instead of laces.

As for me, after the collapse of the warren of tunnels that I dug for my large stone marbles – my treasured 'taws' – I run shivering to my mother. The tide is rising again, she says, rubbing the warmth back into me as the first puffy clouds form over the dunes behind us. The wind sweeps over the dune tops, as if to muss their grassy hair, and those large, sand-coloured creatures brace themselves for the night ahead.

My grandfather, his gleaming cane of varnished elm wood already in his hand, is waiting restlessly for us to reach the promenade. Then he takes the lead; he is not a tall man – five foot six, I often hear him say – but wherever he goes, people make way. With his head erect, his black boots polished to perfection, a sharp crease in his trousers, arm in arm with his unspeaking wife and his cane in the other hand, he strides out ahead of us with slight impatience, glancing back now and then and calling out that we'll miss our train if we don't pick up the pace. He walks like a retired soldier, which is to say not pounding his heels oafishly into the ground, but always landing on the ball of the foot, as a soldier should, the habit of more than half a century. Then he somehow slips out of view in my memory, and overcome by the sudden radiant clarity of this scene from all those years ago, I'm so tired I could fall asleep on the spot.

Without any transition, the next image I have of him is that of a man silently weeping. He is seated at the small table where he painted and wrote, in his grey smock, his black hat on his head. The yellow light of morning shines through the small, vine-framed window; in his hands I see one of the many reproductions he tore out of art books and used to practise copying (pinning the reproduction to a board that he attached to his palette with two wooden pegs). He holds the picture in his hands; I cannot see what it is, but I see that tears are running down his cheeks and he is silently mouthing words. I climbed the three stairs to my grandfather's room to tell him about the rat skeleton I'd found; now I quickly, quietly back away, my steps muffled by the carpet on the stairs, and close his door behind me. But later, while he's downstairs having coffee, I slip back up to the room and find the picture on his table. It is a painting of a nude woman with her back to the viewer, a slender woman with dark hair, lying on some kind of sofa or bed in front of a red curtain. Her serene, dreamy expression is visible in a mirror held up for her by a cherub with a blue ribbon over his shoulder; her bare, slender back and round buttocks are prominent. My eyes drift to her frail shoulders, the delicate hair curling around her neck, and then back to her derriere, which is thrust almost obscenely towards the viewer. Shocked, I put down the reproduction, I go downstairs, there is my grandfather in the kitchen, beside my mother, singing a French tune he remembers from the war.

My childhood years were overrun with his tales of the First World War, always the war and nothing but the war, vague heroics in muddy fields under a rain of bombs, the rat-a-tat of gunfire, phantoms screaming in the dark, orders roared in French – all conjured up from his rocking chair with great feeling for spectacle – and always barbed wire, shrapnel whizzing past our ears, sub-machine guns rattling, flares tracing high arcs across the dark heavens, mortars and howitzers firing, billions of blistering bombs in ten thousand thundering trenches, while the tea-sipping aunties nodded beatifically and about the only thing that stuck with me was that my grandfather must have been a hero in days as distant as the Middle Ages I'd heard about in school. To me, he was still a hero; he gave me fencing lessons, sharpened my pocket knife, taught me how to draw clouds by rubbing an eraser over shapes sketched with a piece of charred wood from the fireplace, and how to render the myriad leaves of a tree without drawing each one separately – the true secret of art, as he called it.

Stories were meant to be forgotten, since after all, they always came back again, even the strangest stories of art and artists. I knew that old Beethoven had worked on his ninth symphony like a man possessed because he was deaf, but one day a disturbing detail was added: he didn't even go to the trouble of visiting the toilet while he was working, instead he did 'his business' by the piano. Consequently – and I quote – 'the man who wrote that lovely song about all men becoming brothers did his composing next to a heap of dung'. I imagined the great composer, deaf as a post, seated in a Viennese interior with the capitals of the columns painted gold, wearing his luxuriant wig, gaiters and galoshes, next to a towering pyramid of excrement, and whenever the miraculous adagio from the *Pastoral Symphony* drifted through the house on one of those long dreary Sunday afternoons, while my parents and grandparents nodded off on the brown floral sofa by the radio, I would picture a mountain of crap next to a glossy lacquered spinet as a cuckoo from the Wienerwald warbled along with the woodwinds and violins and my grandfather kept his eyes tightly closed. He was a firm believer in romantic genius; his reverence for it ran so deep that he could not face the mundane world of his home and family at such exalted moments. Not until many years later did it dawn on me that he himself had spent about a year and a half next to a real dung heap in the miserable trenches, where as soon as you put your head above the parapet in search of a better place to do your business, you were punished with a bullet through the brain. Thus the things he wished to forget kept coming back, in shards of stories or absurd details, and whether hell or heaven was the subject, shards and details like these were the puzzle pieces I had to fit together before I could begin to understand what had gone on inside him all his life: the battle between the transcendent, which he yearned for, and the memory of death and destruction, which held him in its clutches.

At home, my grandfather invariably wore a smock – always the same short white or light grey garment, the length of an old-fashioned dressing gown – over his white shirt and bow tie. No matter how my mother and her mother washed and boiled those old cotton smocks, which he wore with a certain flair, they remained mottled with stains: scattered swipes of oil paint in all the colours of the rainbow, criss-crossing fingerprints, a composition of careless, intriguing smears, the raffish graffiti left there after the real work.

That real work, which he had carried out uninterrupted since his early retirement as a disabled veteran at the age of forty-five, was painting for pleasure. The small room where he stood in front of the small window day in and day out smelled of linseed oil, turpentine, linen, oil paint. Yes, even the odour of the large erasers, cut down to size with a knife, could be detected in the irreproducible mixture that gave the room its ambience, the glamour of the endless hours he passed in silence, zealously yet fruitlessly emulating the great masters. He was a superb copyist and knew all the secrets of the old materials and recipes that painters had used and passed down since the Renaissance. After the war he had taken evening classes in drawing and painting in his home city of Ghent, despite all the times his late father, a painter of frescoes in churches and chapels, had warned him against it. Although he was still doing heavy manual labour at the time, he pressed on, and just after reaching the usual marrying age, he earned a 'certificate of competence in fine-art painting and anatomical drawing'.

From his window he could see a bend in the Scheldt river, the slow cows in their pastures, the heavily laden barges chugging past low in the water in the morning, the faster-moving empty riverboats leaving the city with a shallow draught at day's end. Countless times he painted that view, each time in a different light with a new set of hues; another time of day, another season, another mood. He painted each leaf of the red creeper from nature – apparently, art sometimes demanded exceptions to its great law of illusion – and when he copied a detail of a Titian or Rubens, he knew himself to be practised in patience, in sketching accurately with charcoal or graphite, in the secrets of mixing colours and thinning pigments, and in waiting just long enough for the first layer to dry before adding a second, which gave the impression of depth and transparency – another of the many great secrets of art.

His grand passions were treetops, clouds and folds in fabric. In these formless forms he could let go, lose himself in a dream world of light and dark, in clouds congealed in oil paint, chiaroscuro, a world where nobody else could intrude, because something – it was hard to say what – had broken inside him. His warmth and generosity were always tinged with shyness, as if he were afraid that people would come too close because he had been too friendly. At the same time, he exuded a higher, nobler strain of friendly guilelessness, and that naivety was at the core of his good humour. His marriage to Gabrielle seemed idyllic, if you didn't know better. Intertwined like two old trees forced to extend their branches through each other's crowns for decades in their struggle for scarce sunlight, they passed their simple days, which were punctuated solely by the frivolous-seeming gaiety of their daughter, their only child. Days vanished into the folds of distracted time. He painted.

The room that served as his studio, three steps up from the small landing, was also their bedroom; it is hard to believe how unremarkable it once was to live in cramped quarters. The bed was by the wall behind his small, makeshift desk, so that his wife would have something to lean against in her sleep – she slept far away from him despite their narrow bed. Clouds and folds in fabric; treetops and water. The finest paintings in his staunchly traditional body of work each contain a few shapeless smudges, strange abstract masses that he regarded as tokens of fidelity to nature, as if he were painting from the model that God laid out before his eyes and bade him unfurl in the meticulous patience of his daily work as a lowly copyist. But it was also a tribute he dutifully paid, his way of mourning the untimely death of his father, the lowly church painter Franciscus.

For more than thirty years I kept, and never opened, the notebooks in which he had set down his memories in his matchless pre-war handwriting; he had given them to me a few months before his death in 1981, at the age of ninety. He was born in 1891. It was as if his life were no more than two digits playing leapfrog. Between those two dates lay two world wars, catastrophic genocides, the most ruthless century in all human history, the emergence and decline of modern art, the global expansion of the automotive industry, the Cold War, the rise and fall of the great ideologies, the popularization of the telephone and saxophone, the synthesis of Bakelite, industrialization, the film industry, jazz, the aviation industry, the moon landing, the extinction of countless species of animals, the first major environmental disasters, the development of penicillin and antibiotics, May '68, the first Club of Rome report, rock 'n' roll, the invention of the Pill, women's lib, the rise of television and the first computers – and his long life as a forgotten war hero. This is the life he asked me to describe by entrusting his notebooks to me. A life that spanned nearly a century and began on a different planet. A planet of villages, cart roads, horse-drawn carriages, gaslights, washtubs, devotional prints, old-fashioned cupboards, a time when women were elderly at forty, a time of all-powerful priests who smelled of cigars and unwashed underwear, of rebellious bourgeois girls in nunneries, a time of major seminaries, of episcopal and imperial decrees, a time that began its long death throes when the small, grimy Serb Gavrilo Princip sent the enchanting illusion of Old Europe crashing to pieces with one not-even-that-well-aimed shot, ushering in the calamity that would engulf the world and with it my short, blue-eyed grandfather, determining the course of his life for ever.

I had resolved not to read his memoirs until I had plenty of time for them, in the belief that the experience would fill me with the overpowering urge to write his life story – in other words, I felt I would need to be free, with nothing else to devote myself to but him. But the years slipped by, and the time approached when the inevitable hundredth anniversary of the cataclysm would release a flood of books – a new barrage alongside the almost unscalable mountain of existing historical material, books as innumerable as the sandbags on the Yser front, thoroughly documented, historically accurate, made-up novels and stories – while I held the privilege of his memoirs but was too scared to open them, didn't even dare to open the first page, in the knowledge that this story would be a farewell to a piece of my child-hood; this story, which, if I didn't hurry, would be published just when readers turned away with a yawn from yet another book on the blasted First World War. I left the notebooks closed, even though I knew that this exceptionally rich and detailed account belonged in a First World War archive – knew, in other words, that my scandalous indolence was actually keeping a vivid eyewitness narrative out of the public domain. At this thought, I felt a fear of failure descend on me, making it even harder to move forward. And when I called to mind some of the stories I had once heard him tell and began to understand their true meaning and import for the first time, a feeling of power-lessness and guilt washed over me. Again I wasted precious years, diligently working on countless other projects and keeping a safe distance from his notebooks: those silent, patient witnesses that enclosed his painstaking, graceful pre-war handwriting like a humble shrine.

But during those years of stalling and suppressed guilt, something came to light that only seemed to make the matter more urgent. My uncle, having come by to help my father replace a few rotting boards in the old parquet floor of the front room, found, in the dust at the darkest end of the crawl space below, a gravestone. He called to my father to join him, and the two men crept over to the stone on their hands and knees, lighting their way with a torch. It was the grave-stone of my grandfather's mother. I heard my father say, Well, I'll be damned. So that's where he hid it! They dragged the heavy stone to the trapdoor and lifted it out. Even then, I didn't fully understand

the situation. My grandfather had died some ten years earlier, and I couldn't see why anyone would hide a gravestone in the furthest corner of a crawl space, in the apparent conviction that it would never see the light of day again. Years later, I noticed that my father had mounted the stone on an ivy-covered wall of the garden with heavy metal brackets, about three feet from the ground, behind the old garage where he used to park his car. For the first time, I read the inscription carefully:

PRAY FOR THE SOUL OF
CELINA ANDRIES
B. 9 AUG. 1868
D. 20 SEPT. 1931
WIDOW OF
FRANCISCUS MARTIEN
WIFE OF
HENRI DE PAUW

Two notebooks lie before me. The first is small and thick; the edges of the pages are stained red. Its cover is light-grey linen, as if it had been fitted with a pre-war tweed jacket. The second one is larger, almost the size of a modern legal pad, and has an old-fashioned marbled cardboard cover, a bit like the faux marbling he loved to paint on walls. In the first notebook, he recorded his memories of growing up poor in Ghent and some of his experiences in the First World War.

He was seventy-two when he started using the notebook – the date is 20 May 1963 – possibly so that he could go on telling the story of how his life had been deformed, since his family and relatives had grown tired of his anecdotes and would cut him off, saying, I've heard that one often enough, or I'm tired, I'm off to bed, or I have to go now. His wife Gabrielle had died five years earlier; somehow, through the act of writing, he completed his period of mourning. His firm handwriting hardly evolves in this first notebook. Usually writing in midnight-blue ink, he strings his stories together cheerfully, with a flood of memories from his days in a grey provincial town – I can still picture his Waterman fountain pens on the small, nineteenth-century dressing table that he'd painted in fanciful woodgrain patterns in the hope of making it look a bit antique. The original marble tabletop must have cracked; the clumsily attached wooden replacement is slightly too small. He wrote at this small dressing table for years, even though it was too high and he sat uncomfortably. The table, with its simple drawer smeared with colourful streaks of oil paint, is here behind me in the room where I am writing; I still keep the two notebooks in it. The second notebook, which he started because he regretted having described the humiliating poverty of his childhood in such copious detail, opens by explaining that he had put too many personal anecdotes into his first notebook and would have to start afresh, this time confining himself to his memories of the war. Besides, he had come to the end of the first notebook after only six months.

He writes, *My war diary is more than half filled with tedious stories of childhood and scores of irrelevant pages. Now I shall write only about the war, truly and sincerely, not to glorify it. So help me God. Only my experiences. My* <u>*horror.*</u>

So he summarized a number of stories he'd already told, adding fresh details here and there, and went on until 1919. The second notebook contains some of the traumatic scenes on the Yser, the particulars of his wounds, his recovery periods in England, and the discovery of the fresco in Liverpool that meant so much to him. After the year he was shot for the second time, he becomes more terse, because the descriptions of his squalid life in the trenches can only be repeated so many times, the scenes of killing rats with your bare hands and roasting them over a fire in the night, the cries of wounded comrades, fumbling with rolls of barbed wire in the mud as your hands bleed, the rattle of machine-gun fire, the bursting of shrapnel shells, and the eruptions of soil and torn-up limbs. But he lingered over his third stay in England – in Windermere, in the Lake District. In the final pages of this second notebook, when he comes to the personal tragedy he experienced a year after the war, during the Spanish flu epidemic of 1919, his handwriting disintegrates. Yet despite this loss of discipline, his tone as a narrator remains surprisingly reserved. The lines in this section cross the page diagonally, teetering to the left and to the right; sometimes he returns to his old, regular script, and sometimes it all goes reeling. He must have been well into his eighties by the time he laboriously scrawled the final pages. By that stage he was writing with ballpoint pens in different colours, and his eyesight had greatly deteriorated – as far as I'm aware, he never bought a new pair of glasses in the decades that I knew him, and he may hardly have been able to see the page he was agonizing over. Seventeen years of work on six hundred manuscript pages in total. His memory was still so clear and retained so many details that I believe some form of post-traumatic clarity must have been at work; the details in the second notebook, laid beside the first one, show that he descended ever deeper into the trenches of recollection. All his life, he could not escape those details, not the fluttering leaf at nightfall just before he yet again stared death in the face, nor the image of his dead comrades, the smell of the mud, the mild wind over the blasted countryside in the first days of spring, the scraps of a blown-up horse in a bullet-riddled hedge. On the last page, there is a stain where liquid seems to have soaked through the paper; on one side of the gap is the word *night*, on the other the word *panic*.

I gave myself time to absorb what I had read and then began numbering the pages and noting the scenes where the first and second notebooks overlapped. It took me almost a year to type up his memoirs, and in the process I gained insight into how the many events and suppressed stories were interrelated. It was taxing work: on the one hand, I was at a disadvantage, because I could not reproduce his combination of old-fashioned grace, awkwardness and authenticity without falling into mannerism; and on the other hand, when I adapted his long-winded narrative into a modern-day idiom, I felt as if I were betraying him. Even correcting the often endearing errors in his writing filled me with a vague sense of guilt. This task confronted me with the painful truth behind any literary work: I first had to recover from the authentic story, to let it go, before I could rediscover it in my own way. But time pressed harder than ever, and somewhere in my head the idea had lodged that I must finish the job before the centenary of the Great War, *his* war. My struggle with his memories.

Like a clerk, I ploughed through the hundreds of handwritten pages, cursing my own mediocre style, the result of my equivocal attempt to remain faithful to him while nevertheless translating his tale into my own experience. Then I compiled an index of scenes and key words, made a list of the places I needed to visit, had the notebooks copied for fear they might be lost, and locked them away in a fireproof safety deposit box. I spoke with the few remaining survivors, who could tell me just a few uncertain details. I asked my father, his son-in-law, who by this time was living alone in the house on the riverbank, to write down everything he could recall; still clear-headed and energetic in his nineties, he helped me find the glue I needed to put the fragments together, to take the apocryphal versions that my grandfather had cheerfully strewn about for decades, hold them up against the versions in the notebooks, and learn to see everything in truer proportions.

When I look at the old dressing table here behind me, I see a small, stocky figure who exudes an unparalleled intensity. His bright blue eyes still twinkle, more than thirty years after his death, under a scalp wreathed in thin white hair, a bit like that famous photograph of the aged Arthur Schopenhauer: tough, outsized personalities that could no longer exist, we tell ourselves, because life has lost the spartan sobriety that allowed their temperaments to ripen and flourish. I can still hear his booming voice, his infectious crescendos, the tessitura of his stories, but no longer the specific words or sentences. There are the scents that clung to him: the smells of an old-fashioned painter, and something undefined, *his* scent, his one-time physical presence in the world, distant from the moment when I write this. Now that he has receded in time like the figures in ancient myths and stories, he has become tangible in an entirely new manner, in the way of an intimate history. And when I search for traces of his life, and am usually thrown back on my own devices because almost everything has vanished, I wonder, time and again, what it is that connects us to our grandparents in this ambivalent way. Is it the absence of the generational conflict between parents and children? In the yawning gap between our grandparents and ourselves, the battle for our imagined individuality is waged, and the separation in time permits us to cherish the illusion that a greater truth lies concealed there than in what we know of our own parents. It is a great and powerful naivety that makes us thirst for knowledge.

Strange as it may seem, there were details of my own world that never offered up their historical secrets until I read his memoirs: a gold pocket watch shattering on the tile floor; an oval cigarette from a silver case, smoked in secret, which made me nauseous when I was fifteen years old; a worn reddish-brown scarf on one of the discarded cupboards in the dilapidated greenhouse, covered with the thin droppings of the disoriented blackbirds that would throw themselves against the glass in panic until by chance they escaped through the open vent; a little old-fashioned shaving kit, silver in colour, giving off the penetrating odour of alum and antiquated soap; a folder from Liverpool unfolded and refolded so often it had torn along the creases; the small metal box containing his medals and decorations, which I did not find until years after his death; the brass casing of a heavy shell, which he kept on the newel post and carefully polished every week, and which I had mistaken throughout my childhood for some kind of squat vase for flowers.

Time gradually unravelled my grandfather's secret for me – the story of his long life, most of which had been a mere epilogue to his practically medieval childhood, the horrors that filled his young manhood, and the true love he found and lost after the war. It was a story of dogged resignation, excruciating forbearance, childish daring, inner struggle between devotion and desire, endless murmured prayers as he kneeled with his hat on the pew beside him, his white-wreathed head bowed before countless figures of saints and flickering candles in shadowy houses of worship – the passionate inner life of a world that appeared on the surface to be anything but stirring.

I roam the streets of the city where I was born, which I see through very different eyes now that I've lived elsewhere for more than a decade. It's a cool spring day with clouds of the kind he liked to draw. The old façade of the bicycle shop where I got my first red bicycle is still there, but the letters have faded. Bourgeois houses stand in a forlorn row along an asphalt road that has little to do with the life of ease for which they were designed and built. It starts to drizzle; queues of cars crawl down Heirnislaan. It must have been close by, the lightless alley where he spent his early childhood, with railway sidings on one side and a canal on the other. These days Heirnislaan is part of the city's ring road; back then, it was an elegant avenue, shaded by dense foliage in the summer, when the 'young ladies of the *haute bourgeoisie*', as he respectfully called them, would titter as they peered through the windows of their light calèches at the ashen-faced guttersnipes who showed up on Sunday afternoons to gape at them. On misty winter mornings, he crossed Heirnislaan in his clogs, like the young hero of a Dickens story, toting a large bucket, on his way to beg coal from the jet-black men who loaded the tenders of the locomotives behind Dampoort railway station. Back at home, he'd set down the heavy bucket behind the coal stove, where his mother, when she returned exhausted from working for a bourgeois family in some other part of town, would be delighted to see that they could heat the house and eat a cooked meal that evening. Then he'd skip straight off to school, where he would be scolded for tardiness. His sisters made fun of him because he struggled to keep up in mathematics and languages. Somewhere along the side of the railway line, on a slope overgrown with butterfly bushes and elder, he had once planted a grain of maize, coming back every day to give the young shoot water from a dented bowl, until he found it snapped and torn off – a scene he describes with the gloomy reflection that 'bit by bit, our family was left isolated in that alley'.

I pass the uninspired apartment buildings where the Ghent livestock market once stood; the memory of the place lives on in me like a potent smell. The old livestock market was a covered hall with regularly spaced iron pillars beside which stomping bulls tugged at their chains, their eyes bloodshot, saliva dripping from their mouths. Watery blood flowed through the trampled straw under the cutting tables, and the formless, light pink mounds of stacked lungs seemed slippery with life. The hearts lay piled next to the tongues, the heads were sold by weight, and the eyes that watched you from the copper pan of the 'steelyard' (my grandfather used the old word for the butchers' scales) seemed to gaze, meditative and glassy, from beyond the borders of death, which was all around, a death closer to the heart of life than anything I, innocent of war, have ever experienced. I expect that thoughts of this old livestock market sometimes leaped to mind, unbidden and revolting, when he witnessed the slaughter along the banks of the Yser, thoughts of innards poking out, of borders transgressed – the borders within which life should be safe from the grasping claws of death. The mix of panic and resignation in the eyes of the sheep waiting to be slaughtered was blithely overlooked by the sellers. It was a placid time in a provincial town around 1900; everything had its place; that penniless ragamuffin, my grandfather, strolled from table to table, knowing that if he could show a touch of childish sadness in his deep blue eyes, sooner or later they were bound to toss him something: a few ounces of blood pudding, a sloppily boned rib still good for soup, or a scrap of stringy meat to

boil for broth. Later, when the two of us were looking at art repro-ductions and came to Rembrandt's slaughtered ox, he said, 'He painted this one so well you can smell the livestock market.'

His mother, Céline Andries, had had the privilege of going to secondary school, he writes. Her parents – grain and potato merchants, like his future in-laws – had sent their daughter to Piers de Raveschoot, a chic private school for girls, which in the nineteenth century was affordable only to the wealthy elite. She spoke not only Dutch but also French and English, she could recite poems by Prudens Van Duyse from memory, and she read Hendrik Conscience's *The Lion of Flanders*, which won her over to the Flemish Movement. During her studies, she had spent time 'in service', as a housemaid for an aristocratic family in the Potter de Veldewijk, an outlying neighbourhood of Antwerp. There she had become acquainted with the lifestyle of the upper classes and acquired an air of dignified reserve, which she never lost. She must have been a woman of exceptionally strong character; my grandfather's admiration for her was utter and absolute. In his memoirs, he writes of her with a mixture of detached love and warm affection.

His father, Franciscus Martien, was a 'church painter', a talented lower-class youth Céline had met one day when she entered her parish church and inadvertently walked into his ladder, almost knocking down the lowly painter, who had just been restoring the fourth Station of the Cross. Before I read the notebooks, it had always been a mystery to me how they could have met, and though my grandfather shrugged off my questions with a laugh, he wrote down the story with love. When she accidentally bumped into his ladder, something must have fallen off the top, just missing her: a brush, a palette knife, one of the tools he hung from his belt – it's not clear. It clattered on the stone floor of the empty church; the young woman looked up and saw the startled man about to lose his balance; the ladder tilted away from the wall for an instant, forcing him to throw his weight against it as quickly as he could to keep from plummeting. A smile crept over her stern face, and she walked on. She sat and prayed next to the two candles burning for the Blessed Virgin and later said it was as if those two small flames were their souls quietly burning side by side. An encounter between a scruffy young man and a statuesque young woman in an empty, silent church – in their day, it was not often that young people met without chaperones. He looked down, saw the black lace mantilla draped over her long, straight shoulders, descended the ladder, and waited for her, shyly and awkwardly, at the gate. She shot him a brief glance as she brushed past him: ironic, light grey eyes, as if she were pouring clear, cold water over his soul. Light grey eyes, but black hair – that must have caught his attention as a painter; it's a rare combination, a category of beauty, my grandfather liked to say in later years, and he knew what he was talking about.

The encounter left Franciscus reeling – for weeks, he awaited the return of the dark apparition in vain, becoming desperate, feverish and ill. He stayed home from work for a few days, until the curate came to inform his parents that Franciscus would lose his job if he did not go back. When Céline finally reappeared, on an ordinary weekday when most people have no time to go to church, he knew she had come for him. Reading between the lines of my grandfather's story, it's obvious this must have sent her family into an uproar. They would not have embraced the idea of their well-bred daughter going about with a pauper. But that proud young woman had evidently lost her heart to the dishevelled, romantic artist, to his thin, El Greco-like face, to his bony, paint-stained hands and the way he looked when he walked, hunched and thin, yet boyish. Her wealthy merchant family had unwittingly reproduced the dynamic seen over and over throughout history: when the farmer grows rich, he gives his children a middle-class education and exposes them to culture, and as a result they reject his material obsessions and turn to higher things. It took months of quarrelling with her parents before she won their consent to the marriage. She had threatened to take off, enter a convent, run away to God knows where; she had shut herself in her room, made their lives miserable, and secretly thought, I want him, my blue-eyed church painter, I want him, and I shall have him. Even for a devout potato merchant, the thought of his beautiful daughter vanishing into a nunnery was too much to bear. So her parents finally gave in; the proud, well-bred Céline got her penniless painter.

He came with all sorts of strings attached: a life of poverty, money troubles, Franciscus's poor health, his nightly coughing fits and asthma attacks, the damp in their run-down house, the cramped rooms where they passed their days, the hunger and endless bawling and snivelling of five urchins in a row. And she doted on her husband as if he were her sixth child. 'Oh, my dear sweet painter,' she would say to him, shaking her head, when she wanted to poke gentle fun at him. And he adored her – the knot in her lustrous hair, her throat, her straight shoulders, the gracefully curving joints of her wrists, the perfect shape of her fingernails, the strange pale glow she gave off when she spoke.

The proud Céline's new life was filled with toil and painful sacrifices to make ends meet. She was always dressed in black; like her husband and children, she wore ordinary clogs, because the tall, stylish boots she had worn in her parents' home stood out beside the rest of her family and the other residents of the alley. So she buried them deep in the old cupboard and tottered around on hollowed-out blocks of wood like everyone else. To contribute to the family budget, she took all sorts of odd jobs. For a while, she mended clothes for the better families, until her old treadle sewing machine broke down and she couldn't afford a new one. She composed letters for her illiterate neighbours when they had to reply to official correspondence, write to a family member or request legal assistance – in those days, such letters had to be written in French, never in Dutch. When her husband was ill at home for weeks on end, she did charity work with the nuns from the convent to stay in their good books so that he wouldn't lose his job; she raised her five children as properly and decently as she could.

My grandfather, who was second in line, was soon followed by two little brothers and a sister. For a while, Céline cleaned the house of a French-speaking family in the centre of town, and the little money she earned seemed to slip through her fingers like water. At the same time, their house was becoming overcrowded, but they weren't able to start looking for a larger one till spring, when her husband regained some of his strength, and of course their new home, once they found it, was in worse repair, since they could not afford to pay any more rent. For some time, Franciscus worked in a monastery for the Brothers of Charity, who uncharitably paid him starvation wages to repaint their entire refectory. Even so, the family remained devout and strictly loyal to the Church. The priest paid regular visits, listened to Céline's tales of drudgery and domestic crisis, and sent a few students a couple of days later with scraps from his well-spread table.

Franciscus fixed up the damp old house as best he could, replacing crumbling putty and broken door frames, reinforcing mouldering beams, and repairing the rotten steps of the cellar staircase. Their new neighbourhood, around Oostakkerstraat in Sint-Amandsberg, was more to their liking; in the summer they could see a few fields over the low garden wall, and a little further away there were wild flowers in bloom along a canal. They could put a goat out to pasture there, so that the children could at least drink milk regularly and they could make their own fresh cheese. In the evening, in his narrow bed in the packed children's room upstairs, my grandfather could hear his parents talking in the old kitchen, his father's low rumble alternating with his mother's soft replies, the call and response of a large bluebottle and a turtle dove, lulling him peacefully to sleep. It was a marriage, he wrote, based on 'deep and genuine love, and when my mother stroked her coughing husband's thin cheeks, she would sometimes call him "my down-and-out darling", and her light grey eyes would grow moist'.

Their son Urbain Martien, named after Céline's grandfather, was the kind of lad who stole everybody's heart. He was solidly built, with long, curly hair, sturdy hands, and guileless blue eyes. Waddling after his statuesque mother like a duckling, entertaining her with his whimsical ways and irrepressible urges to cuddle and play the fool, he would dance in his clogs or walk around the washhouse with his tin cup, secretly drinking the soapy water in which his own dirty underwear was soaking. During Sunday car trips six decades later, still happy as a child in his old age, he could stare at the perfection of a Boeing gliding through the air high overhead and say it was all so beautiful, everything he saw in the world. His *joie de vivre* had sprouted in the darkest soil – he says plenty about that in his memoirs. Urbain Martien, predestined for everything and for nothing (because he had many indefinable talents, his mother once said, laughing). Urbain was a hardy survivor, but sensitive and sentimental. Standing in the sun on an Easter Sunday morning at the age of seventy, he could blurt out with tears in his eyes that the blue of the flowering irises in the backyard was so unfathomably deep around their bright yellow hearts that it gave him palpitations — something like that — and it was a shame a person had to die without ever understanding how such things came to be.

When it was explained to him as a seven-year-old in catechism classes that you simply could not see God — not even on a cloudless day — because God was invisible, and on top of that, even on clear nights you couldn't look past the stars to the place where He reportedly dwelled, and accordingly, faith could not be verified, because then it would no longer be faith, he broke in: 'Yes, but, Reverend Father, then you might just as well say that there are millions of sea horses floating around in Heaven, since nobody can see it anyway.' The astonished priest's jaw dropped open as if the hinge had snapped. Those sea horses, drifting through dark and infinite space, between the stars, sometimes light years apart, have never left my imagination, and they still come floating by, numberless hosts of them in sublime silence, whenever I hear talk of proving God's existence. Yet Urbain Martien was a man of faith, and more than that; after returning from the Great War, he began to show signs of religious mania. He got up at five thirty twice a week to attend the early mass, shuffled through ice and snow to church in his spotlessly polished boots on days when even the priest could not be bothered, sat in the cool silence of the parish church in summer as the rosary beads slipped through his fingers and his lips moved slightly, murmuring Latin prayers. He lit candles for Our Lady of the Seven Sorrows and went to confession once a week with bowed head, he who seemed too pure of heart for the mildest of venial sins.

The world he grew up in before 1900 was full of smells that now have largely disappeared. A tannery gave off its tenacious stench in the thin September mist; the tenders with their loads of raw coal pulled in and out of the station in the dark winter months; the odour of horse droppings in the streets in the early-morning hours could create the illusion, for the half-slumbering boy by the draughty window, that he was in the countryside somewhere, as could the smell of hay, herbs and grass that still pervaded the city. The penetrating odour of old wood and damp sackcloth prevailed in the dimly lit shops where salt, sugar, flour and beans were still sold *en vrac*, in bulk, scooped into sacks and canisters brought by the women who shopped there. The closed courtyards smelled of Brussels sprout trimmings, horse manure scraped off the streets and drying tobacco leaves. Describing his own grandmother, born in the first quarter of the nineteenth century, he said that her black apron – he called it a pinafore – smelled like the offal of young rabbits.

As a white-haired elder surrounded by an admiring circle of my aunties and cousins, he could spend hours lost in the particulars of that life in the last decade of the nineteenth century, his childhood years wrapped in the sulphurous fumes of early factories, the memory of the street hawkers' cries, the slam of the thin wooden door of the public toilet at the end of the alley beside an ivy-covered wall that smelled of urine and nettles. The everyday dreariness of the first wave of industrialization had thoroughly shaped the contours of his thinking, although he also began early in life, after leafing through the few books his father owned, to dream of the colour palette of Tintoretto and Van Dyck.

It's the spring of 2012. I've been to London with my son for a few days, not only to show him the original model for his beloved city of New York, but also in the interest of male bonding: the connection a father must renew every now and then with his fifteen-year-old son to overcome all the discord of an upbringing. I don't want to club him to death with culture, so we stroll through Covent

Garden, have a bite at Carluccio's, drink pints of bitter in a wood-panelled pub, and hash out our differences in an amicable tone, later roaming along the South Bank at night, hopping from one Tube line to the other, and enjoying ourselves immensely.

Still, the next day I want to show him a museum or two, carefully dosed so as not to alienate him, because I know that despite the distrust of everything highbrow inspired by his ever-flickering iPhone, he is susceptible to painting. He was only eight when he squatted in front of the portrait of a young sixteenth-century man in Venice and said, Papa, come sit with me, this is so beautiful. So as we stroll through the airy rooms of the National Gallery, I have no desire to force anything on him, although I do make sure that, as if by chance, we end up in front of the spectacular anamorphosis in Holbein's *Ambassadors*. I explain to him how you can see a perfectly proportioned skull with the aid of a conical mirror, but he wonders why the painter decided to distort the image. Maybe because you can never look death straight in the eyes, I say, but he seems only moderately convinced. Then I show him *The Four Elements*, those famous market scenes by the Flemish painter Joachim Beuckelaer, once the pride of Ghent's Museum of Fine Arts, and explain that despite the religious subjects in the background – which are so small they hardly seem relevant anyway – the barely concealed erotic scenes are the real point. I draw his attention to the tell-tale symbols used in those days, the variations, the positions and the suggestions. Now his attention takes on a pensive quality: has his father become such a hopeless intellectual that he sees pimps in vendors, whores in fishmongers, phalluses in leeks and fish, and vaginas in jars of butter and half-open pea pods? We continue our stroll, and suddenly there it is, and because I am totally unprepared, it lands a frontal blow to my consciousness.

There she hangs, flagrantly nude and inviolable: Velázquez's *Venus at her Mirror*, known as the Rokeby Venus. The painting is slightly larger than my grandfather's copy – that is, if I recall correctly; I saw his version only for an instant, somewhere in that small room of his.

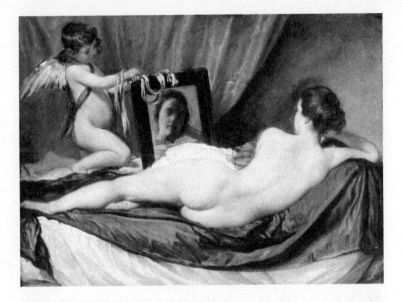

Venus's hair is also lighter in shade than in his copy – I don't know why my grandfather, meticulous copyist that he was, painted her hair almost black. I am catapulted back in time – to the day in my childhood when I hopped up the three steps to his room and found him crying silently with a reproduction of this painting in his hands. I remain standing in front of the masterpiece for a long time, under the spell of memory. My son stands some distance away, fiddling with his iPhone, and asks, 'Are you done yet? It's kind of embarrassing to see an old man standing and staring at a naked woman like that.' Realizing that my true motives are a bit too complicated to explain, I nod and tear myself away from the painting I yearn to investigate in more detail, glancing over my shoulder as we leave the room. I'll have to go to my father's house and have another look at the copy when I get home. I remember what he always used to tell me: your grandfather saw his own wife naked only once, by accident. She was washing herself on a Saturday afternoon and he came home earlier than anticipated – she never washed without sending him out of the house first. And she called him every name in the book that day, wept and wailed and later complained to his mother about his shamelessness, demanding that he apologize at length (his mother was probably wise enough not to take sides). The nudity of Velázquez's Venus, so warm and natural, so unabashed, perfectly at ease with herself, with her idle, aristocratic figure – such a thing could be found in painting alone, solely and singly in the consolation of art. Never have I understood the depths of that bitter consolation more fully than there, on that spring day in the National Gallery, and since I've started thinking about how the details of a copy can add something to the original painting, I have come to suspect that other secrets lie veiled behind what I once saw merely as clumsy copies. Again, I see his tear-streaked face before me, so long ago. The sun breaks through the clouds over Trafalgar Square and makes the fountains sparkle, a spreading prism of hues that emerge and vanish: madder, white lead and a sheen of cobalt, am I right? I wish I could check with my grandfather. Nelson stands high and unassailable, a dark angel on his sun-ringed pedestal; on the stairs of St Martin-in-the-Fields, a young woman is playing a Bach partita. St Martin, I'll be damned, I say to my son, this church is dedicated to my grandfather's patron saint, you know Martien was his family name. You just figured that out now? he asks, his eyes locked on the b-boys breakdancing on the pavement in front of the National Gallery. And suddenly it pains me to think that they will never meet, my line of descent and my descendant. I look at my son, suppress the urge to lay my hand on his shoulder, and ask, Where shall we go tonight?

As the Eurostar comfortably whisks us back to Brussels, deep below sea level, and I'm telling my son how long the journey used to take when I was young – the night ferry from Ostend to Dover, bobbing on the waves with its engines slowly pounding – a different story flashes into my mind: my grandfather's disastrous wartime crossing in 1915. He had been wounded on the Yser front for the second time and carried off with a bullet wound in his thigh, just below the groin, and was sent to the coastal village of Dinard in northern France to recover. He decided to cross from nearby Saint-Malo to Southampton, with several other convalescent soldiers, to visit his brother-in-law in Swansea, but a violent storm struck almost as soon as they reached the open sea, and raged on for a day and a half. He arrived in England broken and drained and later referred to it as one of the greatest ordeals he had endured in the war. I have my own vivid memories of the night ferry, the slurred shouts of the drunkards on deck, the hard benches where we lay rocking for much of the night, the chalk cliffs illuminated by the morning sun, the relief that the night had passed without a storm. The voyage to England was still laden with symbolic meaning in those days; when you arrived in London after a half day and full night at sea, everything looked more exotic. I recall a sunny room in Kensington Gardens where I once stayed. I read poems by the Irish poet William Butler Yeats there. My son listens to these stories, which must sound nostalgic to him, sits in silent thought for a moment, and then says, 'Funny, I used to imagine the Channel Tunnel was made of glass and you could see the seahorses swimming above your head, and now I don't even feel like we're crossing the sea at all.'

My grandfather so often told me how his passion for painting was born. But only after reading his memoirs did I understand how palpably that love was etched into his soul in childhood. He describes in detail how his father – seated on a wooden stool, with his paintbrush and a cotton swab on a wooden handle in his right hand, his palette with its carefully applied dots of paint on a small stand next to him, one eye half shut, back bent – retouches the fingernails of the Angel of the Annunciation in the Chapel of Our Lady of the Seven Sorrows. Then he goes on to restore the colour of a faded leaf on a clumsily painted date tree in the sixth Station of the Cross. He leans back for a moment to evaluate the result, half turns towards his son, and asks for a finer brush to fix a contour. He mixes most of his paint himself, since he cannot afford to buy it readymade in tubes. In the open pear-wood box are clumps of pigment, toxic cobalt powder, and sweet-smelling sienna, sepia and sinopia; flasks of refined linseed oil, turpentine, methylated spirits and siccative; thin knives and palettes; old brushes made of rare squirrel hair; round brushes, flat hog-bristle brushes, and a pair of soft hair brushes made from sable marten, for which he had scrimped and saved for months; cloths of diverse fabrics, from coarse to fine; pencils, charcoal, and asphaltum – the appurtenances of the endless, silent hours that Urbain spends with his father. He sits obediently in a church pew all afternoon, watching Papa's hands in motion. Sometimes his father stands at the top of a ladder and performs death-defying feats: removing the candle soot from the cloud on which the Virgin Mother stands in a tricky corner above a side altar; accentuating the plague sore on St Roch's thigh with a swipe of brownish-red, adding a new set of eyelets to St Crispin's old-fashioned shoes, sprucing up St Eloy's flaking emerald-green jacket, and brightening the three lilies in the desert sands by St Giles's feet with a thin layer of deadly poisonous white lead.

High on the converging lines of the ladder, he sees his father's legs, his ragged trousers, his worn 'mules' – old-fashioned slippers – and it's as if his father has joined the Oriental figures in the background of the frescoes on the wall. He hears the soft sweep of the brushes, which occasionally grows more intense – the eternal blue sky of faith is sometimes large and requires broad strokes. Tinted rays of sunlight descend from the stained-glass windows, casting patches of colour on the black marble tiles. He watches dust motes dance in those transparent columns of light. His father asks him for a size-five brush; Urbain digs down into the box, retrieves the brush, carefully climbs halfway up the ladder, and hands it to his father, who leans forward perilously to grasp it. Then Urbain climbs back down and returns to the hard pew, where he sits with his hands between his knees. Franciscus awkwardly straightens his back, clears his throat and wipes his chin on his sleeve, dips the brush into the iron bowl attached to his belt, and adds a few strokes of light yellow to a pale cloud from which the angel of the Annunciation is descending. Silent, endless days. At noon, he and his father share the sandwiches his mother made for them: dripping and fatty sausage when they can get it, hard mature goat's cheese at the end of the month. They chew and swallow, passing a dented flask of water back and forth. The church is locked; no one can walk in on them. This is Urbain's little heaven. Noises from outside are muted. When the clock strikes the hour, they hear the creak of the swinging beams and the flapping of wings as the birds in the peak of the roof take flight.

Clattering home on their cheap willow clogs, they sang silly tunes the whole way, like the merry tramps they were. The quaking aspens and white poplars along the ash-covered road rattled their leaves, and the father said to his son that the leaves in the wind were like a crowd of tiny ballerinas. My grandfather looked up in surprise and saw that the trees, which until then had formed one whole, were now fragmented into innumerable unknown forms that were waving at him, a stage with unimaginable scenes. He gulped and felt the warmth of his hand clasped in his father's.

He stands in the cemetery sixty years later, his hat under his arm, tears in his eyes, and the rosewood beads of his rosary between his fingers, praying with something like obstinacy for his dead wife Gabrielle Ghys. There is a shrine on the grave in the form of a chapel, with a stained-glass window depicting the Holy Ghost as a white dove. The niche in front of it holds a white marble statue of the Blessed Virgin, spreading her arms wide to receive the wretches and sinners who seek her out. He designed this statue himself and had it carved by a stonemason. He hisses at me to settle down and stop running all over the place. He has just raked the soil in front of the grave into gracefully converging lines, and here I am crashing clumsily through them again. For me, the cemetery is a playground. In the warm June sun, I race past the gladioli and the lilies, the early roses and the beds of violets, beneath the robinia trees and the young ashes; I leap at the patches of light that the delicate leaves cast on the cinder paths, I give the bronze angel at the start of the row a slap on the back each time I pass, I lie sprawled on the sun-warmed stone of an old grave until my outraged grandfather orders me to get off it at once. Out of nowhere, with a child's blunt innocence, I ask where his parents' grave is. He stares at me in disbelief with his piercing old eyes, starts to say something, seems to think better of it, picks a speck of dust off his royal-blue sleeve, and says, 'Come on, we're going home.' Not until half a century later will my father uncover the secret, when to his surprise he finds the old gravestone in the almost perfect hiding place where my grandfather once left it. When I visit the family grave, many years later, there is a thin layer of snow on the ground, and the white figure of Mary shines like opal in the lustre of the day.

My beloved Gabrielle,

It's a beautiful June day. I can see the barges passing from where I sit, at the little table that I later painted in wood-grain patterns, you would remember it. I visited your grave this afternoon. There was a very light rain at first, as if the drops were blowing down from the blue sky. Right after that, the bright sun broke through, and the light shining through the stained glass in the back of the small shrine onto your gravestone reminded me of the rays of colour in the churches of my childhood. The grandchildren followed the paths, passing the large, bronze angel at the start of the row where you are buried. I watched them go over the hill towards the Campo Santo Cemetery. It means so little to them, they play and chatter and are never quiet. On my way back, I saw a dead marten lying next to a crooked old gravestone, and it was as if all the sorrow I've felt since your departure was packed into that stiff, dead creature with dirty streaks of mud on its cold pelt. I thought to myself, they make such fine brushes out of that. I am still the good soldier I always was, Gabrielle, and showed no trace of emotion to Maria and the children.

At home, I opened the drawers in which it all lies untouched – your prayer book, your linen, the caps you wore to bed. It will remain there, as if in a household shrine. Our marriage was not easy, and you know how I wrestled with the devils deep inside. Our Lord gave us so much, Gabrielle. Less than we'd hoped for, perhaps, but still, more than enough to merit silence.

The fencing lessons he gave me, between the ages of eight and twelve or thereabouts, took place in the corridor and in the little entrance hall just inside the front door, always from eleven to twelve on Saturdays – we could smell the soup being made in the kitchen. Behind us was the wooden newel post that bore the gleaming, polished case of the large shell from the First World War. On his lathe in the old greenhouse, my grandfather had, with patience and dedication, made two wooden copies of slender foils, with thin handles that he cut from a sheet of metal and beat into a fairly graceful form with a small hammer – a technique he referred to, with restrained pride, as 'cold smithing'. We did not wear masks, so he covered the tips of the foils with pieces of cork from wine bottles. Standing before me in his greyish-white smock, he snapped his feet together and ordered me to do the same. '*En garde!*' he cried. 'Straighten your feet! Back straight! Look straight ahead! Raise your foil! *Un, deux.*' Everything about us was straight, as straight as a poker, just as they had taught him in the military school where he was educated in the picturesque years from 1908 to 1912. Advance, retreat, lunge . . . ready? *Tierce . . . Pronation! . . . Sixte en supination! Eh hop-la! Dessous! Reculez! Repos!. . . En garde!* I jumped around like a marionette in a costume drama, taking pains not to rotate my feet outwards or inwards, keeping my knees carefully bent, but always ready to leap forwards or backwards, evading his practised thrusts as I tried to hold my wooden floret in *sixte, quarte, octave* and *septime* – the terms for upper and lower left and right – while making sure to avoid an admonishing tap on the wrist by using the motion of my wrist, instead of my forearm, to guide the foil.

This went on for an hour; sometimes he would provoke me into attacking and then, instead of parrying, he would neatly dodge the thrust, so that I would charge forward like a young calf, straight into the wooden newel post, where he would deftly catch the shell case before it hit me on the head, saying, 'You still have a lot to learn.' I later found one of the foils in the greenhouse, broken, in the large box of soil holding the roots of the nearly centenarian grapevines, on which hardly any grapes grow any more. He would stand beneath those grapevines on summer mornings, picking a grape when he felt the urge and spitting the skins and seeds out into the soil. And as he spat, he made a noise, a slight coughing noise, which may be one of my deepest childhood memories, because it is surrounded by otherworldly calm. The edges of this image, so to speak, are stained with summer sun, warm earth, the faint odour of carbolic acid and lubricating oil.

S cenes from his childhood, 1900.

In his baggy old socks, oversized clogs and grey smock, with his rumpled, girlish curls and naive blue eyes, he stands dutifully waiting for the nurse to arrive at the small side gate of the convent courtyard with two pans of food for him, one brimming with soup, the other filled with slices of meat. With vague triumph in his chest, he saunters through the dusk, along the illuminated windows of the shops by the city's eastern gate, stepping over the railway line by the main dock in the harbour, passing the station where the train comes chugging to life, wending his way through the narrow streets between Land van Waaslaan and Dendermondsesteenweg – Biekorfstraat, Zeemstraat, Wasstraat, towards the béguinage of St Elisabeth – past a little square with tall poplars that will be chopped down a few years later. Somewhere around there is a small sweet shop, where he puts down the pans for a moment to catch his breath and to examine the goodies in the poorly lit display.

There are elderberry balls, boiled sweets with paper mottos, Katrien's caramels, candied anise, liquorice chew sticks and black liquorice laces, sweet-and-sours, and tart strawberry drops, all lined up in large glass jars. A man appears next to him, glances down at the guttersnipe with his smudged face, sees the pans from the convent, and tosses a couple of pennies into the soup. 'There, snot-nose, fish those out and you'll get your sweets.' Urbain looks up at the man in astonishment, hesitates for an instant, then rolls up his sleeve and gropes around in the greasy, tepid soup until he feels the coins. He takes them out, puts them in his mouth to lick them clean, pulls his sleeve down over his soup-slicked arm, licks his fingers off, and buys some sweets. He makes his way home, sucking on a sweet, but just before he gets there he twists his ankle on the curb, the soup gurgles out of the fallen pan, and no story in the world can convince his mother that he did not exchange his soup for sweets. He sits out his punishment in his musty bedroom, brooding, hungering for his missed supper, staring out through the twilight at the sagging rooftops across the way where a pigeon is mounting its mate.

Twice a week, a few young men stopped by – recent seminary graduates sent to the working-class neighbourhoods by the Society of St Vincent de Paul, an organization for poor relief. They sometimes just came by for a chat, asked how the children were doing in school and whether there were any complaints, and usually brought along something to eat. One day they turned up unexpectedly yet again. Céline was working as a cleaning woman in the neighbourhood at the time, for an Italian woman who called her 'Donna Cilla', so Urbain was home alone with his brothers and sisters. They were bored; without their parents around, the afternoons dragged on. They were holding a kind of competition to see who could bite off the most sandwich without swallowing, and my grandfather was on his way to an easy win. He had just taken four huge bites, one after the other, and his cheeks were as round as a beaver's, when the young men from St Vincent's were suddenly in the kitchen, their dark grey overcoats draped over their shoulders like drooping wings. His brothers and sisters fled full-mouthed into the sheltering darkness under the stairs and left him gagging in front of the two-man tribunal. They politely but formally asked him whether his mother was at home, bending their tall, thin forms over his; their smirking faces bobbed in the air above him. The taller of the two bared a row of irregular, yellowed teeth. The large mass of bread congealed into a clump of slimy dough against his palate. His mouth was too full to chew, he knew it would also be impossible to swallow, and spitting was out of the question. His head was spinning. Under the stairs, he heard the coughs and sniffles of his brothers and sisters. A wave of nausea rolled through his body. He had the feeling his eyes were bulging; the two men stared at him with raised eyebrows.

Well, lad, cat got your tongue?

He was choking. Tears welled up in his eyes.

The boy's not normal, he heard the taller man say.

A large hand, bony and clumsy, patted his small shoulder. My grandfather had the feeling this hand was not attached to anything, that it was floating out in space somewhere, that it kept getting bigger, and that it was headed for his throat. He shook his head, fought back his tears, walked out into the courtyard, and heaved up the doughy clump, along with the leftover soup he had eaten first. Still hiccupping, he went back inside. The two men were already gone. A rectangular card lay on the kitchen table, stamped in blue ink with the words GOOD FOR 1 LOAF.

He grabbed the card, stuck it in his smock, and ran out into the street. It was more than a fifteen-minute walk to the bakery where he could pick up the bread. He had forgotten to put on his coat and was shivering. His clogs rattled noisily through the streets. By the time he arrived at the bakery, it was about to close. He rushed inside to the counter and brandished the coupon: 'One loaf for my mother, please.'

The baker's wife studied the ticket, gave the red-faced, shabbily dressed boy the once-over, and said, I can't help you. I just have a few loaves left, and they're for my regular customers.

Once he was out in the street again, he heard the woman turn the key in the lock behind him. In the distance, a locomotive blew its whistle, somewhere near the city's eastern gate. The sound seemed dampened by the drizzly air. When he looked up, he saw a flock of wild geese in a V formation, winging majestically over the drab city. The primeval sound of their cries calmed him a little. The V seemed to form an arrow pointing towards the harbour, where a hazy band of brightness had formed over the rooftops and the trees, a slowly opening fissure of low raking light in the cold, descending dusk.

Only now that I'm reading his memoirs am I gradually forming a picture of his childhood, and as I do, just as many of my own memories are springing to mind, coming to light, gaining significance, meaning, colour and odour. For instance: I see him before me now, already an old man, about to go to bed. He has taken off his smock, shirt and undershirt, and I see, for the first and only time in my life, his bare, white back. From his shoulders to the hollow of his back, his skin is pocked with dark blue pits and scars. He turns around and says sternly, Run along now, little man, away with you. I close the door behind me. The next day I ask where the scars came from. Was it the war?

The iron foundry, he says curtly, I was thirteen years old when I started working there.

I read that he could not keep up at school because he was so frequently absent. This was partly because in the morning he was often sent to the apothecary's shop for the poor, to pick up medicine for his ailing father. He would bring a doctor's handwritten Latin prescription to the old shop and take his place on the hard bench where there were usually a dozen people already waiting for the apothecary to stick his impressive bald head through the wooden partition and call out, 'Who's first, please?' Then bedlam would break loose, as they all began quarrelling about who had arrived first. Some people sprang to their feet and elbowed their way through the crowd. The hatch was slammed shut with a muttered curse. Once the uproar had subsided, the apothecary opened the hatch again and asked if they would please behave like halfway civilized people. Then they shuffled one by one into his office and came out again murmuring under their breath. The boy was usually at the end of the queue and did not return home till the late afternoon, bringing stramonium – the poisonous powder of the thornapple – and nitre paper, the dubious medicines prescribed to asthma patients in those days. His father sat by the blazing stove, gasping for air, his hand on the warm bar; my grandfather placed the package wrapped in thin paper next to his father's hand, where it would remain until the next coughing fit a few moments later.

Elsewhere, he describes the empty church after school on weekdays, his father atop a small wooden stepladder, retouching St Peter's left foot.

Give me that azure blue again, son, I'm going to touch up that fold in St Peter's jacket, and then hand me a little cobalt for that shadow, there, to your right, on the palette. Then his father paints a fresh layer over the flaking white of the lily next to the Virgin Mother, behind the altar. It's another Annunciation. The young woman with a Flemish profile – a small chin, high pale forehead, thin nose and serene blue eyes – stands in the glow of a luminous cloud, a sticky, silver mass of mist around her pious face. Next to her is the angel with the lily branch, his features masculine and dark; he has a golden band around his waist, a glittering ribbon that swings up over his back and into the sacred cloud. Illegible words are written on this banderole; a few letters can still be made out, old-fashioned Gothic characters meant to keep God's secret. Sometimes his father needs to mix a little plaster on a board with a raised edge – he stirs it quickly with the worn-down scraper until it's a creamy mass, a poultice to be applied right away – ideally in one smooth stroke. A few minutes later, he smooths out the surface with a bit of sponge wrapped in a rag, and as it dries he adds the retouch, with brushes, a scrap of cloth, a fingertip or a thumb, moving swiftly from one to the other in wordless concentration. The devotional nature of those hours is sacred to Urbain. When it's cold, he blows puffs of mist into the beams of light, and they rise like incense during Sunday mass. His faith is fired by the magic of the colours on his father's old palette, by the privilege of being alone with him there, after the large church gate is locked behind them with the heavy iron key, by the sound of his father humming, there at the top of the stepladder, as if he is part of the scene he is painting, with one foot in heaven already, a heaven of plaster and paint, of old smells, of cold and damp, of filtered light from above shining down on their arms and shoulders, as if they are rising above themselves and into a biblical scene. It is the adoration of painting, a personal allegory, a conspiracy between a father and his son.

If those afternoons in church were his childhood heaven, the hell was soon to follow. After a few failed attempts to find an apprenticeship, he goes to work for his uncle Evarist, a 'smith/iron-turner/mechanic'. At first he is put in charge of greasing the lathes and drilling machines and hauling the iron: round and square bars of iron, heavy pieces of cast iron, sections of angle irons, and sheets of iron he can hardly move. After a month he is permitted to do jobs outside the workshop with his boss or another assistant. After a year and a half, he earns fifty centimes a day.

He witnesses a grisly accident at work: his cousin, the smith's son, comes to work blind drunk and falls face down into the blazing furnace. He sees how the smith – who was oblivious at first, hammering with his back to the furnace – roars profanities as he pulls his son out of the flames, but it is too late. They take in the sight of a ruined face, a charred lump with vaguely human features expelling a slimy fluid mixed with saliva and blood. The eyes are burnt white like the eyes of a fried fish; the mouth is a black hole in which the exposed upper row of teeth glimmers. An assistant brings a bucket of water and pours it over the dying boy's head. With an excruciating gurgle and hiss, the water soaks deep into the burnt flesh, and he chokes out his last breath, his body writhing and twitching. A dark stain forms in the crotch of his work trousers. The father throws himself on his son, snatches up the unrecognizable head, grips the body by the shoulders, and says nothing, but sits motionless, minute after minute, mumbling an endless stream of nearly inaudible curses under his breath. He does not look up at anyone, as if trying to bore his gaze into those white eyeballs. The workers and apprentices stand and stare.

'Piss off, every one of you, before I kill you too,' he snarls, without looking up. One by one, they drift outside, where a low sun shines over the rain-swept sheds and stables.

It is the first time my grandfather has seen a dead man. There was no psychological counselling in those days; he goes home and says nothing all evening.

In the days that follow, he returns to the smithy each day and finds a locked door. He dares not ask when his cousin will be buried. He hears about the burial a few days later, when he runs into another worker near the city gate in the morning twilight: 'They chucked him in a damn pit, same as an animal, somewhere out back of their property. The reverend went to see, but the smith took him by the throat.' The smithy stays closed for over a month, and the orders pile up. When it finally reopens, only two workers show up, and one apprentice: Urbain. The men work listlessly, the place is a shambles, more and more orders are cancelled, the smithy is often deserted, and the lathes go untouched. The last journeyman tenders his resignation, and Urbain leaves a few days later. The smith doesn't even look up from his workbench as the boy stammers his apologies with hunched shoulders and stumbles outside, lurching as if he has soiled his trousers.

Then time moves fast. After another few weeks of searching, he ends up in the iron foundry. Heavy labour. A boy of barely thirteen, he spends the first few days wandering disoriented through the deafening racket, among the men carrying heavy hunks of iron, in the burning heat of the furnaces, amid the yelling and shouting, the crude jokes, and the poisonous vapours that fill his lungs. Some of the men have a pale gloss over their eyes from working in the glow of the hot metal. Others have what resemble club feet from stepping in molten iron by the furnace. They are like mild-mannered demons roaming their underworld, tough and long-suffering, dogged and withdrawn. Young boys like Urbain aren't allowed to drag the heavy baskets of scrap metal along the narrow gangways; instead, he is put to work at the furnace's mouth, balancing the large wooden basin with all his strength as it fills with the molten iron spilling out of the clay troughs. The men gather round with their long wooden ladles, which they hold up to the basin; my grandfather's job is to carefully tip the heavy crucible, so that each man carries just the right portion of iron back to the dies. The heat cuts off his breath; it's as if his eyes are melting in their sockets. When the gush of iron subsides to a trickle, the conduit is plugged with a pointed mass of clay on a lance. The fire crackles and hisses and seethes at the edges of the stoke hole. Sometimes the plug flies out, like a devil spitting wide spirals of fire, fans of sparks, molten metal that winds a loopy path over the pounded earth floor, a volcanic eruption in miniature. Then the men hurl large scoops of wet clay with all their might, so that the fire will not spread throughout the building. One day it happens: the plug falls out of the worn-out stoke hole, there is not enough damp clay in the bucket, and the men shout at Urbain to shift the basin back in place and keep it upright until they return with clay from the courtyard. The river of fire is soon spurting over the edge of the crucible, which he tries to hold steady with all his strength. They call out that he must not let it tip, he feels the heat swallow him up, he is blinded, burned alive, his head goes hazy – and then, after some sort of rush of wind inside his ears, there is a deafening silence. The fiery river spills over the rim of the basin; his hands seem to have disappeared. The molten iron winds its way around his clogs, he feels them cracking under the searing pressure – he thinks of club feet, he cannot move, behind him is frenzied motion he no longer notices, the heat enfolds him like a mother, cradling him, numbing him, the yelling and shouting ebbs away again. Dark patches appear in the vast, divine light that beckons him, great shovelfuls of earth all around him and into the blazing stoke hole, and then a plug on a lance after all, the return of something like consciousness, hissing and bubbling, a nauseous feeling, large hands reaching out to him and voices calling, Come here, lad, quick. But he stays stock still, his head spinning; the handkerchief sticking out of his trouser pocket has caught fire and is burning like a faint blue flower beside him. He sees the upturned eyes of a saint his father painted in an old fresco in a silent Sunday church; he wants to keep sitting here for ever. Then someone comes running across the strip of earth, tugs at his shoulders, grabs him by the armpits, and pulls. His clogs are clenched and trapped in the cooling iron; a man with a crowbar starts breaking them off his feet. It all feels like part of a dream, and when he is finally lifted out of the broken clogs and carried off, he retches up what little he has eaten that day. He is laid in the courtyard in the lukewarm drizzle, where he slowly returns to his senses and watches the grey clouds drift by.

At that moment, something in me changed, he writes.

I imagine his mother noticing the change that very evening. He walks differently; there is something about his newly muscular neck, his hunched shoulders. He is short and burly, and says little since he started working in the foundry. The first pits and scars have already formed on his back, left by sparks that leap onto the workers when the flames rise high. That evening, his mother sees the introverted glimmer in his eyes as he sits at the supper table staring into space, not hearing a word the other children say. He's not hungry, he tells her; he goes out into the courtyard, where over the low wall he sees a few nuns go mumbling by in their fluttering black habits, strange birds from another world. The back door creaks, his father comes to his side; he has lost a lot of weight in recent weeks, and his fragile form contrasts with the sturdy young man around whose shoulder he silently puts his arm.

I see in the paper that a young Ghent politician has a new master plan for the city. He says that the overpass built in the 1960s, which penetrated deep into the city centre and reduced the once-proud Zuidpark to half its size, should be demolished and replaced with a tunnel. Then the park – originally conceived in a traditional nineteenth-century style but later sapped of its soul by the motorway – can become Ghent's own Central Park, the proud herald of a new, ecological age. This motorway slip road was controversial from the start; critics saw it as proof that the proud provincial capital had traded in its pride for filthy lucre. Luxury apartments had popped up along Frère Orbanlaan and Gustaaf Callierlaan, the graceful avenues by the park, but ever since the 1960s those apartments have looked out over the motorway. A bust of the great Flemish poet Karel van de Woestijne used to stand in a modest flower bed, looking somewhat lost; a short distance away, in the surviving half of the park, is an equestrian statue of King Albert I; and at the end of the park – where a splendid railway station, Zuidstatie, once stood – a fountain spurts behind a modern building. I recall the colour of the begonias in spring before that building was there. A great deal of history has vanished around this city park – in particular, the nineteenth-century zoological garden and the graceful old station. The zoo with its ponds and flower beds, its cafeteria in the Byzantine style, disappeared when my grandfather was fourteen. In Muinkmeersen field, where it had stood, came working-class dwellings clustered around little courtyards. The only vestige of the animal park is cosy little Muinkpark, with its arched bridge and artificial boulders, in a once-residential neighbourhood shaken up in the past decade by the arrival of a megaplex cinema. I imagine my grandfather and a neighbour boy walking through it – the carrion smell from the predators' cages, the performing elephants weary of their tricks, and the happy faces of the bourgeois visitors, under the spell of an exoticism untainted by our modern pangs of conscience.

Zuidstatie, at the far end of the park, was the pride of the early-twentieth-century city, a palatial railway station with a large front square where the bronze statue of a gladiator stood beside a fountain ringed with flowers. My grandfather spent his free Sunday afternoons there – Saturday was a working day, the last of the six long days in the working week – strolling around with his friend, sliding down the bluestone parapets, watching the arriving and departing trains from a platform above the tracks, taking pleasure in being sprinkled by the clouds of soot and ash that spewed fitfully out of the broad smokestacks of the engines. The interior of Zuidstatie was a sensational sight: a spacious concourse with a steel framework, a sloped roof with large windows in the style of the day, and an impressive indoor garden of palm trees, azaleas and all sorts of ornamental shrubs filling the middle of the space beneath the glass dome. The front square was bright and open too, radiating self-confidence. The station was demolished in 1930. When I emerge from the underground car park now, I face the modern city library on one side and a shopping centre on the other, where the chic Parkhotel once stood opposite the station. Younger generations do not even feel the loss; normality is a by-product of forgetting. I try to imagine what it was like here a century ago:

a row of carriages, the horses patiently waiting with nosebags of oats, the coachmen – moustached, of course – drinking beer out of earthenware tankards in the café, the smell of horse manure everywhere, passengers going in and out under the stately pediment of the façade, possibly a barrel organ, and, on the gladiator's bronze head, a pigeon. No one even remotely suspects what will happen barely ten years later.

Walking uphill from Zuidpark, you arrive in Sint-Pietersplein, a large square where, back then, the latest novelties were regularly on show. On a Sunday afternoon, a couple of five-cent pieces would buy you a ride in the wicker basket of a large hot-air balloon that rose into the air along a set of cables, hovered for a while so that you could see the medieval roofs of the old city in the distance, and came back down again. Newfangled tomfoolery, the older generation said, pride goeth before a fall, but it thrilled the boys and the soldiers with upswept moustaches. My grandfather proudly reports that he shook the hand of the Belgian aviator Daniel Kinet there one day, as the balloon was buffeted by a gust of wind. Kinet, already famous then, was a backer of the project; he would turn up again later at unexpected moments.

While Zuidpark was based on traditional geometrical shapes, Citadelpark was inspired by the Romantic philosophy of the natural-looking landscape, much as the old zoo had been. Ghent sensed that it was shaped by the historical forces of rationalist planning on the one hand and picturesque romanticism on the other, and expressed that fact in its recreational areas. The neo-classical citadel vanished long ago, making way for the park named after it; all that remains is the Roman-style gateway. In fact, this so-called citadel had been little more than an old barracks, fallen into decay; few traces of the foundations can still be found – but the cement-lined romantic grottos behind the waterfall are still there, and I can imagine my grandfather strolling here as a young man, in his clogs, with his head of coarse, straight hair, his hands in his pockets. Over the waters of the pond, where the ducks are cackling, he and his companion skim flat stones.

I have my own memories of passing under the Latin motto on that gateway – *Nemo me impune lacessit*, 'No one provokes me and goes unpunished' – on my way to the museum on Sunday afternoons, hand in hand with my almost seventy-year-old grandfather, to learn about the paintings he admired: most of all, perhaps, the large, luminous winter scene *The Skaters*, painted by Emile Claus in the year 1891, an image in light yellow and white of a pond frozen solid in the powdery snow, where three boys in clogs are preparing to ride their simple wooden sleds. Their clothing is thick and grey; there is a snowman by the edge of the pond; in the distance floats a line of pollard willows, and a farmhouse lies sunk in the landscape. The freezing-cold silence roars from the paint, a feast of light and clarity; he passed down his deep delight in these things to me. Only later did I realize he had shown me a painting from the year he was born – and wasn't he born in February, sometime in the frosty winter

months when Claus painted this scene? I request the record of the weather on that date from the Royal Meteorological Institute in Ukkel and discover it was a day of chilly mist, just below freezing; I imagine the wisps of fog at the confluence of the Lys and Scheldt rivers, his mother in childbirth, the smell of the stove, which isn't drawing well on that low-pressure day, the new-born swaddled in wool and laid down by the midwife in the primitive cradle next to the stove, and Claus the painter at work on his evocative, eggshell-white painting of a frozen pond nearby, on which a few boys are skating, lads my grandfather may have run into as a child, when they were young men.

In front of me, on my writing desk, lies a heavy grey rock with an unusual shape. It's long and thin: almost seven inches long, three inches wide, and an inch and a half thick. Its rounded corners are perfectly symmetrical; the top and bottom are absolutely smooth; millennia of aimless tumbling in the breaking waves have shaped this stone into an ideal thing, as if human hands had fashioned it; it's hard to imagine a more tangible illustration of the chance origins of natural perfection. My grandfather painted a folkloric scene on its flat top after returning from his trip to Italy: a man and woman in dark clothes against a background of looming hills, the sea, and a childish sailing boat. In slightly shaky black capitals above it, with a thin brush, he wrote 'Rapallo'.

He gave it to me at a time when I was collecting rocks – I must have been about twelve years old. The scene on the stone was not of immediate interest to me; what mattered was the simple fact that my grandfather had painted something on it, including a word I did not understand – for I quickly forgot he had told me it was the name of a city in northern Italy.

A decade and a half after his death, at a time when I was trying to read the poet Ezra Pound's unfathomable Cantos, my wife and I visited the town of Rapallo on our way to Florence. We walked on the small, stony beach near the old tower and there I found, to my surprise – how often you are blind to your personal history – rocks of the same shape and size. So he had simply picked it up right there.

There are moments in life when everything inside you starts to shift; I remember my arm around the shoulder of my lovely young wife, the feeling of weightlessness and freedom; the sun, the wind, the smell of salt and seaweed; the sudden feeling that I was almost physically inhabiting my grandfather's body, in a place where he had stood beside his faithful, timid wife Gabrielle in her black mantilla. They were on their way to Rome; it was one of those pilgrimage tours arranged by some Catholic organization, and Rapallo was merely a quick stop along the way, where they probably just had time for lunch and a short walk. He must have picked up the stone while they were combing the stony beach, all dressed in black, and Gabrielle must have said, 'What are you doing, Urbain? That's much too heavy to put in your suitcase.' And he, stubborn in these little things, kept it in his hand, boarded the bus with it – it must have been sometime in the mid-1950s – and lugged the three-pound stone all the way back home, where he later decorated it with this souvenir-shop scene, as the talisman of a journey of which few photographs have survived. Oddly enough, when he painted the stone he felt no desire to depict a particular experience of his own, but instead painted a sentimental, folkloristic cliché, which apparently encapsulated the happiness of that moment for him. Of course, it's always possible that he really did witness such a scene; who knows, maybe there were people walking around in traditional costume that day, perhaps it was a holiday, there's no way of knowing.

That trip to Rome was the only time in his long life that he went abroad, except for his journeys to England and France to convalesce during the First World War and a trip to Oslo that I know frustratingly little about – only that he often claimed people there spoke a dialect that sounded like the crudest Ghent patois, but was nonethe-

less impossible for him to understand. I once checked this while conversing with the writer Jostein Gaarder, and it turns out my grandfather was right. In any case, the rock from Rapallo with the painted scene is my only keepsake from his travels, and of course, rocks tell no tales. Because his memoirs end in 1919, two-thirds of his life is buried in stony silence.

Rapallo is provincial, but open to the sea. The philosopher Friedrich Nietzsche was wandering the beach there when he came up with the idea of writing a heroic epic not about Empedocles (whom he apparently read about in the poems of Friedrich Hölderlin), but about Zarathustra. The poet Ezra Pound, scarred by the First World War like my grandfather, went to live there in 1924, in a period when his mistress, the American violinist Olga Rudge, became pregnant and after giving birth sent the child away to live with a wet nurse, a German-speaking peasant. Pound roamed about restlessly, kept returning to Rapallo, worked on his Cantos there while railing against Jewish usury on Italian radio, and became a follower of Mussolini. Through Olga's offices, he even met Il Duce in person and tried to sell his ideas about the evils of Jewish finance to the Fascist dictator, who is said to have waved him off, calling the Cantos *divertente*, entertaining – an anecdote that Pound, showing a sense of irony, later incorporated into one of his Cantos. Yeats wrote about astrology in Rapallo, Kokoschka painted an almost Impressionist view of the bay, and Joyce once came for a visit; Elmore Leonard set his thriller *Pronto* there.

On 2 May 1945 – four days after Mussolini was publicly lynched, while his mangled body hung like a slaughtered ox next to that of his mistress in the open air next to a petrol station in Milan – the Fascist poet was arrested by partisans and taken away from his home in idyllic Rapallo. Before he left, he threw a copy of Confucius and a Chinese dictionary into his travel bag. In an interview just a few days later, he likened Hitler to Joan of Arc and called Il Duce a leader 'who lost his head' – you can say that again. Regarded as a genius who had descended into madness, he was penned up in an animal cage near Pisa. Later, back in Rapallo, the old and chastened Pound, ashamed of his anti-Semitic bluster, said to Allen Ginsberg, 'I was not a lunatic, I was a moron.'

There is no way of telling which of the Cantos' many cryptic passages about the sea refer to the small town of Rapallo. But standing there, I do know I am in the place where that man, as stubborn and blue-eyed as my grandfather, was eclipsed for a moment by a devout pilgrim in a black fedora with a heavy rock in his bag. They have almost nothing in common, and I assume my grandfather never even heard the name Pound in the course of his long life. Nevertheless, one thing connects them: a fleeting, enigmatic association inspired by the most intangible of relationships, like my association with the photo of Schopenhauer – something that will always be beyond my grasp and pertains to other customs, other morals. People from the age of Europe's great catastrophes – how much sense can we make of them today? I take another look at the stone, run my fingertip over the meticulous brushstrokes, and realize that nothing ever returns to time unless it is stored in mute, voiceless objects; rocks do tell tales after all. Tracing the brushstrokes, I touch the motion of his fingers on this cold, quiet stone, as years ago I touched his forehead after he died and was seized by the thought: Have I ever felt anything colder than this forehead? Why won't he open his eyes and speak to me?

There are also objects that have disappeared, but which haunt my memory all the more. The one that comes to mind most often, and torments me most, is the golden pocket watch he gave me for my twelfth birthday. As soon as I saw him coming down the stairs into the living room, his face beaming, I knew he had something special in store for me. Open your hand, he said, and he carefully placed the precious gift in it. I thanked him, looked up, and was just about to put my arms around him when the timepiece slid out of my hand and shattered on the tile floor. I have relived the scene countless times in memory: the expression on his face, his shock, the sight of him muttering curses, shaking his head, squeezing his eyes shut, and then the suppressed anger with which he swept up the fallen pieces, shoved them into the pocket of his smock, and went out into the garden, not to return until several hours later. It has often come back to me on sleepless nights, and every time I felt like slapping myself on the forehead, and sometimes I did.

But now that I have read the true story of this watch in the first notebook, which describes his childhood experiences, I know the debt I incurred to him at that moment can never be repaid.

The watch had belonged to his father's grandfather, and whenever the family's poverty became too oppressive to bear, his father and mother had their son take a few of their valuables to the pawnshop, which bore the impressively cynical name of Mount of Piety – a Christian phrase that brought a touch of grandeur to a mundane operation. The Mount of Piety still stands; the construction of that Baroque pile began in 1620 by order of the sanctimonious monarchs Albert and Isabella and was completed in 1622, in a time when religious wars had led to grinding poverty. The building – now beautifully restored, still bearing the inscription *Mons Pietatis* on its façade – is on Abrahamstraat, near Gravensteen Castle and the pleasant Prinsenhof district. Since 1930, it has held the city archives. With one of the city's earliest Baroque façades, the building is somewhat reminiscent of an Italian palazzo. For a working-class boy, it was a long walk from the edge of town into the historic centre, and I imagine the building intimidated him.

One day, his father had reluctantly given him the watch in question, urging him, for God's sake, not to drop it. He entered the gate beneath the words *Mons Pietatis* with this treasure clutched in his hand and placed the watch on the table in front of the scowling nun, who in return gave him some money and a receipt, which he took home. In those difficult years, when his father's bouts of illness grew more and more frequent, he brought to the Mount of Piety his mother's few French books, her necklace and the ivory cameo of the girl with the ponytail, set in silver, her own mother's gilt hairpin, silver tableware, and a lace tablecloth in the Bruges style handmade by her grandmother around the mid-nineteenth century. Years later, when Franciscus had saved a little money, he instructed my grandfather to return with the same amount they had received – the *Mons Pietatis* lent to the poor without charging interest, that too is written on the façade. As he began to rant that those buzzards wouldn't get away with stealing that blasted watch after all, his wife, who was thinking of her mother's pawned pearl necklace, said, 'Please, Franciscus, it's not Christian to curse.'

The watch was reclaimed, and after his father's premature death, Urbain's grieving mother placed it in his hands, telling him he was now the man of the house. He put it in his pocket, wore it as a talisman throughout his military training, and kept it with him for all four years of the war. Its delicate mechanism survived the nightmare of Schiplaken and the horror of Sint-Margriete-Houtem; it lasted through the legendary retreat to Jabbeke and Ostend and the hellish years on the Yser front that followed, from Mannekensvere to Stuivekenskerke. It was in his pocket when he crossed to Southampton and thought he would die. It was missed by mere inches when he was shot through the groin while erecting a barbed-wire entanglement on the Yser front. And it met an inglorious death at my clumsy young hands on my twelfth birthday, a day that will always remain burned into my memory. Now that I'm checking the dates, I see it happened only two months before he set to work on his memoirs. Just before he started writing, in other words, his most valuable keepsake slipped out of my hands and was lost for ever.

On a grey day, I drive to Ghent for the sole purpose of walking aimlessly past that building, turning around, walking past it again, crossing the street, and squinting at the beautifully restored façade. Thoughts hammer in my head: once it was kept here, once he brought it through that door. And I broke it, an heirloom that was nearly an antique when he was young. What could he have done with the shattered pieces? A man walks by with a panting Dobermann straining at the lead; I hear pigeons cooing. It's too late now for the remorse that holds me helpless in its grip.

On Sunday afternoons in spring he would take me with him to Kouter, Ghent's main square – where the weekly flower market was even more modest in size than it is today – and stand with me in the front row, usually by the vaguely Viennese façade of the Handelsbeurs, in a spotless dark blue suit with his cane planted in front of him, just as beneath the canopy the band began to play. He knew their entire repertoire by heart, note for note, and I often saw him humming along or rhythmically nodding his head as they played yet another march or a tune from Bizet's *L'Arlésienne*, the wobbly tone of some instruments making it seem as though the oboist, the clarinettists, the buglers and the red-faced man blowing the bass line on the tuba were crossing an unsteady bridge high above the fast-moving river of the challenging score. He would often say to me, as we walked home in satisfaction, 'I once sang in the choir there, conducted by Peter Benoit.'

Benoit, the great Flemish bard and composer of an oratorio about the Scheldt river! He won the illustrious Prix de Rome, the highest honour a composer can receive, conducted in Paris, in Jacques Offenbach's Théâtre des Bouffes-Parisiens, and founded the forerunner of the Flemish Opera. Benoit, invariably referred to by my grandfather as the Flemish Brahms, died in 1901, so my grandfather must have been under the age of ten when he sang in the gala choir. A brief search turns up the celebration in question: when Princess Elisabeth, Duchess in Bavaria, and Prince Albert of Belgium visited 'the proud City of Ghent' in 1900 as part of the celebration of their recent wedding, a large mixed choir was formed that included a number of carefully selected children's choirs. It must have been a magnificent event; the orchestra that performed in Kouter was impressive, and undoubtedly suited to the refined musical tastes and enthusiasm of the young princess. Already well known as a music lover, she would later lend her queenly name to one of Europe's most prestigious musical competitions, the Queen Elisabeth Competition, about which I once, a few years back, heard a famous Flemish conductor ask the king, 'Sire, isn't it time you shut down that old-fashioned circus once and for all?' Upon which King Albert II, the grandson and namesake of the musical Queen Elisabeth's husband (who died tragically in an accident), winked affably at his dining companions and replied, 'You *are* a little rascal, aren't you?'

In any case, the great Flemish composer's performance in Kouter in Ghent in the year 1900 made a lasting impression on my grandfather; Benoit could wield his authority over the Ghent children's choirs just by indignantly raising one of his legendary bushy eyebrows. In the well-known portrait by the painter Jan Van Beers Jr., a superb character study, you can still see how impressive those eyebrows were, and how deep the circles under the eyes of the great, exhausted tone poet. A certain likeness to the famous portrait of the ageing Brahms cannot be denied, and yet Benoit's head is far more Brahmsian than that of Brahms himself, so to speak. I later listened to Benoit's piano concerto, which did sound a lot like Brahms, and it was impossible for me not to picture my grandfather sitting by the radio with his eyes closed and one finger in the air, softly whistling along with the stately melody, which is not easy considering the slow tempo. The whistled tune would sometimes shoot upward just as the music plunged into the depths, but that's how it goes sometimes when the spirit is profoundly moved.

From Kouter, we would go on to Veneziana, the old ice-cream parlour and restaurant near the medieval castle Gravensteen. It was a quaint, old-fashioned establishment, where he always treated me to melon ice cream. Veneziana was an institution. Poets went there for coffee and gossip, and to brag about their secret mistresses in the nostalgic canal houses on the Coupure, read the newspaper or gripe about the weather. The elderly Ghent composer Louis de Meester, who was affiliated with Schönberg's modern school but could nevertheless glare just as impressively as Peter Benoit, often held court there, side by side with his much younger wife, who was said to have once been a waitress at that same cosy ice-cream parlour. Veneziana, a Ghent highlight for several generations of satisfied ice-cream eaters, unfortunately shut its doors in 2006, and I have always suspected the beginning of the end came when its owner, Nikki Zangrando, decided to renovate the interior, remove the brown panelling, and replace the endearing 1930s furniture with soulless modern pieces. Zangrando – who was not precisely Venetian but did come from the Veneto region, near Cortina d'Ampezzo – had apparently underestimated the power of his own invented tradition in the provincial Flemish town, and in retrospect it seems clear that by rashly giving in to the urge for the new that prevailed in those days, he delivered the death blow to an establishment that will for ever be linked in my mind to the taste of melon, a fruit then eaten only by the wealthy. Once, when I told my grandfather I didn't even know what a melon looked like, he led me to the nearby vegetable market and bought two fragrant cantaloupes then and there. When we returned home, Gabrielle said, 'Are you out of your mind, Urbain? Who on earth would eat a thing like that?'

My grandfather's love of music usually swept over him like a fit of melancholy. The soaring wind section in Bizet's lyrical suite *L'Arlésienne*, the wistful melody from Schubert's *Rosamunde*, the notorious chorus of slaves in Verdi's *Nabucco* – they all had the same effect: his blue eyes grew moist. Wagner, on the other hand, filled him with anger and disgust. Unbeknown to him, this feeling was shared by the great philosopher with a hammer; Nietzsche wrote late in life that he preferred Bizet's southern light-heartedness, his affirmation of love and life, to the Teutonic opium dreams of Wagner's murky mysticism. Offenbach put my grandfather in a cheerful mood, and military marches lifted his spirits. He knew Beethoven's *Pastoral Symphony* by heart, especially the movement with the cuckoo calling in the cool Wienerwald; I've already described the malodorous details with which, thanks to his stories, my childish imagination embellished that piece. But no other music was as dear to him as the overture to Bizet's *L'Arlésienne*, with the infectious rhythm of the March of the Kings, the wistful melody that follows in the wind section, and the dramatic, even tragic, melodic turn, all in such swift succession that it may have been the perfect expression of his whole personality. While listening to it, he would sometimes say, 'Oh, the light in the south, you have no idea!' and then sink into rapt, wordless attention. Who knows, maybe he was thinking of the beach at Rapallo. Of course, this Arlésienne, a girl from Arles who causes the death of her admirer, was remarkably similar to the dreaded femme fatale Carmen, from Bizet's opera of the same name, who calls love a rebellious bird and gives her lover a choice – love me and you'll have to look out for yourself, or don't love me and you'll have to look out for yourself all the more – but given the timid moral climate of Flemish living rooms in those days, he passed over that resemblance in silence. What choice did he have? A life-consuming passion had come close to devouring *him*, and had burned him badly enough. That much I could sense intuitively during the dark turn in that unforgettable prelude, which contains the force of an entire opera.

Places are not just space, they are also time. I look at the city differently now that I carry his memories with me. My thoughts go on circling Kouter, which I have seen ever since my childhood as a place of celebration, associated with Sunday mornings, the fragrance of the cut flowers my parents bought, and the old-fashioned band music performed in the perfectly restored bandstand. But now I am scanning the private language of the façades to find the house where once, for the few months that my grandfather was apprenticed to the Brussels tailor Mr Tombuy, he would report to work at the door of a Monsieur Carpentier, 'garment reseller'. As my grandfather described it, the house was 'adjacent to the renowned literary Club des Nobles situated in Kouter'. That's easy to find; since 1802, the Club des Nobles had been housed in what is known as the Hotel Falligan – a rococo building

beautifully restored in a hue approaching the 'Maria Theresa yellow' of the Habsburg family – which still stands proudly on that main city square. The façade is flanked by Apollo on the right and Diana on the left, a well-known pair; he represents the arts, and she the hunt – art and hunting, two favourite pursuits of the nobility since time immemorial, chiefly because of their aura of distinction. But I learn from a website that the statues were once 'reheaded' in the course of restoration, and funnily enough, Apollo ended up with Diana's bow, while Diana had to learn to play the harp. This forced exchange of occupations is nothing if not remarkable, and undoubtedly attests to the widening horizons of the city's cultivated aristocrats. To this very day, the building hosts the meetings of the French-language Falligan Literary Circle, one of the last remnants of Ghent's moribund Francophone bourgeoisie, an exclusive, nostalgic world chronicled by authors such as Suzanne Lilar in *Une enfance gantoise*. Lilar was also the author of *La confession anonyme*, a novella skilfully adapted by André Delvaux into the dark, passionate film *Benvenuta*, with the unforgettably sensual Fanny Ardant in the lead and an exquisite score by the discerning composer Frédéric Devreese; the beautiful setting is one of the most evocative buildings on the Coupure – a large, mysterious canal house with a walled garden, which I would have loved to purchase if I'd had the money.

The garment reseller's house on Kouter is not as easy to identify; was it to the left or right of the Club des Nobles? To the left is a shop that invites me, in eye-catching toxic green letters, not only to step inside, but also to come right back out again with instant internet access. The ground floor has been blemished with some kind of cheap black marble facing in the bad taste that appears to come naturally to retailers all over the world. But the four upper storeys, each with a beautiful loggia, still leave no doubt that this is an almost palatial nineteenth-century bourgeois townhouse. To the right is an immense building now owned by a bank. With a frontage of more than ten windows, this building is so large that it may not have been designed as a private dwelling, even if it does date from the years before the Great War, when the blatant display of personal wealth to the hoi-polloi in the streets was still considered a sign of a refined moral character. So my money is on the building on the left, and as I visualize how attractive and stylish the now-hideous ground floor must have looked a few years after 1900, I begin to form a picture of the thirteen-year-old kid who, for ten centimes a day, ran from one end of town to the other in his clogs and sagging black stockings with heavy stacks of finished garments, and who came here to ring Monsieur Carpentier's doorbell. A servant opens the door – a woman, let us suppose. She takes the heavy package from him, thanks him in French with a Ghent accent, and shuts the door – or maybe she slips him an extra centime or two first, I don't know. The boy runs back to the tailor's house – the address has been lost – where his employer's demanding wife makes him split logs, start a fire and fetch coal, and then runs back to the sewing workshop, where he is scolded for being gone too long and returning with dirty hands. The tailor gruffly sends him off to pick up his son from school. After a while, this becomes a daily routine, and he has to carry the young bourgeois gentleman's book bag, making sure to stay two steps behind him to avoid being rapped with his walking stick, which the twelve-year-old boy already wields with Proustian panache.

He did not write down the following anecdote, but I heard him tell it often enough: how his mother came to fetch him from the sewing workshop after two months. The bashful Urbain was alarmed to see her standing in the middle of the room; he took enough abuse already, it seemed to him, without also paying the price for his mother's obstinacy. But no, she did not even stop to glance at the tailor, who was squinting at her over the rim of his pince-nez. She looked her son straight in the eyes, as he sat cross-legged at a large cutting table trying to sew buttons to an odd scrap of cloth, and said, 'Come on, son, you're done here, we're going home.' The tailor looked down at the proud working-class woman as if he had discovered a cockroach on the floor and said haughtily, '*Madame, voulez-vous avoir la politesse—*' She broke in, 'Monsieur Tombuy, you can stick your ten centimes a day where they'll stay warm, *avec politesse*', and dragging her astonished son by the hand, she strode out of the workshop and slammed the door behind her.

All these stories expressed an admiration for his mother that ran deep. Again and again, he spoke of her attitude of pride, her self-control, the impressive knot in her black hair, the way people would step aside as she passed, how she looked straight through every fast-talker with her light grey eyes, without saying a word, till he slunk off in shame. That day, his heart pounded as he walked beside her, and he was filled with an overwhelming sense of freedom regained. He is more docile than she is; he will never outgrow his meekness in the face of higher social classes. All the events of his life reveal his sense of humiliation and self-doubt, which often clashed painfully with the sense of pride he had inherited from her. Even at an advanced age, when he knew the family doctor was coming by, he would set to work an hour in advance, polishing the large knob of the bell pull, the handle of the front door, and the old shell case on the newel post, so that all the brass in and around the house gleamed in the sunlight for the triumphal entry of the Doctor of Medicine, during whose examinations he always stood stiffly to attention as if a surly medic were deciding whether to approve him for military school.

He never fully recovered from the traumatic moment, one evening at the age of about ten, when he was awakened by knocking on their flimsy front door, the sound of his mother screaming, and men's anxious voices in the house. He scrambled out of bed, tiptoed down the steps – and there, in the kitchen, in the dim lamplight, his father was seated in, or draped over, a chair, 'his head covered with bleeding wounds', as he never failed to say when he told the story, so that from childhood I associated this scene with

Bach's well-known chorale about the tortured Jesus. One of the men held a damp cloth and was dabbing at the blood that welled from his split eyebrow; another was muttering words of encouragement to Franciscus as he fished a broken tooth from between his bleeding lips. His father's head dropped onto his chest, and his mother cradled it. Because Urbain had rushed into the kitchen shouting 'Papa! Papa!', one of the men grabbed the struggling boy and told him to go back to bed, but his mother, still holding her husband's head as he slipped in and out of consciousness, said that he could stay, since he'd already seen it. His anxious questions went unanswered; they were too busy attending to his battered father, moving him over to his wicker chair, and bringing him a drink of water. His nose was swollen, and there was blood running over his split lips, blood flowing down his neck and dripping onto his brown velvet waistcoat, and even blood sticking to his hair.

Blood everywhere, his father, his gentle friend, the hero of the frescoes in the church! My grandfather caught snippets of the story, as if in a daze, but it was only after his mother had said that she could handle the rest on her own and the men had left, assuring her they would return the next day to see how Franciscus was getting on, only after his father had begun to return to his senses and his head was bandaged, that Urbain calmed down a little and was given the whole explanation.

His father and a few old friends had gone to the annual pottery fair in Schellebelle that day, and on their way back – they did all their travelling on foot, so they didn't reach Ghent until nearly dusk – they had gone for a pint in their old neighbourhood off Heirnislaan. He hardly ever did that sort of thing, but it was the kind of early summer's day that called for a celebration, and one little glass of beer was not about to kill him. In the pub, they were overcome by the urge to sing, and all of a sudden there was a waiter at their table, telling them to shut their ugly mugs. Then the waiter knocked one pint off the table. He shouldn't have done that; it belonged to the giant Louis Van den Broecke. He drew himself up to his full height, grabbed the waiter by the throat, and asked what the problem was. The waiter shouted, 'I don't have to take orders from you, you filthy Papist' and tried to throw a punch, but before he could swing his arm, he received a blow that slammed him into the bar. He staggered outside, swearing, Louis ordered a fresh pint, and that was that. When they left half an hour later, it was dark. Near the Rietgracht canal, they were assaulted by five men, led by the waiter, who attacked Louis from behind. Louis seized hold of the man and flung him into the canal like a doll. When he crawled back out and came at him with a knife, Louis punched him again. By this time, the other men had got hold of Franciscus. Two of them were sitting on his chest and the others were kicking whatever parts they could reach. The giant raced over, slammed them aside, picked up the waiter's hat, placed it on his own head like a trophy, and together with two friends, who had made a run for it and then cautiously returned, dragged the half-conscious Franciscus home. In the kitchen, Louis saw that there was a name in the hat, which turned out to belong to a leading socialist. The man was given a year's probation by the justice of the peace, which did nothing to ease the tensions between socialists and Catholics.

To people like my great-grandparents, socialism meant nothing but danger, violence, fear and mayhem. For a few years, the city had been in the grip of social unrest – my grandfather describes with horror and disgust how the 'Reds' sometimes marched through the working-class neighbourhoods in the evenings. There were people singing, resounding cries, gendarmes on horseback charging into the crowd. Then the fighting began: a gendarme was pulled off his horse and mauled. My grandfather was out in front of the marchers, fleeing from them in his clogs. He arrived home panting and slammed the door behind him. *We lived through the uprising of the rabble*, he wrote bitterly in his notebook.

Discharged soldiers were called to arms again to break the massive strike in La Louvière and Charleroi and to put down the popular uprisings that accompanied it 'with drawn swords'. There was talk of the great mine disaster in Hornu, a town in Wallonia, and the inhumane conditions in the mines there, of the drowned fishermen in Ostend, of the children worked to exhaustion in the textile factories, whose fingers were torn off by the huge carding machines as they gathered up the ends of the flax fibres, of the maimed metal-workers and cripples who could no longer work and were wasting away at home, and of the countless other disasters that befell working people in those days. But working-class Catholics did not protest in the streets; they abhorred the idea, and withdrew into their quiet little lives.

Even right there in Ghent, there were bloody clashes between socialists and gendarmes. Tempers ran high; there were deaths on both sides of the conflict. On long summer evenings, they would hear the 'goading voices of the Red orators in the dead-end alleys where the low people swarmed together to voice their hatred of anyone a hair's breadth higher in rank or station'.

Sometimes there were hotheads who bellowed that it was time to seize the money from the people who had it, that they would march to the homes of the rich to demand it, why not now. That made my grandfather's ten-year-old heart contract with fear; soon all the fine ladies and gentlemen would be angry, and then his father and mother would never find work again. So the Catholic dogma of the day took root in their household: the Reds were envious, common people who had forgotten their place in the world, who blustered, made trouble, and drank themselves into a stupor instead of humbly doing their jobs. The earliest demonstrations seemed calculated to strike even greater terror into the hearts of the timid working people; each procession 'was preceded by two rows of twelve muscle-bound brutes, who emptied the streets, from the thoroughfares to the footpaths. Any family that wanted peace and quiet slammed its door shut.' The Church, too, did its best to undermine any possibility of better relations with the socialists; conflicts of this kind formed valuable fuel

for both propaganda machines, and the priests in their pulpits spewed as much gall as the protesters in the streets. On Sundays, Father Vandermaelen's theme was the godless heretics who once again, my dear congregation, as in Roman times, seek to murder Christians and throw them to the lions. Although my grandfather came from the common people and, in a way, remained proud of that fact his whole life, he expressed nothing but loathing for the 'Red clique', a dangerous enemy that he accused of possessing no culture, no respect for God or his commandments, and no sense of justice. He was sickened by their coarse language, their disrespect for God's name, their failure to use more than three hundred words in their whole lifetime, the way they polluted the canal sides with quarrelling and cursing, how they drank up their wages at the alehouse as soon as they got them instead of dutifully coming home, as his father did, and sharing the money with their families: 'They shouted, "Down with the tyrants", but they themselves behaved like beasts, taking unflagging pleasure in other men's misery.'

In his memoirs, he noted bitterly that socialists were later appointed as city councillors, members of Parliament, and even ministers, but that this new class of representatives was barely literate and required assistance from the very kind of people they once had cursed. While

67

events like these certainly widened and deepened the rift in the working population, all my grandfather saw as a child was his father in bed with a bandage around his swollen head. And his young heart hardened against the people he would later describe as the enemies of law and order.

For a while, in the 1950s, this trauma manifested as paranoia. There were microphones all over his house, he said, planted there so that the socialists could monitor his conversations, and when he started telling anyone who would listen that the Christian Democrats had offered him a post as minister, but the Reds were spying on him in his own house, it was time for the family doctor to intervene. He was admitted to Sleidinge psychiatric centre, where he received shock treatment five times. He returned home a broken man, said nothing to anyone for weeks, and sat and cried in the greenhouse under the small, green grapes. Now and then it would resurface, and he would pound his fists on the table, fulminate against the 'riff-raff' from the back alleys – even though he came from the same place – and call his proletarian neighbours toss-pots and drunkards. Then the only way to preserve the peace was by keeping all newspapers out of his sight and avoiding the radio news as much as possible.

His old wounds were reopened again and again – by the controversy over King Leopold III in 1951, and later, in the 1960s, by the daily television news. The old animosities between socialists and Catholics seemed to merge with the tensions between the regions of Wallonia and Flanders, and between French and Dutch speakers, reminding him of long-ago humiliations at military school. He heard that Russian Communists had destroyed the old church icons, scratched out the eyes of saints, murdered priests. And every time, it seemed to him like a plot to kill his dead father again; yes, even to destroy his murals if they got the chance – sacrilege, no more and no less. Madness struck a second time; he began to talk nonsense and was readmitted for more electroshocks.

68

He left no autobiographical account of the years after the Second World War, because he refused to talk about the things that really mattered. What remains are apocryphal puzzle pieces, an assortment of anecdotes and memories recounted by my aunts, cousins and parents. The pain all this had caused him went on smouldering when he saw me fall under the sway of left-wing ideas at university, and he snapped that I was throwing away everything my parents had done for me. In his eyes, it was the second time I was letting my family heritage go to pieces.

I later realized how fitting it was that his birth year also saw the publication of the notorious papal encyclical *Rerum Novarum*, a pamphlet by Pope Leo XIII about Catholic social teaching, which was a new and unexpected development after centuries of support for nobles and aristocrats. This was an attempt by the Church to head off the rise of socialist unions, partly by parroting the demands of the socialists, interspersed with precepts calling for just the kind of rigid morality and obedience that had created such a barrier between my grandfather and his non-religious fellow working men.

In the small scullery, he stands in front of his father's white-painted bathroom cabinet. He is trying to shave the downy stubble on his cheeks for the first time. He looks into the small, speckled mirror and sees a stocky, robust young lad with a thick head of wiry hair, bright blue eyes and a couple of sizeable pimples poking through the blond fuzz along his jawline. He stands with a straight razor in his hand, which he first sharpens the way his father showed him, on a leather strop hooked over the doorknob to pull it taut. He is almost fifteen but will never grow tall. Even in his old age, he will claim that he never reached his full height because of all the heavy lifting he did in the foundry as a fourteen-year-old boy. He picks up the shaving brush, dunks it in the large bowl of soapy, lukewarm water, and lathers his right cheek. He scrapes the razor awkwardly over his skin, clenching it in his large fist with black-rimmed fingernails. It is as if an unknown animal awakens something in him, something still slumbering that half-opens its eyes, rudely aroused from childish lethargy; a slow, warm dream still sweeping through his shivering body like the first gust of summer wind in May, there in the cold scullery, a warmth that spreads from his mouth to his ear and wounds him, cuts him, makes him aware of his own vulnerable body. He feels how warm and hard it is growing in his trousers. He wipes the soap from his cheek, dabs at his burning skin with the alum set out on the crude wooden rack, lathers the other cheek, and pulls the skin taut as he has seen his father do. Just then, with one cheek covered in white, frothy soap, he sees a face behind him in the mirror: his mother, staring at her son with bated breath and a light in her pale eyes. She notices that he has seen her in the mirror; their eyes meet. He stands with the blade in front of his face and gazes at her steadily. He sees her expression soften, as if she smiles without moving a muscle, changing only the look in her eyes, like a brief burst of sunlight through a veil of clouds, drifting away and gone before you've truly seen it. Then she steps back and softly shuts the door.

In the adjoining house, a young woman is dying. She has been sick for months, complaining of pain in her back, pain in her belly. Her four children have a neglected look. Her husband, the surly Henri, a cabinetmaker by trade, gets drunk and stays out late. The young woman, Emilie, is thirty-five years old. She stands in her kitchen, wasted and pale; she pounds on the thin walls for help; she shrieks in agony and asks for death. Céline holds the new-born on her lap, a premature baby girl named Helena. She nurses the child at her own breast, since she is still breast-feeding her own youngest daughter, Melanie. Years of breast-feeding were no exception in those days; it saved a mouth to feed. In the weeks that follow, Emilie wastes away rapidly. When Céline brings her something to eat, she throws it up almost at once. She screams with pain when anyone tries to tend to her swollen midriff. As far as I can tell from my grandmother's story, the cause of her death may have been an undetected tumour somewhere in her bowels; at the time of her death, she had a black boil on her belly.

Henri places the other children under Céline's care, not knowing what else to do with them. It must be a heavy burden for her to bear: her own five children, plus the youngsters from next door. After a few weeks, she is worn out. Franciscus, unable to bear the sight of his wife falling apart, walks in on his drunken neighbour Henri as he dozes in his armchair – the houses had no doorsteps to separate them from the street, and the doors were never locked in the alleyways – and insists that he send his children to one of the city's many charitable institutions. Henri grudgingly agrees and later moves away himself. He takes his eldest son with him, and his eldest daughter Leonie comes to mend clothes with Céline twice a week, another small source of income. For my grandfather, this means four new foster brothers and sisters, and for his poverty-stricken parents it means even more mouths to feed when the charity schools are closed. He never told me much about them, except that the eldest, named Joris, attended secondary school a few years later with financial aid from some Christian organization, a stroke of good fortune of which my grandfather was secretly a little envious. Joris grew to become a somewhat fretful boy, perpetually smitten with girls he was too shy to talk to, stiff and fussy, always finding fault with one thing or another, but once in a great while they would walk by Zuidstatie together and recall the idyllic days gone by, when they spent their Sunday afternoons strolling around the serene city. They would see each other for the last time amid the feverish turmoil of London in March 1915. One of them, my grandfather, was a war hero by then, returning to Belgium after his first convalescence; the other, the educated stepbrother he admired, had fled the war after the death of his anaemic wife and would die in obscurity somewhere near London.

He was my friend, the learned scholar, the elderly Urbain wrote in his fine, shaky handwriting. *I still idolized him, as I always had. No matter whether he was ill or in the pink of health, he was my hope of a better life.*

In the small chapel of the girls' boarding school run by the Sisters of Charity of St Vincent, Franciscus stood for months on scaffolding he had built himself. He whitewashed the walls, carefully added a thin golden layer to the ornaments on the pillars, restored the old biblical scenes, and even painted a few new ones. He received permission to consult books in the school library with etchings and plates depicting biblical figures. He made sketches on paper, exercises in which he drew hands in all conceivable positions. He also drew countless heads – tilted heads, listening or watching, faces staring at a child, a dead snake or a burning heretic, faces that had to be pensive and unrevealing. He learned to recognize that the great painters can be identified by the expressions in the eyes of their figures, and he did his best to approach that effect: how do you draw an intelligent look? What lines is it composed of? He often worked with a piece of charcoal that he held in a pair of metal pincers. Attached to the other end of the pincers was a tiny India rubber, which he used to draw lighter areas by rubbing out traced surfaces to varying degrees. Look, he said to his son, I can draw by erasing. This was the same technique my grandfather would later pass on to me when we went to parks and gardens to draw together.

Franciscus bought everything he needed, sending an errand boy, who had been assigned to him, to fetch an order of expensive pigment. He measured, sifted, dosed, blended, diluted, experimented and refined till he had the right mixture. He made trial brushstrokes on some boards he had sawn for that purpose and compared, deliberated, started over. It snowed, froze, thawed, rained, gusted, milder weather came, and all that time Franciscus was climbing up and down his scaffolding, day in and day out. Lying on his back, he painted the ceiling: a jumble of clouds and windblown robes, of streamers and vague faces, a divine epiphany that brought heavenly music to mind, the music of the spheres, imagined music, music in his cold, cramped knuckles, the music of lines, scratches, streaks, surfaces, folds, beams of light and hair, of fabulous creatures standing or lying around the main action: a small dog with a light brown snout, looking up at a saint; a fleeing stag with thin, delicate antlers in front of a mulberry tree – it hardly even seems to touch the ground, as if it were transubstantiating into the sacred unicorn of his wondrous superstitions. Music of the age, music of colour and nuance, music without sound, just a distant rumble, the rush of the city around the silent chapel, where he was all alone with his thoughts and dreams. Week after week, he came home with a stiff back from leaning over backwards to paint. There were days when the paint trickled into his beard and formed painful clots; sometimes it dripped onto his mouth and he had to spit out the bitter liquid. That gave him the idea of diluting paint with saliva, which created a truly splendid effect here and there, especially in Our Lady's sky-blue mantle, which, honestly, you'd like to pull off her shoulders and take home for your wife.

He finally finished the job after months of labour, and showed off the result with modest pride to the dour abbess, who brought in an abbot from some nearby monastery for the occasion. They scrutinized his work, looking pleased, but trying not to show it – if you praise a simple fellow like that, it'll only go to his head, and he'll stop applying himself. The 'good little sisters of St Vincent' showed less reserve. Turning their eyes to heaven, with their heads tipped back like Bernini's St Teresa in ecstasy, they stood beside the diffident church painter and made him blush with their cooed compliments and rolling eyes. The city's Christian institutions heard the success story of the humble painter who was capable of such miraculous things. He was promptly summoned by the Father Director of the

73

Asylum for the Deaf and Dumb, who informed him of his next assignment.

Franciscus, I have good news for you.

Yes, Reverend Father.

There's an opportunity for you to work in Liverpool for a year. It's a major assignment in an institution there.

Where is that, if you please, Reverend Father?

In England, Frans. You'll see.

But Reverend Father, how can I leave my wife and children?

You'll be well paid, Frans, and you can send your family more money every month than you'd earn here in six. You have eight days to decide. Talk it over with your wife. We'll send an expert woodworker and an interpreter over there with you. Go on, then, it's twelve o'clock now, you may go home to your family early today.

Yes, Reverend Father. Thank you. *Merci*, Reverend Father.

When he shows up in the kitchen at twelve thirty, Céline nearly dies of shock. What's wrong? Why are you home at this hour? Has something happened to the children?

He takes her in his arms, comforts her, and tells her what he has been told.

You're out of your wits, Frans, there's nothing but fog and vile factory smoke there. You can't handle that, not with your asthma.

No, no, don't fret, the director says it's a large estate, with a park where I can go for walks. I'll have short working days, no more than eight hours. I'll recover my health there, you'll see.

Céline's face is pale; her lower lip trembles. She does not know how to react; she turns away, straightens her back, walks to the far end of the kitchen, bends over, fills the coal scuttle, picks up the hook for lifting the lid of the stove, and heaves the coal into its smouldering mouth. A cloud of fine sparks drifts towards her face, her squinting eyes. It suddenly occurs to Frans that she looks something like a she-devil, a beautiful, captivating she-devil, with that fiery light reflected in her pale eyes. And he feels a little afraid of what will happen.

All right, Frans, all right.

They say no more that night.

For the next few weeks, Céline is at the sewing machine day after day. She makes three pairs of work trousers, three dark grey jackets of coarse linen, a suit for weekdays, and a suit for Sundays. One Saturday, she goes with him to a shop near Sint-Jacobsplein to buy a suitcase for the voyage.

Will you be faithful to me, Frans.

You silly fool. Come here.

He takes her in his arms and strokes her back, right there in the middle of the street, where people can see and are bound to speak ill of it.

The following week, they spend several days visiting his relatives and hers. There is no end to the asinine questions and droll remarks. He exchanges a resigned look with Céline. It's as if they've developed an entirely new relationship over the past few weeks, something larger yet more fragile, which makes their hearts beat faster when their eyes meet. At night, they cuddle close together, saying nothing. He caresses her in the dark and feels that one of her cheeks is wet. Even in bed, she keeps her back straight, he thinks. One day soon she'll snap like dry wood. He goes on caressing her. All right, now, Frans, I've no need of another baby whilst you're in England. So they lie still in the dark, side by side on their backs, both filled with longing, listening to each other's regular breathing, keeping themselves in check until morning comes. During the day, she sits on the sofa with her hands in her lap and does not hear the conversations around her. She sees herself in that large bed alone and is already shivering; she imagines the mean, cold, dirty dusk; she turns onto her side and squeezes her eyes shut.

On the day before his departure, she offers him a present: a razor, a piece of shaving soap, a leather strop, a block of alum and a cloth bag for his few toiletries.

Oh, Céline, my dear, you shouldn't have.

Don't lose it, Frans, you know I'm superstitious.

It's hard for my grandfather to part with his father. In his notebook he describes it as if it were yesterday: that 'delicate man, with his tender disposition' sitting across from his mother in a dark, rattling carriage with just one crack of light seeping in, bringing a faint, intimate glow to the faces of the silent husband and wife, like faces in a painting by Georges de la Tour. It is raining in Zeebrugge, he does not cry, nor does his mother, but he feels as if he is losing something for ever. High on a bank by the railway, under a lean-to where rain wets their stained faces, amid clouds of smoke and soot from the engine, they say their goodbyes and watch the stooped figure drag the suitcase onto the train. On the long trip back, as they jolt down the endless cobbled streets, she places her hand on his arm and says, Now you are the man of the house, my big strong lad.

A great gap had opened in our family he writes. The slow, interminable ticking of the cuckoo clock – a gift from a distant cousin to his father, who would carefully pull up the brass weights every night – fills their days, wearing away the time they must endure, ticking away the difficult mornings when his mother sits waiting for a letter and the postman does not slow his step as he passes their door. But when he does, she leaps up, grabs the letter from the floor, and goes to the shadowy front room to read it alone by a single small oil lamp while the children leave for school. Her heart pounds in her throat. A loose lock of hair falls in front of her face as she reads her husband's clumsy scrawl: *I have a long night ahead and am wholly alone here. It is very hard for me to find the right words, pray forgive me. I shall compose my letter to you in pencil first and then copy it over. The second time I shall find better turns of phrase to tell you how I am faring here. I start the day by cleaning myself thoroughly, dress up as if to visit some distinguished personage and put on that handsome waistcoat that you sewed for me. I am not lodged far from the chapel that I am to paint. It is a cold, bare place, but I mean to turn it into something sublime. When the weather is bad I say a Pater Noster for you. Each evening at nine thirty when I go to bed my thoughts are of you. To the west I see the changeless grey sea in the distance. May God bless and keep you, Céline, and our children too.*

He grows ever closer to his mother. The memory of a summer thunderstorm lingers, an image of their lives together. One night after the younger children go to bed, he's sitting in the small court-yard with his mother, telling her about the seedy cabarets where his pals from the foundry go after work, and she's teasing him, asking if he looks at girls too, when suddenly, without warning, a bolt of lightning shoots through the warm dusk, followed a few seconds later by a deafening thunderclap, just as he is telling her that he would never, ever do such a thing, because he only has eyes for her, and his sentimental confession is drowned out by the sudden tumult. Along the lane behind the house, wood pigeons flap from the swaying tops of the white poplars. As they run inside, the rain pours down on the roof, the courtyard, the street and their intimate world, which glows with an ethereal light. On the landing, just as Céline is soothing the frightened children roused by the storm, a window slams open, the frame hitting her full in the face as the rain spouts in. She stumbles, but regains her balance; the water floods onto the steps. In the flashes of lightning, he sees blood on her forehead, they push at the window together, the latch is broken. He tells her to hold the window shut to keep out the howling wind and the torrents of rain, runs down the stairs, and searches the firewood for a piece to wedge between the hinges. He leaps back up the stairs, taking them three at a time, and jams the wedge into the crevice, while above him the wind roars across the roof, the loose tiles rattling in the night. They stand together in their vulnerable house, soaked to their bare skin. Céline takes her son in her arms.

Aged seventy, he writes: *When she, my beautiful mother, clasped me to her breast, a great emotion washed over me and my heart raced. I missed my father so much, I saw the blood on my mother's forehead, I wiped it away and couldn't help weeping. Nothing makes a deeper impression on a boy than seeing his strong mother suddenly girlish and hurt. My mother laughed softly and said, 'You're as tender-hearted as your father, you are – it's just a scratch, silly boy', and she ran her hand through my rain-drenched hair. And now as I write this down I can't help weeping again when I think of my mother that night in the blue lightning, standing before me for a frozen instant like a lovely old portrait.*

Reading these lines, I recall something he once said to me: I have tried several times to paint my mother from memory but never succeeded, I couldn't capture the exact expression on her face, I smashed the last attempt to splinters and threw the canvas into the stove. On the other hand, he copied Raphael's *Madonna with the Chair* at least five times, and the look in the eyes of the child taking shelter in his mother's arms grew a little mistier each time.

A while earlier, he and a friend from the iron foundry had visited his friend's eldest cousin, who worked in the old gelatine factory.

You have to come and see it sometime, the cousin had said, it's unforgettable.

So one free afternoon they set off for the factory. It was in the blue and gold month of October, and the old chestnut trees along the avenue stood so leaf-still in the mild air that it seemed the world itself was holding its breath, so that not one detail of the day's fleeting beauty would escape the notice of the living, who had eyes, and noses, and senses for experiencing it all. My grandfather, who was always elated when he could pass an idle afternoon with a friend, twirled about madly, singing a song about pearls and joy – or something else that rhymed with 'girls' and 'boy' – and dancing by the banks of wild flowers gone to seed by the roadside: cow parsley and ground elder. With a final sprint to see who would reach the large, rusty factory gate first, they arrived at the supervisor's booth. He stared out at them through a small, dusty window and asked what their business was.

We're here to see Alfons, my grandfather's friend said. He's my *kozze*.

Have you got sturdy shoes?

My unsuspecting grandfather pulled off one of his clogs and held it up to the window. The man growled something inaudible and nodded his head towards the gloomy building. That very moment, the rusty gate swung open, and an enormous cart rolled out, its iron-shod wooden wheels rattling deafeningly over the cobblestones. The Brabant carthorse that pulled it was heading straight for them. They leaped aside. Foaming at the bit, the animal swung its large, gloomy head, its eyes gleaming with yellow obsession between the leather blinkers. The boys slipped inside, and the gate groaned on its heavy hinges as a man in a sleeveless leather jacket pushed it shut. He looked at them without expression, waving them away.

It wasn't until they turned around that they saw the large pile in the courtyard, and froze. Animal heads of all shapes and sizes lay in the centre of the filthy yard, heaped into a pyramid. The heads of horses, cows, sheep and pigs shone there in a viscous, spreading mass, freshly dumped from the cart. A swarm of fat flies, so dense and infernal they looked like a gleaming blue mist, droned around the heads with their huge extinguished eyes like staring boils, their bleeding eyes, their sunken eyes with dead gazes and blind pupils where maggots squirmed. But not only those eyes – there was also the mass of muzzles, jaws and snouts that dripped brown slime, the protruding tongues, bloody nostrils, broken horns and formless lumps. A swirling stench took away their breath. A man came closer. He was wearing a spattered greyish-brown coat and thick gloves with sleeves that reached up to his elbows. He grabbed a few heads carelessly by the horns, the ears or the snout, buried his fingers in a severed throat for a better grip, hooked his thumb around an empty socket, and pitched ten heads or so onto a long wooden wheelbarrow. The bloody slop oozed off the barrow as he rolled it through an open gate into the brick building. The boys remained transfixed by the towering heap of slowly spilling heads. It was as if the oxygen – that invisible substance they had never even been conscious of before – was being driven out of their blood vessels, their lungs, their eyes and their hearts, and replaced with a thick, asphyxiating ooze that would cling to them for ever.

Without a word, they stumbled over the slick cobblestones towards the factory building, from which they heard a confused hubbub of voices, metal blades sliding back and forth, continual thundering crashes like bodies falling into large tubs, and somewhere in the darkness beyond the noise, a sonorous clanging and juddering. When their eyes had adjusted to the dim light, they saw dozens of men in a row, standing before long tables on which the heads were sorted by animal. Horse heads next to horse heads, sheep with sheep, pigs with pigs, the muted tumble and thump of bony masses that seemed to disgorge more and more fluid as they were tossed and rolled, until, at the end of the long row, they were hacked into three pieces by burly men with cleavers.

The meat-cutters' jackets were so thickly spattered with muck that they seemed to have been hewn from some kind of liquid stone. They threw the pieces of head into large cauldrons on fires fuelled half a storey below, where men with shovels were piling on coal, their faces shining in the yellowish glow of the fire pits.

Only then did the boys realize that something around their feet was moving, shifting, sliding to and fro. Legions of white maggots that had fallen out of the heads were crawling over the floor in a thick layer. They looked at their open clogs, and then at the men's tall boots. They stamped in disgust, realized this only made the slime thicker, shifted uneasily from one foot to the other, and dared not proceed any further. A man sorting heads one-handed, while casually eating a sandwich with his other grimy hand, saw them there and motioned to them to make way. The man with the barrow streaked past them, nearly running into them again, and dropped his load at their feet. A black bull head rolled into one leg of the table, and the white maggots immediately went for it, like an invincible army sent from another world to cover everything and gorge themselves till nothing was left. This was a total eclipse in broad daylight, a dark substance out of which something unnameable was pressed, refuse transformed into refuse, death into sludge.

Just as the boys were about to go back outside, they were stopped by the cousin, who clapped Urbain on the shoulder and shouted, 'It's a sight to see, ain't it!'

Gagging at the rancid smell of the hand that had touched his shirt, Urbain nodded, a meek sheep that has stopped bleating and is willing to do anything if somebody will only make this stop. But it did not stop. The cousin dragged them along to the back of the building, where the thudding of heads in tubs and the dry, rhythmic banging of the cleavers was drowned out by the sound of grinding wheels and the whipping of huge leather driving belts. Here the boiled sludge was poured into tanks where it sloshed and eddied like bubbling magma as it drained away into a hole. What ran out of the rusty, filth-encrusted spout at the other end was – the cousin shouted in their ears – the basis for gelatine. It was poured into fifty-litre barrels, which were then fitted with round lids screwed on by men with large leather gloves.

The nephew, who was apparently the factory foreman, made a sweeping gesture towards the courtyard, where sparse grass grew between the rocks, and animal hides awaited tanning in another building. A large horse cart hurtled past, filled with barrels. They're taking that wonderful stuff to a processing plant, he said, where they filter it and take care of the smell. From there, it goes to every corner of the country, where they use it in all sorts of products. It's in all the fancy lotions for French-speaking ladies. It's what they rub on their noses and their dainty little cheeks. He sniggered. It's in your bottle of gum arabic, and it's in the sweets you suck on like manna from heaven. It's in the jam your mother makes for you; she spreads it on your sandwich, you're none the wiser. You're full of the stuff that comes pissing and dribbling out of those heads, dear boys, you're full of that rot, but you don't know it, because they can deodorize and filter and disinfect it until you no longer realize it's death you're sucking into your hungry little mouths, it's this sludge that those ladies of fashion are rubbing into their tender bosoms – fine bubbles of saliva sprayed from his mouth – it's all one and the same thing, but nobody knows. Good thing, too, otherwise the world would stop turning. He laughed, exposing his yellow teeth, hiccupped, and gave the thunderstruck boys a look of pity. The diabolical gleam in his eyes reminded my grandfather of the senseless idiocy of the goat in their small city courtyard. It was that senseless, slow-witted smile that would come back to him later, under circumstances then unthinkable, as he drifted between sleep and waking in the ice-cold mud, mulling over the things he had seen that day – the sludge of the world, which he absorbed for lack of any choice.

And all the cow parsley and ground elder, all the swaying plants that lined the avenue like a host of wayward angels, calling out to them that the world was not so bad, all things that rustled, moved and lived by the roadside that late summer, the turtle dove cooing monotonously to the soft sighs of the silver poplar, the last of the tortoiseshell butterflies and red admirals, a garden warbler in a pear tree – it was as if they could not hear it, could not see it, as if they had been robbed of all their senses. They walked side by side in silence, only nodding goodbye when their ways parted, in the late sun slanting over the first crooked houses of the city, bathing them in yellow evening light as if someone were shining a huge lamp on the world to illuminate a secret that nobody wanted to see.

*

One thing sticks in his mind in the days that follow: the sight of the animal heads in the gory courtyard. In his memory, the gentle glow of afternoon is falling over that heap of breathtaking ugliness, and what he sees are colours, tones, the subtlest transitions of light and shade, greys and red, sepia and midnight blue, crimson turned almost black, the delicate yellow, nearly white, of a scrap of undamaged hide by a dead snout. He thinks back to one of the old books he's seen his father leafing through – more specifically, to one painting that made a strong impression on him even as a small child: a skinned bull, painted by the famous Rembrandt. In that painting, a thing that in itself could not be called attractive was altered into a spectacle possessing power and beauty. This antithesis gnaws at his innards. It slowly dawns on him, as he stares into the roaring stoke hole in the iron foundry and the sparks dance around him like fireflies, that his shock of revulsion at the sight of that apocalyptic heap of rotting flesh filled with gaping dead eyes has awoken something that tugs at him, that hurts, that opens a new space inside him – that for the first time he feels a desire that seems greater than himself. It is the desire to draw and paint, and the instant he becomes aware of it, just as he's picked up another heavy ladle filled with molten iron, it's as if his knees fail him. The sudden realization washes over him with overwhelming force, in which there is an element of guilt. The realization that he wants to do what his father does – mingled with the bitter, shooting pain of missing his father – makes him want to drop that ladle of glowing fire on the ground, immediately, right now, and run to a place that is bright and quiet, like the churches and chapels where he spent so many days of his childhood at his father's side, and where his father retouched an angel's hand, while light descended in a glass-stained ray of colour and the silence was so complete that the minuscule scrape of the brush against the wall filled the whole interior. It wells up inside him like a sob, like a painful, electric shock from deep within, where his unconscious has taken its time to ripen before coming to light, there – amid that hellish noise, the hammering and shouting, the dragging and heaving, the rattling and clanging – he dreams of a heavenly silence, there in the heart of the dark, fire-smouldered vault of the workshop filled with toiling phantoms.

And he cries. He wails as he clasps his stinging hands around the rough wooden handle of that damnable ladle of fire and tries to concentrate, to behave himself, to do what he ought; but in that flash he knows that he no longer wants to do what he ought, that he wants to be like his absent father. I want to draw and paint, booms the voice within him, I want to draw, I want to learn to draw, and he fights with the dark force that shakes him and refines him. And all through the day, as he sorts iron, as he eats his sandwiches or makes his way over the precarious gangways down which all the men in the foundry saunter and shuffle the whole confounded twelve-hour day, all that day not another word comes out of his mouth.

Are you ill, Urbain?

He shakes his head no.

They leave him alone.

As he arrives home, hours late again because a demanding customer just had to have his mouldings delivered to his house that very day, his legs feel wobbly. His clogs have cracked in the heat, and a splinter is poking painfully into the arch of his right foot. He goes to his room without saying a word and creeps silently into bed. He thinks of his father and lets his tears flow freely.

Even though his father has often advised against it, in 1906 he begins taking drawing classes at St Luke's night school, where *Le Frère Professeur de Dessin* teaches him to draw 'line after line, no end of lines'. This soon starts to irritate and discourage him; it is not what he dreams of doing. With some guilt, he remembers his father's command: 'Do whatever you like with your life, but for God's sake, don't start drawing and painting. You can see what's become of me. This is not sixteenth-century Florence – remember that.' But what makes up his mind is the memory of the hours spent in churches with his father, whom he finds himself missing more and more. So in the months that follow, he spends two evenings a week bowed over his drawing paper, red-faced, in his clumsy fist a piece of graphite sharpened with his pocket knife. First exercise: straight lines. Lines slanting to the right. Lines slanting to the left. Vertical lines. Intersecting lines. Lines of different lengths. And when he begins to get the hang of that, they start over in charcoal.

Recommencez, Urbain! Begin again!

Lines, lines, lines. He sees lines through the window, lines through the clouds, lines through the eyes of his friends, lines through his dreams.

He falls asleep over his paper and dreams of a cast-iron sea from which breakers with fiery crests roll onto an endless white beach. After class, he barely notices that the other boys are striking up conversations, stopping off for a drink. He goes home and sees lines, he hates lines, he falls behind at work, he has ruined two moulds in the past few weeks, and the foreman shouts at him. After a while he starts missing classes and is reprimanded by *Le Frère Professeur* on the rare occasions when he does show up. He swallows his disappointment and lies in bed worrying as his mother's sewing machine rattles downstairs, because she has to earn extra to pay for his lessons. Is it really worth all that? For an endless series of stupid lines? How will he ever restore an angel's hand if he has to spend for ever and a day making lines on third-rate paper? When he tells the foreman he can stay at work longer again in the evenings, he bears the man's knowing chuckle in silence. But during those classes, he at least made a friend: a boy who had lost his right arm in an accident with a textile machine, but could draw left-handed with the best of them. He even made something of those lines: whole compositions, rhythmic variations, changing lengths, thicknesses and weights, lines varying from faint

85

to pitch dark, lines with personalities, lines long and short, armies of lines speaking a language inaudible but all the more visible, layer upon layer – it was as if he saw whole spaces inside them, endless dimensions and perspectives. They became hordes and armies, advancing throngs. They became buildings that existed only in that one-armed boy's mind, posts along roads, side views of endless rows of barrack windows, a futuristic city, architectural fantasies, level upon level, a world of vanishing points that pulled you in, while Urbain's drawing paper was filled with nothing but straight lines. At the end of the term, the boy was moved up to the next class: drawing blocks, cubes, rectangles, diamonds and then volumes. And again, he turned those mindless exercises into miracles, storehouses of mysterious boxes you longed to break open so that you could discover his secret – blocks and more blocks, open rooms and galleries in miniature, concave and convex blocks, how did he do it? It seemed as if the boy was carried away by visions, like musical variations for charcoal and imagination, his upper body slightly turned as if he were always ready to leap inside, into the secret depths of the world he was drawing. The stump on the other side of his body, that puny stump inside his pinned-up sleeve, gently moved along with him, describing small circles, entirely of its own accord, driven by some strange force, and it somehow seemed to charge the exquisite lines drawn by the other hand with hidden meaning and power. My grandfather had seen how pathetic his own exercises looked by comparison, and maybe his admiration for the boy had led to his discouragement. But he did not forget the feverish determination of his one-armed friend, who might well have made up all those patterns even without the *Cher Frère*, since they weren't even part of the assignment, but flowed directly from his hand, a world without cause or reason, simply taking shape.

On Friday evenings he sometimes strolled by the display window of De Gouden Pluim, the venerable art supply shop still open for business in Vrijdagmarkt today. Sable brushes, compasses and pencils, brushes and cases, linen canvases and sketch pads all lay in the dimly lit display, and my grandfather would stand with his hands in his pockets and a hangdog look, staring at all those beautiful things, at the dream that had spat him out.

One day, the one-armed boy pops up beside him.

Urbain, why don't you come to class any more?

He shrugs and says nothing, his eyes glued to the display.

The boy says, Come with me, start over.

He stubbornly shakes his head no.

But after the one-armed prodigy is gone, he takes a deep breath, gathers his courage, and uses his scanty pocket money – since he hands over practically all his wages to his family – to buy a sketchbook and a few new pencils.

The following week, he wanders into the elegant bookshop on the corner of Voldersstraat and Veldstraat, which has art books in the window. He leafs through them a little, glancing around nervously now and then, taking in the illustrations, absorbing them into his mind, gazing at the hands and eyes in Van Dyck's sublime portraits, at Tiepolo's coiffures, turbans, windblown garments, muscular shoulders and copulating snakes, at the meek, downcast eyes of a girl in a painting by Jordaens, at the odd expression of an onlooker in a Piero della Francesca, at the delicate Palladian arches of villas in the background of frescoes, at the proud peacocks and parrots in De Hondecoeter's imaginary avian parks, at colours and shapes that danced in his confused mind's eye.

The shop owner, Adolphe Hoste, a well-known figure in Ghent, is suddenly at Urbain's side, inspecting him top to bottom, observing his soiled clothes, sniffing the penetrating odour of iron and crude grease that clings to him, eyeing the wooden clogs on his store's fine parquet floor. He says, How much longer do you intend to paw at my expensive books with those grubby hands? If you don't mean to buy anything, *monsieur*, then make yourself scarce.

Humiliated, he steps outside, cursing under his breath, and feels such strength welling up inside him that he could draw all those sketches and etchings, all those paintings and frescoes from memory, just you wait, he'll show them a thing or two. He walks home, takes his sketch pad out of the drawer, sits down at the kitchen table, and while the other children are playing tag or hiding behind his legs under the chair, he tries to draw a biblical head, a thunder god, a patriarch, one with enough power to break the curse. He makes a terrible mess of it, a twisted face with clownish features, an unsightly thing that resembles the battered head of a dead bull. He throws the precious paper with its confused smudge of lines into the glowing belly of the roaring stove.

That entire winter, whenever he has a little energy left after dinner, he sits and draws. He starts by placing his left hand on the table and trying to draw it. The result is a distorted, evil-looking claw, the paw of a gryphon or some such creature, and he has fun transforming it into a genuine, blood-curdling set of claws, which he shows the children: Look, a monster! Their shrieks sound like encouragement. He draws the stock pot. It comes out as a crooked, ridiculous lump of stupid charcoal lines. Two onions turn into peculiar lumps of coal. Well, then, he'll draw lumps of coal, from memory, a big heap of them. That's not so easy either. Now he has to make sure the coals don't look like onions. Slowly, an apple starts to resemble an apple. A drawing pencil lies on the table. He copies it – oh, all right, draws it – with a thin shadow beside it. So that's what those lines were good for. Ever so gradually, he gets over his intimate humiliations and begins to enjoy himself. He even takes pleasure in the drawings that don't work, because they give him new ideas. And in that constant shape-shifting, those drifting metamorphoses, anamorphoses and variations on related forms, a new world opens up to him in those long winter months, something he can come home to after a long working day, something he starts to look forward to during his lunch break, as he washes down his sandwiches with lukewarm coffee and tries not to listen to the roars of laughter and the macho tales of hands up women's skirts, holes in toilet doors, randy serving girls in the scullery, the shapely buttocks of the mares by the inn, and other charming subjects of that nature.

He sits down in front of the mirror and tries to copy the lines of his own head. After an hour of scribbling, erasing, shading and trying to grasp the outlines, the face that grimaces up at him from the paper is so hideous he has to laugh. When his mother comes to peek over his shoulder, he whisks the piece of paper away.

Come on, silly, let me see.

No, Mother, please, don't.

He thinks of the one-armed boy, and of the dream world of lines and cubes.

He stuffs the densely scrawled sheets into the bottom of a drawer in the old cupboard in his bedroom, beneath his socks and underclothes. The next day, he starts over. Over and over, all winter. Spring comes, the other boys go out walking and swimming, on the first warm spring days they go boating with the girls on the Lys, but he sits at home alone and draws, while everyone else is outside, under the scudding white clouds and the warm air working its magic on the city. He is drawing and making progress, and as he sits there, all alone, he sometimes feels a kind of power inside him, a great, deep power that makes him feel like someone, someone who can do what others can't. After his months of effort, it's like reaching the top of a mountain. Don't be naive, a different voice inside him says, there is no summit, you've barely begun, it's a little clearing on the mountainside, a place to catch your breath, look down, and say, Just look how far we've come already. The thought fills him with quiet pride. But when he looks up – in other words, when he thinks of the reproductions in the bookshop he was asked to leave – he knows he has a long, steep road ahead. And even that doesn't scare him any more. He realizes how much he longs to see his father again so he can show him some of the sketches – there's no doubt in his mind that his mother gave away his secret months ago in her letters. He wants to see his father, he wants his father back. He falls into a deep, dreamless sleep.

Our outings to Herckenrath, the successor to Adolphe Hoste's bookshop, were like a solemn ritual. Never did my grandfather polish his black boots brighter than when we 'visited Herckenrath'. Never did he make a more dignified and impressive entrance, while Mr Herckenrath – known for his long-ago friendship with the late, great poet Karel van de Woestijne – was reshelving a few books pulled out by customers, somewhere in the back of the shop. As Mrs Herckenrath looked on benignly, my grandfather would leaf through a few books in reverential silence, standing in front of the rows of glossy spines, sniffing discreetly when he saw one that appealed to him.

He never left without buying something. The eyes of the French-speaking woman, weary with refinement, drifted over his fedora, his cane, his midnight-blue suit and his bohemian tie with a blend of affection and pity. Running her graceful ringed hand over the cover of a novel by Suzanne Lilar on the stack by her cash register, she waited until he had unrolled his banknotes and proffered two of them. She wrapped his book in beautiful paper with the name of her elegant, aristocratic shop and handed it to him with a measured smile and a barely audible *Au revoir, monsieur*; a sign of her willingness to see him as fully human, even if he did speak old-fashioned, hyper-correct Dutch. He took the book of paintings by the School of Fontainebleau, made a slight bow, took me by the hand, and said, Come with me, lad, it's time for a *crème à la glace* at Veneziana.

I later went to Herckenrath on my own more times than I can count and bought a few expensive bible-paper editions in the Pléiade series, my first books on philosophy, a few sumptuous volumes of art reproductions, and a monograph about Tintoretto. Not many Dutch books were available, and although some were laid out in a side window, it looked more like a hiding place than a display. Once I found a copy of my own first book there, lost among travel guides and a book about outer space, and was caught up in nostalgic thoughts of the ragamuffin in clogs who came in to leaf through the books and was sent packing, and later returned so often in the guise of a little gentleman. My first book was published six months after his death. He never dreamed that I would publish anything. Across the street, in the Viennese patisserie run by the Jewish baker Benjamin Bloch, well-born ladies partook of buttered croissants and coffee from a silver pot while perusing books they had purchased at Herckenrath; the wrapping paper lay neatly folded next to their ringed hands. They were so posh that even their Dutch sounded French.

One warm, windless day, his father returns from Liverpool. They all go to Zuidstatie to meet him. Decades later, my grandfather could still describe it in detail, like a scene from an old film unspooling before his eyes. The wheels of the train hiss and thunder as it rolls in under the roof of the station and comes squealing to a halt in a cloud of smoke and vapour. They are standing on the platform in the middle of a swarming crowd, and before they can even start to look around his father and the moustached woodworker, Mr Bracke, come striding towards them, waving. Céline rushes over to him; little Melanie clings to her skirts and stumbles along with her. She throws herself on her husband with such passion that the little girl falls to the ground. Franciscus looks down at his smallest child, who seems to recognize him only vaguely. He takes some sweets out of his coat pocket. In the calèche on the way home, the husband and wife look at each other like strangers. The coachman cracks the whip. Conversation is impossible over the rattle of the iron-shod wheels and the clop of the horses' hooves. When they enter their street, they see that a crowd of neighbours has gathered in front of their house. Some are clapping their hands. But when Franciscus gets out of the carriage, with a pale face and tired smile, supported by his wife, they fall silent. A couple of them reach out as he passes, to squeeze his fingers or lay a hand on his shoulder. Céline thanks them with a nod, the coachman lugs the large suitcase into the hallway, and she presses a few coins into his hand. They enter their humble home and shut the door behind them. Inside, an aunt and uncle have decorated the living room with home-made garlands, and in the kitchen, a large pot of soup is steaming on the stove. Franciscus takes a long look around, saying nothing, as if surprised to find everything just as he remembered it: the meagre patch of grass in the large courtyard, the goat pen, the hopping canary and the finch in their simple cage. He barely hears the questions his wife and children are asking; he turns to them in surprise and picks up little Melanie. Still uncertain of him, she lays her hand against his stubbly cheek. His eldest child, Clarisse, is a little jealous and moody; Jules and Emile are giggling; Urbain swallows and is silent. Céline doesn't know what to do with herself. Then she and her husband fall into each other's arms again. The children look on in embarrassment as their mother runs her fingers through their father's hair and covers his neck with kisses. He pulls away, goes into the corridor, undoes the belt around the large suitcase, and gives the boys a leather football, the girls a kind of board with hooks and numbers and a ring to throw over the hooks, and the smallest children a strange wooden horse with holes in it – the Trojan Horse, made by Mr Bracke, he explains. He pulls the tail out of the horse and shows them what to do: you shut your eyes and try to stick the tail in the right hole. The children stand and stare in wonderment. Then he takes out a small box and presents it to Céline. With his limited means, he has bought her a cameo and a necklace. She holds the cameo to her chest and looks in the mirror.

You fool, you. Come here.

When he sits down in the wicker chair where he always used to sit, the girls squabble for a place on his lap. He runs his stubbly chin over their cheeks, making them squirm and giggle in his arms.

Clarisse goes to untie the goat and bring it in. Their father pats the animal on the back and rubs the spot between its horns with his knuckles. She's getting on in years, our Betty, he says. And he falls silent again, staring out of the window.

Look at your eldest son, Céline says. He missed you most of all. He stood by me and made me proud the whole time; he neglected his friends so that he could help me to keep this family going. And he learned something that will amaze you.

Go on, Urbain, she says, show him your drawings.

At first, my grandfather turns white and shrinks back, shaking his head no. Then he sees the questioning look in his father's eyes, and goes off with a sigh to fetch his drawings. Franciscus takes the stack of paper and examines the sheets one by one. The self-portraits, the studies of hands. The sketches in which he tried out different poses: a bent leg, a foreshortened torso, a rag in the wind, gnarled trees, an angel with a trumpet. Some are clumsy, but now and then they are skilful and expressive.

My grandfather could not possibly have expected what happens next: his father bursts into sobs, puts the sheets of paper down on the table, and clasps his son so tight he can hardly breathe. Then he pushes the boy away, looks him up and down, starts to say something, bursts into tears again, and makes another attempt to speak, but gets no further than garbled fragments.

All right, Frans, all right, dear, Céline says. Sit down.

He squeezes his son's hand and looks at him in silence.

I'm sorry, he says finally. You can't imagine what it's like to be back. Everything is so familiar, but different.

He looks out of the window again and seems lost in thought. Then he coughs – a raw, scraping sound. Céline gives him a bowl of soup and feels how cold his hands are.

Frans, you're so cold.

Don't I know it, dear. Been cold for months. It's like it's in my bones.

Somewhere out in the street, they hear the hurdy-gurdy man. So he's still alive too? Franciscus says. The doves beat their wings on the low roof of the scullery, the male cooing and scratching. Céline hands him a drink.

Here, get that into you, it'll warm you up.

He downs it in one swig. It makes him choke and cough. Céline slaps him on the back with the flat of her hand.

You want another?

He nods, and sips from the refilled glass. His breath scrapes and squeaks.

Then, unexpectedly, he stands, as if struck by a thought. He wants to finish unpacking his suitcase. But Céline says he has to rest now, so that he can go to the *Frère Econome* the next day to ask for work. He protests at first, but then notices his wife shooing the children out of the house: Go play outside for an hour or so, your father's tired. She unbuttons her black apron and says, Right, upstairs with you, and her eyes light up. She leads him by the hand, and he follows her, almost meekly, up the stairs.

My grandfather writes, *So it was that my dear father came back into our lives. I saw, as his hunched back climbed the stairs behind my overjoyed mother, how thin his hair had grown. He was old for a thirty-seven-year-old man, with sharp features and dark shadows under his eyes. Amid all the joy of our reunion, fear had crept into my heart, a fear that would never leave me.*

He ambles through the streets. It is the autumn of 1907. In a few months, he will turn seventeen. The streets of central Ghent are quiet; the people there are living their placid, anonymous lives filled with trivial concerns. There is news from America of the Knickerbocker Crisis, a great panic unleashed by a scheme to corner the market in United Copper shares. J. P. Morgan and Rockefeller pour money into the failing banks and just barely manage to stave off a stock market crash. In Egypt, Lord Carnarvon receives permission to begin the excavation of Thebes. In the Netherlands, the visiting German Kaiser Wilhelm II arrives by warship. He informs Queen Wilhelmina that, should war break out, Germany will respect the country's neutrality. But why this talk of war? The Italian minstrel in the byway sings *Vissi d'arte, vissi d'amore*: I lived for art, I lived for love, I never hurt a living soul. Urbain tosses two five-penny pieces into the tin box dangling from a leather strap under his cart.

In the evening, he writes, he would go to his father's bedside and make the sign of the cross on his forehead, saying the magic word *Gobbleskipya*. This was all that remained in their everyday language of what had once been 'May God bless and keep you', said while crossing the forehead with your thumb – a time-worn formula, foolish and incomprehensible to the outside world, a secret code to soothe the heart when thunder roared at night. *Gobbleskipya* also accompanied the countless evenings of my own childhood, as a stone on the shore is a water-smoothed vestige of what once was a great rock jutting wildly out of the sea, traversing the millennia to end up on a bedside table, left behind while the sick man was sleeping, sick with the memories into which he always, irresistibly, strays in the night.

The soft, regular creaking of the springs in his parents' bed through the thin wall is like the music of the spheres, rocking him to sleep, without thoughts, without dreams.

On the distant west side of town, in yet another institution run by the Brothers of Charity, Frans received an assignment that would take him two full years. The rough woodwork in the sheds and storehouses needed a fresh coat of paint, and the broken panes in scores of old windows had to be replaced. Frans, who had regular asthma attacks, accepted the job with reluctance. He often had to spend hours on tall, rickety ladders, picking the shards of glass out of an old window frame in the draught that blew through the opening, removing the old putty with blunt knives, cutting new panes of glass, and putting them in place. He occasionally lost his balance while reaching for some tool or other, and cut himself several times on the brittle glass while flinging out his arm to keep from falling. On top of that, his work was constantly being interrupted by the priests, who came to him for all sorts of other odd jobs. This prolonged the unpleasant work in the chilly sheds.

He was counting the days, because he had been told that after he was done he could restore a fresco in the Brothers' main refectory and add his own 'paintwork and decorations'. The large fresco, damaged by damp, dated from the eighteenth century. The job seemed made for him. He decided to begin the restoration work even before finishing the first, more physically demanding job, and established an alternating rhythm, which allowed him to recover his strength at regular intervals. In the evenings he would sit by the stove in the kitchen and sketch: new figures, based on engravings he had found in the Brothers' library. The large fresco depicts Christ as a young man, against the backdrop of a vaguely Oriental building in a garden of trees and bushes hung with festive wreaths of foliage. Young men and maidens approach, bearing baskets of fruit and vegetables. At a long table in the middle ground, shabbily dressed peasants are served food and drink. Christ himself is in the foreground, greeting the bedraggled old folks and the children with a gesture of welcome. Beneath this scene, Franciscus repainted a quote from Luke on a gently curving ribbon the colour of oxblood, picked out with an edge of gold. It comes from the story of the rich man whose friends will not come to his supper. He says to his servant, 'Go out quickly into the streets and lanes of the city, and bring in hither the poor, and the feeble, and the blind, and the lame. Go out into the highways and hedges, and compel them to come in, that my house may be filled.'

On the internet, I go through all the addresses of Brothers of Charity monasteries and institutions, picking out the ones in Gentbrugge, Oostakker and Ghent. I find one named after St Francis, like my great-grandfather, but it's in Mortsel, out near Antwerp. Nowhere do I find a monastery that lies or might have lain to the west of the city and where he might have worked. Was my grandfather mistaken? I call a number of monasteries and hospitals. Not one has ever seen a fresco of that kind in the refectory: the walls were repainted before the Second World War, or there's been a renovation; it's always possible there was something of that kind a century ago, what do I expect, they can hardly scrape off the paint for me, I do understand that, don't I? And no, there's nothing in their records or archives about anything of the kind, they're terribly sorry, but they really must go now, thank you for your understanding, goodbye.

A fresco is a painting executed on freshly plastered walls. The colours are applied to the wet plaster and combine with it as it dries. The art lies in anticipating how the colours will look after they dry, because all hues are darker when wet; the moisture makes blues and reds brighter and more intense, while yellows and greens look matte. Suppose one of the maidens in the background of the large scene that Franciscus is restoring has had one of her legs eaten away by damp. Then you first have to coat the wall with highly diluted plaster until the dark patch of moisture disappears or at least is well hidden, all the while making sure to keep the surface perfectly even. No strokes of paint should show through the fresh layer of plaster, and this can be very tricky, since they are sometimes visible only in light from a certain angle, and then you have to retouch them with fine sandpaper. The next step is to repaint the leg, but not in the same shade you see in front of you. You have to try out various mixtures on carefully numbered boards brushed with plaster. Once these test boards have dried – it can take more than a week in damp weather – you can see whether the result is approximately the right colour. If not, you have to try again on a new test board.

Soon, the refectory was filled with dozens of test boards, all in different colours. Using this method, my great-grandfather carefully restored a missing leg, the greyish-blue folds in a white garment, a pale yellow apple on a serving dish, a patch of grass in the shade. Each time, he had to study his test boards carefully and hold them up next to the spot to be filled in. When the evening sun bathed the east wall in a treacherous red light, he could not work unless he first covered the high windows with old newspapers. But even that had its dangers: in the morning, when the light contained more blue, some additions seemed not entirely successful, subtly different from the original. Then the only solution was to apply a little more diluted paint, as inconspicuously as possible, or, if the shade was too dark, to cover it with a very thin, watery layer of white, most of which he then had to wipe away again with a fine sponge, a few days before the plaster was completely dry. One stroke too many and he would have to do the whole thing over again.

So weeks passed as he restored a few figures on a single wall, without any model or engraving to use as a reference. But the priests were enthusiastic; they brought Frans a cup of hot soup now and then and showered him with praise. Then he would become flustered and hardly knew how to respond.

In his memoirs, six decades later, my grandfather wrote, *Now that I'm old, and having painted all my life, I believe I have something of an expert eye. Well, then, I have a document in front of me – a coloured drawing of the restored frescoes showing what he added. And I am filled with even deeper reverence for my father, who died far too young, and I feel a pang in my heart when I see the love and devotion with which he retouched an old farmer's hand. For he saw each individual, however humble, as equally worthy of his attention. And I miss him more than ever now that I myself am nearing the end.*

And I wonder, as I have wondered for years, whether he delib-erately failed to mention that his father had once asked him to pose as the young Christ, whose shoulder and neck he had to restore. I eventually put this question to my fierce old Aunt Melanie – my great-aunt, really – who lived to the age of one hundred and three and remembered no more than vague details from back then, in her spacious apartment on Frère Orbanlaan along Zuidpark, where she held court, lucid and dignified, the last witness of a bygone age. No, she wasn't sure where that monastery was either, she had been far too young when her father died, and she'd never heard him talk about a coloured sketch of the fresco, but her brother had told her about it. As my Aunt Melanie spoke to me, daintily holding her teacup in her wizened hand, adorned with a single diamond ring, I pictured my grandfather, the little foun-dryman, with a ratty old blanket draped over his stocky shoulders, posing as Christ in that cold refectory in the quiet years before the Great War, with his father in front of him, sketching away without a word, and it's as if the scene in my imagination becomes a memory, the painter painting a painter, something I seem to have truly experienced and can call to mind right now, right here, now that I too feel the stealthy approach of old age, and the dead grow more and more alive in an ineffaceable fresco, an allegory no living soul can ever revisit or recover, but which has been burned into my being.

Dans le ciel il y a une danse, says plucky old Aunt Melanie, the youngest of them all, the baby of the family, and she laughs her girlish, centenarian laugh.

My beloved father is going downhill fast. I lie awake at night. In bed next to me, I hear and feel the regular breathing of my eldest brother Emile. My two sisters, Clarisse and Melanie, are sleeping in the alcove in the furthest corner from my bed behind a folding screen. Next to the door, little Jules lies in his little bed. My nervous fatigue keeps me from falling asleep – images of the foundry flicker through my head. The streetlamp sends its pale beam slanting down beside my headboard. In the half-light of night, the window draws a black cross on the whitewashed wall.

The fumes of the small oil lamp fill the room. I can still hear clogs rattling down the pavement outside, and I try to guess from the cough of a passer-by what kind of person it is – a man or woman, young or old. My mattress is torn at the foot of the bed, and the shredded straw filling sticks out between my toes like pipe stems. Further down the street is the foundry, its heavy gate shut for the night. Next to it, across the street from the working-class houses around their little courtyards, is Café De Muyshond, where the fancy women are. I can hear the muffled music. Someone is singing along in the street: 'Tick-tock goes the mill . . . it never fails to turn its sails.' After a while I hear my father gasping for breath as he clambers up the stairs. Soon after that, my mother goes into the children's room again, puts a warm cover over the little ones, makes crosses on their foreheads, and puts out the oil lamp on the mantelpiece. Then I listen to the howling of the sheepdog in its kennel in the back of the foundry courtyard, to the whistle of a distant train, the screech of the iron wheels as the heavy locomotive tilts, rounding the sharp corner to the harbour. But most of all, I listen to the wheezing, panting sound of my father drawing breath. I can hear it distinctly, because my parents always leave their bedroom door ajar to let in the fresh air he badly needs. And I pray, for as much as an hour, pleading with God to protect my father, to save his soul and, if possible, cure him of his illness. I pass the rosary beads between my fingers as I murmur, and some nights my face is wet with tears. Dear Lord, please save my father, please, Our Father who art in Heaven, hallowed be Thy Name . . . I sink into a kind of stupor, and when I awake, I hear my mother downstairs in the kitchen, shaking the ashes out of the stove grate and heating the fire with the bellows so that she can quickly prepare a cup of warm milk for her husband. She comes upstairs with the milk, and I hear her say to my father, 'Here, drink a bit, it'll do your throat good. And rest a little longer, everything will be all right.' When I get out of bed, I peek furtively into my parents' room. My father is sleeping peacefully on his side. The old sheets have slid off him. I tiptoe into the room, cautiously rearrange the sheets, cover up my father, and creep downstairs. My mother gives me such a reassuring look that all the weight is lifted from my shoulders. I embrace her, wash my face at the pump, drink a cup of chicory coffee, put on my jacket for work, pick up my knapsack, in which my mother has already put the sandwiches she's made for me, sling it over my shoulder, slide my feet into my clogs at the front door, and step out into the early-morning street. It is late January, Christmas and New Year's Day are just a memory, and soon it will be Carnival – a whole week of people in masks whooping down the streets. Shreds of paper blow over the footpaths like a final flurry of snow, pale and smudged. Café De Muyshond is bursting with drunken merrymakers. At the end of the street two mounted gendarmes, their swords at their belts, keep an eye on the festive crowd.

The city is strangely quiet in the days that follow, as though all the people are staying at home to lick their wounds.

The first warm days are on their way. A hint of spring, a blue sky with white clouds sailing over the grim factories. Hope sails through the streets and alleys. The locals buy tubs of brown soap and clean out rooms grown sooty from months of heating. The windows are wide open all around. Jars of paint and buckets of whitewash are at the ready. They whitewash the walls of the small rear courtyards to keep the damp out and apply a shiny black stripe of tar at the bottom to keep pests away. The smells are familiar, the neighbours more cheerful, and chirping sparrows fly in and out of the hedges. The poor, black soil in the urban courtyards is fertilized with horse manure, which you can scoop right up off the streets. Amid this humble, hopeful world, my fears about my father's condition swell to such paralysing proportions that I feel like telling them to the trees and bushes. He has been at home with a nasty cough for three days. He sits shivering by the blazing stove during daylight hours and lies in bed wheezing at night with three pillows to support his aching back. The blue line along his gums is a symptom of lead poisoning from the white lead he uses so often at work, a condition that may worsen his shortness of breath. The doctor comes to see him every day, and friends and relatives stop by to ask my mother how he is. By our front door, the neighbour women whisper to each other. My courageous mother slams the door shut with a bang. A nauseating smell fills the house – the smell of illness. Over the past week my father's coughing fits have left dozens of bloodstains on the whitewashed wall beside the bed. Next to the bed are untouched bowls of broth and tea, biscuits grown damp and stale, and unnoticed fruit. The Prior and the Frère Econome come from the monastery to visit him: 'You've been doing such fine work recently, Frans. We hope to see you back again soon. Your trial boards are all dry now.' My father breathes more and more heavily, trying with each exhalation to tell them he knows how far gone he is – 'yeh . . . yeh . . . yeh . . . yeh . . .' morning, noon and night until everyone in the family is climbing the walls. In the afternoon, my mother sits behind the wicker chair where he sits groaning, holding her hands up against the back of the chair. Her eyes wander out to the treetops in the courtyard, swaying against the dull grey sky. The budding branches whip back and forth in the April rain like bare arms raised to heaven. My mother's eyes are ringed with red, but not a word of complaint passes her lips. The Prior and Econome are impressed. 'We shall do our best, Madame Céline, and remember your husband in our daily prayers. He has grown very dear to us.' My mother shrugs.

I stay up with her the following night to care for my father. In his exhaustion, he has come down with pneumonia, a potentially fatal condition. In the early twentieth century there was no available method of easing his suffering – no antibiotics, no penicillin. In 1908 the medicines on a terminal lung patient's bedside table were stramonium, camphor, ether and tar pills. My mother makes him another cup of milk with sugar to build up his strength and orders him to drink at least a little – but he has great difficulty swallowing and immediately coughs half of it up again. The sugar irritates his throat, and the milk makes his body produce even more asphyxiating mucus, but we did not realize that in those days. Breathing has become an exhausting struggle for him. His entire upper body twists and strains for the slightest sip of air. The shortage of oxygen in his blood makes his heart beat more than 120 times a minute, twenty four hours a day. His mouth is parched, his lips have split. His eyes seem to bulge every time he can't get any air – sometimes for a full half minute. He grows thinner by the day. His face is sunken, his nose as sharp as a mummy's. He sits up in bed: 'Urbain . . . you must . . . fetch my cane – the smooth cane . . . to stick into my throat . . .' My mother shrieks: 'Frans, please, you're driving us mad!'

I have never seen her like this. She tugs at her hair, wrings her apron like a rag, kicks the headboard of his bed, stomps across the wood floor in her black-stockinged feet, seething with helpless rage. In the twilight before dawn the priest comes to the door with the consecrated oil. Just then something inside my mother snaps. She leads the Reverend Father upstairs. By my father's bedside she sinks to her knees as the clergyman murmurs his prayers. Our delirious father is hardly aware of what's going on around him. The soot-black oil lamps go on fuming – a cloud of smoke hangs in the small, suffocating room. The neighbour women have gathered around our front door, 'blabbing and yammering', as my mother says with suppressed exasperation. An hour later, the doctor arrives in his little chaise and orders immediate admission to the hospital. The hospital staff, three nuns and two orderlies, do not arrive until late in the afternoon. They lift my father onto a wooden stretcher, and my mother wraps him up in two coats, his and hers. 'There you are, my boy – we can't have you catching another chill.' He lifts his upper lip in a wan grimace meant to signify a smile. He looks into our eyes and, panting, says to his wife, 'Goodbye, sweetheart. Be back . . . soon . . .' The rest is lost in a coughing fit that has him heaving up phlegm.

The stretcher is loaded, with difficulty, onto the back of the horse cart. My mother and I sit down on the bench in front. My father reaches forward to clasp my hand and stammers a few words I can't make out over the rattling wheels and clopping hooves. I nod my head yes. My father squeezes my fingers.

After he is admitted, the file cards filled in and his clothes handed over, my mother and I silently walk back home. She pulls me into the chapel of Our Lady of the Seven Sorrows, where she lights a few candles, falls to her knees, and sinks into mumbled prayer that seems to go on for ages. After a while, she falls forward and stays in that prostrate position. I sit next to her with my hand on her back. I can see the sky darkening above us through the stained-glass windows. I hear sounds of children playing on the little square in front of the chapel. The flames of the candles in front of the Virgin are so motionless they seem frozen. Under the statue is a clumsily painted inscription: 'Vous qui tremblez, venez à Dieu car Il guérit.' Ye who tremble, take refuge in God, for He will heal you. By the time my mother stands up again, darkness has fallen. Come, she says. We make our way home, where my brothers and sisters have gone to bed without supper. I sit on the edge of my mother's bed for a long time that night. We say nothing. The next morning, we are at the hospital gate before nine. The nuns walk up and down the long, high-ceilinged corridor, avoiding our eyes. They place the clothing we brought the day before on a table where a physician is seated. 'Chère Dame,' he says, 'please do not be alarmed. It was Our Lord's will. Your husband had what we call galloping consumption. He passed away at three o'clock this morning. Be brave now and care for your family. That's what Our Lord expects of you.' He pushes her husband's rosary and wallet towards her. His underwear has been tied up in a package. My mother turns crimson, then ashen. She takes the package, stammers a mechanical 'Merci, docteur', and stumbles outside.

Out in the street I try to hold her up, but she slips out of my arms like a rag doll. I help her over to a bench by a flower bed, where crocuses and daffodils are flowering in bright rows of yellow and blue. She starts sobbing as if just now bursting open inside, sobbing so hard I fear that she will choke. She kicks at the flowers with one clog. 'I won't have it, I won't, I won't,' she cries. I try to quieten her down but that only makes things worse. Her body shakes and heaves as if a devil were loose inside it. I grip her by the shoulders. After more than a quarter of an hour of this, she seems so worn out that she lapses into silence. She looks at me – her light grey eyes seem to wander in her head. 'A widow at thirty-eight,' she says. 'I can't, I won't.' Again she falls into a sobbing, howling fit. Her chignon, done up so carefully that morning, has come loose, and she looks a little wild. I can hardly understand my own emotions. I'm unable to weep – it's as though there's a stopper in my chest, a hard, foreign object that was not there before but is now stuck so firmly in place that it causes me indescribable pain. There comes Aunt Rosa, who was at our house watching the children. She immediately sees what must have happened, helps my sobbing mother to her feet, and drags her along. My mother bobbles like a jointed doll beside her under the trees that line the Coupure. She frequently stops in her tracks and starts sobbing again, and a couple of times her legs fail her. A man rushes over and tries to help her up. She gashes his hand with her nails and screeches at him to go away. I stammer nonsense: that the doctors made a mistake, that our father may just be in a coma, that I'll go back and see for myself, that I— My mother gives me a rough shove. 'Be quiet, Urbain, please, shut your mouth just this once, for God's sake.'

Our mouths will stay shut for weeks on end. Not a word is spoken in our house, because we all live in fear of my mother's madness. She has closed herself off completely to everyone and everything. At the start of the day, she baths her children without a word. She silently gives them their milk in the morning and their buttermilk oat porridge in the evening. She lets Rosa take care of the dishes and crawls into bed even earlier than her children, remaining there until the following morning. She no longer traces the cross on our foreheads at bedtime. She seems like an automaton, a spirit, an apparition vaguely resembling our mother, but unapproachable. She sits down at the table one evening and suddenly yowls like a dog – 'my Frans, my poor boy' – and crumples into a quaking mass, throwing up her dinner next to her chair. We children look on anxiously. Melanie starts to cry. I help my mother upstairs to her room. The spring wind beats on the windows with dull thuds. I listen to the strange creaking, as if the frame of the old house is gently moving in the unbearably long night. At the first hint of dawn, a blackbird sings on the roof. It's as if he is absorbing all the air, all the air in the world, the air our father could no longer draw into his lungs.

After three days, after the pauper's funeral, I return to the foundry. Although no one asks me anything, the men go easy on me, taking the most demanding jobs off my hands. I come home in the evening to find my mother sleeping in her husband's wicker chair. Her long, black hair has come undone and fans wildly around her pale head, as if she were one of the Fates. The goat has got into the kitchen again, and the floor is covered with the gnawed remains of bread and vegetables. My brothers and sisters are not there. I tie a rope loosely around the goat's neck and lead it outside. Going into Café De Muyshond, I ask if the bartender wants to buy our goat. Without any fuss he agrees, thrusting his hand into his cash box. He gives me thirty francs for old Betty – too much, in fact, but it will prove to be a lifeline, just enough to see us through the first few weeks. When I return home and give the money to my mother, at first she stares as if she has no idea what it is.

Merci, Urbain.

She goes upstairs to her room and closes the door. Half an hour later, she comes back down again. I am sitting with my hands between my knees and staring outside. 'Here,' she says. She gives me my father's gold watch, the pocket watch I reclaimed from the Mount of Piety. 'Take good care of it, Urbain — it's the only family heirloom we have left now.' She disappears up the stairs again and does not come out until the next day.

After typing up the pages above, I lay sleepless in bed and saw, in the night, their epoch, their vanished world, their figures rising before me, on a snowy New Year's morning when the five children of Céline and Franciscus, elderly people even when I was a boy, came into the house: Aunt Clarisse, her wavy white hair in a bun, trembling, with her shiny black cane in her hand, and her husband Fons at her side, a boisterous man, always puffing on his pipe and telling jokes and showing up in our kitchen unexpectedly, with old-fashioned bicycle clips around the bottoms of his trousers and the sweet smell of pipe tobacco hanging over him, his greying copper hair stiff and straight on his craggy head; wheezy Uncle Jules, my grandfather's youngest brother, married to Aunt Leontine, an uncomplicated woman who drank gin out of tiny crystal glasses all day long and, no matter what she saw, would lay her chubby hand on her formidable, lace-covered bosom and say, O Lord have mercy ('*Oloramercy*'); Uncle Emile, the middle brother, whom I remember only as a man in a dusty chair, suffering from Parkinson's disease — I see him striking a match again and again, in hopes of relighting the stump of his cigar, but because his hand trembles in slow waves, he keeps putting out the lit matches, until my grandfather, older but in vastly better form, rises from his chair to light a match for him, so that Emile, already short of breath, can puff rhythmic clouds of smoke and inhale fire into his cigar end, appearing each time to draw in the flame for an instant before blowing it back to life in small puffs of smoke — and finally, the baby of the family, my Aunt Anie, with one 'n', as the elegant Melanie called herself in her later years, next to her husband, my over-perfumed Uncle Odilon, who was a hairdresser with wandering hands, as rumour had it, and a full head of wavy black hair well into his seventies. Finally, the man around whom everything revolved, the eldest son, my grandfather, next to his quietly smiling wife Gabrielle, in whose home the whole family gathered every New Year's morning. One after another, they marched through the front door, stamped and wiped their heavy boots on the mat with thumping and scraping sounds, and shouted out to my mother that they were really going to make a pigsty of her nice neat home this year. They brought the smell of snow and cold air with them, the mothball smell of their dark winter coats – loden, mink and astrakhan – and the smell of lavender and Marseilles soap. Their dark forms are larger than life, because memories like that grow along with your body, so that adults from our childhood always resemble an extinct race of old gods, still towering over us. They were constantly cracking jokes; after moaning and groaning into their chairs – 'We're not getting any younger, are we, Urbain?' – they would reminisce, dredging up old stories, often accompanied by peals of laughter that petered out into a pensive 'Yes, it sneaks up on you, doesn't it, my dear . . .' An occasional sigh, and then Fons would call out to my mother that she was not as generous with her liqueur as she used to be, and out would come the glasses, along with another round of madeleines and sponge fingers. Fons would bring smiles to everyone's faces again with a wisecrack in questionable taste, and my Aunt Clarissa, shaking her head, would say, 'Oh, Fons, you dirty man', while the others chuckled discreetly, my grandfather looked disapprovingly out of the window, and I had no idea what they were talking about. Now I wish I could hear their stories again, every colourful detail, because although I lurked unnoticed in the room, seeing and hearing everything, I understood nothing; I, the miscreant who would shatter their late father's watch a few years later. Very soon the room beneath the *lanterneau*, as they called the colourful stained-glass skylight in the roof, would be filled with cigar and pipe smoke. Just as quickly, the bottle of Elixir d'Anvers was emptied, and gin was brought to the table at Leontine's request. 'It's good for what ails you, even better than elixir,' Jules said, chuckling. My mother rushed in and out with 'sweets and savouries', as she called them, they talked about the children and grandchildren, and about who had died in the past year, and how unbelievable it was, and who had one of those newfangled gadgets in the house – a 'telly-vee', Jules said with a sneer – how pointless or wonderful and how expensive they were, and the problems with the city's old-fashioned radio relay system, until Melanie would coyly say that she always made the most expensive choice, because the cheap stuff costs you more in the end, and Jules would cry out, Our little Melanie is every bit as *précieuse* as our dear departed mother, and my grandfather would protest: Our mother wasn't one bit *précieuse*, what are you talking about?

Clarisse stuttered and trembled her way to the age of one hundred and six, as calm and clear-headed as ever; Melanie reached one hundred and three, wistful and elegant till her final day; my grandfather made it to ninety, plucky and sentimental; Jules and Emile died sometime in their mid-seventies. They were all survivors, tough people, hardened by the poverty of their youth and the brutal war years, Christian to the depths of their souls, but pragmatic and coolly ironic about the actual conditions of their lives. Their chronology was as simple as it was efficient, with just one point of reference: 'that was before the Great War' or 'that was years after the Great War'. They never said much about the Second World War. What was there to say? They had gone hungry, eaten bread made of rags and potato peels, seen eels as thick as a man's arm in the Scheldt river; the Germans were polite to them, even when carrying out surprise inspections, no complaints there; and oh yes, they blasted the 'salt mine' (as my family called the salt depot outside of town), but those were mere anecdotes.

*

They sit, they talk, they stop, they sigh, they laugh, they cough, they swallow, they take another sip, they say, Yes, life's an awfully funny thing. I can see their hands in their laps in my mind's eye, one pair gnarled with dirt in the cuticles, another delicate or pale. But I cannot draw them as my grandfather could. A strange kind of unearthly light surrounds their dark forms, the steadfast light of things that can never return. Gone, perished, a scattering of sunken headstones, their houses have been renovated or demolished, the addresses have grown vague, the streets where they lived have changed beyond recognition, the watch has stopped, the cogs are broken, and I fumble with the swept-up pieces, knowing I will never be able to make it run, tick, live again, as it did a century long.

It took half a year before Céline straightened her back and seemed to resume her life. It must have been in late summer, one day in early August. The summer months had slipped by unnoticed – a vague impression of time passing, light slipping by, warm nights of tangled dreams, waking up covered with sweat and feeling the venom of sorrow and grief fill her veins. She had grown thin, which somehow made her look even more dignified. A few white hairs stood out where her chignon reflected the light, making her aura still brighter, hinting at catharsis and inner resolve. She had formed the habit, whenever she passed the coat rack in the hallway, of running her knuckles over her dead husband's winter coat, which had remained hanging there for months. In the sky over the fields behind the house, she had witnessed a fight, a crow assailing a magpie over and over again; the birds made a dreadful racket, swirling around each other, swooping away, sailing together in a death-defying dive, and stabbing at each other with their beaks while in full flight. She had stood and watched the circles in which they moved. The sight was beautiful and strong, she felt, and it brought a new sensation, a kind of clarity, as if a stream of pure, fresh water were running through her numbed, dormant body. She had looked around, heaved a deep sigh, and felt as if she were waking up after months of narcosis. The house was a filthy mess, the windows dull and dusty. The sight of it dismayed her. All that time, she had thought she was as conscientious as ever. Where were the children? Were they playing in the street again? What did they do all day? She had to admit she did not know. They often went to the neighbours' house for supper, and they stayed out so late after school that she had to go from door to door to round them all up at bedtime. Suddenly, it seemed humiliating and unbearable. She had lived on her eldest son's meagre income, and their last reserves had been used up long ago. Urbain had his supper somewhere else too; she didn't even know where.

She looked around again in surprise. And then, again, into the languid August sky. The birds were gone. A few low clouds drifted over the roof, heavy with the promise of rain. She was overcome by a yearning to walk out into the summer shower. She went into the courtyard; the first drops fell. She raised her head and sobbed, silently. It helped, it drew the air in, opening a space inside. She seemed to become one with the air around her. She swallowed and let the rain on her face run down her neck, as soothing as balm on a wound. Her scorched soul, the fire that had to be extinguished. It suddenly began to pour; water fell in torrents. She opened her hands and lifted them, palms to the sky. A distant peal of thunder rolled through the firmament. Her thick, black clothes were soaked. She shivered with enjoyment – a feeling she hadn't experienced in a long time. When the shower had passed, she returned inside. Her clothes stank. She went to her bedroom, took everything off, and put on fresh clothes.

That was the moment when she straightened her back.

She tidied the house. The birdcage was empty – where had the finch and the canary gone? The day her eldest daughter Clarisse had found them dead and thrown them away without a word, she hadn't noticed. She hadn't even noticed that her husband's winter coat had been moved a month earlier, from the hallway to her bedroom closet. It struck her only now. It seemed to her as if she'd just run her hand over it that morning. How could she make sense of that? She remembered nothing, she was empty, but also – for the first time – lighter, brighter.

The next morning at nine, she stood at the gate of the Brothers of Charity in Oostakker. They let her in. She asked the prior if they had work for her. They did. She could make clothes for the insane asylum that the Brothers ran. That very same day, she walked all the way to the Dr Joseph Guislain Hospital near the Nieuwe Vaart canal, where she would receive sewing jobs from that time on. Now and then, she had peculiar instructions; the sleeves were sometimes extremely long and had to be sewn together. In the large scullery she set up two sewing machines, one of which was on loan from the hospital. She bought the other one through hire purchase. As soon as the youngest children left for school – Emile was already working as an assistant in the foundry with Urbain – she was joined by Leonie, the eldest daughter of the neighbour woman who had died young, who had agreed to help her out for a pittance. Then the rattle and purr of the sewing machines began. Leonie filled the day with ridiculous stories and gossip; Céline barely said a word in reply, but it obviously put her at ease, diverted her mind, and the work went more and more smoothly as the days passed. Payment was prompt, and the rates were reasonable. The family's finances were looking a little less dire.

One day, after delivering another fifty garments, she and the talkative Leonie went to the shoe shop in Langemunt. Céline's first pretty shoes since childhood – it took her an hour to decide, even though there were only four pairs for sale in her size. When she thought about it, the expense seemed absurd, but it brought a feeling of foolish happiness deep inside like an itch she had to scratch. She chose a pair of laced boots in matte black.

I feel just like some stuck-up lady, she said, laughing, and her pale eyes flashed with irony for the first time in many months.

Men keep turning up at her door, who just have to sit down with her and have a good talk about life sometime, isn't that right, Madame Céline? They are distinguished gentlemen, they are modest clerks, they are ordinary workers, the city evidently has no shortage of widowers apprised of her husband's death. You're still so lovely, and so all alone, that's no kind of life for a spirited woman like you, so I says to myself, I'll stop by sometime and see –

That's quite all right, don't trouble yourself, she replies, and she passes the man the coat he has just hung over a chair. Sometimes one of them comes to the door, cap in hand, faltering and quaking and going bright red, and offers his hand in marriage on the spot. Sometimes she's amused, sometimes touched, and sometimes she laughs herself silly. More often, she's annoyed and slams the door in their faces. Some slink away, their shoulders drooping, others ask her to think it over, and one or two of them say something truly vicious. Even the family doctor makes an unexpected house call one day, and she can tell why he's there from his furtive chuckling and his comments about how unhealthy it is when a woman has no man to put her through her paces. *Monsieur le Docteur*, she says, have you forgotten your Hippocratic Oath, or should I have a heart-to-heart talk with your wife one of these days? He couldn't get out of the house fast enough.

She goes to the cemetery alone. That's what she prefers. Sometimes she stays there for hours.

Mama, what do you spend all that time doing there? It was dark by the time you came home yesterday.

I talk to your father, Urbain, it eases my mind.

Do you tell him about all the suitors who come to the door?

Yes, she says, laughing, I tell him everything.

The following week she brings along a tin of black paint to touch up the iron cross on the shabby grave. She spends a long while there, thinking the whole time about the body of her beloved Frans, just a few feet away. How must he look now . . . The thought makes her head reel. She wants to scratch away the soil with her nails. Eternal slumber, she thinks, eternal slumber, damn it, damn it, he's so close to me. She grinds her teeth so hard they nearly break. Then she takes a deep breath; the dark urge to dig up the coffin has worn her out. She closes her eyes, waits for her dizziness to pass, and returns to painting. My poor painter, she mumbles, look at me here now, painting your cross.

When she's done, she looks up and notices all the eyes of the faded portraits on the graves. It's as if the countless eyes of the countless dead are all on her. 'What countless numbers death already has undone' – she remembers the line of poetry, but cannot recall where she read it. She shudders. There is no one else left in the graveyard. Has she been here so long? It's already dusk. She'll have to hurry to make it to the exit before the caretaker shuts the gate. She is still squatting, about to stand up, the wind rises, she hears a sudden loud rustling behind her, from far away, approaching between the graves at ferocious speed. O my God, it's the devil, she thinks; help me, Frans, the devil's coming for me; what did I do to deserve this? She shivers, she stands up straight, her whole body is trembling. A large piece of dirty paper flies onto her back, she lets out a shriek, the paper slides away like a great hand, a foul, groping hand that scrapes over her left arm. The next moment, it flies on between the graves until it gets caught in a bush, where it remains, convulsing like a formless animal. She feels her heart pounding in her temples. In utter distress, she runs to the exit as fast as she can. The man lets her out with a mumbled 'G'night to you, madam' and shuts the creaking gate with a bang behind her.

113

From that day on, she brings along her eldest son whenever she visits the cemetery.

You have to protect me from the evil spirit, she says with a smile. Suppose he comes for me, what will you do then? She laughs again, but he sees the fear shining in her pale, unfathomable eyes.

My mother, my elderly grandfather wrote in his memoirs, *was pursued like a rare and coveted butterfly*.

She kept the front door locked for months, even during the day.

It must have been not long afterwards that Leonie's father began stopping by the house to pick up his daughter. One day he sends her home on her own, comes into the kitchen, heavyset and clumsy, wringing his hands, and asks Céline to marry him. She bursts out laughing and says the very idea is absurd. He presses on, saying he earns a good living and she could use a little help, and what with him being a lonely widower and her a widow— She interrupts to say it is out of the question. But Henri keeps coming back; eventually, she forbids him to pick up his daughter after work. Things quieten down for a while, and then the letters start coming, delivered by an embarrassed and somewhat giggly Leonie. Clumsily written letters, brief notes intended to flatter, in a ludicrous, formal style full of grammatical blunders – what is he thinking? She tosses the letters into the coal scuttle and notices Leonie biting her lower lip. After another six months of increasingly curt and accusatory notes, he shows up again, red faced, his hat in his hand. He makes a proposal with an ultimatum: she can take a month to think it over, and otherwise his daughter will not come to work there any more. Leonie, asked for her opinion, refuses to get involved at first, but finally mumbles that it might be nice if Céline were her mama, and her eyes fill with tears.

The proud widow straightens her back in her customary fashion, keeps her own counsel for three weeks, and then says, 'Fine, if I must.'

My grandfather is shocked, outraged, bewildered, aghast. In his memoirs, he rants about the clumsy oaf who came into their home, broke their glasses and dropped his fork, who had no appreciation for music, let alone for painting or beauty of any kind, who never said grace at the table, who bolted down his food and then, seated in his dear departed father's wicker chair, 'gave free rein to his flatulence' – a desecration of dizzying proportions. His mother had suddenly become a riddle, a sphinx, a closed book to him. He could not imagine any intimacy between them.

This goes on for more than a year, until one Sunday morning he happens to overhear them in conversation. They have just returned from church. His mother has on her Sunday best and has placed a white flower in her glossy black hair. She is still in her early forties, in the radiant prime of her life. He hears Henri muttering, Come on over here, you, let yourself go, just for once, Céline, I can't take it any more.

She says, You've got your marriage for the children, just as you proposed, Henri, and I made my condition clear to you. You keep your hands off me. If you're not satisfied, you can crawl back into that hovel of yours and send your children back to charity school.

One of these days I'll break you, my grandfather hears him reply. The blood rushes to his head; he storms into the living room and sees his mother with a mocking smile in her eyes. She winks at him. Henri turns away like a beaten dog, skulks out of the house, and spends the rest of the day in the pub.

So the ham-handed Henri de Pauw, in spite of his plans, became my proud great-grandmother's estranged second husband, and that was how his name came to appear on the gravestone that my grandfather must have removed from the cemetery sometime in the 1950s. Céline died in 1931, the lease must have run for twenty-five years, and instead of renewing it, he took the stone home and hid it in the cavernous recesses under his house. If my calculation is right, that must have been in 1956, when I was five years old. According to my father, he picked up the stone from the graveyard in Gentbrugge with a wheelbarrow, an old-fashioned sloping wooden cart with long wooden handles, an unwieldy monstrosity in which I later carted around my younger sister. The cemetery was almost directly opposite his home, but on the far side of the river. So he had to go all the way to the bridge over the Scheldt, cross the steep bridge with that bulky thing, go back more than half a mile to the graveyard by the church in Gentbrugge, lift up the heavy stone, load it into the barrow, and carry it all the way back over the bridge and home again, about two and a half miles in all, pushing a cumbersome wheelbarrow with a wooden wheel that tended to stick, as well as a heavy load on the way back. On top of that, a single pothole could easily have broken the gravestone; marble slabs are as crumbly as cake when they're not standing upright. In the end, he must have spent half a day lugging the thing.

When I picture him plodding along the banks of the Scheldt with a barrow containing the gravestone of his departed mother, which he felt had been wrongfully desecrated by the name of a stepfather he had never acknowledged, I think of a story he told me many times, whenever Edvard Grieg's *Peer Gynt Suite* was on the radio, which it regularly was. It was one of his favourite pieces; he always sang along. Listen, he would say then, Peer Gynt is carrying his dead mother to heaven in a wheelbarrow: pom-pom-pom pom-pom pom-pom . . . pom-pom-pom, pom-pom-pom . . . Rhythmically marching, carting his dear, dead mother over the mountains and the clouds to heaven, Peer Gynt is taking his dear mother to heaven! And he accompanied the music with the broad sweeps of an amateur director. Years later I bought the suite myself, mainly for nostalgic reasons, a vinyl record with a naive painting of mountains and clouds on the front. When I read the record jacket, I saw to my surprise that the fourth movement, so often pom-pommed by my grandfather, was actually called 'In the Hall of the Mountain King'. I searched for the scene where Peer Gynt carries his little old mother Åse to heaven, and discovered only then that he does no such thing. In the play of the same name by Henrik Ibsen, he simply tells his dying mother the story of the Mountain King's feast, allowing the delirious woman to believe that he is taking her there in a sleigh, past fjords and pine trees, to Soria-Moria Castle, and not to the Christian heaven – although St Peter is at the gate, and in her final moments Åse has a vague image of God approaching. I stood, bemused, with the record in my hands. Why and how did my grandfather come to invent his version of the story? Only after my father had told me the story of Urbain bringing home his mother's gravestone did I begin to understand this perhaps unintentional mishmash of the Peer Gynt story and my grandfather's own guilty journey to pick up a gravestone he then buried in secret. This childish tale concealed a drama whose depths I could hardly imagine: his jealous love of his indomitable mother. In my grandfather's imagination, the evil spirit his mother had believed was coming for her, the great sheet of dark paper that had clung to her back like a diabolical hand, had transformed into Henri's grubby paws, which had tried and failed to gain a grip on his mother. But had Céline herself meant something different that day, something he could not fathom? Why was she so upset, and why did she call it the devil's hand? Did she already feel guilty? Was Henri already in her life, so soon after his father's death? That was impossible and unthinkable.

Abyss after abyss opens in this descending spiral of questions. As I am walking in Gentbrugge Cemetery one lovely October day, on the lookout for names of lost relatives, wondering where my great-grandmother's grave might once have been, I stumble, after long hours of searching, upon the grave of none other than Napoleon de Pauw, a once-renowned Ghent lawyer and bridge-builder, and a sudden smile bursts all my nostalgic memories. On the other side of the river, among the swaying treetops, I see the house where the only surviving eyewitness, my father, still lives peacefully today. The house is surrounded by muddy excavation pits under tall, swaying cranes; a new neighbourhood is rising from the ground. If his house, the romantic house of my childhood, were not standing there between the huge construction sites, as conspicuously out of place as Åse's cottage, I would scarcely recognize the area. Wild geese, a few slug-gish swans in the polluted riverside mud, nervous moorhens in the black, oil-soaked mire. Damaged nature, memory. Pom-pom-pom, pom-pom-pom. Humming, I walk out of the old cemetery. But in the twilight, as I revel in the adagio strains of Edvard Grieg's 'Åse's Death', that superlative mourning music for a dead mother, I see, in my mind's eye, the old phantoms far above me, flickering titanically on the walls of a cave, blown up into eerie shapes by the light of a fire beyond my ken.

Not until years later did I recall that my grandfather once pulled me outside to see the Great Bear. Look, he said, with the happy excitement that sometimes came over him at times like that, look, do you see that big wheelbarrow? That's the Great Bear. At first I stared blankly at his fingertip, smudged with midnight-blue oil paint, but then I saw the large parallelogram gliding through the silent vault of heaven in the mild air of the early September night. This constellation, he argued, does not represent a saucepan, as many people say, but looks more like a wheelbarrow of the old, forgotten kind, with two slanted sides like a primitive cradle (a wheelbarrow transformed into a cradle), and the long wooden handles are also visible in the stars projecting out of the constella-tion. This is the wheelbarrow in which Peer Gynt carried his mother to heaven.

Later I realized that old-fashioned wheelbarrows did not have handles rising from the body, like the ones in the constellation. Instead, they were under the body, supporting the weight, a rational design that uses the power of leverage. Putting away childish illusions, we can see that the constellation most strongly resembles a shopping trolley in a supermarket. But leverage or no leverage, such quibbles could no longer dim the lustre of memory. The image of a large bear seemed even less plausible than the saucepan. I'll take the wheelbarrow. That's how a person becomes a bad poet, I thought later: for the sake of some memory he cannot fathom, he's compelled to pile up saucepans, bears, shopping trolleys, dead mothers, sleds, Peer Gynt and wheelbarrows in his head. And in memory, I keep staring at my grandfather's outstretched finger, each night anew, under the bright, silent stars.

In the left corner of the courtyard, next to the old window, is the zinc drainpipe for the rainwater that runs off the low roof. It ends just above the ground floor. Beneath it is a large barrel that catches the rainwater. The barrel is usually half full, because Mother fetches water from it on Fridays for the laundry, an activity that takes all day. When gloomy drizzle falls, the water splashes into the barrel in halting plops, like a chain of swollen raindrops, some heavier than others. Ploink . . . ploink . . . pling-pling . . . ploink . . . cloikkk . . .

My imagination runs away with me. I hear a piano tinkling in the magical half-full barrel, where the water shines black when the waxing half-moon floats through the clouds, as if it were deeper than the deepest well. I see marbles rolling down a marble staircase in a high, sun-drenched cloister – it's summer, and my father is smiling at me . . . Crystal cones, long, swinging strings of pearls jingling in a chandelier blown by a summer breeze, jingle-lingle-linging like frozen tears at a masked ball . . . But no, it's only water in the barrel, music to my ears, like dancing notes on a musical stave . . . ploink . . . ploof . . . plik-plik-plik . . . splonk . . . plop . . . ploink . . .

I do my very best to shut out the sound of screaming and quarrelling from the kitchen.

*

I take out a well-thumbed card from beneath the old blotter on his desk and stare at it.

Urbain Joseph Emile Martien.

Soldier of the Second Regiment of the Line, age: seventeen years and nine months.

First Company – First Battalion.

Matriculation / number: 55238.

Student in the Regimental School of and in Courtrai-Kortrijk.

Done in Ghent, Wednesday the eleventh of November 1908.

He does not say whether he enrolled in military school in Kortrijk to escape the strained atmosphere at home, but he does write that the work in the iron foundry was taking too heavy a toll on him. He also mentions a new apprentice who charmed the iron founder's daughter, seemingly depriving Urbain of a fair shot at a bright career in the workshop. It was in this uncertain period that he suffered his first episodes of shortness of breath, 'a legacy from my father that lives on in me'. A few weeks earlier, a parish priest had sounded him out: did he have the feeling the Lord was calling him? You see, the priest added drily, for a boy like you, without money or a degree, there are only two paths out of slavery: soldier or priest. My grandfather couldn't see what that had to do with a holy calling; it seemed more like a calculation, which had never before been presented to him so clearly.

All right, then, soldier or priest. At the instigation of Father Van Acker, SJ, a fisher of men, he takes part in a kind of week-long retreat, run by the Jesuits, and has a vision of his father standing under a tiny green blossoming mulberry tree in the monastery garden. He sleeps poorly in his monastic cell – 'soldier or priest' pounds in his head for hours – and when he returns home after days of prayer, sermons and song, he has made his choice: military school, where he will remain for a total of four years. For four years he is well dressed, well fed, well booted; no longer does he have to slog and slave away, but instead he is drilled by bad-tempered sergeants, stands out for his punctuality, reliability and discipline, and for the first time in his life meets boys from the upper classes – lads whose verve and flair, French accent, financial independence and friendly arrogance bring back the sense of profound insecurity he felt in Adolphe Hoste's bookshop. His superiors soon recognize that he has the makings of a true soldier, a man who conducts himself better than the others, with greater discipline and conviction, combining modesty with self-assurance. So they increase the pressure. Sometimes he is punished for a fleck of mud on his boots or trousers, while others go scot-free. He feels no resentment. In the isolation cell, a ramshackle structure under an old linden in the central yard, he sits and sings songs he remembers from childhood. The next day he stands rigidly to attention, unbroken, under the gaze of the hard-drinking, bloodshot-eyed commander.

Très bien, Marshen, now run along back to your post.

Merci, mon commandant. My name is pronounced Mar-*teen*, not Mar-*shen*, *à vos ordres, mon commandant.*

Ta gueule, Marshen, God damn it!

And that – writes the elderly Urbain Martien, sitting comfortably in his small room under the vine-wreathed window that looks out to the east at the barges puffing by on the Lower Scheldt – *brought the first part of my life to a close.* It is spring when he writes these words. He has just had coffee with his daughter. His grandchildren have gone to school, with the usual noise and fuss. The house is quiet. He nibbles at a biscuit. The radio tells of riots in Paris. He barely hears it. Somewhere in the neighbours' overgrown garden, a great tit is chirping its monotonous melody. It is a windless day with white clouds. These days, he is sometimes troubled by melancholy moods. He thinks of his dead wife Gabrielle and wishes he could tell her all his stories again.

About the war, Gabrielle.

I know all about it, you old fool, you've told me twenty times already.

Then he falls silent. He picks up his brushes and stirs the dots of ultramarine, burnt sienna, madder and Naples yellow to get rid of the skins that have formed during the night. He stands at his easel and adds colour to a few leaves of an elm, around a small, crumbling castle that is half finished.

I know, Gabrielle, my dear, it was a long time ago.

But that day, he remains in his chair. Again, he sees himself walking up the hill in Ghent for his physical exam with another boy who was there for the same reason. The boy's name has slipped his mind. What was it again? Albert, Adalbert or Robert? Bert, pronounced the French way – that's right, they called him 'Little Bert' – but he's forgotten the rest of the name.

He masters the arts of fencing and hitting a target from a thousand feet away (an officer he has humiliated orders an inspection of his rifle, suspicious that this raw recruit seems far too experienced). He learns French in the school of hard knocks – from the officers, who humiliate him, and from arrogant bourgeois boys – but at the same time he is appalled by the coarse rudeness of the many bumpkins from rural Flanders, who hang around in bars at night, pinch girls' bottoms, and vomit in their beds. He makes friends with an unassuming Walloon boy, whose gruesome death in the mud at the front he will witness six years later. And he obeys – even when their drunk commander bellows *Silence!* while no one is moving a muscle. But in his memoirs, the French word *Silence* comes out very differently on paper; he makes a slip of the pen; I read, *Cilense*. The word leaps off the page at me. How could he have made such an uncharacteristic error? Then I realize something absurd: he mixed up *Silence* with the name that still haunted him, *Céline*, his mother's name. *Silence*, Céline – *Cilense*.

I sit and stare at that strange word, as if it shone a light into the dark well of my grandfather's soul. A glimpse of his loneliness, his repressed longing for home, a cry for his mother, smothered in the sublime non-word *Cilense*. I see him sitting at his desk, nibbling at his spiced biscuit. He writes and is silent. I'll be strong and silent, Mother; I who braved the summer storm with you that night and was your man in the house, when the rain pearled on our hair and for a moment I was your only darling, the hero of Nowheresville, as you liked to call me. I, who will now be a man in this life I never wanted, far from anything I know and love. *Silence, Cilense. In the hush that fell*, the humble chronicler writes, *I would not have dared cough or blow my nose; on our commander's chest, the medals rattled with a tinny sound.*

After four years of training in subservience, unfailing obedience to a roaring drunkard named Bellière, endless drills in mud and sand, and countless nights of aching muscles, sleep and sleeplessness in the frigid dormitory, he completes his military training. He has become a sturdy, proud and taciturn young man. He is discharged, turns in his rifle and uniform at the depot in Dendermonde, and returns home. A couple of months later, he is called up to serve as a customs officer in the border zone north of Zelzate. His mother throws the letter into the stove; if he thinks he's going to risk his life chasing armed cattle thieves after dark and put his health at risk by spending night after night in a sleeping bag out in the swampy fields, between the drainage ditches, then he shouldn't count on her support. He didn't request a discharge just to turn around and throw away his freedom again. My grandfather nods and says nothing.

A few weeks later, he goes to the railway to look for work and is hired as a metalworker in the Gentbrugge workshops. It is a slow year, a year of calm regularity. He learns to get along better with his stepfather. Sometimes they walk along the bank of the

Scheldt together and say little, but understand each other well. He is almost twenty-two years old now, and his mother says it's time for him to look around for a pretty, well-brought-up girl to marry. He often roams the city, which is being turned upside down for the forthcoming world's fair. La Grande Expo Internationale is expected to put Ghent on the world map. There is some controversy about the organization of the event and the costs. Early on, the French-speaking bourgeoisie takes the lead, mainly because the Germans are thinking about investing in the event. That incites the rising Flemish bourgeoisie to play the German card, in the knowledge that their German brothers support their struggle against Francophone supremacy in their own city. In short, as the Ghent World's Fair approaches, German and French interests are already directly opposed. Amid the cacophony of world's fairs in the early decades of the twentieth century, this is just one more disturbing sign of things to come. No one seems to recognize the squabbling in Ghent as a symbol of anything larger, except perhaps of the Franco-Prussian War forty years earlier and other conflicts of the past. Thanks to pressure from Ghent's Francophone bourgeoisie, the French ultimately gain the upper hand. The Germans withdraw from the organizing committee and it becomes a completely French-language project, chaotic and poorly managed. No one really has any need for yet another international exhibition, except for the ambitious city of Ghent. The Flemish middle class grumbles, complaining that the enemy is now among Ghent's own people – with their Francophone arrogance, the *haute bourgeoisie* are a 'foreign element' in the heart of their community. The first tears in the city's social fabric are already visible, in a project that was meant as a show of unity. Countless plaster edifices are erected to display the glories of the Old World and the New, in all their diversity, to the public. It is the twilight of colonial rhetoric and the kitschy exoticism that accompanies it. There is a recreation of a Senegalese village, complete with villagers, but the entrance to the African village more closely resembles the gate of a German fortress. The Senegalese visitors give rise to rumours about 'certain girls in Ghent' who are said to be hanging around Citadelpark making eyes at the 'well-built Negroes'. When some of them declare their wish to stay on in Ghent after the world's fair, they are quickly escorted onto a ship bound for Africa. There is also a delegation of Igorot tribespeople from the Philippines, described by the great Ghent author Cyriel Buysse as a cross between apes and Mongols. The penniless tribespeople also have a building of their own, which exudes the spirit of the Flemish Middle Ages. After the exhibition, which runs from April to November, some of them are spotted begging in the streets; one young Igorot man dies, overcome by the harsh climate and, the newspapers eagerly add, homesick for the wilderness. His name is Timicheg. In 2011, almost a century after his death, and after all sorts of tussling in councils, commissions and internet forums, the city of Ghent decides to name a tunnel under the railway line near Sint-Pietersstation after this unfortunate victim of the world's fair and its colonial kitsch. The opening ceremony is even attended by delegates all the way from the Philippines, who express their country's humble gratitude to His Worship the Mayor and the big cheese from the Belgian Railways.

In the summer months of 1913, Urbain wanders through the crowds, his hands in the pockets of his Sunday trousers, eyeing the elegant girls from Ghent's best families but too nervous to strike up a conversation. He is a deeply religious, introverted young man. Now and then he sits on a bench with a small sketchbook in his hand and draws what he sees. After his death, I found studies for a small painting that I remember vividly, the portrait of a black man, with a furrowed, abstemious face like a secular Christ and a dark look in his downcast eyes. Did he paint one of the exotic victims of the world's fair, someone he had met in the city? As far as I know, that painting was always in his small room, just over the door, in the spot where you might normally expect a crucifix – when I last visited my father, I saw that it was gone and had, in fact, been replaced by a small wooden cross. Where had the painting disappeared to? My father was as stumped as I was, but that wistful portrait will always remain in my memories. I have never fully grasped the symbolism of that exotic figure, and I never asked my grandfather about it, because only now, as I write, do I realize that there must have been something more, perhaps a meeting or a conversation with one of those people who were shamefully put on display – there were so many things he never spoke of, but which must have run through his mind on quiet Sunday afternoons as the opera programme on the radio lulled the rest of the family into a forgetful slumber.

On New Year's Eve 1913, he celebrates with his family, telling tall tales about military school as his brothers and sisters listen admiringly. In the spring his stepbrother Joris, now resigned to his fate as an anaemic office clerk, marries a girl he describes as 'devout and good-natured', but who simply will not become pregnant. Urban re-enrols for the evening drawing classes and is more successful this time. After three months he is given the chance to draw from living models – boys wrapped in loose-fitting loincloths, posing like Greek sculptures against the dusty plaster of gnarled tree trunks. Le Frère Professeur teaches him that one must keep in mind the muscles under the skin when drawing limbs, that Leonardo da Vinci developed a system of ideal human proportions, and that one must try to make drawings of angels at least a little bit plausible; in other words, one must think about how the wings are attached to the shoulder blades, because there must surely be muscles involved. Flying is no mean feat; anatomy is more than the body, he adds cryptically.

*

126

A young nephew of Céline's dies unexpectedly. It is July 1914. The man, an electrician, was hit by a high-voltage cable in his cabin at work and died instantly. There is no public transport from where they live to the village of Evergem, where he will be buried. Céline asks her eldest son to represent their family. So he walks there on his own, more than six miles, taking the ferry across the Ghent–Terneuzen Canal. There are not many mourners at the modest ceremony, and after attending the church service and offering his condolences, he heads back home without delay. The weather is magnificent. After crossing the canal again, he walks through Port Arthur, an open expanse of sand by the harbour, passing the tomb of the aviator Daniel Kinet, who crashed there in his biplane. He remembers the incident well, even though it was about four years earlier. He had gone to see the aerial show at the harbour, which was announced well in advance, and to which Kinet had invited him after the hot-air balloon ride in Sint-Pietersplein. The event symbolized the new age, the city's boldness and audacity, and the hope of a spectacular future in the new century. On the way to Port Arthur, he had paid a brief visit to the shrine of Our Lady at Lourdes in Oostakker, and just as he was standing in front of the grotto there, his hands folded, the biplane came skimming over his head, less than three hundred feet above him. Kinet was already conducting test flights for the show at the Ghent fair later that day. The actual flight, scheduled for nine thirty, was to follow the Ghent–Bruges–Ostend canal to Ostend. The plan had been for Kinet to come in for a celebratory landing on the beach, just in front of the waiting royal family. At nine thirty that day, 10 July 1910, Urbain was among the crowd peering into the sky when the Farman biplane took off to loud applause and shouts of encouragement.

Suddenly, the aircraft began to swerve, abruptly tipped to one side, and crashed into a tree a few seconds later. With an enormous bang, it bored into the crown. The tree split; branches flew through the air; a cloud of sparrows spread in all directions. In the unearthly silence of that instant, a few people rushed to the scene. The crash had destroyed almost every part of the aircraft. Kinet was pulled out of the wreck, severely wounded. After receiving first aid, he was taken to a clinic on Kasteellaan. He recovered consciousness and could even talk, and surgeons operated successfully on his torn abdomen and damaged kidney the following day, but he died of heart failure later in the month, probably as a result of post-operative stress. My grandfather stood at the entrance to the hospital with a bunch of grapes in a basket, but was not allowed to visit the famous patient. He wrote a clumsy note to wish him a speedy recovery and read the obituary in the paper a few days later. For some reason, he was shaken by Kinet's death. To my grandfather, the aviator had become a model of courage and of what he called 'manly virtue'.

Now, four years later, again in the summer month of July, he stops for a moment in front of the huge lump of stone with a memorial inscription, plonked down in the middle of the sandy expanse. He salutes. A cloud of butterflies flutters around the memorial, and in one of the slender poplars to the right a thrush is singing. A little further on, the landscape has been churned up for the construction of a second large dock. Some distance away from the lonely footpath that leads him through the scattered shrubs and copses, there are construction sheds holding large, newfangled machines. On the side of one shed he reads *Entreprises de Béton armé*. Reinforced concrete. *It was a new product*, he writes in his memoirs, *and back then we had never heard of it before.* (Soon enough he would learn more about it: it was precisely because the concrete forts of Liège were not reinforced with iron that they could not withstand heavy shelling and German mortar fire.) The dirt road is deserted; somewhere amid the trees, he hears the monotonous chirrup of the chiffchaff. He is still about half a mile away from the pilgrimage site in Oostakker. That's just outside the range of a long-distance rifle, he thinks – about 2,300 feet in those days. The sun is sinking; the sweltering heat of the day lingers on the country road and the deserted landscape around it. To the left of the road is a mound, a kind of embankment. He notices young grass poking through the loose sand, a sign of moisture.

Suddenly he sees a small heap of clothing, white and blue. The Blessed Virgin's colours, he thinks to himself. Curious, he takes a few steps towards it, climbs the mound, and finds a sandy pool on the other side. Then he receives what he calls in his memoirs 'the greatest shock of my young life'. A startled girl, about eighteen years old, stands up in the pool. The water barely reaches her knees. He is stunned; it is the first time he has ever seen a young woman naked. As for her, she looks at him as if awaiting his next move, almost apologetic. There before him is something he cannot believe is real, a figure that opens the door to a whole new world inside him, a door he had taken great pains to keep shut, out of Christian piety and the repression it entails. The girl stands in the late sun as if waiting, but does not look scared. He has no idea what to do with himself. *I must admit*, he writes, *I was thrown into confusion; all sorts of thoughts assailed me*. Did she see him coming? Why didn't she stay underwater? Why are her clothes dozens of yards from the edge of the pool, on top of the embankment for all to see? Does she have what he would call 'unchaste' intentions? Isn't she running the risk that some worker on his way home will have his way with her? There is not a stump or trunk for miles around; only the low basin protects her in this godforsaken place on this warm late afternoon. He breaks into a sweat; the girl is almost smiling now. He stammers an apology, feels his collar tight around his neck, gestures as if to say that everything is fine, turns around, and then looks back at the girl. All this time, she has not moved, except to slowly raise her left arm over her chest. He sees the dark blonde tuft on her underbelly, the shadowed slope of her small navel, the curving underside of her young breasts, still visible under her arm, her straight shoulders and the hair tumbling lightly over them – all things he has seen only in centuries-old paintings – or actually, only in reproductions in indistinct books. To think that such a creature now stands before him in sharp focus, naked and breathing! In the wink of an eye, he becomes fractionally aware of his own improbable naivety. He wants to ask if she isn't afraid that something will happen to her. But he can't get the words out, and after an endless minute, he waves goodbye, flees back over the embankment, and rapidly strides away, feeling his head reel. After fifty yards, he looks back. She has evidently left the water; he sees her head sticking up over the embankment, as she watches him recede into the distance 'like a curious squirrel behind a tree'. He hurries on, his heart pounding in his throat. The drowsy afternoon, the bushes and the lonely expanse suddenly seem unreal.

He arrives at the shrine in a fluster, passes the tinkling porcelain tablets hung there by grateful pilgrims, sees the figure of the Virgin Mother, feels a stabbing pain in his chest, gropes in his trouser pocket for his rosary, and launches into a murmured prayer for peace of mind. I am a soldier, he thinks, I saw a virgin, a girl, O Mother of God, not your effigy, but a woman like the ones Giorgione and Titian painted, I saw a nude girl in the flesh, she appeared right before my eyes, her clothes were white and blue, O Virgin Mother, what have You done to me? His head is pounding so hard that several hours later, at home in his room, he is already wondering whether he really saw her: could it have been a delusion, brought on by the heat, the solitude, the funeral earlier in the day, a sidelong look from a distant, dark blonde cousin in a black dress, piously praying in a wicker chair on the other side of the nave? Has he not, in fact, been visited by the wily devil? He tries to draw her from memory – which only adds to his confusion – tears up the paper, and has to say five rosaries before his rebellious nether parts will start to settle down. *I must be pure, I must be pure*; he doesn't know why he must, but he must, he must.

A month earlier, the young Serbian Gavrilo Princip had shot and killed the Habsburg Archduke Franz Ferdinand in Sarajevo, thereby sending my grandfather's whole familiar world hurtling towards destruction, but he was in no state of mind to read the papers. He preferred to look at Raphael and Botticelli's blushing, motherly virgins, while pinching painful dents into the palms of his hands.

It is January 2012. I have just spent a couple of hours in the Alsemberg Vorst cemetery, south of Brussels, because my investigations revealed that it held the neglected grave of Daniel Kinet, the hero who had crashed in the place where my grandfather saw a young girl naked for the first – and maybe the last – time in his life, just a few months before the start of the Great War. Icarus and Aphrodite, I thought, it's too good to be true. So I drove to the cemetery, which happened to be close to the place where I had been sitting and writing all that time. How did Kinet, a Walloon boy from Jumet and an honoured guest in Ghent, end up here in a neglected cemetery south of Brussels? There was nobody I could ask.

It's a clear winter's day. The icy, glinting beeches on the other side of the cemetery wall are moaning in the wind; snapped branches and mud puddles fill the paths after yesterday's storm. Somewhere, a tree has fallen on a few old gravestones; some markers have been smashed, and puddles glitter in the open graves. The light itself seems rinsed clean, purified. The gravestones lean against each other, collapsed and sunken, their inscriptions no longer legible, with white-encrusted patches of moss over the faded letters. Plastic flower buckets have been blown together in the mud on one side of a tomb; three wooden crosses lie in a splintered heap, distinguishable from refuse only by the names that have cracked through the middle. There are deep grooves in the descending paths, eaten into them by the raging storm. Here and there, gravel walkways have been closed off with red-and-white plastic ribbons. The design of the cemetery is very peculiar. The oldest section, with monumental tombs, has a wall around it, and the soldiers' graves are a little way off, in semicircles. There are open, grassy areas that serve no clear purpose. Some of them have a single gravestone at the edge, without an inscription. In another section, a line of cypresses borders a grassy plot with a pile of broken-down machines and wilted chrysanthemums. Nothing here really seems to be grieving; everything exudes calm, detached impermanence. Trudging past graves with names like Corleone, Schiavoni and Devlamynck, names from Mrazek Marasco and Doudou to Jeunehomme, Tobiansky-d'Altoff, Perceval and Culot, I make three loops around the muddy field of the fallen but cannot find Kinet's simple grey headstone. It may be one of the dozens of smaller stones now buried under thick layers of ivy, the only hint of their presence a slight swell in the green overgrowth. There is no one I can ask, since the office is closed. An old woman I approach is so deaf that she doesn't understand me, even when I shout into her fuzz-filled ears. Not until months later, after who knows how many visits, do I find the gravestone, decorated with angels' wings and no body.

That same day, I drive to the harbour in Ghent to find the monument to Daniel Kinet and possibly the pool where my grandfather had his pre-war epiphany, poised at the outermost edge of the old world; there must be some remnant of that idyll that I can still touch. I get caught in the snarl of traffic on the ring road and creep towards the large grain silos by the industrial road, surrounded by lorries expelling clouds of black smoke. The weather has turned cloudy and cold. My satnav recognizes Daniel Kinetweg. It takes me to a no-man's-land in the midst of a desolate harbour zone, with vague industrial sites, warehouses, fences and a tremendous mountain of scrap iron by the side of Farmanweg, a road named after the French aircraft builder Henri Farman, who designed Kinet's biplane. After searching for a while, I find the monument marking the place where Kinet crashed. The forgotten memorial stands by the roadside, next to dozens of yellow-and-red lorries parked in a row. The transmission tower behind the monument looms over it, reducing the rough bluestone monolith to insignificant proportions. A young woman with dark red curly hair, dressed in a leather jacket and jeans, stands in the icy wind taking photographs; besides the two of us, there is not a living soul in sight. The woman gets in her car and drives away. Although we glanced at each other with vague curiosity, neither of us said a word. Who on earth would visit this desolate site on a lost weekday? Who would walk a hundred yards on foot in these parts, in a world that no longer offers a human scale? I look around: nothing but nameless, neglected space of the type left behind by major industries around the globe. Spatial collateral damage. The Arcadian pool where my grandfather must have seen his idyllic apparition lies buried deep under the reinforced concrete of the grain silos. Perhaps it was no more than a slight swell in the old landscape, mindlessly flattened by bulldozers when the harbour was expanded, decades ago.

Driving into yet another traffic jam – rush hour has begun – I go on to the Lourdes grotto in Oostakker, where I stumble into memories of my own childhood: the old-fashioned, exotic style of the

Hotel de Lourdes, the dark basilica with slender Eastern columns along the central nave, and at every turn, inscriptions praising the Virgin – nameplates, votive tablets for that Palestinian girl who was impregnated centuries ago without any stain of human sperm and thereby gave birth to a man-god. I buy a folder of prayers to Our Lady of the Seven Sorrows, my grandfather's favourite. There is nobody here. Outside, wintry dusk is falling, the wind is frigid. I walk to the grotto, which is much closer to the basilica than I remembered. But I recognize the exact sound that's been stuck in my memory for years, the shivery tinkling of the countless porcelain tablets that hang on the fence, swaying and clinking, in never-ending rows beside the gravel path around the shrine, ethereal music from long ago that descends on me with all the force of the forgotten. In front of the grotto with the sculpture of the Virgin Mother is a statuette of Bernadette Soubirous. She too is dressed in white and blue. The girl

mystic sits in an attitude of worship, tilting back slightly with her hands folded together and raised to the apparition in the artificial grotto, the Blessed Virgin herself, surrounded by scores of small light bulbs: bulbs that were undoubtedly not there yet in 1914. This is where he must have stood and prayed, sweating in the late afternoon heat. I try to visualize his route from the pool, from the nude girl and her blue-white clothes, to this place, but it can't be done: the ring road, the buildings, the industrial sites, the fences, the streets, the railway, everything runs straight through it, as if an old songline had been ruptured by the brute force and mindlessness with which modern technology has flattened memories everywhere.

Along the path around the shrine are seven smaller grottos decorated with religious scenes. The cold seeps into my fingers; I have to pull my collar tight around my neck so as not to catch cold. In the yellowish light of the deserted shop, filled with religious knick-knacks, I buy a memorial tablet for fifteen euros, selecting the neutral inscription 'In gratitude'. They are no longer made of tinkling porcelain, but of inexpensive earthenware, possibly made under harsh conditions by devout Catholic children in some third-world country. The dark blonde saleswoman, about fifty years old, asks if I want a hook to hang the tablet on the fence. I say no thank you. She gives me one anyway. I slide the wrapped-up tablet into my coat pocket and walk out of the deserted pilgrimage site. A bantam cockerel struts impatiently beside me, as if warning me not even to glance at the three little hens hopping along behind him. I linger there a moment and look around. Never before have I been so deeply struck by the transience of human life. I know nothing about the girl whose gift to my grandfather was the quasi-mystical memory of a miraculous apparition – not her name, nor her background, nor even what she looked like, apart from his agitated description of her form rising out of the water. She has become the pure apparition of a human figure, so anonymous that she could be the image launched into space to give other inhabitants of the universe an impression of how human beings are supposed to look and what they can expect when they land on this planet. It is the final image of an old, idyllic world, which a few days later was destroyed for ever.

Even though the car radio is droning the news of the day, silence swallows the world as I wind through traffic. I have never been a calmer driver, detached from everyone and everything, as if returning from something utterly fresh and unimaginable, reconciled to the fact that everything is gone. Back in the basilica, I opened a prayer book, read a few lines, and surreptitiously stuck it in my pocket:

> I drew the water
> from the rock for You.
> You gave me gall
> and vinegar to drink.
> Holy, immortal God,
> Have mercy on us.

II

1914–1918

I

Why has that organ been playing in my head all through the night?

Wild geese are flying over, hour after hour. The first birds came just before dawn, in the frigid interval before daybreak. As they soared over the countryside, cackling, their wings shone in the first rays of the rising sun. I'm shivering so hard I can feel my bones creak. In the distance, the sky unfolds a delicate fan of greys, pink, a slight hint of orange. Above it, the thin white of rising mist drifts over the fields.

The date is 5 August 1914. Four days ago, around four in the morning, we heard a pounding on our front door – a city councillor and a policeman; alarm in my mother's soft voice; me, coming down the stairs to find her at the open door, her hair tangled, her dressing gown thrown on in haste. I have ten minutes to present myself at the door 'in full uniform', as the policeman puts it. He says that someone will escort all the lads in the neighbourhood to the nearby square where we are supposed to assemble. I say nothing; my mother says nothing. She clasps me in her arms, holds me close for a long moment; I smell the sleep on her breath, the scent of her skin. She lets me go, her eyes pale, unfathomable.

I jump into my clothes without washing and run a comb through my hair. My name is Urbain Joseph Emile Martien. Corporal, twenty-three years old. I have four years of training at military school. I know what I must do; I know how to obey without flinching; I can stand stock-still for hours in the rain and cold.

More and more geese are flying overhead, cackling geese in the half-light, and that organ music in my head will not stop. Off in the distance, past a low farmstead, I see lapwings over the fields; they seem to swirl in the wind like scraps of paper, but there is no wind, not a blade of grass is moving. The morning chill is rising from the ground. Somewhere beside me, I can hear teeth chattering. The vague smell of cow dung invades my nostrils, mingled with the cold sour scent from the dewy beet fields. Our officers have assured us that we shall be home again before winter sets in. My unit will help to guard the borders. That's all they've told us.

The day of our conscription we walked down our street single file, ten neighbourhood lads in a row. A mood of giggly surprise and excitement soon took hold. Scores of boys were marching into Zuidstatie, thronging together under the high roof. Confusion reigned; everyone was shouting and arguing as if they were just beginning to realize what was happening. As I stood there waiting with the other lads from my street, my Aunt Rosa appeared, bobbing through the crowd towards me. She had brought a parcel of stockings and handkerchiefs and a small flask of lukewarm coffee. Her eyes were rimmed with red. That's from running in the morning chill, she said. Endless processions of railway carriages rolled along the platform, engines hissing, the smell of coal and soot, the swarming of the mass of boys in search of their units – I passed those final moments before departure too unconsciously, everything went too fast. I saw a young fellow weeping at his father's side. I saw a fallen knapsack that had burst open at the end of the platform. A few sandwiches rolled out and were squashed to a pulp by scurrying feet. I saw a chicken in the distance, a white chicken just crossing the tracks, with a reddish-brown cockerel hot on her heels. The compartments were crammed full of bags and parcels; we were packed together like herrings in a barrel. The train chugged slowly into motion and made countless stops along the way. The heat soon became stifling; we couldn't open the windows, as the smoke and soot from the engine would blow inside.

Around noon, we arrived in Dendermonde. In the muddle of soldiers shouting over each other, we were arbitrarily divided into groups of twelve. Everyone was pushing and shoving, trying to stay close to at least one or two familiar faces.

Later that day, the army requisitioned sheds, attics and barns all over town. I ended up in a butcher's attic, along with a few other lads from my neighbourhood. Rays of light seeped through the roof tiles; August was a fine, hot month that year. All around us bugles were sounding, officers were shouting orders, and trucks were honking their horns as they wound their way through the slowly settling chaos. We lay in silence on bales of hay that had been hurriedly tossed into the room.

We spent the whole day waiting. At suppertime, rations were delivered to the billets, just bread and milk for us, too little for twelve men. The butcher had his lanky daughter bring us four fried sausages and some boiled tripe. We gobbled it down in silence, turned onto our sides, and fell asleep before it was quite dark.

For the next three days, nothing happened. Before noon on the fourth day, the whole regiment was called into formation. Long rows of new knapsacks were waiting for us, on top of each one a rifle, bullets and a packet of biscuits. The officers stood watching and shouted orders.

En avant par quatre! Portez . . . l'arme!

We left around seven o'clock the next day, in good spirits because we were finally on the move. None of us could have suspected that one month later the peaceful town we had just left would be reduced to ashes by the Germans. We'd been walking for hours by the time the first faint booming noises reached our ranks; we were marching towards Liège, where 'the enemy' had already gathered around the forts of Boncelles, Flemalle, Hollogne, Lantin and Chaudfontaine, and other fortifications near the city. The Germans were intent on breaking through this ring of forts; some men laughed and said that would be impossible. Others said the ring had already been broken; if that was true, then we would be the first to run up against the enemy. Our officers cut off further questions with a snarl.

We marched all day, till the blisters on our heels tore open and the warm fluid ran into our coarse socks. You milksops, one lieutenant growled, you've gone soft from all those years of sitting at home with Mama. We marched through Londerzeel and Steenokkerzeel, where we rested for half an hour and filled our canteens from a stream. Then we marched through Oud-Heverlee and straight into Louvain. The main thoroughfare, Statiestraat, was deserted, and the sharp echo of our footsteps from the house fronts filled us with a sense of power. We stopped for another rest in the late afternoon, drenched with sweat, our faces crimson, our collars undone, grimacing in pain as we kicked off our boots for ten minutes or so. Our feet immediately started to swell up, which made it even more painful to put the boots back on.

By dusk, after a gruelling march of almost fifty miles, we arrived in Hakendover, a hamlet just past Tienen. The air was so clear and quiet that the trees seemed caught in a kind of half-molten glass. Swallows circled in the sky, mosquitoes danced over the canals. I was no longer thinking about anything. We were billeted in a large farmstead. Cows were wandering loose in the courtyard, milling around the sheds. We asked the farmer's wife for milk; she shook her head no, mumbling that the milk was for the next day. One by one, we scrambled up a rickety ladder to the hayloft assigned to us. Gnawing hunger, confusion and quarrels in French between the officers in the courtyard. The rations had been held up somewhere, no one knew where. One Walloon soldier had the nerve to stick his head out of a window and shout, *Armée bête!* Stupid army! He was put in solitary immediately. Later on, we heard him in one of the barns, shouting and wailing.

An hour later, our commander tried a more polite approach: *Mon capitaine*, don't you have any food for my boys? They're starving.

Taisez-vous, Facherol, the officer said. Shut up. He spat in the sand.

That night we lowered the rickety ladder, crept outside, plundered the orchards in the darkness, ate as much fruit as we could stomach, returned to the hayloft dog-tired, heard the rustle of rats underneath us and dormice in the roof tiles. The monotonous hum of a gnat right by my ear.

B ut now we have been lying here for days, behind a wheat field that blocks our view. We carry out periodic field exercises, which serve mainly to keep us busy and tire us out. Along potential attack routes they had us cut down trees; the logs now lie scattered across the roads to prevent a surprise attack, a prospect that seems unimaginable to us. In the cool quiet of the summer morning, farmers are out in the fields here and there, reaping grain, the slow slash of their scythes approaching and drawing back again – the lonely rustle of the countless falling stalks along the scythe's keen blade interrupted only by the cough of a cow at pasture, the bark of a dog in the distance. In the warm air, the swallows are swirling again, and high in the sky I think I see a lark ascending.

Above that, the blue, the spotless blue that reminds me of my late father's frescoes. There is nothing to confirm what we hear again and again: that war has come. Only the peace of this splendid August, month of harvest, of yellow pears and wasps, of cooler mornings, sluggish flies and weightless spots of sunlight drifting peacefully over the leaves.

As I lie dozing and daydreaming in the sun, the *porte-parole* – as the officers call the messenger – sidles up to the commander. He whispers something in his ear and points at me.

Marshen!

I jump to my feet with a start and stand to attention.

Oui, mon commandant. Je m'appelle Mar-tien*, pas Mar*-shen.

Taisez-vous, Marshen, you idiot!

They resume their mumbling, with glances in my direction.

Then, looking me up and down with a vaguely hostile expression, he says, slowly, in French, *Madame votre maman* has come to say *bonjour* to you, Marshen.

He taps his boot with his whip and shoots me a nasty grin.

I walk out of the courtyard, and there she stands: my mother, as proud and statuesque as ever, her black hair in a lustrous knot, in her best black dress and her worn black shoes. A basket dangles from her arm.

We are sent off behind a hedgerow where the other soldiers cannot see us.

Sit down, Urbain, she says, we have fifteen minutes.

She throws her arms around me and looks at me long and hard. Then she laughs.

I walked straight through the tents, she says, nobody stopped me. I asked if I could speak to the lieutenant. And just look.

She gives me a broad smile.

What? I said. You walked the whole sixty—

Hush now, little man. I stopped for the night in Grimbergen.

But Mother, today's your birthday . . .

She nods and laughs, producing milk and biscuits.

I wolf it all down, while she sits next to me, beaming. I throw the empty milk bottle into the canal. We sit together in silence.

After fifteen minutes the commander returns. He mumbles at my mother, telling her time's up. Then, turning his head, he snarls at me to rejoin my platoon. For my mother, he has another nasty grin.

Désolé, madame.

My mother rises to her feet and makes the sign of the cross on my forehead.

Gobbleskipya, Urbain.

She hands me a basket covered with a towel, sweeps past the commander as if he were air, and vanishes behind the line of trees, while I return to the courtyard. In the basket I find a stack of sandwiches, a smaller stack of underwear, a few freshly ironed shirts, and a tiny figurine of Bernadette Soubirous, which I put in my trouser pocket. It will remain there until the day a bullet bores through both the figurine and my thighbone.

For the rest of the day, I am out of sorts. It's 9 August, a Wednesday, my mother's birthday, the sun is shining. I walk back to the sheds in the rear of the farmyard and find everyone staring at the sky in terror. To the east a Zeppelin, huge and unreal as an image in a dream, floats slowly past us through the weightless blue; a moment later, it glides majestically over the sun, casting its shadow on our upturned faces. My heart skips a beat; this dream-fish drifting silently over our heads is larger, more impressive and more menacing than the battles I had imagined. Fall in! the officers bark. As we grope for our rifles and knapsacks, we hear thunder in the distance, explosions, the thud of dropping shells, an indistinct rumble booming and growling through the air, bearing down on us like a steamroller, biting into our guts, making the walls shake. In the distance, the unearthly apparition slides noiselessly out of sight; black plumes of smoke rise in the east, we hear tremendous explosions, birds wheel down out of the sky as if shot, farm animals pound their hooves in fear and rattle the chains in the barns and, for the first time, our hearts stand still in shock and horror.

An hour later a runner arrives, collapsing in breathless exhaustion in the middle of the yard. He brings the news that the forts around Liège have fallen, along with reports of the Germans torching buildings and murdering innocent civilians. Apparently, there are already many stories of senseless retributory killings like these. We march another twenty miles to the east.

We'll later learn that General von Emmich had launched the attack on the forts around Liège four days earlier, advancing from both the north and the south in an attempt to besiege them, and trying to penetrate gaps like the one between Fort Boncelles and Fort Ourthe. Since we were to the west of the city, we did not see any of that. Apparently, the third division was attacked at Fort Evegnée.

Now an utterly unfamiliar sound is booming through the air with clocklike regularity, and the ground beneath our feet is quaking, making us feel slighter than leaves in the wind. We almost shit our trousers then and there. Not until much later will I realize that we were among the first to hear the sound of the great gun, the famous Big Bertha. In combination with the air raid – a completely new phenomenon, which reduced the massive forts to ridiculous open wounds – this gun annihilated the Belgian defences in Liège, previously thought indestructible, in just a few days. Fort Loncin was destroyed in August when the Germans made a direct hit on the powder magazine. The concrete had not been reinforced with iron; that was the Achilles heel of the old mastodons, the last vestiges of an unsuspecting age. I cannot help recalling the words on the shed near Port Arthur, on that day – it now seems so far away – when I saw the girl in the pool: *Béton armé*.

We are now in battle array, bayonets at the ready. The senior officers are roaring orders in French. After they have shouted themselves hoarse, the junior officers translate. Our orders are to march back westwards. Along the way, we hear that resistance has become impossible. The Germans are using enormous 42-centimetre guns, unlike anything our military has seen before, and have managed to breach all the forts around Liège. Those outdated bulwarks could not stand up to calibres larger than 21 centimetres.

The enemy is approaching, our commander shouts. Show your valour.

My heart pounds in my throat. I feel sick as a dog.

Chickenshits! That's what we are, chickenshits! says cross-eyed Rudy from Lossystraat. We should march east to support the bloody third division.

No one says anything back; it's dreary, this westward retreat over desolate, lonely country roads in dry August – worn-out, sluggish August. Near Waremme, a woman runs past us, gesticulating wildly and shouting something we can't make out. Behind us, we see dwindling clouds of black smoke.

By early evening, we arrive in Tienen. The officers requisition buildings; we lie down on the cool tiles of a school's empty corridors. I take my mother's sandwiches out of my knapsack and share them with the lads beside me. No one says another word; before long, you can hear the snoring of the first exhausted soldiers.

In the days that follow, I notice a change in attitude among my superiors. The officers watch me a little more attentively, and the commanders show me a little more respect, now and then telling me what they're thinking of doing, or asking me which men I'd like in my group of snipers. I know it's not just because I went to military school for four years, and not even because I keep my men under control. It's mainly because the officers were impressed by my statuesque, self-confident mother.

On 15 August we are just north of Tienen, in Sint-Margriete-Houtem. Before nightfall, I am given command of eight men of my own choosing. Our orders are to stand guard at the far left wing of the regiment and establish an eastern sentry position. Somewhere along the road from Vissenaken to Tienen, we pitch a tent against the high wall of a house, so that everyone coming by has to pass us. We carry out rough-and-ready identity checks but look mainly at people's features and how they carry themselves – anyone could be a spy, our commanders warned us. The Germans are offering a reward to soldiers who betray their country. A handful of Belgians have committed high treason, and a few traitors have already been executed.

Today is the feast of the Assumption of the Virgin. A mass is held in the open air. I see refugees on their knees, weeping, or staring rigidly at the makeshift tabernacle in the field. The chaplain tries to offer words of comfort, incantations borne away on the summer wind. We also see the first of the wounded limp into camp today. A boy sits under a tree and vomits blood.

Since the terrain here is slightly hilly, we can see the artillery lines in the field below. Soldiers are coming and going.

We spend the next few days waiting in confusion. From the village of Haelen, we hear shocking news of reprisals against ordinary civilians who were baselessly accused of resisting the occupation and topped off with a shot to the neck in the streets, barns, cellars and sitting rooms. Wounded soldiers are carried in; a field hospital is set up. The boys are made to drink themselves into a stupor so the doctors can amputate their wounded limbs, using strangely primitive-looking surgical equipment. In just a few days, our peaceful August has filled with screams and shouts. We hear the thunder of mortar fire near Haelen; in the evening, the smell of charred flesh spreads over the dewy field. On 17 August, we are told about the destruction of Fort Loncin two days earlier. We hardly sleep, instead falling into a kind of feverish trance. Many soldiers are ordered to march towards Tienen. We do not see anyone return.

On the afternoon of 18 August, the earth suddenly began to tremble. Cross-eyed Rudy from Lossystraat pressed his ear to the ground, leaped up, and shouted, They're coming! They're coming! We reached for our rifles and saw incendiary bombs in the distance, raining down on the city of Tienen. Suddenly a mob of screaming, wailing people literally flooded over us, shouting Save us! Save us! and knocking down our checkpoint in their panic. A nurse in black ran after them, calling out, *Couchez-vous! Couchez-vous!* She tried to make it clear that they should all throw themselves on the ground. But as most of them did not speak French, they paid no attention and kept running – to their deaths.

The German attack was like a *Blitzkrieg*. Less than an hour later, we saw a moving wall of metal, smoke and gunfire rise ahead of us; their numbers were overwhelming, and they approached with a dull rumble that seemed to herald the last judgement. The men from our forward posts came barrelling straight into us, wild with fear, yelling that we had to run. A few of them were stopped by a lieutenant and led away. We knew they would be punished severely for deserting their posts.

In the field below, we saw three of our big guns blown to smithereens, all at once. The shards of metal flew as far as our ranks. One of the lads in my group started whirling like a madman, screeching and sobbing. His lower left arm had been torn off by falling shrapnel. The chief warrant officer came rushing into my post and ordered me to assemble my men and advance without delay to the command post of the 22nd Regiment of the Line, about two miles ahead of us. That's suicide! one boy cried. He was pulled out of the ranks and slammed to the ground. We set off, marching along hedgerows and canal sides and now and then dropping to the earth as the shells landed closer and closer. After about a mile, on the road to Grimde, we truly found ourselves in hell. Soldiers with their heads swathed in blood-soaked bandages lay by the roadside, calling out for help; one boy with a shot-off leg howled that he was bleeding to death. No one had time to spare them a glance.

The attacks now seemed to be coming from two sides and closing in around us. We hurried on. An infantryman came to meet us, shouting that we were crazy: Are you really so eager to die? Look behind you, he cried. Of my eight men, only three were still following me. Hunched over, we continued on our way. I recognized the officers' billet – a farm on the horizon – and ran for it. Behind a wall half demolished by gunfire, wounded men sat moaning on wheelbarrows, side by side with frantic refugees from Oplinter and Grimde, mothers with children. Behind me, my friend Rudy called out, Keep going, Urbain, we're almost there.

When we were a quarter of a mile from the farm, we tried to take cover behind a row of poplars. A strange hissing sound passed over us, like a gust of wind, and felled four trees with a mighty crack. They thundered down on top of each other, forming a pile across the road. One of my remaining three men died instantly. An officer of the 22nd Regiment and his small platoon lay behind a mound of earth thrown up by the bombs. He crept towards me on his hands and knees. I told him that I and my eight trained snipers had been ordered to report to him and that only three of us were left. It seems like madness to me, I said. He looked at me and said, It's pointless. There's nothing left to save over there.

All around us it was raining shells and incendiary bombs; our eardrums seemed about to burst; houses and trees were burning everywhere; the smoke drifted towards us, turning the bright daylight into stifling darkness.

We stayed flat on our bellies until late afternoon; the surrounding countryside was swiftly transformed into a kind of wasteland, a primeval landscape where every trace of civilization had been wiped out in just a few short hours. When evening came, and a red glow blazed and billowed in the sky over Tienen, Grimde and Sint-Margriete-Houtem, we began our retreat, at more of a crawl than a walk. We were a ragged band, like human insects, wailing, sniffling, puking, crying and broken as we crept through the growing darkness, past craters still fuming with shell-smoke, half-dead.

I was supposed to report to the senior officer who had sent us on ahead – Chief Warrant Officer Dugniolle, a severe man, mounted on a slender dapple grey. He had looked down his nose at us as he gave his orders – in French, of course – and then barked, Mar-shen, translate!

À vos ordres, mon commandant. Je m'appelle Mar-tien, mon commandant.

Mar-shen*, je dis, tais-toi, merde!*

Well after midnight, we reached the rear lines. The enemy had advanced in a pincer movement, which by some miracle we had escaped. I held a whispered conversation with the officer there. We had a lot to learn from our enemy, I said. They had weaponry that we not only lacked, but had never even seen before, combined with an enormous supply of grenades, ground troops that fired continuously as they advanced – machine-gun fire, another phenomenon previously unknown to us – heavy mortars, their lightning-fast enveloping movement, the deep trenches where they could herd together hundreds of prisoners of war, and their demoralizing psychological tactics: sowing confusion, arbitrarily executing civilians and prisoners of war, and popping up on all sides at once. The officer nodded and told us to come with him at daybreak. We straggled on past Vissenaken, exhausted, and lay down on the still-warm ground for a few hours of sleep, among the other soldiers sprawled behind a few haycocks near Boutersem.

When we tried to report to Chief Warrant Officer Dugniolle, just after six o'clock in the morning, we were told he had snuffed it, along with his aide-de-camp Denoëlle.

I was foolish enough to ask if there'd been many other losses.

Any more stupid questions, Marshen?

Je m'excuse, mon commandant.

The officers gathered in confusion to discuss what we should do. Since our first engagement with the enemy, our troops had been massacred, and our only remaining option was to launch small surprise attacks on the flanks of the opposing army in the hope of demoralizing them and creating the illusion of an unbroken military force. We did that for a week and were fairly successful, dealing some painful blows to the German lines, but we also made our enemies wary, cunning and resentful. They often killed civilians in blind vengeance. We learned to distrust absolutely everyone; the Germans would send spies in the uniforms of our dead troops. They spoke broken French to the Flemish and broken Dutch to the French, hoping to trick us and extract information. Once, when a soldier shot one of these spies, and the others saw the Belgian uniform, there was a brief outbreak of panic in the ranks. Our officers lambasted us several times a day, blaming the defeat at Sint-Margriete-Houtem on our naivety. We tried to tell them we had done our very best, but they just growled at us to shut our mouths.

Sometimes we were ordered to march ten miles or more at top speed to provoke a skirmish with the Germans, who were invariably ready and waiting. That always cost us lots of men and led to more grumbling.

After a week of this we were dog-tired, underfed and demoralized. We were relentlessly driven back, past Aarschot, Werchter, Haacht, Boortmeerbeek. There we rested for a few days and finally got decent rations. A few of the lads had diarrhoea and gallstones; they had drunk water from canals with corpses in them.

My knapsack was encrusted with mud and dirt; we rinsed off our things at a deserted farmhouse. I found my drawing materials, which I had almost forgotten – charcoal and a pencil. The few sheets of paper I had brought from home were full of mud stains. With a painful lump in my throat, I sat down by a stump and drew the devastated landscape, the piles of debris, the shell craters, the bodies, the blasted stumps, the dead horse I had seen hanging from a broken elm, perfectly straight, its bloody, half-severed head gruesomely twisted against the cool morning sky, its legs tangled in the remains of the tree like strange branches. Under its torn, stinking belly crawling with flies, a few boards from a splintered cart still hung from a length of rope. I thought back to the calm, soothing sound of my father's hands brushing over the paper as he sketched in the peace and quiet of a distant Sunday afternoon, and my eyes were full of tears, so bloody hot and full that I crumpled the paper into a ball, chucked it away, and cursed.

Eh bien, ça va, Marshen?

That same day, the king gave the order for the Belgian troops around the forts of Antwerp to retreat, but we stayed put for the time being in our encampment near Boortmeerbeek. Frantic refugees told us that the Germans had subjected the people of Aarschot to still more reprisals, in the form of summary executions. They would round up the entire population of a village chosen at random, make the trembling men line up in rows, announce that they had calculated the resistance to be one-third, shoot one in three men in the neck, and force the women and children to haul away and bury the corpses of their husbands and fathers. Women who lost control of themselves were beaten to death with a rifle barrel as their children clung to their skirts. The atrocities in Wallonia were said to be even larger in scale; as evidence, one man showed us a sickly-smelling cap with his brother's spattered brains still cleaving to the inside. The losses among the Belgian troops were so catastrophic that their full scale took time to comprehend. The two large regiments had lost so many men that the survivors had been merged into a single regiment, which was not much larger than one ordinary one. This confirmed our suspicion that, within a week, our army had been reduced to half its size.

Then, a few days later, in the last week of that wretched month of August, came the nightmare of Schiplaken.

2

These days, it is almost impossible to imagine the desolation of the landscape through which I marched with my eight new comrades from the third battalion of the 2nd Regiment of the Line. Near Boortmeerbeek, the two gendarmes who were escorting us slunk away, one after the other. The first one came to me and said with a smirk that he had sprained his foot, and a mile further on, the second one frankly admitted that he was scared, because a man on horseback makes an easier target than an infantryman. I didn't waste any words on them, but made it clear with a wave of my hand that they could do as they liked. We continued our cautious advance. I had to remind my men to keep zigzagging, like hares in an open field. German scouts had been spotted near our advance posts. My mind was racing, and I had to make split-second decisions that could mean the difference between life and death. We crossed Leuvensesteenweg and struck out towards Kampenhout in the south-west. From the discarded objects that littered the ground, I could see that our troops had marched past in the wrong direction. Confusion and panic reigned. In the woods of Schiplaken, where the beauty of the summer trees and bushes made me wish I could stop and sketch them, we passed a pool with a lancer's blue coat beside it, thrown off next to a yellow sandbank. From a distance, I thought at first that it was a soldier with his gun raised. Instinctively, I aimed my rifle, but it was only a sleeve outstretched on the ground. The image leaped to mind of the heap of blue-and-white clothes next to the pool at Port Arthur, barely a month earlier.

It seemed like ages ago, a scene from another world that had slipped away from us in only a few days.

We marched deeper into the sheltering woods. Night fell. In the dusk, it was harder for us to advance. We would have to stop before Kampenhout. The earth all around us was covered with what looked like lead marbles, the remains of fragments from a high-explosive shell, which told us that these woods had seen combat. Now and then, a shell hit the ground less than one hundred yards away. The earth shook; we saw soil spurt into the air, trees fall groaning to the ground. Sometimes we heard distant cries. We crept on through the darkening twilight. The gunfire seemed to grow louder and closer. We halted at the prearranged spot. There was our regiment's wagon – God knows where it had come from. I ordered my men to set up their rifles in bundles, with two sentries to the east. I made my report. A few officers arrived in silence, leading their horses by the reins. We all got bread and cheese for supper. A little later, another commando unit arrived. To my surprise, I recognized my cousin René among the soldiers – the second son of my uncle Evarist, whose first son I had seen die in the flames of the furnace. René was pale and exhausted. We had no time to talk. The officers had bundles of hay from the wagon to sleep on; we infantrymen slept on the ground. We were ordered not to light a flame under any circumstances; the only light came from a lantern hung under the wagon, which cast a feeble glow on our regimental colours, carelessly flung down among the bayonets. I could not get to sleep. I saw the faces of the sleeping soldiers glowing like copper in the soft light, with the warm hue you find in some Goya paintings; the shadowed sides of their sleeping faces were as black as Africans. I quietly took my pad out of my knapsack and made a few quick sketches. That calmed me a little. Later, after the war, I used the head of one of the lads as the model for an oil painting of the head of Christ.

I must have drifted off right after that, because I was jolted awake by a tremendous bang. A bomb had made a crater right next to the wagon; the bayonets were scattered all over the place. A few musical instruments had flown out of the wagon and broken to splinters. The golden lion had been blown off our regimental colours. We made sure that no one had been hurt and then lay down again; the moss was soft and cool. Because there were constant rustling noises, one of our officers decided around midnight to put a few soldiers on sentry in the treetops. We didn't get much more sleep after that. At two in the morning, we started to break camp, as quietly as possible. By then the regiment was assembling from all sides; the marching soldiers converged in great, silent waves, advancing through the woods with a soft crackle. In the distance, beyond the trees, we saw a blazing farmhouse. Sparks fanned out in fireworks from the towering yellow flames.

We formed two fronts, one facing Louvain and the other facing Brussels. A while later, a scout reported that we were less than three hundred feet from a German position. Our regiment began digging feverishly to create cover. Occasional bullets flew through the morning twilight. Our spades hit the roots of trees, the work went slowly, and we made too much noise. With growing apprehension, we slogged on. The soil we dug up was used to raise parapets. Next to the farmhouse, we saw the diabolical silhouettes of German soldiers wandering in and out of the firelight. Theo Carlier, a boy I knew from the iron foundry, raised his rifle as soon as he saw them, but a furious officer pounced on him and slapped down his arm, asking if he was really such an idiot that he didn't understand the Jerries were there as decoys, to trick us into betraying our position with gunfire? In the dim light, we saw a few German ambulances pass on the nearby road. Then a deathly silence fell. It was raining; the stench of smouldering ashes drifted towards us. Our pits were not deep enough; we sat uncomfortably, with our legs folded to one side in the wet earth, and awaited further orders.

After an hour, I'd had enough of the boredom and inactivity. I crept over to the lieutenant and asked him if I could go on a reconnaissance mission; there was a thick beech tree a hundred yards away, blown over by a shell. The officer nodded and whispered, Listen, if you make one mistake, we'll all pay with our lives. Theo Carlier joined me. We crawled over to the felled tree on our elbows, with our rifles at the ready. Lying behind the log, we were alarmed by the sight of two camouflaged machine-gun slits in the German position. We counted to three and then quickly shot three bullets into each slit. A long silence followed, but when I stuck my head up over the log, all hell broke loose. The Germans deliberately grazed us with their bullets, not shooting straight at us, but trying to drive us away from the fallen tree. We were trapped. Bullets whistled all around us, hitting the log; wood chips flew past our ears. We had no choice but to leap up and run for our lives, jumping from tree to tree between the bullets. We dropped down into the closest pit. The water in the pits was rising swiftly in the rain; most of the soldiers were already up to their knees in mud. The Germans kept firing systematically – first a few bullets to provoke a response, and then, as soon as they saw a head move, they let fly with their machine guns.

This went on for a whole day, while we sat and waited. The officers kept telling us to keep calm and use our heads. There were no rations; our bellies cramped with hunger. We scooped the dirty water out of the pits, since there was nothing else to drink. When darkness came, a few soldiers made the rounds of the pits to hand out bullets, and others brought packets of damp biscuits. We knew we were surrounded, like rats in a trap. The woods that should have sheltered us had turned into a quagmire.

By morning both sides had started shooting again, but further away we heard much heavier artillery. By midday, a few of our boys lay dead beside the pits they had begun to stand up in. One boy, who had planned to fetch his bayonet from behind the wagon, lay with his eyes open where everyone could see. A bullet had passed through his open mouth, blowing out the back of his skull. His blood gushed into the wet moss.

Night fell again, and nothing changed. The officers were pale as death and whispered anxiously to each other in French. I crept over to them and asked if I could go out on reconnaissance again. They said it was a bad idea; they saw traps everywhere, said the net had closed around us. That night there was rifle fire in the distance, the rumble of the mortars, thunder rolling over the woods, startled pigeons flapping blindly through the branches in the dark, the pale reflection of fire in the distance, the rat-a-tat-tat of the machine guns. In the second half of the night, this all fell silent. Somewhere in the woods, an owl cried. A half-moon slipped out from behind the clouds, casting a perilous light on the sleeping men.

In the early hours of the third day, a morning mist hung over the fields and pastures around the woods; the Germans seemed to have withdrawn. In the hazy distance, we saw the church and houses of Elewijt catching fire under the German shelling. We heard the call to muster in the depths of the woods. Men far and wide struggled to their feet, like golems freeing themselves from the clay, clambering over the corpses of their dead comrades. Shivering, numb, rigid with backache, in mud-caked uniforms, we fell into ragged ranks, half-leaning on our rifles. The circle of enemy troops had been broken, we had no idea how. Apparently the Germans had bigger fish to fry than our 2nd Line Regiment. We cautiously left the woods in ranks of five, one battalion at a time. In the village, we saw the hissing ruins of houses in the rain, the people and animals killed by mortar fire, and the burned-out church, consecrated just seven years earlier by Cardinal Mercier. That was all we saw of the grisly battle of Schiplaken.

We trudged on in our damp, smelly uniforms. Women would come to the roadside with bread, a jug of milk, sometimes a piece of ham. They told us the names of their sons, asked if we had any news. Between the villages, the countryside was stunning. Summer clouds drifted over the waving grain in the distance, the stands of trees in the pastures shaded the grazing cattle, swallows and larks darted through the air, sticklebacks glinted in the clear brooks, lines of willows swayed their branches in the warm breeze. It reminded me of the seventeenth-century Dutch landscape painters, of their peaceful pictures, of treetops painted by the English artist Constable, dappled with patches of light and shadow, of the tranquil existence he had captured on canvas. Our battalion was encamped near Mechelen, in Sint-Katelijne-Waver. We received rations and a fresh supply of ammunition. I passed the days sketching and drawing. Since I no longer had a pencil, I sharpened small pieces of charcoal from the extinguished fires and drew with them. I liked it even better than graphite; the lines were fuller, and I could crosshatch the shadows with greater subtlety. Some soldiers asked me to draw their portraits so that they could send them to their sweethearts. But as I had no way of fixing the charcoal, the paintings quickly smudged. Some soldiers threw them away; I found my blurred portraits crumpled by the roadside.

We had heard that the Germans had set their sights on Brussels and, after a week in the Mechelen area, were headed south-west again, towards Vilvoorde. By this time we had also heard more than enough about the true scale of the catastrophe in Schiplaken, and our bitterness fuelled our fighting spirit. Under a steadily approaching drumfire of shells and mortar bombs, we neared the banks of the Senne river near Eppegem. The Germans had dug in deep on the other side and were guarding the bridge with machine guns. While we were setting up our own machine guns, no one less than our own Captain Maréchal was felled by a bullet to the stomach. A soldier who tried to help was struck blind by flying shrapnel. We left the captain for dead, along with the wailing soldier, and dived down in the grass, cursing, trying to creep closer. The bridge had to be retaken as soon as possible and destroyed if necessary to stop the enemy's advance. The Germans fired deadly salvos three feet above ground level at ever-changing intervals, making it impossible for us to advance. We saw the bullets spark as they glanced off the iron railing of the bridge; earth sprayed up into the air around us. A wide strip of pastureland opened up ahead, strewn with horse carcasses. Their abdomens were torn open, and in the guts that had oozed out of the swollen bellies, crows were scavenging, hopping in fright whenever the volleys moved in their direction. That stretch of the Senne twists sharply, and we hoped the bends in the bare dyke would hide our approach. But the Germans were on to us immediately, and again, the bullets whistled past our ears. Dozens of us ducked behind the dyke. A couple of lads tried to figure out where the shots were coming from, but as soon as they lifted their heads they were gunned down. The fatal shock sent their bodies flying through the air, to fall with a dull thud. We scrambled over them, keeping as flat as we could, and between salvos I could hear the constant *fuck fuck fuck*. There was no escape now. An eighteen-year-old boy lay in the grass, loudly blubbering. I snapped at him to shut his mouth and keep still until further notice. Then I told the troops near me to fire once every ten seconds, holding their guns over their heads, just above the dyke, first the leftmost and rightmost men and the one in the middle, then the others, and then the first group again. The commander nodded his approval and passed on these orders to the ranks further along. Through this tactic, we apparently managed to give the impression that we were in large numbers. To our surprise, about twenty Germans emerged from the woods on the far side of the pastures with their hands over their heads, shouting, *Nicht schiessen!* In their grey uniforms, the spikes of their dreadful helmets gleaming, they approached with dreamlike slowness, grim and menacing even in surrender. They were the first Germans we'd seen up close. Our mouths dropped open in surprise. We could take prisoners of war, seize their up-to-date machine guns – it was an unexpected stroke of luck. The first rank of our regiment jumped up and went out to meet them. Straight away, the first rank of Germans pitched forwards onto their faces, and machine guns rattled in the woods behind them.

About a dozen of our boys were mown down; the others dropped into the grass, quick as a wink. The line of fire was about one foot off the ground, but slanted downward, which told us that at least one machine gun was installed higher up. Now I too started cursing, boiling with rage at the cowardly trick and the dead bodies all around. My rifle at the ready, I crept closer. A bullet pierced the mess tin on my back; I could hear my spoon and fork rattle. A few minutes later, by following the line of fire, I spotted the gunner's nest in a treetop. I crawled behind one of the foul-smelling horse cadavers and took my time to aim; I would not have the luxury of a second shot. The stench made me gag. After fighting back my urge to retch, I carefully pointed the rifle at the face barely visible through the leaves, and fired. I saw the German keel over backwards; his machine gun fell to the ground. I shouted, Fire! Fire! Fire! All the soldiers in the pasture started shooting at the same time, using up much of their ammunition. There was a commotion in the woods, snapping branches, loud cries – it sounded as if they were in retreat. Our commanding officer asked for a few volunteers to go to the riverbank and find out what was happening on the other side; this gave us new hope of escaping the German death-trap. Nobody stepped forward. He asked again. I thought to myself: It shouldn't always be the same people, let someone else do it for a change, I've had enough. But again, there was silence. The commander swore and asked again. Finally, in a gesture of scorn for my comrades, I raised my hand.

Très bien, Marshen. Be careful, Corporal.

À vos ordres, mon commandant.

Bitterly cursing my pals, I crept along the steep bank of the Senne, without any cover, clinging to tufts of grass so I wouldn't roll into the water. It was growing dark. Each sound – a wood pigeon taking flight, the splash of a water rat – made my anxious heart skip a beat. Something inside me had snapped the moment I saw the 'surrendering' Germans dive forward into the grass. The filthy bloody bastards – I felt like killing, stabbing a man to death with my bayonet, my heart thumped in my throat. I heard a sudden rustling behind me, but couldn't even turn my head in that position and knew for sure my number was up. Then I heard the voice of cross-eyed Rudy from Lossystraat: Martien, matey, it's me, just keep moving ahead nice and quiet, and I'll cover you with my rifle. After a hundred yards, lie down, turn around, and cover me. We'll take turns. By this method, at great risk to our lives, and after blowing off every German head that dared poke up over the dyke, we reached the sappers an hour later, far from where our men were trapped. They were building a temporary bridge. The sound of their hammers was muffled; they'd wrapped them in rags, which kept tearing and had to be replaced. We had left behind our knapsacks and kit in the grass; I left my rifle by the river and crept over to the sappers to inform them of the German position. Now that it was dark, cross-eyed Rudy crawled back on his own to let the others know about the bridge. Half an hour later, they arrived, with Rudy leading the way – a hundred men in all, a long, slow snake slithering through the grass. They all crossed the bridge safely. No one gave me so much as a nod, no one had a word of thanks, no one had picked up my rifle. Muttering a string of curses, I crept a few hundred yards along the grassy bank to retrieve it. After that half-hour delay, I joined the ranks, bringing up the rear.

That early September evening, a frost set in. My mud-soaked greatcoat froze stiff as a board, and I was shivering, my teeth chattering so hard that I thought they would crack in my mouth.

We ate a kind of cold gruel scooped into our dirty, battered mess tins. Since mine leaked, I had to hold my hand under it. My palm was covered with the beastly goo.

Eppegem, that bloody sty, I'll love it till the day I die, Carlier said, and he slapped me on the back.

Leave me alone, the lot of you, I snapped, and when Carlier said, Touchy, touchy! I moved about ten yards away and turned my back on him. Just before the chilly dawn, in the foul hole of night where every living creature shivers against the bare, dewy ground, I dreamed of my mother. She was standing by my father's open grave, the rain was streaming down, a large, dark piece of paper was stuck to her back, she laid my father's brushes beside his coffin in an open pit where the water was rising, and she was crying – my mother, who never cried. I stood behind her, cursing and firing a machine gun at the graves in the cemetery, I who never used to curse. Then I woke up with a start, feeling queasy, and threw up the sour porridge on the grass.

Our exhausted and demoralised battalion was granted a few days' rest. In a light rain, sweating at noon and shivering by sunset, we marched towards a cluster of villages whose inhabitants, we were told, had been forced to run away. Under a sulphur-yellow evening sky, we arrived in a deserted hamlet. The lieutenant and senior officers laid claim to the small village hall; the rest of us were billeted in houses throughout the village, in groups of eight men and a sergeant. I ended up with Carlier, cross-eyed Rudy, Antoine Derdeyn, Daman and Boone, Vinus De Bleser, my cousin René and a boy from the Vilvoorde area, in a small farmhouse a hundred yards outside the village. The impoverished villagers must have been driven out of their homes by the Germans, who had apparently moved on almost immediately afterwards. The cows were grazing behind the vegetable garden; the goats and rabbits were ambling around their pen as if nothing had happened. The little house smelled like damp straw and burnt wood. The portraits on the simple wooden mantelpiece seemed to stare at us disapprovingly; country people with squarish skulls, their fleshy hands in their laps, their eyes expressionless. We took off our heavy leather belts; I gave orders to stow the knapsacks in the attic and leave the rifles in a neat row along the wall in the small entryway. Then I checked the cellar to see if we could take shelter there in a bombardment. To my surprise, I found well over two hundred pounds of potatoes and a barrel of salt pork in lard. Long rows of jars on racks held preserved fruit and vegetables, and there were five open earthenware jugs with a thin layer of salt covering the contents. Derdeyn had followed me downstairs. Ha, ha, the farmer's secret stash, he said with a snigger. He found a jug of gin, snatched it up, and said, I want to shit on the floor right here and get plastered. Grinning, he squeezed his crotch. Before I knew it, I had punched him in the face. He fell back into the racks of glass jars; the jug shattered on the floor. His nose was bleeding; I had to stop myself from hitting him again.

Go upstairs and see if there are enough plates and cutlery to lay the table for nine, I snapped at him. He staggered back upstairs, and when I followed, I was just in time to see him turning the portraits of the farmer and his family to face the chimney.

Vinus came in from the garden and asked Derdeyn what he thought about slaughtering and cleaning the rabbits before the Germans came back for them. Ask Urbain, Derdeyn said, he's the boss. I looked into his sly, evasive, subservient eyes.

Fine, I said, we'll have potatoes and rabbit tonight, and there's plenty of fallen fruit for apple sauce in the garden. The boy from Vilvoorde said his aunt lived nearby and asked if he could spend the night there. He said he would bring us fresh bread for breakfast. I gave him permission to go and ordered him to return by eight the next morning. Daman and Derdeyn were outside, searching the sky for the source of the rumbling sound that seemed to be approaching. Then a wall of deafening thunder rolled over the village and the pastures, making the walls shake. Immediately afterwards, we heard two loud explosions. One shell hit the nave of the village church; the other landed in a field. A few moments later, a third came down right next to the little farm where we were staying. The window panes in the front room tinkled and burst into shards; a few rows of roof tiles slipped off and shattered on the paving stones in front of the house.

For an instant there was silence. Then we heard a voice call out, There's a wine cellar over here! One of the shells had hit a bourgeois house; the gaping hole at street level revealed a large collection of costly vintages in stone niches. Daman and Derdeyn were off in a flash, but a lieutenant beat them to it and barred the way. He bellowed in French that there was one bottle for every soldier, and whoever was caught with two would be punished.

Daman and Derdeyn returned with their bottles; Vinus, Boone and cross-eyed Rudy went to fetch theirs. That's plenty for nine men, I said to Carlier, who was peeling potatoes by the back door. He shrugged. A moment later, we heard the booming voice of the lieutenant. He had knocked Geert the fish vendor and Peutie the dog thief to the ground; the bottles hidden under their jackets had broken and dyed their uniforms purple. Lumpy Segers had forced his way into the small village bakery and now emerged triumphantly with a large, shallow basket of rolls and pastries. He held them high above his head and shouted that everyone could grab one without looking. He was soon knocked off his feet by the onslaught of young soldiers, and the basket fell onto the cobblestones. Everyone grabbed what he could, laughing, kicking, swearing and whooping. The commanders did nothing to stop them.

By ten o'clock, the chimneys of the occupied village were smoking peacefully, far from the tumult of war. The smell of stewed meat filled the streets; we dined on rabbit with brown gravy. The wine flowed; here and there, you could hear singing. We sang too, and toasted and feasted and laughed as if at a village fête.

After the meal, I sat outside on a stool just behind the cowsheds and, for the first time in a long while, felt almost at peace. The sky was clear; Venus hung low over the orchard, casting a penetrating light; the Great Bear shuffled across the night sky with his old wheelbarrow; the grass smelled fresh and made me a little light-headed. My thoughts wandered back to my home, where my mother was now on her own with my two sisters. My other two brothers were still too young to be conscripted; I didn't even know where they were staying. I saw my dead father huddled beside the stove, the black-rimmed fingernails of his slender hands, his pale eyebrows. I was just thinking I should be able to draw his face from memory, when a few seconds later pandemonium broke out. A machine-gun strafe from a low-flying aeroplane was accompanied by running groups of Germans firing in all directions. We had never seen anything like it. It was raining bullets from all sides. Daman, who had been smoking by the front door, lay dead in the hall an instant later, his blood pooling on the tiles. His throat looked as if it had been torn to shreds, and only a few thin strands still connected his head to his body. At the same time, we heard mortar fire. A bomb hit the cowsheds I'd just run away from, and I heard the cattle lowing and rasping in agony. I charged into the house. The men were cowering in the cellar; their rifles lay in a heap by the front door. I scooped up the guns from the floor, threw them down the hatch at the top of the stairs, and shouted to the lads to come out at once.

We heard shouts and cries in the darkness all around us; in the heart of the village, orange smoke was rising over the low roofs. A new explosion set what remained of the church ablaze, moans of fear and agony filled the air, flocks of starlings burst into flight just over our heads, somewhere a well had been hit, doors and house fronts were spattered with sludge, not one windowpane remained whole. I got my men to creep behind the farmhouse, single file, towards the centre of the village, and I took up the rear. We saw about twenty Germans ahead, dark against the blazing pyres, and ran through the gardens till we reached the village square, where we had a clear view of them. They were about to storm the village hall where the officers and the lieutenant had barricaded themselves. I leaped forward and signalled to my men that they should all fire at once. The volley hit the Germans in the back; they fell before they even had time to be surprised. Two of them managed to turn around; Vinus dropped to the earth, screaming in pain; we all fired again; the last Germans toppled to the pavement. The pandemonium died down. Suddenly all we could hear was the flapping of wood pigeons and the crackle of the fires. Somewhere in the distance, a dog howled like a wolf. The Milky Way twinkled, endlessly far away from the black hole where this stupid planet was spinning. We edged along the house fronts with our rifles at the ready and our bayonets fixed, suspecting an ambush, but it was all over. An officer peeked through a window on the upper floor of the village hall. Next to him, I saw the machine-gunner who was always at his side. I waved to him and shouted that it was safe.

Here and there we heard the groans of the wounded.

The officers came outside one by one, and the men began to emerge from the houses too, some still blotto. We had lost about twenty lads. The officer swore under his breath, posted sentries on both sides of the main street in extended order, and stationed machine-gunners on the upper floors of two houses, one on each side.

The others must sleep now, he said. Tomorrow is another day.

To me he said, Marshen, I'll see to it you receive a promotion for this.

I saluted and returned to the house with my men.

Boone lay by the front door, wailing and praying for death. His uniform had been blown open at chest level, and his organs were bulging out between the gleaming buttons of his jacket. He had thrown up all over his face. I wiped it off with my dirty handkerchief, cursing Derdeyn for a fool because he had smashed the jug of gin in the cellar earlier that day. Boone's misery didn't last long. Blood came welling out of his nose and mouth, gurgling and sloshing, his eyes rolled vacantly, a moment later he was unconscious, and a few minutes later he was dead. I shut his eyes and told the men to dig a hole in the backyard. We laid Boone and Daman side by side and covered them with a layer of straw before we filled the hole. Theo Carlier made a primitive cross out of a couple of boards and carved their names into the wood with his knife. The night was well under way, the grass, leaves and branches wet with dew. The world was silent and inexplicable. The rising moon appeared, gleaming, timeless and vast as in a dream, like a yellow wheel of cheese behind a line of rustling poplars. I prayed to Our Lady of the Seven Sorrows, I asked her why she had turned her face from our world. I inhaled the earthy odour of the autumn night, still laced with a faint whiff of gun smoke. We went inside; I slept on some straw in the cellar. Cross-eyed Rudy, Carlier and Derdeyn settled down on the floor. One by one, we fell into a bottomless sleep, sleep like the slow extinction of a light, a large and distant light that stabbed through the small cellar window again just a few hours later, while the birds sang like maniacs in the old apple trees and a cockerel crowed on the dung heap by the bombed-out barn.

We milked the two cows in the courtyard before we moved on. I took Boone's canteen out of his knapsack and filled it to the brim. After Daman's death, I had taken his mess tin, which was still in perfect condition. We moved on in marching order, with heavy heads from the wine the night before, still bearing west towards Humbeek. After a few miles, the plugs popped out of a few canteens; some soldiers had filled theirs with the leftover wine, and as the liquid sloshed back and forth in the rising heat, it started to foam. Wine gushed out past their collars and into their hair, dripping down onto their necks and jackets. To the hilarity of the other soldiers, they walked the rest of the way in purple-stained uniforms that reeked of sour alcohol.

That afternoon it drizzled, and the morale of the hungover troops dropped by the minute. We struggled to keep our footing on the greasy clay of the country roads and the mud-slicked, uneven paving stones of the shot-up streets. A few nuns came rushing out of a boys' school partly demolished by a shell. They had heard we were coming and prepared huge quantities of soup. They also handed out tins of beef and sardines. The officers bellowed that we had no time to lose. We all filled our knapsacks and marched on, grumbling. The rain was chilly by this time and pelted our faces. Behind a sandbank somewhere along the route, we found traces of earlier fighting. Shutters and doors had been removed from abandoned houses and laid across canals and pits. Beyond them were deserted trenches, partly covered with boards and scrap metal. In the boggy ground we saw footprints, wheel marks and hastily dug ditches. The last company to pass this way must have left no more than an hour and a half earlier. We were ordered to drag all the boards, doors and shutters along with us and then use them in digging a trench a few hundred yards further on. We had no idea what the point of this exhausting labour was, until we saw energetic movement in the bushes several hundred yards away. The order came for everyone to crouch, immediately, and work on all fours. In this awkward position, we continued digging the shallow pits. Sweat and rain trickled down our necks and over our backs. Since I had done well on the banks of the Senne, I was sent on another hands-and-knees patrol, this time as far as the next canal, on the other side of the pastures. I knew the lieutenant now in command, Laurens de Meester, from the military school in Kortrijk; he respected me, and showed it without a lot of pother by giving me assignments like this one.

Carlier, Derdeyn and I crept around the German camp until after five. I made a sketch showing the possible locations of their trenches as precisely as I could. That cost me my last few sheets of smudged drawing paper.

Around sunset, I was sent out on reconnaissance again. The officers distrusted the silence, after the signs of frantic combat that we had found. In the cold evening mist, the mud dried into hard, irregular serrated edges that made crawling difficult. As we were nearing the outskirts of the village to the left of the woods, a gigantic black horse came out of nowhere, charging towards us. As it galloped past, barely missing us, it became aware of our presence, veered away with a loud flapping of its horse lips into the pasture to our left, and bucked wildly, spilling the contents of its saddle bags. We could see from its harness that it belonged to the enemy troops. The animal vanished as suddenly as it had appeared. We heard the fading thud of its hooves on the grass. I immediately crept closer and found a volume of topographical maps, a compass, field glasses and a notebook. As we returned to our post, walking upright under cover of darkness, we suddenly heard the horse approaching us. When we turned around, we saw its large brown eyes shining brightly in the gloaming. The animal followed us at a walk, obediently, as if it recognized us as its masters. Carlier, a farmer's son who knew how to handle a horse, took it by the reins. Snorting, it twisted its fierce head back and forth a few times, kicked at the mud with its hind legs, and then meekly followed. We arrived at our trenches with the horse in tow, to the intense interest of the lieutenant, who closely inspected everything we had found. The men looked on, listlessly spooning up what the nuns had given them earlier that day.

Dark gaps formed in the pale sky; stars pierced through them; it soon grew cold. The earth gave off a chill, like an unknown planet of cool soil, and we, absurdly small and shivering, were stuck to it like flies in syrup. That night I dreamed of the smith's son with his eyes burned white in the fire; he spoke to me, but I could not understand him. *Whazzat?* I asked him again and again, he sprayed bubbles of saliva in my direction, they seared my face like white-hot iron. When I awoke, I realized that they were raindrops. In the biting morning mist I pulled the hood of my capote over my head, ill-tempered and trembling.

Sunday morning. Not a church rang its bells in all the countryside around us; the crows swarmed over the broken poplars and the collapsed houses beyond them. We were each given two army biscuits and a mug of hot coffee. I eagerly grabbed the warm mug and started to drink, but burned my lips. I jerked my head back and was about to blow on the coffee when two bullets, one after another, flew between my mouth and the mug towards the barn door where a sergeant was pouring the coffee. The bullets pipped him in the neck and throat; he died instantly, keeling into the door and crumpling like a puppet. Everybody screamed and ran for the trenches, scrambling for their rifles. Lieutenant De Meester barked commands. He ordered me to run two hundred yards to the right with twenty-four men, lie flat, keep watch and shoot anything that moved. We slithered through the grass like eels and found ourselves in a potato field – a stroke of luck, because the raised beds gave us cover. When we cautiously rose to our feet, we saw only deserted fields and an empty farmhouse hundreds of yards away. But when I looked through the German field glasses that De Meester had entrusted to me, I saw tufts of grass shifting and quaking, an advancing meadow, noiseless and treacherous. The enemy regiment must have been following us since the day before, determined to catch us unawares and kill us all.

Then the small attic window of the farmhouse swung open with a flash in the rising sun. They're setting up a machine gun there, I whispered to my men. I ordered all twenty-four of them to fire at the window simultaneously, on my count. The salvo rang out as if from a single rifle. Through my field glasses I saw six or seven men come rushing out of the little house. That very same moment, bullets started flying in all directions through the green of the potato field, but our ridge of earth sheltered us. I could see the meadow shifting towards us, rippling, wriggling and squirming. My heart skipped two beats. We had wasted a lot of ammunition and only had about ten bullets each. To make matters worse, we were isolated from the body of the regiment. I ordered the twenty-four soldiers to fire a fan of bullets low to the ground, one bullet each. Confusion broke out in the living pasture; no shots were returned for some time. Suddenly we saw projectiles overhead, which hit the ground a few hundred yards behind us. The Germans had guessed that we had reinforcements on the way and were trying to cut them off. For the first time, I felt afraid of dying. A penetrating odour told me that the young soldier next to me had soiled himself. His whole body was shaking, and he had laid down his rifle at his side. Corporal, he said, may I—

Keep your mouth shut, I said, we have bigger problems than your trousers.

There was silence again for a while. It was almost nine o'clock. I suspected the Germans would not venture into the potato field.

We started to breathe again. I gave the panicked boy a reassuring nod. Suddenly, a German officer leaped up less than ten yards away and aimed his pistol at my head, which had poked out just over the greenery. He fired twice. As I ducked, the soil sprayed into my face. I leaped up immediately and shot before he could shoot again; caught by surprise, he fell onto his back and lay motionless.

Now we had five bullets each, and no place to run. Mortar bombs and whizz-bangs dropped a hundred yards behind us; the entire landscape was being ploughed up. Ahead of us, an unknown number of Germans were preparing to slaughter our little group of twenty-four. I looked at the lads' faces. They were tensely squinting through the grass and leaves, expecting another spiked helmet to appear before their noses any second. We didn't have enough ammunition to scare them off by shooting blindly into the grass.

It occurred to me that the lieutenant had promised to signal with his drawn sword when it was safe for us to crawl back. But not a sound or signal came from Molenheuvel, the hummock by the barn where they had taken cover. Then we'll return at our own risk, I thought, and I ordered the furthest soldier to jump up and run back. After three strides, he fell down dead. Following another long interval of silence, I again ordered the soldier in front to jump up and run back as fast as possible. He stumbled to the ground after ten yards, riddled with invisible bullets that whizzed low over the potato field. I felt hate burn like acid in my throat, a bitter gall that surged through my body and dizzied me with furious, death-seeking energy. I had two bullets left. I shifted my knapsack to my right side for protection, jumped up, and ran for my life towards the edge of the neighbouring field. I could feel the bullets whistling past. The collar of my coat flew off; a hot streak shot across my neck. Right after that, the straps of my knapsack were shot off. I stumbled, tripped over my own rifle, and landed face first in the soil at the edge of a beet field. My rifle lay three steps behind me. My heart was pounding frantically. I inched backwards, belly up, and pulled my rifle closer by the strap. The men looked on, paralysed with horror. I waved to them to throw me their bullets. Ten bullets landed in the loose soil around me, and I crept over to pick them up, one by one. Once I had them all, I carefully wiped them clean, loaded my rifle, and fired horizontally, just above ground level, whenever anything moved. After the third shot, it stayed quiet for several minutes. I let out a loud cough and ducked behind the ridge between the fields. A bullet promptly flew in my direction. I returned fire. A dark silhouette sprang up, screaming, and fell backwards. Then there was silence. I signalled to my men to creep towards me on their bellies, one at a time. After the first hundred yards, we started crawling on our hands and knees, and after another hundred yards we jumped to our feet and ran for our lives, but there was nothing moving any more.

We sat down by the barn, panting. Nobody said a word. Soldiers were arriving from all directions, some wounded, with dark red bandages round their arms, legs, chests – bandages they had made from strips of their own underwear. Others straggled into camp covered with mud, like zombies, the living dead, their eyes glittering in their blackened faces. Here and there, not far away, we could hear rasping and wailing in the fields. We didn't know where it was and would not venture beyond our sheltering wall again. The German horse had already been slaughtered; a few soldiers had skinned it with their bayonets and hung large slabs of meat on a stable door. We could not start a fire to cook the meat, which gave off the nause-ating smell of blood. In the evening we went back for my two dead boys, groping blindly through the pitch darkness. Ambulance workers went in search of the wounded men moaning in the fields. My cousin René had fallen in battle less than a hundred yards from the place where we had fought. I didn't have a chance to see him; the ambulance men had already carried him off. I was assured that he had not suffered and that he had 'perished on the field of honour', an empty formula we heard time and again for all the ghastly deaths around us. Someone else had laid claim to his shoes – the shoes left behind by my cousin René, the pasty-faced swanker who had dreamed of becoming a shoemaker. How would they break it to Evarist, the old smith, that his second son had gone the way of the first?

We went on to Zaventem. I spent a long time in the church there, kneeling before the side altar with the painting of my patron saint. The lieutenant gave us extra rations and congratulated us on our courage and cold-bloodedness. For me, he had a friendly clap on the shoulder.

'You did your best, Marshen. Don't dwell on it.'

When I lay down to sleep that night, I bawled like a baby, with my rosary clutched in my fist. I prayed in utter turmoil, to drown out the deafening screams that had risen like a storm in my reeling head, and it was as if my prayers were swept away in that unbearable inner bedlam. After an hour of compulsive prayer, I heard it again – the distant drone of the organ – and fell asleep.

3

Battle of the Yser, October 1914

From a fast-moving army of one hundred and twenty thousand troops in constant military action, we had been reduced to a ragtag band of soldiers, surviving as best we could. We had escaped death countless times and become hardened to the sores, blisters, diseases and wounds we picked up from the crude equipment that we lugged through miry fields and past deserted villages. In the first week of October – weary in body and soul, with rifles that still went bang but had no precision left in their worn-out barrels – we made a forced march to the besieged dykes near the southern coast of Flanders. We passed Jabbeke after three days, tramped on to Ostend a day later, and split up in Middelkerke. We were billeted in empty houses; we devoured our sandwiches and hot coffee and went to sleep on the thin layer of straw scattered over the wooden floor. A couple of hours later, we woke to the sound of the battalion's buglers and drummers. To perk up our dazed, debilitated group, we were given mugs of coffee and a couple of dry biscuits, which we gulped down in doleful silence. Right after that, we were sent on another forced march – destination unknown. A messenger told us the fall of Ghent was near; fear gripped my heart when I thought of my mother. There were whispers that Middelkerke was a death trap; with our backs to the sea, there would be no escaping the advancing German troops. The officers growled at us to shut our big mouths and keep marching.

My feet were in shreds; the clotted blood in my coarse socks kept rubbing against the wounds and reopening them, wider than ever. Every step of the way, I was limping in pain. I heard that British and French relief troops might be coming. But what did we know? A scruffy, hobbling pack, we had long ago cast off, shot to pieces, or trampled our tall shako helmets and replaced them with looted hats or policemen's forage caps, our tangled hair poking out below. We wore boots found on farms, the shoes of dead Germans, knapsacks of knotted rags. We were a mud-spattered bunch of battle-numbed saps, groaning and grousing our way to the unthinkable, plodding down mucky roads under the low clouds of our rain-lashed country.

Just after noon, we arrived in Ichtegem, where we had to await orders from the general staff. After more than an hour of deliberation, the brass hats decided to send us back the way we'd come. The men's protests swelled to such a point that the officers drew their swords and shouted themselves hoarse, ordering the mob of emaciated ghouls to simmer down. The lads swore and stamped; some flung themselves into the grass, pulled the shoes off their wounded feet, and shouted that they would not go another step. A couple of Walloon boys started bleating like sheep: *Armée bête, armée bête*. The officers were clearly taken aback. I stepped forward, feeling resentful because I'd just heard that my mother and sister Clarisse had come to Jabbeke the day before and been denied permission even to say hello to me. I told Lieutenant De Meester that the men needed a couple of hours' rest first. Request denied; our orders had arrived. I said it might be a good idea to let us know what those orders were, so we would at least see the point of all this.

De Meester said, Martien, don't you get uppish, now.

Furious, we gathered our courage, and our regiment marched past Mannekensvere and crossed its one bridge to the other side of the Yser, where we were finally ordered to halt at the Tervaete Loop. The officers had relented a bit along the way and permitted us a couple of stops to rest. By the side of a brook, we rinsed out our dirty, bloodied socks and lingered for several minutes, dangling our feet in the cool water as long as we could, sharing talcum powder and puttees. At the end of the long march, we collapsed in exhaustion on the banks of the Yser.

The soft cries of the wood pigeons in the evening echoed from the smooth surface of the moving water. In the mud, I saw the fresh prints of women's shoes and children's feet. But the area seemed utterly deserted. The empty fields were dotted with lost-looking cows and horses.

Biscuits were handed out again – large aluminium tins of Biscuits Parein, tins we fought over even when they were empty, because they were so convenient for storing all sorts of little things. That night, instead of sleeping, we worked at a feverish pace. With the blunt saws given to us, we had to cut down a row of willow trees, sawing through the trunks just above ground level. The fallen trees and their branches were supposed to protect us from the wind and rain. The thickest logs were sawn in two lengthwise, so that we could use them to cover some of the trenches. The officers gave orders to dig ditches that could be defended from attackers on both sides. I asked what the point of that was, and was told that because this stretch of river snaked back and forth, if the Germans crossed the Yser, we would immediately be surrounded. In a farmhouse, coffee was brewed for us; we slurped it greedily from our iron mugs. It was six in the morning, and all of us were longing for a couple of hours' sleep. Just as Segers and Lievens came out of the house with yet another canteen full of coffee, all hell broke loose again. A howitzer shell hit the ground next to them and blew one of them to bits. We couldn't even find his body; the other man died instantly too. As if to show off their accuracy, the Germans immediately followed up with a few well-aimed bombs that landed right on the horses and cows in the pasture behind our backs. We saw the limbs of the animals sticking up out of the craters into the sky, the swirls of blue shell-smoke dispersing over them. The enemy had managed to build a pontoon bridge across the river. Panic broke out; there was close combat in some places with bayonets. Then the shells started shrieking over us. In less than no time, the farmhouse and the barn next to it were razed to the ground. By ten o'clock, nothing was left of the charming countryside. In the mass of rubble and upturned earth surrounding us, there was no sign of life. We fired back with machine guns in the direction of the battery fire. A large-calibre shell struck our machine-gun nest. We saw our friends' bodies soar into the air; severed limbs went flying over our heads.

The days wore on, and we were tossed back and forth between sudden alarm and long hours of quiet when everything seemed just fine. Most of our artillery never showed up, and there was no point in opening fire anyway; the barrels had worn out in the heat, and our light guns didn't have a long enough range. Some days we couldn't see a thing through the icy fog.

A raft came drifting silently down the river one night, laden with large crates of fresh munitions. We had no idea how it had reached us.

But what we saw the next morning staggered us all: a mass of dogs, cats, polecats, weasels, rats and rabbits, swimming across the river like an otherworldly army, their snouts just above water, trailing countless triangles in the smooth black surface. The locks had been opened in Nieuwpoort, and the countryside was gradually flooding, as far inland as Diksmuide and Tervaete. It slowly dawned on us that this might halt the enemy advance. We watched with pounding hearts. We had strict orders not to shoot at the fleeing animals, because that would betray our position. So we looked on as those sharp-nosed messengers from a doomed world, fleeing an unimaginable Armageddon, came on land, shook the water out of their pelts and rushed past our trenches without a glance, fleeing blindly like lemmings. No one grabbed at the animals; as hungry as we were, no one wanted to kill and eat one. Like disguised angels of judgement, the bedraggled ghosts passed out of sight again, bounding over the slick black fields of mud in the drab morning light. We gaped at the ripples they'd left on the river's dark surface. In the distance, we saw the pale glow of water rushing through the fields in our direction. The commanders passed through the ranks, repeating that provisioning would be difficult and we would have to pull through for many days on our own, without reinforcements from the area behind us. The only food they gave us was tins of sardines and damp biscuits. The men cursed and gagged at the flavour of the salty sardines after the coffee they had just drunk. We were forbidden to leave the trenches to 'heed nature's call'. Plenty of soldiers had been heeding the call right where they sat for the past week, some even pissing their pants for a moment of warmth in the blasted morning fog. In the corners of our trenches, the mountains of faeces grew by the day. We tried to forget they were there. Sometimes one of us would scoop a little soil on top, but the penetrating odour was already in our heads, our breath, our bones. We're more primitive than cavemen in this bloody place, Carlier said, and he spat into the mud.

One morning, a week later, we heard a child crying. A boy of about ten years old was standing on the opposite bank. The commander forbade us to go and fetch him. Carlier said it was a bloody shame, pulled off his uniform, dived into the water, and swam to the other side. Just as he was reaching out his hand, the child walked away. The Germans all opened fire at once; we had no idea where from. Carlier fell backwards, rolled down the bank into the river, dived underwater, and did not resurface until he was on our side. We had all watched this spectacle with bated breath. Carlier was pulled out of the water. The commander said he deserved to be punished severely, but considering our outrage at the German trickery, he decided to leave well alone.

We were thunderstruck by the realization that our enemy no longer had any moral scruples whatsoever. This kind of psychological warfare was new to us. We had been taught a strict code of military honour, ethics and warcraft. We had learned to fence skilfully, to conduct rescue drills, and to think about the honour of our country's soldiers. What we saw here had nothing to do with all that. It stirred up our thoughts and emotions; we sensed, with fear in our hearts, that we were becoming different men, ready and willing to do all the things we'd once abhorred. A few of our officers were quarrelling in French. One of them wanted to order us to cross the river; the other one was roaring that it would be madness.

A waste of munitions and of human lives! De Meester bellowed.

But soon afterwards, they seemed to have concocted a plan. We were sent down the riverbank in groups of four to ten, to see if from the bends we could observe any manoeuvres on the other side. Near the ruined farmhouse, about a hundred soldiers stood in a circle, ready to fire. We had been issued with shovels and started digging our way towards each other; after a few hours, we had a new hundred-yard trench. Now we were told to drop into the trenches immediately and stay there without moving until further orders. Night fell; we slept on a thin layer of straw that we had collected from the demolished barns. Others slept on the muddy ground, half standing, bowed over their rifles, or in a foetal position, their faces turned towards the shallow earthen wall. We wished we could smoke, but the smell of cigarettes could have betrayed our position to enemy scouts.

I thought of my mother again that night and suddenly, I don't know why, of the fact that I had never been with a girl – something the other men often teased me about. I thought of the girl in the shallow pool – had that been such a short time ago? I saw her rise to her feet in the warm haze of summer by the harbour, her clothing on the bank, blue and white like the garments of Bernadette Soubirous. Her soft, naked skin burned like a patch of light in the darkness. What miracle permits us to see light and life in our dreams when darkness is all around? Restlessness surged through my body, lust took hold, and the demonic desire for self-gratification caught me in its grasp. Here and there, I heard the rhythmic shifting of fabric in the dark; I knew what that meant. I understood why the others did it, but I could never forgive myself if I gave in. I found myself in the stranglehold of a limitless desire to release my seed, just once, after all this time, out of sight of the Almighty and his priests, out of range of the confessional, here in this hell of death and mud where even the animals had fled their Eden. Would it be all right, just once? Before I could make a move, the thought alone sent a hot, blissful spurt down my army-issue trousers; I flinched, grew dizzy, and started to cry in silence, begging Our Lady to forgive my weakness. I saw the girl; my lust raged on; I turned with a sigh to the dirty straw and, burning with shame, surrendered to my own touch, wept, prayed for forgiveness, and fell asleep.

When we were shaken awake, I found next to my head a piece of roast pork, still slightly warm, handed out to us just before we had gone to sleep. It must have been less than three hours later. The buglers sounded a muffled call to arms; once we had fallen into formation in the trenches, still stumbling and groggy, we received our orders.

Soldats, portez-vous en avant! Flemish soldiers, forward, double-quick!

An immediate cry of panic: Bloody hell, the Huns are in our trenches!

The clarions blared. Shivering with cold, we surged forward, some of us already leaving the trenches, and charged four abreast at the Germans, who had crossed the river in the night. A grenadier with his black busby under one arm, a chasseur with a green beret, a gunner formerly assigned to the fortification belt, a sapper – each time, the commander shot a couple of bullets past their heads for cover. Running and shooting, we advanced almost a mile.

Form ranks!

This way, this way, this way, join the ranks, goddamn it!

Death and disaster hung in the frigid air.

Martien and Kimpe, first sergeant majors, effective immediately.

Merci, mon commandant.

Stand to attention.

Oui, mon commandant.

Private Marroi.

Oui, mon commandant.

The three of you will stay in a parallel line, one hundred and fifty yards away from each other. Mark any place where we can take cover from the enemy. Try to mark a jumping-off point for our charge on the enemy front.

Martien: fifty yards ahead, on the right. Kimpe in the middle, Marroi on the left. If you meet resistance, withdraw and rejoin us. Fix your bayonets. Now!

I was the first to charge, head over heels, out of our position, clumps of grass flying past my head, debris blown out of cellars. I ducked from shell hole to bomb crater, leaped behind tree trunks, expecting to hear the signal that the others would follow. But we heard nothing behind us; over our heads was the shrieking of bullets and bombs, high-explosive shells and shrapnel. To my left, I could no longer see Kimpe. He was supposed to be fifty yards behind me, but the ravaged landscape made it impossible to tell what was going on. Confused, I dropped to the ground and crept forward as fast as I could. All around me were mangled barbed-wire entanglements, dead cows, sections of wall, twisted iron, deep pools and craters, and a dying horse, desperately flailing its head. The foam frothed and burbled around its mouth, and its hooves scraped at the mud. I shot the animal to put it out of its misery, pressing the barrel of my gun against its sensitive, brown-haired head. Blood and ooze spattered through the air. The enemy fire was now so close by that I could make out the machine-gun nests, hellmouths that barked and clattered and rattled till I could no longer hear or see. Then I came to a slope. Ahead of me, about five feet up, was a pasture. This would be a safe spot for our men to gather for the attack. But how could I let them know? The river bend was a treacherous place. Turning back would mean certain death; even my own comrades would shoot at me, not realizing who I was. My only choice was to go over the edge and see what lay beyond it. Suddenly, far to my left, I saw Kimpe climbing the slope. He leaped forwards and ducked underneath the shot-up fence. I did the same; one hundred and fifty yards apart, we ran towards the enemy line. This is madness, I found myself thinking. The bullets were flying around me at knee level; I ran and leapt over bodies and more bodies, so thick on the ground that my throat clenched shut; but I knew it had to be there eventually, out ahead of us: the *parallèle de départ*, the jumping-off point that we had been ordered to mark. I hopped back and forth like a madman, dodging the whistling bullets, dancing like an idiot for my life. Finally I reached the last fence. Now I had to act fast. I jumped, but felt a shock run through my body – I couldn't tell where – a white flash before my eyes, the feeling that my belly was tearing open. Between the falling bombs, I dived into a dry ditch and lay shivering there, flat on my belly, with my left groin in such pain that I could not breathe for a full minute and thought I would suffocate. I could not cry for help, or cough, or reach my rifle, which was lying right by the edge of the ditch. I could not undo my heavy knapsack, which had fallen on top of me. I was completely paralysed. I saw the blurred image of the Yser dykes about one hundred yards ahead. Just before losing consciousness, I mumbled, Mission accomplished, *mon commandant*.

Then everything went black and silent.

Much later, I woke up. It was twilight. Drizzle was falling straight down on me; I was drenched. I lay next to the ditch; apparently I had climbed out, but I couldn't remember a thing about it. I might have been lying for hours in full view of the enemy riflemen. On my throat was the heavy boot of a dead man. I coughed and very slowly turned my head. All around me were my lifeless comrades. Apparently our stunt had ended in death. Pain tore through my body. I lay there motionless until the last light faded and the shooting stopped. I was parched with thirst; the pain in my groin tormented me. In the dark, I probed the crater of soft flesh somewhere in my underbelly, sticky with blood. For a while I lay sobbing, convinced I was going to die there. Frantic with despair, I crawled through the mud on my elbows in the depths of the night, dragging my numb legs behind me. But even that apparently made some noise; bullets came hurtling blindly through the darkness in my direction. With my elbows scraped raw, blood dripping from the cuffs of my jacket and trousers, praying to the Blessed Virgin, I crawled past dead cows, horses with torn bellies gaping open, dead soldiers with shot-off faces, and saw not a living soul, except perhaps for that one boy whimpering somewhere in the darkness. Sometimes I brought my hand down flat on the lacerated body of a dead man; I shuddered and crept far behind the deserted trenches.

As the first glimmer appeared in the sky, I crawled on through an endless series of trenches, weeping and, so I imagined, dying. As if by some miracle, I saw two Red Cross stretchers. A doctor and two young priests were huddled together beside them. Apparently, I was hundreds of yards behind the front line. I rolled into the pit. They gave me first aid, the medical officer muttering as I lapsed back into unconsciousness. When I awoke, there was a piece of cardboard pinned to my chest; I couldn't move enough to see what was written on it. Along with other wounded men, I was loaded onto a cart and driven away. We trundled down the broken roads, our destination some place beyond the deadly Tervaete Loop. That same morning, the rest of our battalion was massacred by the machine guns and shells of the exceptionally well-entrenched German forces. From Nieuwpoort to Diksmuide, one hundred and fifty thousand young soldiers fell in less than a week.

I spent several days in a kind of barracks, gasping in agony. There I heard what had become of our proud *parallèle de départ*. Our commander had awaited our signal for two hours; not one of us three had made it. In desperation, they had gone over the top, sabres drawn and bayonets fixed, and, almost without exception, had been mown down. We lost about a thousand officers that week, just on that side of the front. Countless boys were left, unidentified, to die in the mud; others were wounded or taken prisoner, or died in the horse cart on the way to the barracks where I lay. Bumping and thumping over the shattered paving stones, a wagon brought me and the other wounded men to the rear of the front lines. In a ramshackle house, we were examined by another medical officer. The commanders were distrustful and always on the lookout for shirkers; some lads would put on the blood-soaked uniforms of dead comrades and make a show of moaning and groaning, so that they would be taken away with the wounded. The two young chaplains were in shock. They kept crying and crying and eventually had to be carried off themselves. Every time we were taken to a new aid station, still further away from the front, we underwent yet another medical examination and received first aid again. There were fewer of us left each time; I watched boys die next to me in the open bed of a wagon. The grey sky was void and empty, and the crows that rode the chill wind etched their triumphant cries deep into my broken body. We finally arrived in Calais. In a requisitioned hotel, we were placed in beds for the first time and given soup and bread. After that we were taken to a hospital; I had no idea where. A bullet was removed from my groin. The army doctor was standing by my bed when I awoke. He handed me the bullet as if it were a medal.

You were lucky, *mon ami*. One inch closer to the centre, and it would have hit your spine. Then you'd have been crippled for life.

He gave me a pat on the cheek. I couldn't move. I slept for days without eating. Then we were fed a watery vegetable soup, which gave me immediate diarrhoea. I felt as frail as an autumn leaf on the wind. In my nightmares, dead horses rose from the blood-sodden mud and started trampling soldiers. One morning, as I watched the nurses come and go in their grey uniforms, those quiet young women who cared for us with hushed voices and careful hands, to my embarrassment, I burst into sobs. The next day, fifty of us were put on board a ship. Liverpool, we were told, Liverpool was where they were taking us. I slept through the entire crossing.

4

When I was thrown back into the fray six months later, what I remembered most about Liverpool was a shock of recognition that would stay with me all my life. But first we were carried through sleet and storm, in an ice-cold wind that howled across the wide, choppy waters of the Mersey, to a hospital right next to the large cathedral under construction on Hope Street. After that I spent the spring in two auxiliary hospitals for recovering soldiers – the first in Wallasey, across the river, and the second back in Liverpool, somewhere near Toxteth. The days drifted by like a vague dream of rest and relief. For the first few weeks, I was in a wheelchair pushed by a taciturn nurse named Maud. I had trouble finding words in those early weeks, and would lie awake at night, ashamed of my awkwardness. After a while, I could hobble up and down the corridor on crutches. I would no longer be able to locate the auxiliary where we stayed; Maud told me it was a ten-minute walk to the banks of the Mersey. I do recall that the hospital was next to a park with a few old oak trees behind low walls. That first weekend, every movement hurt. Every moment of the day, it was painfully clear to me that even moving a single arm activates the muscles in the lower abdomen; it was as if every gesture I made was driven from that tender spot. I had trouble urinating and was embarrassed for the statuesque nurse who had to help me with my catheter, a brown tube through which watery blood kept running into the white enamel basin that she would hold up for me; I cursed under my breath whenever I tripped on a doorstep.

But after a month and a half I was feeling well enough to start on the first exercises meant to get me back into form. I took short walks, and then progressively longer ones. I sat and sketched under the trees in St James' Cemetery, in the shadow of the unfinished cathedral, where construction had stopped for the duration of the war. Soon, a few soldiers were asking me for portraits. I drew them in charcoal, and taciturn Maud leaned in for a look. It was a spring day, mid-March. I caught a whiff of violets, and when I looked up I saw her green eyes fixed on my hands. I gulped and, without thinking, mainly to hide how nervous and tongue-tied I felt, blurted something I'd just figured out that instant: years earlier, towards the end of his short life, my father had stayed somewhere in Liverpool too, sent by the Society of St Vincent de Paul. After a moment's reflection, she told me there was a Church of St Vincent de Paul on St James Street, and then continued her rounds.

From that moment, I could not rest. How could I have been so foolish as to forget that my father had spent almost a year of his life here? Had the war shaken me so badly that I had lost my memory? I spent the sleepless nights that followed racking my brains. Where had my father worked? And what had he painted? Soon after he returned home, his health had deteriorated rapidly. We'd barely had time for questions, and he had volunteered little, because he had such difficulty talking. Why hadn't I drawn him out about his trip?

Full of self-reproach, I wrote my mother a long letter describing my doings in Liverpool. As soon as my health and the weather permitted, I went out searching. Maud was right: in St James Street I found the Church of St Vincent de Paul. My heart was pounding as I entered its damp, sparsely decorated interior. On the dingy walls to the left, there was no sign of any murals my father might have worked on. On the right, I found the Stations of the Cross on panels. There happened to be men at work in the church, whitewashing walls. They couldn't recall any frescoes under the whitewash. In the days that followed, I visited almost every church in Liverpool, astonished at the number of Catholics living there; Maud told me many of them were Irish immigrants. I visited the Sacred Heart Church, the St Philip Neri Church, still under construction, the Church of St Luke, later bombed in the Second World War, the Church of St Thomas of Canterbury, St Anthony's Church, and the smaller churches and chapels in outlying districts. Nowhere did I find any trace of the murals my father was supposed to have restored and extended. He had worked in a monastery, or a school, I vaguely recalled. So I walked all the way to Everton Valley to visit Notre Dame College. But I still could not find what I sought, and my guilt and obsession mounted by the day.

One morning in late February, I went for a stroll along the docks, turning into one street and then another as the fancy took me. I strayed into run-down areas on the outskirts of the city, lost my way, arrived at a walled garden, and found a kind of cloister with a small church. I walked in without any hope, simply intending to pray for my dear departed father. I knelt down on a hard, simple bench. A few candles were giving off smoke, and a woman lay prostrate on the stone floor, praying. I took my rosary beads from my pocket and sank into a long, repetitive prayer that soothed me, as if all my cares slipped away. When I stood up, cleansed, I noticed behind the altar a mural that appeared to portray St Francis; a wreath of small birds flew around his half-bald head. I climbed the two steps past the altar and felt a kind of electric shock run through my body; the saint's face was, unmistakably, my father's. I could not believe my eyes, but there he stood – he had painted his self-portrait, here, where no one would think worse of him for it, in the certainty that no one would ever know or see what he had done. Here, far from everyone who knew him, my father had immortalized himself in the guise of his patron saint . . . This was his face, a few months before his death, a death he might already have felt skulking in his thin frame. Dumbfounded, I gazed at the mural. This was just how his face had looked when he stepped off the train at Zuidstatie in Ghent, that far-off day in the quiet years before the war.

To the right of the saint was a shepherd boy, and this gave me a second shock. It was undeniable: the boy reaching out his hand affectionately to the saint – had my own face. I looked again, feeling sure that my overwrought imagination must be playing tricks on me. But no, he had painted me from memory precisely as I was in those days, a boy about fourteen years old, with coarse, bristly hair, a short thick neck, the blue eyes I'd inherited from him – there I was, in a humble corner next to my father, shrouded in the half-darkness of a small church. Had he sketched me while I was sleeping behind the coal stove? Could he really have painted this purely from memory? In a flash, it occurred to me that I had posed for the Christ figure in the monastery of the Brothers of Charity not long before he left for Liverpool. Had he taken a number of sketches along with him? Either for this purpose or simply the way people would later bring family snapshots along on their travels? He had never said one word to me about this. It must have seemed inconceivable that I would ever find out. I remembered how he had burst into tears when he returned home and saw my sketches: who knows, maybe he was thinking of this fresco then . . . I was immediately overcome by the memories of churches where I had sat next to him, my whole childhood long. I could still see it all before me – his movements, his quiet coughing when he was intent on his work, the smell of turpentine and oil. Overwhelmed by melancholy, I sat and took in the fresco for many long minutes. After half an hour, I went back outside. Immersed in memories, in the grip of confused emotions, I returned to the centre of town. In a sudden burst of sunlight, I saw the statue of Pallas Athena light up like an otherworldly apparition on the dome of the Town Hall. I heard seagulls squawking over the streets, I stopped to pray in St Nicholas' Church, I walked to the terminus of the Great Western Railway along the banks of the choppy, dark grey Mersey. I sat on a mooring post by the docks, staring out in disbelief at the vague strip of blue sky over Birkenhead. That night I hardly slept. I wrote my mother another letter to tell her what I had seen, but it all seemed so improbable that I started to doubt again; what if the whole thing was a figment of my imagination?

The next day, I tried to reconstruct my winding route. I roamed the streets and parks, crossed squares and avenues, but to my dismay, I could not find the little church. I didn't have much time left; a few days later, we would return to London. We had already been spending full days on preparatory exercises. I became extremely fretful about my latest stupid mistake – I hadn't thought to jot down the name of the church or the street! I had one last afternoon off, and in the few remaining hours before I had to report for embarkation, I took one last walk through all the neighbourhoods I thought I had passed through. Before I knew it, I had looped back to my starting point. I returned to the hospital, wheezing. Maud gave me a sceptical look and asked if I was really ready to go back.

A soldier must obey orders, I said to her, and almost before I knew it I'd saluted. A spark of amusement seemed to light up in her eyes.

As we set off for London, I was in a state of confusion, consumed with fretfulness and self-reproach. I swore one day to return to Liverpool and find the little church. Many years later, realizing I would not make it there myself, I asked the Brothers of Charity in Ghent for a list of all the churches and monasteries in Liverpool. That was in 1939. One small Welsh church more or less matched what I remembered, but I found out it had been demolished – and couldn't imagine he would have painted there in any case. I will never forget the impression that faraway, vanished mural made on me. It may even have fated me to become the man I am today, wavering between a full, difficult life and the quiet consolations of painting.

We marched to Lime Street Station. The drab carriages, some riddled with bullet holes, were waiting for us. Past high, dark walls, soot-black tunnels and bridges, the train rolled out of the city. We had soon left the nautical atmosphere of the Mersey's banks far behind us. Along the way, I saw the peaceful hills and the pastures at Wolverton, bordered with ancient trees. I felt I was being pulled away from my life's rediscovered centre of gravity; it was also then that I finally realized I had been in love with my nurse Maud the whole time, and too bashful even to say goodbye to her as we marched in formation to the army van. My groin was still tight; I could feel the scar when I tired myself out walking, and I sometimes had muscle cramps I'd never had before. But I also knew that I was well enough to return to duty and had no means of prolonging my stay in the heavenly peace and quiet of the hospital. I had buried my sketchbooks deep in the sackcloth bag issued to us on departure. As our journey took us further from the coast, the sky clouded over, and it started to rain over the grey suburbs. Wriggly lines like glass worms streaked down the windows of the carriages, which were abuzz with conversation and laughter, boisterous song, tobacco smoke, and the smell of booze. We had already returned to our crude life as soldiers.

In London, I saw my stepbrother Joris. After his anaemic wife had died in a bombardment, he'd become one of the many Belgian refugees. For weeks he'd been wandering the city, regularly checking the military dormitories for familiar faces. When he recognized me, he burst into tears, urged me to be careful, and said his life was ruined, that he saw no point in carrying on. I asked what he'd heard about my mother and sisters and told him to go back to Ghent – that was where he belonged, living in London would destroy him. I was relieved to hear from him that my two brothers were back at home. Emile was nineteen, Jules sixteen; they could be called up any day. His own brother Raymond, my younger stepbrother, was also wandering around somewhere, Joris had no idea where. It was March 1915. In a few days, we would cross the Channel to the battlefront.

Before leaving London, I received a letter from my mother, sent on from Liverpool by military post. She wrote that she was deeply moved by my story about the mural and would like to go on a pilgrimage to see it, but that Henri was bound to say no. He had escaped conscription thanks to his lame right leg and was making her life miserable with his gruff, temperamental ways. Never before had she written about Henri so openly and explicitly. Touched, despondent and fearful all at once, I watched the chalk cliffs of Dover slowly sink away behind our ship. We had been on the open sea for only an hour when we clearly heard the rumbling of heavy guns in the distance; it was like the growl of some gargantuan animal lying in wait for us on the horizon, opening its hungry jaws wide to devour us. We were heading back to hell.

When I report to the medical service, the examination does not take long.

Eh bien, mon brave, try walking a little. Come on! *Un, deux*, faster!

The thump of a stamp slamming down on the desk.

Bon pour le service actif. Fit for general service. Next!

To my surprise, the package presented to me includes my capote with the shot-up collar. As soon as I try to put on that steam-cleaned, threadbare rag, it is taken away from me.

I am issued with a blue overcoat with domed black buttons, a pair of old, worn-out shoes, and a hat with ear flaps. Apparently, the stock of military uniforms has been used up. In this outlandish outfit, perhaps from the wardrobe of a dead civilian, I walk the last leg of my journey to the rear of the lines alone, past batteries of reservists, past farmhouses standing solitary in the countryside, with soldiers tramping in and out of them. I do not see a single familiar face, and begin to worry. But as I make my way down a long lane of half-obliterated poplars, I am struck by the sound of bellowed commands. My heart lurches with shock; for the first time, I clearly see last year's closing scene in my mind's eye – the charge towards the riverbank with Kimpe, the shot that took me down. Through a privet hedge, I see a high-ranking officer in the inner courtyard of an open farmstead. His soldiers stand in a large circle around him, listening in silence. As I step through the open gate, most of them turn their heads towards me. I step back, not wanting to interrupt the captain's speech, but he snarls, *Approchez!*

I try to push my way through the men, but they tug at my clothes, somebody clasps my hands, tries to embrace me: Martien, you bastard, are you still alive? What are you doing here in that queer outfit?

The man who throws his arms around my shoulders is Kimpe – Lieutenant Kimpe now.

Rompez les rangs! the captain barks. Fall out! The soldiers salute and march off to the barn.

The captain tells me to come with him and Kimpe. In his office, set up in the stuffy sitting room of the farmhouse, he asks me to state my identity.

C'est Martien, mon capitaine, Kimpe says, beaming.

Stow it, Kimpe. *Nom?*

Sergent-Major Martien, mon capitaine.

There is no paperwork to be found, so it's up to Kimpe, after all, to report on my military record. I am assigned to the *quatrième section*. Inquiries will be made to confirm that I truly received the rank of first sergeant-major for my conduct at the front. I am placed in command of twenty men at the front in Noordschote and told to pick up a uniform and a new rifle in the scullery.

Apparently, the front has been quiet. A 'quasi-status-quo' has been reached, as Kimpe officiously puts it.

This section has just returned from the village of Boesinghe, where yet another two recruits were felled when the Germans attempted to capture the lock.

Just stay as brave as you have been, the captain says, and he gives me a meaningful nod.

I salute and walk outside. About a dozen soldiers rush up to me and slap me on the back, all shouting at once.

Hullo, old sweat, we thought you must be pushing up daisies . . . De Meester saw you fall, and that was the last we heard of you.

I tell my story, leaving out my father's fresco.

That afternoon, there's a strict inspection of rifles, ammunition and rations. We are told to watch out for barbed wire and unexploded shells when we crawl through the mud, and we learn of a new type of shell that contains tear gas. Apparently, the French were the first to use it, and the British soon followed their lead. Bromacetone, Kimpe says. Foul stuff. It keeps on blowing back in our direction. If you inhale that filth for more than a second, you puke up your lungs a few days later and die like a dog.

We spend the first week ceaselessly filling sandbags. Any conspicuous movement sends a machine gun on the other side rattling for minutes on end. We must be prepared for surprise attacks at any moment. The whole regiment is in a peculiar state. After a while, being ready for combat twenty-four hours a day is much like being totally paralysed. At the same time, it often stays quiet for days, so quiet that we forget the constant threat to our lives. Apathy takes hold of our minds and bodies. Some lads sit for hours, staring at nothing in particular, as if they have willed themselves blind. The earth warms up; after the chilly morning hours, vapour rises from the miry fields, which shine in the strange light. A blanket of lapwings ripples over the horizon; sometimes we hear the hoarse cawing of wheeling crows by a line of trees; in the sultry afternoon we hear seagulls in the distance; but otherwise our world seems devoid of animals – that is, except for the rats that infest our trenches. They are everywhere, their shrill squeaking never stops, they dash between our feet, they gnaw on anything they can get their teeth into, they stink, and they mate, bear young and flourish, eating our biscuits and gnawing on our dead comrades, walking over your face at night, and whenever you knock one dead, five others take its place. Sometimes we roast them, but their flesh is vile, muddy and gooey. A commander roars that we'll catch the plague. We spit out the revolting meat and rinse our mouths with brackish water.

Rations arrive at night and have become increasingly scarce – tinned food, soggy biscuits, no vegetables or fruit, hardly ever any fresh meat, now and then a damp, stale loaf of bread, and unclean water in dented canteens that reek of iron. After a few days in the trenches, my gums are bleeding again, and a few days later my diarrhoea is back. White clouds glide overhead like the backdrop to some idyllic scene. We occasionally have an hour's rest and lie daydreaming in a spot where grass is starting to grow again, propped up on one elbow, enjoying the scent of the spring and fresh greenery. But mostly we inhale the odour of rat piss, the stench of wet straw and the improvised open latrines. We would be better off if we could burn the contaminated litter and rotting scraps, but the smallest wisp of smoke provokes a frenzied salvo. After a few days of peace and quiet, an officer visits the trenches, bellows that this is no town fair, grabs a rifle, and deliberately fires several shots into the air, setting off another hellish onslaught of German fire. It is like the wrath of God, minus God: every action is weighed in some unfathomable balance, and at any time, the most trivial movement may be punishable by death. The slightest misjudgement could easily be the last judgement. Not that this makes death trivial, but dying does seem more absurd than ever – the hellish pain, the formless horrors that bulge out of the body, the unbearable wailing of the lads in their final moments, their hands on their torn-up bodies as they clutch at their own entrails and moan for their mothers. They are children, countless wasted boys of barely twenty, who should be out in the sun, living their lives, but have sunk into the muck here instead.

I pray every day. Like an automaton, I drone prayers without end, because the rhythm of prayer, more than any unshakeable faith, helps me through the bouts of despair and mortal fear. The others try to scrounge scarce luxuries, a plug of tobacco or a slug of filthy distilled brandy, which they obtain from each other through extortionate barter: your wristwatch for a glass of brandy or ten cigarettes – trades of that kind, all through the days and frigid nights, as the booming of the guns resonates in our rumbling guts. I cling to the only thing that ties me to my far-off childhood: my father's pocket watch, which by some miracle is still running. It ticks in my pocket like a second heart, and when I take it in my hands, I see the fresco in Liverpool, and I speak to my father in my thoughts, as long as it takes for my heart to calm down and beat with the soothing rhythm of his timepiece.

What remains to us here, behind the Yser, is not much more than a strip of land almost impossible to defend; a few rain-soaked trenches around razed villages; roads blown to smithereens, unusable by any vehicle; a creaky old horse cart we have to haul ourselves, loaded with crates of damp ammunition that are constantly on the verge of sliding into a canal, forcing us to slog like madmen for every ten yards of progress as we stifle our warning cries; the snarling officers in the larger dug-outs, walled off with boards, where the privates have to bail water every day and brush the perpetual muck off their superiors' boots; the endless crouching as we walk the trenches, grimy and smelly; our louse-ridden uniforms; our arseholes burning with irritation because we have no clean water for washing them after our regular attacks of diarrhoea; our stomach cramps as we crawl over heavy clods of earth like trolls in some gruesome fairy tale; the evening sun slanting down over the barren expanse; infected fingers torn by barbed wire; the startling memory of another, improbable life, when a thrush bursts into song in a mulberry bush or a spring breeze carries the smell of grassy fields from far behind the front line, and we throw ourselves flat on our bellies again as howitzers open fire out of nowhere, the crusts of bread in our hands falling into the sludge at the boot-mashed bottom of the stinking trench.

Just over our heads, we suddenly hear the small aircraft flown by our two airmen, our heroes Coppens and D'Oultremont, skimming over the enemy positions, throwing shells, then ascending as fast as those rickety machines will go, quickly veering around, firing while under fire, and always escaping at the last moment, leaving the Germans to gnash their teeth and plot vengeance in their rancorous, entrenched strongholds, their impregnable fortifications and deadly machine-gun nests beyond the still surface of the river. Many of the men feel weak and fatalistic; they sing to keep up their courage; and we wake up in the midst of an ear-splitting racket or fall asleep at the first rays of sunlight, worn out by the paranoia that afflicts our ranks by night. Already, several boys have potted their own pals when spooked by an unexpected noise at dusk. It gnaws at us, we can't go on, we must go on.

Oddly enough, my spirits are not usually bad at all. On the contrary, fresh energy flows from some inexplicable wellspring every day. It's not just soldiering on, but pure, absurd vitality: the strong bonds of friendship between the lads, their crude humour and stupid jokes that often have us all leaning against the filthy trench wall, hiccupping with irrepressible laughter, until again, someone is careless for a moment and gets his hand shot off and we have to stifle his cries of pain by stuffing a rag in his mouth, as the officers in their rickety shed keep hissing, *Silence! Silence là-bas!*

From the trenches, we see a swathe of blue sky with tall white clouds drifting like a dream, we alternate guard duty in squalls of drizzly rain, we creep more than a mile through the dark for a jug of milk, we stomp through the clingy clumps of clay in our leaden boots, slipping constantly and watching as our mess tins are trampled by careless feet. Those who are good with their hands kill time by cutting small brass women's rings out of bullet cartridges with the blades of their bayonets, sharpened on bomb shards, and try to sell their creations – the going rate is about five cigarettes.

Once a week a newspaper vendor comes from goodness knows where all the way to the rear dug-outs, hawking *Le vingtième siècle* and *De Legerbode*.

I've had it up to here with the *vingtième siècle, merde alors*, keep your newspaper, grumbles Kimpe, *mon* bloody *oeil*.

I try to maintain discipline as well as I can. Sometimes when I order a few men out on patrol, the response is a spiteful, *Do it yourself, Sergeant Shithole*. I snap at them to keep their mouths shut; one time I give the incorrigible Maigeret from Liège a punch in the face. That restores order and discipline; there's no other way. A thought sometimes flashes through my head: How far I have strayed from what I once hoped to become.

The season of the first cherries has begun. Sometimes a farm girl comes all the way to our positions, saying she has fruit to sell, but no one has a penny here, so they push and pull till all of the protesting girl's merchandise has been knocked out of her hands. One day when a few of the lads are feeling under her skirts and rubbing up against her coat and she starts to scream, I threaten them with punishment and smack them on the head. To my surprise, they instantly turn meek and back off. My heart goes out to the lads, who have nothing to occupy their minds here, while I often sit and read the few French books that the newspaper vendor has brought for me. Occasionally an officer gives me something to read as a token of gratitude for my unit's discipline. In the gloaming, when nostalgia strikes, we sing the songs we remember *sotto voce*; the infantryman Laurent Mordin from Charleroi, who studied music, teaches us to sing notes that go together in chords. It sounds so lovely; he says that after the war we'll start a big choir, and everybody takes him at his word. Until the next patrol, when we have to leave yet another tenor voice behind in the barbed wire, shrieking. We sneak out at night to drag the victim into a shallow pit like an animal, glad that at least we can bury him, but not until we have stripped him down to his underwear, taking everything that might still come in handy. We turn tough and get sentimental; we laugh as we cry; our life's a waking slumber, a slumberous wake; we quarrel with our arms around each other; we lash out at each other while shrugging our shoulders; no part of our bodies or minds remains intact; we breathe as long as we live, and live merely because we are breathing, as long as it lasts.

Hicketick, a soldier from Antwerp who has served since the start of the war, used to be a cook in an officers' mess; now he lies here grousing about the filthy crap we eat. Sometimes he slips away and returns with a wood pigeon, a stray chicken or a pheasant. Then he scrapes the dripping off a couple of slices of bread, builds a fire behind an earthen wall far behind our trench in the dusk, and fries the chunks of meat in the lid of his pan, until we go wild with craving and beg for a bite. After we chew and swallow, the flavour lingers like a nagging hunger for more; we munch on our bread and drink the weak beer that the supply base now sends us at irregular intervals.

I feel a powerful urge to write everything down, but I don't have time. Sometimes I daydream about how we could possibly get out of this, or I sketch with the charred tip of a dry twig. Drawing soothes me. The lads keep their distance then, showing a kind of reverence. So I tend to go off on my own towards nightfall, which comes early to the dispirited landscape. I draw the bare tree stumps where once the lanes were overhung with green; the protruding shaft of a covered wagon in a crater; the remains of a roof, which looks like a sagging wigwam; a ruined wall, overgrown with grass and stinging nettles. Clods of turf hang from a tile batten jutting out from a collapsed roof, looking like impaled heads in the twilight. I shudder and commit the scene to paper. A flock of partridges passes overhead, filling the air with their staccato cries of 'roof-roof'.

Somebody shoots one out of the sky; a few seconds later, the artillery lets loose an ear-splitting volley; we duck as earth flies everywhere; inane laughter spreads through our ranks, foolish chortling and giggling because we've squeaked by yet again. Look, Hicketick says, there are two partridges on that wall. Martien, who's going to shoot them, you or me? You have to hit both with one shot or you'll lose them. I aim and fire; the birds seem to dive away; a salvo comes screeching in my direction; I lie flat till it's over. The Germans are getting tired of this game too; they fire distractedly, as if out of habit. Hicketick curses; I creep through the half-light to find them; one partridge is dead, the other still twitching. I pull off their heads and crawl back. Hicketick tells me we can't cook them straight away. It takes a couple of days for the meat to soften. I shrug and stuff the birds into a dead pal's mess tin.

I head off with five of my men to keep watch at the most forward post; twenty-four hours of vigilant observation, noting any changes in the German positions. We are lying so close together that we can hit each other with pebbles. Even when we see a spiked helmet surface above the wall, we don't shoot. There's no point in provoking serious combat here; it would only cost us all our heads. But towards nightfall, when a German unexpectedly throws a grenade that goes off close to our dug-out, I lose my temper. I grab one of our grenades, pull out the pin, and throw it furiously in their direction. We stop up our ears and wait for the explosion. Nothing. And then – nothing. We wait in disbelief; the grenade must have landed right next to their forward post without going off. Once darkness falls, I send one of the lads out to have a look. A moment later, we hear a boom, followed by a furious blast of rifle fire, screams and cries from the other side and our own, shells flying back and forth. We run for our lives, away from the German trenches. After ten minutes, everything is quiet again. An owl cries in the tilting trunk of a willow beside a drainage ditch that gleams in the vague moonlight. The boy I sent ahead did not return; his death is on my conscience. I order my men to reoccupy the forward post as quietly as they can, while I crawl over to the dead soldier's body. I am so close I can hear the Germans talking. My heart pounds in my throat. I try to drag the boy back through the mud, but it proves impossible. His whole chest has been shot open; he is lying on his back. I cautiously take his rifle and ammunition and make the sign of the cross on his forehead.

Gobbleskipya, I hear in my head. *Gobbleskipya*, pal, God damn it.

I return to my place among the men in the dug-out. Their disapproval takes the form of a crushing silence. Stiff with cold and damp, we are relieved ten hours later.

Back in the trench, I see Hicketick again. He asks me where the partridges are. I open the mess kit and out comes a sharp stench. Twenty-four bloody hours and they're already rotten, he says. Maggots writhe in their sunken eyes.

'I'll stew them up for the officers, with a whole bottle of red wine,' he says with a wink, and then he's gone.

It is May 1915. *Le vingtième siècle* writes, Still quiet on the Belgian front.

5

Time rolls on into bland duration, duration loses direction, direction gives way to stasis and boredom, boredom makes us sluggish and apathetic, the days creep through our fingers. There are, in fact, whole weeks when nothing happens, weeks when the commanders try to distract their men with petty projects, like building a better dug-out for the officers or putting on a 'war circus' behind the front lines, where one summer evening we witness an absurd spectacle: an infantryman, Jef Brebants, stumbles across the flimsy stage like a grotesque ballerina, dressed in a tutu, with puffy skirts over his knobbly knees and thick plaid slippers on his flat feet. Two wads of rolled-up socks swell like lumpy breasts under the straitjacket he wears as a bodice; soon, one sinks to his belly and the other rolls out in front of his feet. As a couple of soldiers sing a dirty song, he loses sight of the edge of the stage and falls off in the middle of his dance like a seasoned slapstick artist, his white legs in the air and his filthy underwear visible to all. The men roar with laughter, slap their thighs, whoop, and toss their louse-infested caps into the air. An explosion of pent-up mirth, a liberation from the stifling apathy of time. But as we return to our trench, the bungling Jef Brebants, who is over the moon after his successful performance, is pipped in the right eye by an enemy bullet. Half his face is blown away, he lets out a bestial death rattle, shits himself, pukes, and falls over. Somebody shoots him again to put him out of his misery, because his brains are hanging out of his head. We all lie flat on the ground and crawl the last hundred yards till we can roll into the trench.

The Huns are always close by; those filthy brutes are always lurking, and they seize any opportunity to demoralize us. This sometimes provokes outbursts of blind hatred; one of us charges forward with his rifle in a fit of rage, only to fall seconds later, riddled with bullets, somewhere in the marshy field out ahead. After dark we risk our own lives to find the daredevil and accord him at least the dignity of a hole in the ground, so that his name can be added to the roll of those who 'perished on the field of honour'.

I write letters for the others, as my mother once did in my childhood. Most of them are for the wartime godmothers who hosted them during their convalescence. I do the best I can, in French and in English, learning new words every day from the two small dictionaries I've been given, and as I leaf through their pages or write rough drafts, the lads pass by, slap me on the back, and jokingly ask me, *Marshen, ça va bien?*

I also draw posters for theatre and music performances organized for our entertainment in 'gaffs' far behind the lines. Sometimes my portraits of clowns and actors, sketched on cardboard or rendered in watercolour, are posted here and there on the trees, with the names of the performers listed at the bottom. Then the lads josh me, asking me where I found a mirror so I could draw such a silly face. The ensemble performs arias from *Cavalleria Rusticana*, Mendelssohn's 'Spring Song', Handel's 'Largo' and pieces from Bizet's *L'Arlésienne*. Three bars of music are all it takes to make some boys start crying their eyes out.

Sometimes we have to stand guard right after a strafe, without a pause. For three days and nights, the bullets whistle past our ears – grim days, when all of us think in silence: When will it be my turn to die like an animal? During roll-call, some men shout out, *Mort pour la Patrie!* or Choked on straw! Bitter laughter and murmurs, the commanders shake their heads and grin, but bellow less and less. I look on in silence as the lads around me sink into fatalism. Most are younger than I am – sturdy lads, meant for worthwhile occupations, with their hearts in the right place, lads with degrees who should be establishing households and having children – and here they lie, their scabrous bodies reeking in the tepid rain, with no hope of any change, mired in cynicism and death-lust, numbed by the stupid jokes told by the regimental idiots, scratching like apes and crying like babies, shivering with stomach cramps and the fear of a fatal infection, or living in dread of a stray bullet, of the shaft of a rickety cart accidentally snapping, of long nights filled with the snorting of horses dying slowly.

Around mid-August, the time comes again: we stand in a circle in the dark, summoned by a French-speaking officer.

A brave volunteer! *Une fois, deux fois* . . .

Nobody.

The officer coughs, looks flustered, repeats his question.

Someone scrapes his shoe against the ground.

The stars are twinkling above us; the moon is rising, still low in the sky. An owl cries in the distance.

Again, I lose my patience with my own men.

Yellow-bellies, I murmur. I step forward and salute.

À vos ordres, mon commandant.

My orders are to build a fortified advance post to end the stalemate that has dragged on for months. In the submerged fields ahead of us, we are instructed to string four lines of barbed wire in a semicircle extending below the surface of the water. The water is muddy and stinks; the slightest careless move sends you sprawling into the layers of slime dredged up by the shells.

The job will take about twenty nights, for me and eight men I'm told to pick myself. I go to sleep and wait till the next morning to choose my men. It's not easy to persuade them to join me; they are only too aware of the risks of the operation. By the time they have given up quibbling and protesting, it's late afternoon, and the eight of them follow me to the rear of the front lines to pick up the first loads of boards, pickets, hammers, pliers, nails and rolls of barbed wire. We are issued with work gloves, thicker uniforms, waders. We pick up tickets for emergency care at the dressing station.

The first night, we start building a floating platform; at the first cautious taps of our hammers, a spray of bullets zings past our heads. In the darkness, we load all the boards and beams back onto a cart, drag it two hundred yards back, and, sheltered by a dyke some distance behind the front line, spend the next day rapidly putting the platform together with hammers wrapped in rags. By noon we are about to collapse with fatigue. We are granted a few hours' rest in a small farmhouse behind the lines, where they bring us a pot of soup. We return to the trench, where men are playing cards and smoking. They stare at us in silence, with a blend of mockery and admiration.

The next night, we drag the platform to the forward post and tie it to the trunk of a tree. Then it's time to start driving the pickets into the ground. Again, it takes only two hammer blows to set off a volley of machine-gun fire from the other side. Ducks take to the air, quacking and flapping their wings, and bullets whistle past our ears. We lower ourselves into the water; again, blind volleys burst forth. The waxing moon rises over the broken landscape, a faithless, silent moon that could cost us our lives. We can't stand around all night without working, so we go in search of stones that we wrap in rags, moving as carefully as we can so as not to startle the waterfowl. The pointy noses of swimming rats puncture the pale mirror of the water's surface; we look like zombies performing nonsensical acts in slow motion.

After two nights, fear has a firm grip on us. The Germans seem to suspect that something is going on; sometimes they send a few flares soaring over our heads. Then we stand perfectly still, blinded, our hearts thumping. Any movement means certain death, I've taught my men: don't panic, think lightning-fast, and make as little noise as possible. Like a flock of spooked sheep, we huddle close together behind a few fallen trees every time they open fire. Then I give them permission to drink lukewarm coffee and eat a hunk of hard, sour bread. We sit side by side, chewing and swallowing, the smell of mud mixed with the smell of summer night as the shell-smoke clears. A bullet whistles just past Bonne's head as he's rising to his feet; goaded to exhaustion, he shouts, Kiss my bloody arse, you filthy Hun! – and returns fire. Another salvo immediately follows, Bonne falls bullet-riddled into the shallow water, whizz-bangs go off all around us, the shooting continues for more than a quarter of an hour.

Now all our work has been for nothing, I say to the trembling men.

They want to go back to the trench; I raise my pistol and say, I shall personally shoot down the first man who leaves. They stay on their bellies, grumbling, and tell me they'll pay me back if we ever get out of this alive. Make all the empty threats you please, I say. It's madness, I agree, but it wasn't my idea.

Morning comes, and we collapse into exhausted sleep in the field, roused from time to time by orders shouted in the distance, a cart rattling down the ruined road, the endless swarms of mosquitoes buzzing and whining around our heads in the afternoon heat, until we are out of our minds from slapping our own cheeks again and again.

It takes us more than a week and a half to put up the barbed wire, four rows thick.

On a night with a waning moon, while resting after a few hours of work, we see something wondrous: thousands of little eels wriggling through the grass in the silvery light, twisting and glistening, an opaline army in the vast silence of the night. They must be coming from spawning grounds in the submerged polders, with their ungodly stench of brackish water. They form one great current as far as the eye can see, a primordial ritual unfolding in perfect silence. The legion of eels glides through the grass in waves, as if on command, exuding a slimy odour; more and more follow; the wondrous ritual goes on for over an hour. The lads watch, their mouths agape, and one begins to pray. The moon sinks below the horizon, the last eels glide past the sleepy soldiers, we think we're dreaming. We wake up hours later with sunlight in our eyes and wonder whether we all had the same dream.

After three weeks, we've completed our forward post. Our hands are torn, our backs are broken, the mud has seeped into our bones, and our breath has a boggy, bilious smell. The last morning, after a night of feverish toil to finish the job, I am standing next to the post with my back to the enemy, checking whether all the barbed wire is taut, when I hear a sudden bang. An electric shock runs down my spine, my whole body is tingling, fat drops of sweat come running off my forehead and into my gasping mouth. Close one, eh, Martien? someone says next to me. From a hole near the top of my right wader, blood is gushing. Here I go again, I mumble, and pitch forward into the water, flat on my face. A volley bursts out, I know I shall choke to death there in the mud. Images flash through my mind. I raise my head out of the water, roll onto my back, throw up, nearly choke on it, somebody rolls me onto my belly, pulls my head up by the hair and pushes it down, I heave and sob and retch and pant for air. Then everything goes black.

I awaken in hellish pain that shoots all the way up my back and neck, as two men carry me limping to the dressing station. I see the officer coming out of the tent.

Our work is done, *mon commandant*, I say, and then I sink into a feverish dream.

Two stretcher-bearers lay me on a stretcher, wash the wound, clean the mud and dirt out of it, and disinfect it with alcohol that makes me jump with pain. A male nurse brusquely pushes me back down onto the stretcher. Panting, I pound my head against the canvas in agony as they apply the first bandage. The stretcher is loaded onto a flat trailer. The automobile thuds and creaks its way over the bumps and potholes to the field hospital in Hoogstade. I am moved to a bed, the pain is driving me crazy. It is 18 August 1915.

You're the darling of your regiment, you are, the nurse says as she washes me with lukewarm water. An officer came to say we have to give you very special treatment. The nurse has coppery curls peeping out from beneath her white and grey bonnet. She looks at me with large green eyes and smiles. I hear you'll be receiving a Medal of Honour from the king himself.

I hiss in pain whenever she comes near the surgical scar on my thigh. I try to smile.

I'm just an ordinary sergeant-major, I stammer.

You get some more rest now, she says. You have to recover your strength first.

She tucks me in under the starched sheets, pulls them tight, and runs a flat hand over them. Then she rustles away in the sunlight through the large ward filled with wounded men, a number of them moaning and groaning. I sleep like a log from sometime in the late afternoon till mid-morning.

The next day, all fifty soldiers are lifted out of their beds in the large ward and laid on stretchers in a field of grass.

To our surprise, a brass band is playing. The instruments gleam in the afternoon light; a baritone sings '*J'aime le son du cor*'; this is followed by Luigini's *Egyptian Ballet*. The sun breaks through the clouds; the fragrance of flowers comes drifting over the dewy grass. September is already in the air. The silky mildness of the afternoon, combined with the music, melts my heart. All this unimaginable luxury, harmony and tranquillity: no lice, no rats, no muck, no reeking uniforms, no thundering mortars, no dying men, no swollen feet in tight, soggy boots, no swarms of buzzing mosquitoes – it makes my head spin. Looking around, I see the nurses a little way off, in a row, listening. Some of them have their heads cocked; one has her arms crossed over her chest; another is laughing at something whispered in her ear. The andante grabs me by the throat. I remember the bandstand in my faraway home town where I heard this music as a child, while strolling through Kouter with my father and my mother. My bed sheets smell like Marseilles soap. In the intervals between the acts of the ballet, we hear, far in the distance, the dull thundering of guns at the front. To think this light, bright heaven is built on the sounds of that hell in the distance . . . I think of my men who are still back there, and of cross-eyed Rudy from Lossystraat. You've got a cushy one now, matey, he said, laughing. Out for another six months. Make the most of it. You'll be back here with the rest of us soon enough.

A week later, the ward is in commotion. It starts early in the morning, when the nurses bathe us more hurriedly than usual, giggling and saying they mustn't give away the secret. But all is revealed that afternoon, when who should come into our ward but – we can't believe our eyes – the Queen herself, in a simple nurse's uniform. She goes from bed to bed, asking each wounded soldier if he wants chocolate or cigarettes. But she gives me both, saying, 'You're a courageous man, I hear, a credit to our nation.' I stammer, 'Your Majesty, I . . .' I want to tell her I sang for her in the main square as a boy; the green-eyed nurse is standing next to her; she brushes a few coppery curls from her forehead and offers an encouraging smile. The words catch in my throat; a sort of sob wells up inside me. Then the Queen has moved on; I urgently have to use the toilet; I cannot move; I am sweating in consternation and embarrassment.

After three weeks, I still cannot lift the wounded leg so much as a hair's breadth.

After examination by the attending physician, I and twenty other men are sent to northern France in two army vans. We ride along the coast, laid out on stretchers, each bump and thump causing fresh torment. We arrive at the casino in Dinard, which has been converted into a hospital. There is one large infirmary with a view of the sea. Silence, crashing waves, salt air, seagulls in the morning, the distant tooting of fishing boats. The absence of booming guns in the background echoes in our ears. It's a strange sight: beds and more beds in a circular ballroom, with pathways cleared between them for the nurses, and here and there a chair topped with medicine bottles and all sorts of clutter.

For the first few days I am invisible, nobody talks to me, even the nurses who bring the meals don't say a word. Only after three days does a soldier come to ask for our names. Flemish names drive him crazy, he tells us. We have to write them down on slips of paper for him. A few hours later, boards with our names on them are attached to the beds. Soon after that, two army doctors enter the room and spend a few minutes examining each soldier.

When they come to my bedside, one of them flings away the sheets.

Levez la jambe.

I can't lift my leg.

Levez la jambe, Sergent. That's an order!

I just can't do it, *je suis désolé.*

Bon. We'll see.

The next morning at eight, a bear of a man with rolled-up shirtsleeves strides up to my bed. My last sip of coffee goes down the wrong way.

He produces an iron pot of Vaseline and screws it open. After briefly consulting a notebook, he pulls the sheets off my bed.

Let's have a look, by Jove! he says, in French laced with laughter. He holds his flat hand an inch or two above my big toe.

All right, old man, give us your best kick, right into my hand.

I cannot move my leg a fraction of an inch. The muscles are completely paralysed.

Now the bruiser leaps into action. He rubs Vaseline into my thigh and starts pinching, pressing, chopping and pounding with his brutish paws.

I am sweating, coughing, drooping and panting, almost choking with pain.

Look, old man, you can go ahead and scream. Bawl it out! For the love of Jesus, breathe!

He grabs my wrists and makes me clasp the iron bars under the mattress. I pull with all my might. The torture continues for another five minutes or more.

When I am thoroughly spent, he gives me a whack on the rear and says, There, that's enough for the first time. Chin up. See you tomorrow.

The next morning, when I see his villainous face approaching, I break into such a sweat that it runs down my forehead into my eyes.

He grins broadly.

Not *scared*, are you?

He pats me on the cheek and resumes the torture. Again, he pushes my hands to the bars of my bed frame.

Afterwards, I notice I've bent the bars.

I won't break your thigh, so don't you break your bed, he says with a chuckle.

After ten days, life starts to trickle back into my leg. Even the orderly seems surprised. He admits that he thought the muscles were too severely torn ever to heal.

It takes another full week before I can cautiously stand up next to my bed and try to support myself on the wounded leg. I instantly fall to the floor. But from that moment on, I can do slow little exercises in bed; soon I can lift my leg more than an inch. The brute is delighted; the Vaseline is flying.

One day in October I stumble outside on my own for the first time, leaning on a crutch. The sea air overwhelms me; it's thick with a strange light; seagulls sail over the park and the stately houses; the sea is calm and blue-green; I sit on a bench by the promenade. People walk by, chatting, a few boats are bobbing just outside the Baie du Prieuré. Out to the left, in the distance, I can just make out the medieval silhouette of Saint-Malo. The leaves crackle, yellow and dewy, on the trees; a breeze sighs through the grass; it's as if there had never been a war.

*

Every day I sit there for a couple of hours, looking around and making quick sketches. A girl with a round hat box walking against the wind; an old woman swathed in flapping black garments, scattering bread for the seagulls, which dive dangerously close to her hands; a soldier passing on two crutches, the stump of his lost limb wrapped neatly in a freshly ironed trouser leg.

Suddenly, an old man is standing behind me. My hand comes to a stop.

'*La prestidigitation est un art très peu apprécié,*' he says, and he walks on.

For a moment I sit staring, mystified. Why would this strange man call drawing an under-appreciated conjuring trick?

The boats ply peacefully between Dinard and Saint-Malo. One day I make the crossing. The sea is flat; fish leap out of the water; seagulls dive and screech in the ship's white wake. I sit on deck and am free of all my cares. But as soon as that thought comes to me, my heart pounds in my throat, and I remember my comrades, crawling through the mud, fed up and comfortless.

As I walk back to the casino that evening, carefully balancing on my crutches, step by tiny step, a nurse comes running up and scolds me: Why must I take such risks? Besides, there's a message waiting by my bed. I tear open the envelope marked with a crown: my name is listed in the Military Order of the Day. I am to be made a Knight in the Order of the Crown. The next day, a letter arrives from Britain; my stepbrother Raymond invites me to spend a few days with him in Swansea, where he is staying as a refugee.

It is already mid-November when some twenty of us soldiers board the ferry to Saint-Malo in the early morning, have our travel passes stamped by the British consul, and, in the early afternoon, are escorted to a ship whose skipper greets us with a salute.

I spend an hour strolling around Saint-Malo; the narrow streets, the cliffs along the coast. A dead seahorse tumbles back and forth in the breakers, bright and opalescent. I am alone in life, I think, when I see a young woman approaching from the other end of the beach, and I do not know if I shall ever see my mother again. The woman is elegant, although dressed entirely in black; she has a small umbrella with her, which she thrusts into the hard sand at every step like a cane. I do not dare look her in the eyes. After she has passed, I turn around, and see her doing the same. For an instant, our eyes linger on each other.

My leg still cramps with pain sometimes; I have overexerted myself. Exhausted, I board the ship, which is scheduled to depart around four o'clock. A few soldiers are already blotto; they wolf down their allotted rations immediately. The ship's bell tinkles, the steam whistle blows, the sound echoes from the house fronts, I wonder where the young woman lives, and loneliness crashes down on me like a boulder.

We sail to Southampton, the city that lost nine hundred young men just three years ago in the *Titanic* disaster. Most of them were crewmen: sailors, labourers, dishwashers, pursers. A lot of lonely ladies who need our services, one soldier says, before spitting on the deck. The skipper comes and reprimands the drunken, rowdy soldiers. He orders them to spend the entire voyage on deck, with cork belts around their limbs, and strictly forbids them to go from the forward deck to the port side. He knows what he's talking about – the heavy trunks with metal parts that the ship is carrying to England could come loose and crush a careless passenger against the gunwale.

I take a seat on a canvas-covered bench on the port side.

At first, everything is fine. We bob peacefully past the small island of Cézembre, less than five hundred yards away, with its infamous prison where more than a few Flemish soldiers have been sent by military tribunals.

After an hour, dark mountains of cloud appear over the purple sea ahead. A strong wind starts to blow; the men curse; the skipper comes on deck and gives us all strict orders not to walk around. Just a few minutes later, the ship begins to buck like a wild horse; eddies form in the water like pits, some more than fifteen feet deep, and the bow topples into them as if dropping onto metal plates. We grimace at each other, clinging tightly to the bench as we are shaken back and forth. A few minutes later the storm breaks loose above our heads; the ship seems lost in the churning water. We see the skipper heading for the pilot house – he smacks into the railing, slips to the deck, scrambles back onto his feet, and hurries into the compartment. The wind shrieks and moans; all the devils in hell are on the loose. Gigantic waves crash onto the deck, sending great fans of water in all directions and leaving us thoroughly disoriented. I lie down flat under the bench; a soldier immediately vomits all over my feet. From that moment on, there is nothing to be done: everyone is seasick, deathly seasick, we puke the very souls out of our bodies, some soldiers still recovering from their wounds cry out in pain, the storm grows even fiercer. The prow of the ship sometimes rises high above the waves, only to fall into a huge eddy with an enormous crash, making us think our final hour has come. It is night; there is no direction, no land, no world, no up or down, no left or right; there is vomit and salt water; there is noise, a cracking sound as if the ship is splitting open, which goes on for hours and hours and never stops.

By morning some soldiers, whose friends lashed them to pipes or masts, are rolling numbly back and forth like limp sacks, broken and half-dead. The ship is no longer sailing, but surging on the waves, sustaining blow after blow, adrift on the swirling sea. The skipper is sitting it out. As lash after lash beats down on us, we pray, convulsed with cramp, for the end to come. We should have reached the other side last night at ten. In the sparse light, we can tell there is no land anywhere in sight. Some boys, certain we shall perish, whimper like dogs as they expel the last bit of gall from their bodies, drooling and gnashing their teeth in pain and misery.

By nine in the morning, the storm has mostly passed, but the sea is still so rough that when the motors start pounding again, it's enough to make us all dizzy with agony. We proceed at a snail's pace, angling into the wind, until we're near the coast. Swaying ships in the harbour sound their horns to warn us not to dock; our ship would be smashed to pieces in seconds. So we go on swaying and surging until late afternoon; the endless torment froths blue and white over our wrung-out bodies, like the foam that bubbles on our lips, and we crawl in circles to escape ourselves, with twisted visages like devils and demons, as we hold tight with our final scraps of willpower.

This is worse than anything we went through in the trenches, a soldier hiccups in my ear. It is six in the evening before the skipper carefully manoeuvres his way towards the harbour, moving astern, yard by yard. A tall wave lifts us up and hurls us down, narrowly missing the quay wall. Again, we sail a hundred yards away from the quay; all the swaying ships are honking like mad to warn us.

Around seven o'clock, the ship is tied up at dock, still swaying, and we, the sick animals, the lice and the rats crawl and roll ashore like dying creatures and lie in the wind and rain for another hour, our trousers stained with shit and the stench of gall around our heads.

By the time we stagger to our feet, the sun has set.

The skipper calls us together for a head count. One soldier is missing; no one has any idea where he could be.

'It's the same damn thing every time,' the captain growls. 'Now they'll hold me accountable for the drunken swine who got knocked overboard.'

He takes us to a small café to get over the worst of the shock.

Only now do we look at each other, because the waitresses clap their hands to their mouths. We are as yellow as Chinamen, thin and haggard from spewing gall, hollow-eyed ghouls with trails of dried saliva on our cheeks.

Nobody feels like eating; a little later, when we are shown to small attic rooms with bare wooden bunks to sleep on, we immediately fall into a dreamless sleep, while outside in the darkness the November storm rages on, pounding dully against the roof.

The next day I sit and doze on the train to London, where I wait for my connection for two hours, numb and drained, like a man who has lost all purpose and direction in life. I feel homesick for my friends in the trenches. From London, I travel on to Swansea by way of Bristol. I sit alone with my misery, downhearted and chilled to the bone, as the train rattles slowly onwards through the deserted hills. The trees and hedges drip with melting snow. No one says a thing. At each station that slips past, we see huddled soldiers, some smoking, obviously fully recovered and on their way back to the front. Others look like me, pale and wasted, on their way to a few weeks of convalescence. Long past midnight, we pull into a dilapidated old village station. I ask the way to the refugee home where Raymond is staying, spend the next hour trudging through the snow along a coastal path, and arrive at a tiny seaside resort that has one long street with some shops and low houses and three hotels overlooking the promenade. There is no sign of life anywhere, except for the sentry posted by the wooden barracks along the seafront, who mistakes me for an officer in the darkness and springs to attention.

Good evening, sir.

Good morning, you mean.

He laughs and asks, 'How's the war going in Belgium?'

I mumble a few words and ask him the way to Home Rest Cottage.

I continue down the seafront; waves froth on the snow-dusted beach.

Seven o'clock and still no light in the sky. Feverish and fed-up, I notice a deckchair under a lean-to by one of the large houses and decide to lie down on it. My leg tingles and throbs and burns; I am utterly spent. I curl up like a child and tumble into a hell of remorse: I should have gone back to Liverpool to search for my father's fresco, why did I come all this way just to visit Raymond? My friends have gone to the south of France to recover, I'm a first-class idiot, my feet are frozen so solid they could snap off, I never should have crossed the bloody Channel, I am sick with fatigue and trembling so violently I can feel my bones creak.

In a stately old-fashioned mansion that rose up out of the chilly mist, I finally found my younger stepbrother and asked him about my mother and sisters, being careful not to hurt his feelings, since he knew what I thought of his father as a husband to my mother. We were probably sitting too close to the fireplace – I fell to the floor unconscious around eleven in the morning and did not wake up until two days later. My body was covered with red blotches, a sign of blood poisoning.

I have now spent six weeks in this backwater, living in a daze. Early on, I went out to sea with a fisherman. After many hours, the huge creature that tugged at his crude line turned out to be a dogfish, a thrashing, inedible monstrosity that stared at us with a crazed grin as the fisherman cut the hook out of its throat with his knife and slid the colossal creature back into the churning water. A trail of blood, nothing more, wet snow in our faces again.

Port Talbot, the smell of silt, of sackcloth, of rope, of poverty. The coal mines in the mountains in the distance.

Bad fish, bad coffee, bad bread. We have rotting teeth and a nasty taste in our mouths. We chew in silence, sometimes gagging, looking at the bare trees against the line of the grey-green sea. Christmas brings wet snow and driving rain. Two nurses join us for a scanty meal. We hardly speak. New Year's is barely celebrated. In a small chapel, long, monotonous prayers for the dead and wounded. The next day, under a blinding winter sun, in the cutting wind, we find an emaciated horse beaten to death next to the seawall. Everything seems unreal. I am homesick.

The last day of my trip, we visit a munitions factory in Swansea; one of the directors gives us a guided tour. I come to life again as we pass the glowing furnaces; I reminisce about the iron foundry; the conversation bucks me up. I see new technologies that amaze me – in the wink of an eye, a hunk of red-hot iron is pressed into hundreds of paper-thin sheets for tins and soldiers' cups. Something in me can no longer distinguish between what I think and what I see.

Rocking back and forth in the same maddeningly slow train, my stepbrother and I sit in silence across from three English girls, who see no need to lower their voices as they keep up a running commentary on the two callow Belgian soldier boys, who have obviously never touched a woman. That one, there on the left, would make the perfect model for a bronze statue of the Simple-Minded Soldier in some grassy plot, sprinkled with pigeon droppings. They squeal with laughter, until I rise to leave the carriage and wish them a pleasant journey in my very best English. Then they clap their hands to their mouths and cry out all sorts of apologies, all at once. We shrug, and as we walk away down the platform with a friendly wave, I feel a surge of dizziness, something that sweeps through my bowels, anxiety and desire running together into a kind of nausea that will stay with me for the rest of our journey back to the front, on yet another dirty, rickety train, chilled to the bone, peering through grimy windows thick with the soot of greasy candles. There are signs of vandalism everywhere, on the seats and on the floor; the toilets are covered with filth, too vile to use. Soldiers are destroyers and bitter men when they return from furlough to the front.

And once again, months pass in which utter boredom – we sleep half the day away – is suddenly broken by two hours of sheer ghastliness, an unexpected advance, shouted orders, panic, confusion, the cries of the wounded. Afterwards, the dead are carted off – mutilated hunks of human flesh, where not long before, a young man was smoking and swapping stories with his pals in the trenches.

My story is growing monotonous, just as the war grew monotonous, death monotonous, our hatred of the Huns monotonous, just as life itself grew monotonous and finally began to turn our stomachs.

One thing does make a deep impression in those murky days. One evening a dying soldier is being carried off; I hear he has only one arm, yet distinguished himself through his bravery as a volunteer medical orderly. He was struck by a falling beam in a burning barn. I walk over to the stretcher and recognize the boy from my drawing classes, my much-loved, brilliant fellow student who constructed new worlds out of lines. His neck appears to be broken, at an odd angle to his body. He lifts his eyes for a moment and recognizes me. He wants to say something; he strains forward; I see what always used to strike me about him: the stump of his arm moving as he moves, under his torn uniform. Then he falls back. I walk along next to the stretcher, unable to help. By the time we reach the field hospital, he is dead.

Sometime in June 1916 I am sent on my third mission, this time to a forward observation post, a cowshed between the two lines. Every night, our commander dispatches three men. None of them return. The soldiers grumble and protest; the officers respond with punishment and intimidation. After a week and a half, I and two of my men are ordered to keep watch at the forward post. I salute and say I'll do whatever I'm told, but this is a fool's errand. The commander snaps that I can expect to be punished if I happen to come back alive.

Around midnight, we creep cautiously towards the post. In the dim light, we see dead boys all around us. Their ammunition is still inside the shed. I order the two men to gather as many bullets as they can and position themselves ten feet away from the shed, one on either side.

They cover me as I creep forward and sketch the spots where I suspect machine guns, the length of the trench, the height of the defensive wall. I creep back. Where did the other lads go wrong?

We snatch up all the bullets and put them in our bags. Now that we have an unexpectedly large supply of ammunition, I order the men to fire in turns through the night, after carefully calculating how many bullets we'll need and how frequently we should fire. No Germans pop up that night; we are not taken prisoner; we return towards dawn, triumphant. But just as we think we've made it back safely, the bullets start to fly. In a few seconds' time, I see the two lads next to me leap up to escape, one after the other, and drop to the ground dead; I remain perfectly still, flat on my belly. After a few minutes I cautiously rise to my feet and am immediately shot in the back, a cowardly shot that enters at an angle, passes through the small of my back, and comes out at my hip. I staunch the gushing torrent of blood, throw up, press the gaping hip wound shut with all my strength, and am carried away through the darkness to the field hospital, where the medical officer says, *Marshen!* You have a subscription, *ou quoi?*

I grin, the world goes blurry, and not until three days later do I wake up, with a brown-stained bandage around my belly and agonizing pain in my back. I have been heavily sedated for days, because the pain would otherwise have been unbearable, a nurse tells me. I am also told that after I heal, I shall face a court martial for using ammunition not issued to me by my superiors. I shrug and say that they can go to hell.

Bed rest, flat on my back, boredom, frustration, thoughts of my men in the mud. This time I am sent to the Lake District to recover, to a small estate in Windermere. There I befriend the lady of the house, Mrs Lamb, who plays cards with me and tells me tales of her ancestors over afternoon tea. Towards evening we often walk together in the park. Her husband is also at the front. We fall into an intimacy that perplexes us both. I am just a common soldier from Ghent, I keep telling myself, as I lie alone at night in my large room on the first floor and hear her footsteps in the corridor.

During my convalescence in Windermere I see in the newspapers that a new kind of poison gas has come into use: mustard gas, apparently even more gruesome in its effects than the shells filled with chlorine gas to which we were introduced in 1915. I read about the mass casualties and cannot sleep for several nights. How many of my comrades have died by now? I can only guess. I sometimes look back on our trench as a sheltered, relatively safe place, despite the weekly deaths. More and more, in every conversation, I hear how disgusted everyone is with the absurd, meaningless carnage that drags on without cease; it is said that even the Germans have had enough and are deserting in droves. Are there any young men left in Europe? asks Mrs Lamb of Windermere, and she places her hand on my shoulder. I am reading English newspapers, which report very different things from the French-language Belgian newspapers occasionally available to us at the front.

She has two farewell gifts for me: a carton of English cigarettes, yellow and oval in shape, and a scarf she has knitted for me, a long scarf – you'll need it in the winter months at the front, she says fretfully. She takes me in her arms.

I shivered with distress the day I had to leave Windermere. In the distance, I saw the Langdale Pikes against the brightening grey of early morning. The front awaited me again; we were beginning our third winter.

When I returned to the front, I heard that my commanding officer still wanted me punished for insubordination; when I had come back wounded from the post by the cowshed, I still had masses of ammunition with me that I had collected there. We are forbidden to use ammunition not allocated to us by our superiors. I was guilty of a serious transgression.

I first had to report to a lieutenant, who gave me a stern lecture and explained the possible penalties. When I did not move a muscle and remained stiffly at attention, waiting for him to decide whether or not I would be court-martialled, he gave me a long look, straight in the eyes. He must have read the bitterness in my face. He reviewed the file again for a couple of minutes, stamped it, signed his name, and then said, The matter has been dealt with, Martien. Return to your men. Dismiss.

I saluted without a word. But I lost my will to fight that day – and what is worse, I lost my faith. The more human lives are sacrificed, the harder it is to bear the contempt of the French-speaking officers, the public humiliation and discrimination that they inflict on Flemish soldiers. They stand in sharp contrast to the Walloon lads from humble families who show us their friendship, and usually their solidarity. We're all cannon fodder together. While we sit in the trenches with half-frozen fingers, thick woollen hats and shreds of flannel in our worn-out boots, spending entire days trying to rub some warmth into each other so we won't freeze to death, the officers sit in their well-heated farmhouses. Once a week a lieutenant performs a cursory inspection, his nose in the air, joking about how healthy this frosty weather is: it kills all the pests, and if it goes on this way, it'll kill the Boches too. No one laughs. The lieutenant turns his back on us disdainfully and says, audibly, to his adjutant, *Ils ne comprennent rien, ces cons de Flamands.*

One day I'm told to report to another commanding officer, a French-speaker from Brussels who demands that I salute after every sentence. As he humiliates me in this way – at the end of every sentence, I lift my hand to my head and click my heels – he looks on with a smirk and haughtily informs me that I am soon to be transferred to another section, because I fraternize too much with my men and thus form a threat to military discipline. I ask whether the order comes from his superiors. He bellows in French that a *Flamand* has no business asking questions. I salute and make a quick exit. As I silently pack my things, the boys look on in confusion: What are you doing, Martien? I'm being transferred, I say curtly. Then something happens that I could never have anticipated: my men fly into a rage, rush off to the commander's office in a body, and stand by the doorway shouting and shaking their fists. Soon, a few of them start throwing stones. The commander comes out and bellows at them – to no effect – telling them to shut their mouths and warning them that mutiny is grounds for immediate execution. The racket continues to swell, as soldiers come from all sides to join the uprising. Somebody shouts, Flemings, unite!

The commander goes red in the face, withdraws into the farm-house, and returns with a senior officer. They talk to each other and point at me. I am on the other side of the mob of mutineers, still packing my things. Two lieutenants come to get me; they grab me by the arms and roughly drag me forward like a condemned man. When we reach the senior officer, I straighten my back and salute. It's the same one who saved me from a court martial. He scrutinizes me closely again, with narrowed eyes.

Eh bien, he says, and he cracks his whip against his gloved left hand.

I salute again, produce from my pocket the iron case that holds my medals, open the case, and display them one by one to the senior officer, without saying a word.

He understands my point. He examines the medals and takes a long look at me.

Then he removes my Knight's badge from the case and says, slowly and distinctly, *Sergent-Major Marshen*. You have earned some remark-able distinctions. But you have been misled. This decoration is a counterfeit.

My most prestigious badge of honour, a counterfeit. Maybe the commander who awarded it made off with the real one. The senior officer glances around him and sniffs.

The commander flinches and tries to intervene.

Taisez-vous, Delrue, the senior officer snarls. I've had enough of seeing the Flemish soldiers humiliated. *Et vous tous* – he points at our commanders and at the sub-lieutenants who rushed over when they heard the noise – You are all to blame for this fraud, you idiots. *Tenez, Marshen*, you may remain in your regiment with your troops.

He promises me that the genuine badge will be delivered to me in just a few days and tells me to hold on to the forgery as evidence until then. The men cheer and toss their caps into the air. I salute, thank the officer, and try to calm down my men so as not to create any more bad blood. We return to the muck, the stench, the tedium, the sudden explosions, the frayed nerves, the occasional man dropping dead before our feet. A Walloon boy in our trench says in broken Flemish that he is ashamed. That night a bottle of Holland gin turns up in our trench – I don't know where it came from. I pass it around, the boys sing softly, a light rain brushes over our heads under low-hanging clouds. A shell drops close to our funk holes, burrows deep into the ground, and does not explode. We wait in fear; nothing happens.

Time has abandoned us; we have slipped into a dim, unreal fold in its fabric, with no beginning or end in sight. Season follows season, the clouds drift overhead, fabulous white beasts and capricious gods in the noonday light; we are old before our time, we behave like housebound, fatalistic children, numbed and indifferent to life and death.

Winter, 1917–1918. Still more boys have died of deprivation, cold, pneumonia, typhus, sorrow, intestinal disease, syphilis, anger, despair, who knows what else – but the most horrifying story we've heard took place in Passchendaele in October and November of this year.

We are sitting in the trenches when we see our stretcher-bearers called away one by one. The word Passchendaele is on everybody's lips. The officers scowl and stare at the ground when we ask for information. The mortar fire in the distance is heavier than any we've ever heard before. They're using mustard gas; the tales we hear are so gruesome that we're almost grateful to be sitting here rotting away in the mud, where our only concerns are hypothermia, enemy machine guns and the whims of the military mind. Mustard gas burns turn out to be more painful than anything we've ever experienced before, and no medicine or ointment at the army's disposal will ease the suffering of the howling victims. Morale sinks even lower than the night-time temperatures. There is another spate of thinly disguised suicides, lads running into enemy fire and shouting, Shoot me, you filthy Boches, go on and shoot me. Their wish is usually granted. Somehow, more and more strong drink finds its way into the trenches; according to rumour, the high command is responsible. Blustering, spluttering soldiers spend all night sobbing under the stars and fall asleep at sunrise, drained and sedated, and in those early hours, when the cold that bites into our bodies is at its most savage, they freeze to death.

Spring brings more and more rumours of the imminent German surrender; sometimes we see a muddled file of pointed helmets marching towards the horizon, like black silhouettes against the red evening sky; we have no idea what they're doing. Summer comes again. The mosquitoes, hornets and infections return; in a dead-end sap trench, a mountain of excrement lies stinking to high heaven; when we try to bury it, we keep digging up corpses, severed limbs, and shrapnel. So we leave the whole mess as it is and slink off, gagging.

In the autumn, I receive permission to spend a few weeks at home on leave. In the course of the war, we've learned how to sneak in and out of the occupied zone, wearing mufti. Now the German soldiers have begun deserting. On the way home, I see the damage inflicted on our country, the houses shot to pieces, the vagrants and looters, the poverty. But also the relief that peace has come. Ghent lies partly in ruins and makes a strange sight, but here and there the Belgian flag is flying. People come out to greet us with beaming smiles. Traces of the most recent fighting are visible everywhere.

There are sporadic attempts at looting and acts of retribution against collaborators. Some houses are attacked and practically demolished. I am reunited with my mother, sisters and brothers – heart-wrenching moments. My mother, who comes limping out of the house with a slipper on one foot and a clog on the other, sees my medals and bursts out weeping. She has changed and looks more sensitive, more fragile. My stepfather Henri has become an old man, nipping at his drink in glum silence: raw moonshine he distils in secret from rhubarb and half-rotted pears. Living in wartime poverty has ground them all down. My mother's hair has turned completely grey, her proud, straight back is bent, but the force of her mind is undiminished. My sisters have become charming young ladies; Clarisse is going about with a loud red-haired fellow, Fons, who pollutes the air in our home with his pipe but makes everyone laugh with an incessant stream of jokes, amid the poverty and bitter hardship the war has brought upon the city's people.

When I return to my regiment, the air is thick with rumours: there's been a popular revolt in Germany, the front has been crumbling for months. During our final march homewards a month and a half later, as we pass heaps of all imaginable kinds of rubble, refuse and abandoned artillery, I find an undented shell case in a ditch somewhere near Merelbeke, large calibre, 215 millimetres. My comrades rag me for wanting to bring the heavy thing back with me. I arrive home that afternoon, covered with sweat, and give the brass case to my mother, who says she will grow flowers in it.

She never did; I later placed it on the newel post of our new house, and Gabrielle, who didn't like polishing, said, You can shine that brass for yourself, Urbain. So that's what I did, my whole life long, every Friday in the early afternoon, before the weekend began and the children came home.

I hear the latest stories from our neighbourhood. A starving woman got pregnant by a German who had promised her a loaf of bread in exchange for 'carnal intercourse' – after the war, she was dragged out of her home, shaved bald and kicked. Soon after that, she had a miscarriage. A farmer's daughter who had hidden a German in the barn spent her nights making love to him. When her father found her there and kicked her to death, the German crushed the farmer's skull and fled.

Suddenly there are fervent patriots all around us, many of whom made a tidy profit from clandestine trade with the Germans during the war. All around us, people are hiding evidence and covering their tracks. All around us, I see discord, envy, backbiting, betrayal, cowardice and looting, while the newspapers trumpet the praises of peace. We returning soldiers know better. We keep our mouths shut, wrestle with our nightmares, and sometimes burst into tears at the smell of freshly ironed linen or a cup of warm milk.

Here and there along our street, the flags are raised, flapping in the wet wind.

A merchant and his family have recently moved into the house behind our own on a cross street, Aannemersstraat. He's a farmer who made his fortune in wartime, trading in grain and potatoes. People often wonder where all the money comes from, my mother tells me. His trading company has a large storage area behind the house, a long, narrow courtyard separated by a wall from our back gardens. From my bedroom window, I can see the workers and customers come and go. The farmer has two daughters. The younger of the two resembles my mother: a proud, black-haired beauty who strides slowly and confidently across the courtyard. Without meaning to, I find myself keeping watch at the window in the evening, to see if I can spot her. One evening I open the window and strum on the old lute that Jules brought home, years ago. The young woman looks up. She sees me. I play a soldiers' tune. She laughs. She has pale, bright eyes, like my mother's, and the same black hair. My heart pounds so hard and my nerves are so strained that I can feel the scars from my bullet wounds throbbing.

During my final weeks at the front, that image never leaves my mind for an instant. The first thing I do after the sudden armistice – after we storm the packed trains like a crazed mob and return home, singing all the way – is go to my room to keep watch. The war is over. I see the young woman at work in the courtyard below, with her back turned. As if she senses something, she abruptly whirls around, and I look directly into her luminous, pale eyes. Nausea and dizziness wash over me; I seize hold of the foot of my bed.

III

———

He would never have believed, he observed, how long the days, and time, and life itself could be when one had been shunted aside.

W. G. Sebald, *Vertigo*

III

He looks up again from his seat at the old dressing table, wondering what he should write about next. His tale of the war is finally finished, after all these years; now he has to describe how he met Maria Emelia and lost her.

It is 1976, summer, a summer that will be etched into the memory of a generation as exceptionally hot and dry. He is old; he has spent the past thirteen years working on these memoirs, on and off. There were times when he left the notebook unopened for weeks, once for as long as six months – that was when the time came to write about his third wound, and the officers' treachery, as he called it. Beside him are his medals, which he went looking for today because his memories were so vivid. Coincidentally, his first encounter with Maria Emelia has brought him almost to the end of this second notebook; there is not enough room on the remaining pages to tell the rest of the story. He hesitates, puts down his pen, pulls a folder from under his blotter, and starts a letter:

My beloved Gabrielle,
When I contemplate the death of your beloved sister . . .

He puts the pen back down; the words won't come.

It is oppressively hot, late June, and the whole world seems to be wilting. He removes his black hat from his bald head and wipes the sweat off his forehead with a handkerchief.

Should he ask his daughter to buy him a third notebook?

The thought is unappealing. These last few pages have taken a lot out of him. It's all starting to fade, anyway, his handwriting is wobbly, he has gout in his fingers. He can still paint, an hour a day, but he finds it increasingly tiring to stand at the small easel.

His grandson will soon become a father. He lives on a small farm somewhere near the Dutch border; they rarely see each other. Going off to university really changed the boy; once God-fearing and obedient, he's now become rebellious, mocking God and his commandments and causing his parents no end of distress. That's how it goes; parents scrimp and save so their children can have a university education, and then the children use what they learn to make their parents feel small. He has hair halfway down his back; it looks dreadful. In his day, boys had to have character, keep their hair close-cropped, show discipline. His grandson thinks of nothing but having a good time, listens to those halfwits from Liverpool – yes, Liverpool, can you believe it – and is full of big ideas about politics. His blue denim workmen's trousers are ripped and worn. That's not how the boy was raised – with politics, and certainly not with the politics of the Red Menace.

The heat is making him a little queasy. Or is it his heart? He shouldn't have thought about Maria Emelia. But he can't help it.

Over the next few days, he will jot down a few brief thoughts about the early months of his engagement. After that, the second notebook contains a few stray sentences and dissolves into something about night and panic; the ink has run, as if the pages were stained with tears. There the story of his life ends. In a sense, his life itself ended there too.

Something about the lost ethos of the old-time soldier is almost unthinkable to us today, in our world of terrorist attacks and virtual violence. The morality of violence has undergone a seismic shift. The generation of Belgian soldiers driven into the monstrous maw of the German machine guns in the first year of the war had been raised with exalted nineteenth-century values, with pride and honour and naive idealism. Their military ethics were based on the virtues of courage, self-discipline, honour, the love of the daily march, respect for nature and their fellow men, honesty and the willingness to fight man to man. They read aloud from books they had brought with them, sometimes even literature – often poetry, in fact, however bombastic it may have been. They adhered to Christian morals, had an utter horror of sexual deviance, and used alcohol in moderation, or abstained. Soldiers had to set an example for the civilians they were sworn to protect.

All those old-fashioned virtues bit the dust in the trenches of the First World War. Soldiers were deliberately plied with alcohol before being driven into the firing line (this is one of the greatest taboos among patriotic historians, but my grandfather's stories leave no room for doubt). Towards the end of the war, clandestine cafés – seedy outfits, which my grandfather called tingle-tangles – were popping up all over the place, and soldiers were encouraged to relieve their frustrated sexual urges there, not necessarily in the gentlest of ways. Cafés like these were a novelty, especially in this institutionalized form. The atrocities and massacres changed the morals, the world-view, the mentality and the manners of that generation for ever. The battlefields redolent of crushed grass, the soldiers who saluted even in their dying moments, the rural scenes of hills and glades in eighteenth-century military paintings gave way to a heap of psychological rubble choked with mustard gas, ravaged pastures filled with severed limbs, the physical annihilation of an old-fashioned breed of human being.

The royalist Flemings returned home traumatized. Although the military parade that marked the entry of Albert I into Brussels seemed triumphant, many returning soldiers were bent with fatigue and disillusion, despite their relief that peace had finally come to their ravaged country. Some were scarcely able to keep up the appearance of patriotism required for the occasion. In the drawer of my grandfather's old dressing table, I found a small folder with twelve picture postcards by the Brussels photographer S. Polak. The decorative script on the plain cardboard envelope read, 'Historic procession for the triumphal entry of King Albert and the Allied Armies into Brussels, 22 November 1918' – but by that time, patriotism already left a strange taste in the mouth. How could a person identify with higher ideals after they had been blown to pieces? The fields of West Flanders were strewn with the remains of naive credulity and romantic notions. There was music presented in cooperation 'with the American delegation', a picture of a reception for 'Dignitaries', a crowd of men in togas gathered around the king on the steps, a photograph of the American artillery parade, a cavalcade of the Belgian carabiniers, a procession with the flag from the Yser, Scottish and French marching bands, the solemn return to Brussels of the heroic mayor, Adolphe Max, the procession of cars with the royal family, and finally, a photograph of an excited, jostling crowd.

But somewhere a gasket had blown. That much was clear to the soldiers who looked on mutely, without joining in the cheers: the cosy intimacy of Old Europe had been destroyed for ever. The war had shot humanism full of holes, and what came rushing in was the infernal heat of a barren moral wasteland that could hardly be sown with new ideals, since it was abundantly clear how far astray the old ones had led us. The new politics that would now flare up was fuelled by wrath, resentment, rancour and vengefulness, and showed even greater potential for destruction. But the old soldiers would never return, the men for whom marching was a point of honour, who had learned to fence like ballet dancers, who made absurd half-bows before skewering their enemies. In the muck of the trenches, in the clouds of lethal mustard gas and the sadistic reprisals against defenceless civilians that were carried out by the Germans wherever they went, a spark of old-fashioned humanity died out. When a peace-loving German writer commented during the Balkan wars, towards the end of that same century, that the violence had become so horrific because the ethics of warfare no longer left room for honour, because there was no human respect for the enemy, because combat no longer aspired to style or grace, what he brought to light was merely one small corner of the sense of style that Europe had lost. The press tore the author to shreds, accusing him of politically incorrect nostalgia.

My grandfather never abandoned his touching, old-fashioned view of life; it had been hammered too deeply into his psyche. But the suspicion that would seize hold of him in later years, his paranoia in the 1950s, his fits of temper and rage at no one in particular for no apparent reason – rage at his own lost innocence, perhaps – spoke silent, tight-lipped, bitter volumes to us, the people who lived with him.

A few years after marrying Henri, his mother moves into a house on Gentbruggestraat, not far from the Vijfhoek, a five-way junction that was a local landmark. The first of the five ways leads to his roots, across the Gentbrugge bridge over the Scheldt to where his mother came from. The second is the way to the world of painting: the Prins Albertstraat, where his friend the painter Adolf Baeyens lives. The third is the way to his memories: Gentbruggestraat to Steenweg towards Dendermonde and on from there to the Dampoort, the setting of his early childhood. The fourth is the way to the future: Destelbergenstraat, where he will later build a house on the banks of the Scheldt. The fifth is the way to love: Aannemersstraat, perpendicular to Gentbruggestraat, where a trader in potatoes and grain, Mr Ghys from Sint-Denijs-Boekel, has made his home.

Each day he sees her from his window, the younger daughter, walking back and forth among the trade goods heaped in the back garden, her bearing stately. Their gazes meet. One evening he gathers his courage, goes around the corner, and rings the Ghys family's doorbell. They let him in. After an hour he comes outside with her, takes her home with him, and introduces her to his mother. Mother, this is Maria Emelia. Long silence. A lump in his throat. Two black-haired women with pale eyes examining each other ironically, the one like a younger version of the other. All right, Urbain, his mother finally says. She squeezes his hand. The girl embraces the woman with the stiff smile. 'Would you care for a cup of milk, young lady?' 'No, thank you, very kind of you.' Silence. From that day on he visits the home of his future in-laws daily and is accepted by the trader as a son.

Ghent's first cinemas open their doors. He goes out in the evening with his statuesque fiancée to watch the newsreels, images on greyish screens that symbolize a new age to them. He is mad about her. For her sake, he wants to buy a car, a Fiat, an eccentric plan for a man of his limited means. His mother and the young woman look like an older and a younger sister. The horrors of the war begin to recede, though he still has panic attacks, shortness of breath and nightmares from which he wakes up panting and sweating. Trauma counselling has not yet been invented, so he swallows his emotions and reassures his mother when she asks him how he's getting on. Love agrees with him. The preoccupation with religion that seemed such an essential part of him has largely disappeared. But he still prays his fingers to the bone every Sunday, seated in front of the side altar of Our Lady of the Seven Sorrows.

He shows the lovely Maria Emelia Ghys, who is twenty-five years old – he himself is twenty-seven – his father's frescoes and murals, and describes the painting that he saw in Liverpool. He talks a mile a minute; they are inseparable. It's as if the love his father felt for his mother, until his premature death, is reborn in his love for this proud, beautiful young woman. The thought calms and settles him, he worships the ground she walks on, the horrors of war fade away, and believe it or not, he is happy. They plan their wedding; by this time, he has found a job in the Belgian Railways workshops on Brusselsesteenweg in Ledeberg and is taking classes again at the art academy. He promises that he will paint her if she will pose for him.

In his memoirs I find the following passage:

> *I have found a heavenly girl with whom I can join in wedlock and forget the horror. I have said and sung it:*
>   *Sighing, breathing / Chests heaving / Be my love.*
>   *Et cetera.*
>   *We run errands together. What I like best of all is to go out into the pasture with her and see the young foals frisking and kicking their legs. On Sundays we go dancing in Het Volk Concert Hall and I tell her that she is like a foal.*
>   *When Maria is ill, I bring her books by Courths-Mahler, but she says she'd rather read something else, and then laughs and throws her arms around me. I am concerned about her health. She is as pale as an alabaster figurine, but her cheeks still have their glow, and she is always good-humoured. Courage, she says, courage, my little soldier, we shall be married in the spring.*

It is 1919. The Spanish flu races through exhausted Europe. The virus is said to have been brought to the old world by American soldiers and, ironically, to have spread like wildfire because of the crowds that gathered all over the continent to celebrate the peace. Around the globe, the virus claims more than a hundred million lives, taking a toll ten times heavier than the brutal war that Europe has just put behind it. Strangely enough, the flu hits young adults hardest, and at one point my grandfather fears that he has caught it. He has a cough, a fever, a sore throat – the first symptoms. He is confined to his bed, everyone waits in fear, but after a week he pulls through. The next person to fall ill is his lovely Maria Emelia; she looks pale and feels exhausted; she has dizzy spells and low blood pressure. One day she loses consciousness for a moment as they are leaving the cinema; he holds her up until she comes to. It's nothing, she says, those war scenes in the newsreel, I had no idea how much you've been through. The following Sunday, they are strolling past the flower beds in Kouter when she starts to feel sick. He takes her home, where she is put to bed immediately. After a few days she develops a racking cough and can no longer keep her food down. The illness leaves her drained and thinner by the day; every evening, he sits beside her bed and holds her hands in his. They talk about their future in worried tones. Then disaster strikes: Maria Emelia develops pneumonia. Nothing available at that time can relieve her suffering. Antibiotics will be invented in 1928, penicillin that same year, cortisone will be discovered in the adrenal cortex in 1935, and fenoterol, which opens up the bronchioles, will not come into widespread use till the end of the twentieth century. In the space of a few weeks, he sees the proud woman he loves waste away into a coughing, emaciated wisp, and when she begins to gasp desperately for breath, as he remembers his father doing, he thinks he will lose his mind. The doctor says she has water in her lungs. A fatal complication.

One day she says to him, 'I give you back your freedom. You have no future with me.'

'Maria, please,' he begs her, 'don't say such a thing. You have a fever, that's all.' He takes her hands in his. Her pale, exquisite eyes gaze into his own, so long and piercingly that a chill comes over him, and he feels the horror flooding back that he thought he had left behind at the end of the war. He feels himself becoming nauseous, and grows dizzy, gulps, and throws himself upon her, his face in her loose black hair. As he cries in desperation, she goes on silently staring, stroking his hair with an absent look in her eyes.

I heard stories of her death only when my grandfather was nowhere nearby. It must have been gruesome. The water made her lungs swell to such a size that her heart was pressed flat, which is said to cause unbearable pain. She spent her final days begging for death, and in her last hours once again told my grandfather that he was 'released from his duties towards her' – words it was said could still bring tears to his eyes fifty years later. She died in his arms, convulsing in pain that grew with the pressure on her heart; after she fell unconscious, he held her motionless form in his arms until she had let out her final breath.

His grief was too terrible for words. He considered suicide, and his mother threw the pistol he had kept after the war into the Scheldt. He fell ill again and hoped the Spanish flu would permit him to 'join her in the presence of Our Lady and our dear departed father'. But he did not die. He was as tough as an alley cat, hardened by the foundry, his life of poverty, the war, and all his other hardships, and he lived on against his will, like a plant on a rock. In any case, he was too devout a Christian to kill himself: we must humbly accept the fate that the Lord has chosen for us. On Maria Emelia's memorial card, which does not show her photograph but a crucified Christ – that sweet, sacred heart of Jesus – she herself wrote words of consolation for him the last day she was fully conscious: *For you, my heart's beloved, with whom I hoped to make a happy hearth, I pray that the Almighty may give you strength in your hour of need.*

Her parents had befriended his mother and went on visiting regularly. They invariably brought their eldest and sole surviving daughter with them: the shy, unforthcoming wallflower Gabrielle, already well into her thirties and therefore an old maid, as they still said unselfconsciously in those days. After a few months, her father Ghys had a man-to-man talk with my grandfather and urged that splendid young fellow not to let the family down. He got the message. Urbain pulled himself together, asked for a week to think it over, and then the soldier in him did what he'd always done: he said yes, because he'd been asked. *À vos ordres, mon commandant.*

So it came to pass that in 1920 First Sergeant-Major Urbain Joseph Emile Martien – decorated veteran of the Great War and recipient of three medals of the Order of Leopold including one Cross with three palms, and one badge of the Order of the Crown with one palm, as well as the Knight's Cross for exceptional merit, the Military Decoration with a striped ribbon, the War Cross with three palms and two lions, the Yser Medal in the colour of the Order of Leopold, and various other medals and decorations – was married, just before reaching the age of thirty, to the timid Gabrielle Ghys, three years older, who would remain his wife for almost forty years, and for whom he would always cherish a sincere affection, as he might have said.

On the feasts of All Saints and All Souls, regardless of the weather, they would wend their way to Maria Emelia's grave, where he would force his wife to say the Lord's Prayer for her dead sister for hours on end. His own prayers grew increasingly fervent; Our Lady of the Seven Sorrows became the icon of his own dead Maria Emelia. Once, when he heard the name Maria sung in Scarlatti's *Stabat Mater*, it left him so short of breath that he needed a cortisone injection on the spot. But that takes us far ahead of our story, into the mid-1950s, when he was committed to the psychiatric ward. Because there is no photograph on the memorial card for her funeral, I wondered for many years what Maria looked like exactly, in spite of all the stories I had heard. However precisely language can describe a person's appearance, it never adds up to a physical identity.

When his daughter, my mother, was born, he insisted that she be named Maria Emelia – and what could Gabrielle do but say yes? Why shouldn't she pay homage to her dead sister, who had been better, smarter, more graceful, more dazzling in every way? Many years ago, my father told me in confidence that Maria Emelia Ghys must have been a passionate woman, like my mother, and he left no doubt as to what he meant by that; I know that throughout their marriage my parents remained intensely and physically enamoured of each other, and perhaps my grandfather would have found the same intimacy with Maria Emelia. Instead, he whiled away his life at the side of a good-natured but passionless woman, who wore a raincoat to bed because of her husband's occasional animal urges, which sometimes made him so reckless that he tried to embrace her. My family strongly suspects that he only had sexual intercourse with the woman a couple of times. Those were his only experiences of physical love, and one might wonder how satisfactory they were. According to family legend, Gabrielle went to his mother after becoming pregnant to insist that she rein in her son, because there was no more call for that kind of vulgarity now that she was pregnant.

The rest is buried in silence, piety, prayers before countless altars of the Virgin Mother, devotional prints, reproductions of seventeenth-century Venuses, Aphrodites, Salomés, Majas and Dianas, Madonnas, Our Ladies in white and blue, the young girls of Ingres, finely drawn damsels, dryads and rustic fairies, oil paint, art and mortification, guilt and atonement, knowledge of sin and repentance, sorrow and transcendence – endless silent Sundays like the one when I caught him with tears in his eyes, staring at the reproduction of Velázquez's Rokeby Venus. Allegories of the sorrowful body. The greatest irony of this whole story may have been that he met the same fate as his stepfather – his mother, at least, must have grappled with mixed feelings. The constant refrain in our house was that we must humbly accept the fate meted out to us by the Merciful Lord. In any case, the Maria Emelia who became my mother, cheerful, warm-hearted woman that she was, wept for her father in silence, bowing her head and saying, 'Maybe I should have had a different name. That might have helped to ease his mind.'

The image of the aged couple sitting side by side, chastened and peaceable, is permanently etched into my mind. It is Saturday afternoon; they are about to go into town together. She has draped her black mantilla over her head, and it falls over her shoulders and grey coat, complementing her stern features. He sits up straight, looking dapper in his midnight-blue suit, turns his intent gaze on her and says, 'You look good, Gabrielle, come on, let's go.' And with a wistful smile, she stands and says, 'Oh, Urbain, you're such a charmer.'

They pull the door shut behind them. The house is quiet.

Driving, by the way, was a skill he never chose to learn. Gabrielle was opposed to it; he was much too nervous for that type of thing, she explained.

What must it be like, spending your whole life with your true love's sister? Seeing flashes of the flamboyant Maria Emelia in the timid Gabrielle, a woman who spurned his embrace? Did it allow him to stay close to the love of his life? Or when he saw some of her features, her mannerisms, resurface in that other woman, did it torment him? Should he have avoided the situation at all costs? Isn't love's illusion built on the principle that the beloved is irreplaceable and unique? Doesn't the near-duplication of the beloved, and the accompanying sense of not-quite-rightness, strike at the heart of this notion? Isn't it intolerable to the other woman, who is doomed to resemble her predecessor and doomed never to resemble her enough? Does that explain my grandmother's civil disobedience in the bedroom – did she wordlessly sense this fact, understand it, suffer the sting, and feel the humiliation? In his efforts to be more intimate with his wife, was he really courting his fantasy of her dead sister? And if so, wasn't he committing a kind of adultery whenever he tried to embrace his wife, an embrace that was tragically rejected time and again? Did that add a second torment to the original loss, a torment that recurred throughout his life? How did he make the shift from his early infatuation with the flamboyant Maria Emelia to his deep personal bond with the restrained Gabrielle?

I don't know enough about neurology to say exactly what happens when you're knocked off your feet by the particularities of a person's figure, the look in their eyes, the way they hold themselves, something that instantly sets that person apart from all others for you. I suspect that very complicated things coincide in that instant, a kind of associative explosion that produces the impression of uniqueness, the feeling that all this has absolute, immediate and unconditional meaning and depth. A person in love sees symbols in the most trivial things. What seems trickiest to me is the seamless merging of the physical appearance of the beloved with a tangled mass of psychological and emotional effects on the lover's brain. In my grandfather's case, there was a third factor: the resemblance, in physical appearance and character, between his adored mother and the object of his passion. Or was that resemblance partly his own fabrication? But what about my elderly relatives, who remember her as looking like his mother?

My grandfather spent his life within this tetragon of women – his mother, his dead love, her older sister and his daughter with the fateful name. His only escape was into the fantasy world of painting: Giorgione's and Raphael's idealized, eternally youthful figures, the young woman in Palma il Vecchio's exquisite portrait or his nude *Diana with Callisto*, Titian's *Venus of Urbino*, the scores of sensual young

women in Tiepolo's frescoes, Ingres's *Grande Odalisque* – yes, they were a different sort of woman, yet in the sheaves of torn-out reproductions he left between the pages of his books, I found mainly dark-haired beauties, worldly women of bygone days, posing in mythical settings, as well as portraits of proud bourgeois women, sometimes laying one hand on a bodice of gold brocade or resting their fingers on a delicately illuminated throat, one simple pearl turned towards the viewer under their pinned-up hair in a small, half-hidden ear.

There are few records of his life in the 1920s. They lived in a small place at first, 'across the river'. In 1929, the year of the great stock market crash, he was able, with financial assistance from his parents-in-law, to buy a long, narrow plot of land on the other side of the Scheldt, along a disused towpath. The land was cheap; it was on top of an old, buried pre-war dump. There was no such thing as soil remediation in those days. The snug villa with its Dutch bonnet was built on what may well be an ideal late-nineteenth-century arch-aeological site. I remember how often I dug up the skeletons of small animals from the lean black soil. I laid out rows of bones in the jerry-rigged tent that my grandfather had made for me out of coarse canvas 'left over from the war'. I can only assume he meant the Second.

My mother was born in 1922. She was a frail child, and asthmatic, like her father and grandfather, but lively, light-hearted, in every way the opposite of her taciturn mother: a dancing, frolicking bundle of energy with wavy blonde hair, an entirely different creature, who gaily subverted and contradicted the muffled world of her parents' home. As she grew up, she was confronted with the strict morals of her prudish parents. When she announced at the age of thirteen that her first period had begun, she received a box on the ear from her father for using such shameless language and a stack of flannel cloths from her tight-lipped mother.

The house was comfortable. The kitchen was in the back, with two metal hand pumps over the sink, one for rain water and one for well water. They drank the well water – which came directly from the buried dump – as much as they pleased, without boiling it. In fact, the well was also right next to the cesspool, which was under the blackened coal shed. I remember the spring days when my grandfather would empty the cesspool with a bucket attached to a six-foot pole. The manure was used to fertilize the grapevines, the roses and gladioli, the irises and tulips, the plum and pear trees, and the currant and gooseberry bushes. It had a sweet, penetrating odour, bound up with spring and sunshine.

It was there, in that dreamy house on the banks of the Scheldt, that my grandfather should have found happiness and peace. He remained at the Belgian Railways until the mid-1930s, when he started to show symptoms of his first psychological breakdown. He was examined by doctors and, in 1936, at the age of forty-five, pensioned off owing to signs of mental exhaustion. They lived frugally. Ever since the war's end in 1918, the Ministry of Finance had paid him a pension for invalid soldiers, listed in the 'Ledger of Disbursements Pertaining to the National Knightly Orders'. The amount of this pension was 150 Belgian francs a year, which comes to about €3.75. My grandfather's old *carnet de pécule*, or savings book, lists precise figures by date – figures that varied from two to five Belgian francs. A note accompanies the last recorded payments: *Arrêté à la somme de cinq cent quatre-vingt-un francs septante centimes, le 23–12–1919, Le Quartier-maître ff.* On 17 January 1922, he received a pension certificate and an updated listing in the Ledger as no. 954. This document was drafted in Mont-Saint-Amand-lez-Gand, the French name for the Ghent neighbourhood of Sint-Amandsberg in the days when the Dutch language was taboo in official correspondence. By 1939, seventeen years later, that war pension was many times the original amount, but it remained modest. In a yellowed document dated 9 November

1939 (a day after the attack on Hitler in Munich, and exactly fifty years before the fall of the Berlin Wall), I find a specification of the annual payments to my grandfather: a military pension of 1,269 francs; a premium of 2,248 francs for soldiers who fought in the front lines; and a payment for members of knightly orders of 748 francs a year. This adds up to 4,265 francs a year, or 106 euros. His military pension remained so small because his meritorious service during the war had never been rewarded with promotion to a rank above sergeant-major. That filled him with bitterness: all the Walloon sergeants had been promoted to lieutenant on merit, he said, and so had his own Flemish brother-in-law David Ghys, just because he lived in Wallonia, and even though (according to my grandfather) he had never been wounded. Meanwhile, despite my grandfather's medals and his wounds – he sometimes spoke of a fourth and even a fifth wound, but these go unmentioned in his memoirs – he remained a sergeant, 'like so many Flemish lads'.

That may account for his new-found sympathy for the Flemish Movement. He began spelling his name in the Flemish way, 'Urbaan', and sometimes spelled his wife's name 'Gabriella'. He griped that the Flemish lads had been royalists in the trenches and the Walloons republicans, but the royal house had rewarded the French-speakers, and not the Flemish, after the war – and since this shameful act of discrimination, he fumed, the French-speakers had acted as if they were God's chosen protectors of the royal house against the Flemish. 'Here is our blood, when will we have our justice?' he would say then, quoting the notorious words written on the Merkem Stone by an anonymous Flemish soldier, and he would bite his lower lip in anger.

Painting was a comfort to him, but he never went beyond still lifes, which are too finely painted to have any character. His penchant for displays of virtuoso skill deprived him of a certain force that might have made his work more intense. He despised Cézanne, Van Gogh, and all the other 'daubers'; they paint with the wrong end of the brush, he would say with a sneer. He made a warm and loving portrait of his daughter Maria with a doll in her arms, sitting wide-eyed in a wicker chair. Her blue eyes, which she inherited from her father, gaze into peaceful nothingness. He seems to have painted every hair, but realism, as he well knew, is a question of well-planned effect.

Strangely, I can find no mention of the death of his beloved mother Céline – there is not a word in his memoirs, and the few surviving family members have no stories to tell. By the time of her death in September 1931, he is a man of forty, employed in the workshops of the large Belgian Railways complex in Gentbrugge, the father of a nine-year-old girl, the husband of his true love's sister, and the owner of a house under construction on the banks of the Scheldt. A photo passed down in the family shows him next to his wife, who is next to his mother; it may be the last photograph of Céline.

This picture could easily have been the work of Henri Cartier-Bresson, at least judging by the atmosphere and the setting. The three of them are sitting in a row: my grandfather, his wife Gabrielle with a fashionable hat in the late 1920s style, and a portly old woman with a moony face, who in no way resembles the stylish lady of his youth. In this stage of her life, Céline looks more like a matronly farmer's wife, with her pudgy hands in her black lap and a vague shadow on her upper lip that suggests a light dusting of hair. She too is wearing one of those round hats from the final years of the Roaring Twenties, and she smiles broadly in his direction, looking highly amused. He himself is wearing his fedora, black boots, white shirt and dark suit, a badge on his lapel, and of course his indispensable bow tie with tails like a dress coat – albeit fairly short ones in this picture. They are seated on a grassy slope, with dozens of people behind them who are staring at something we cannot see. My grandfather's still-young face contrasts strangely with the clothes so familiar to me from his later years – this image of a man of forty in those dark, severe garments says something about the regimented emotional world in which he lived. Today, the average forty-year-old man looks completely different: in his jeans, T-shirt, trainers and optional baseball cap, he radiates a boyishness that shows we find it much harder to give up life's illusions. My grandfather, wearing the uniform of that strict, middle-class epoch, seems to have put away childish things with an almost thoughtless ease. He is sitting and looking at something outside the picture frame; I think he is talking; he has his hands in a strange position, as if pinching an invisibly thin conductor's baton between the tips of his fingers. The scene brings back my summer memories of the beach in Ostend, and I realize his appearance must hardly have changed in the twenty-seven intervening years. On the back of the photo he wrote, in a fine dip pen:

My Dear Mother was one of the first two hundred to make the Pilgrimage of the Yser to Diksmuide Cemetery: we see Her here at the last meeting that She attended there, in August 1930. 250,000 Flemings paid tribute to their dead that day.

Until 1924, the gatherings known as pilgrimages took place at various sites of remembrance around the Yser. After that, these pilgrimages were held in Diksmuide, where the photograph in question was taken. The IJzertoren (Yser Tower), erected in Diksmuide to commemorate the Belgian soldiers killed on the Yser front, was also a symbol of Flemish pride (and still is today). A little detective work reveals that the original, smaller, IJzertoren was consecrated on 24 August 1930. My grandfather is said to have been listed on this tower, with a photograph, among the heroes of the Battle of the Yser. That tower was blown up in 1946 and replaced with the present, larger, one. All traces of the list of war heroes were wiped out in that attack, which is officially 'still unexplained'. The demolition is said to have been ordered by senior French-speaking army officers, in cooperation with Resistance veterans, to take revenge on those among the Flemish who collaborated with the German occupiers in the Second World War.

When I visited the IJzertoren, I observed that the only slope on the site is right next to the location of the original tower; this suggests that my family was at the focal point of the event. That makes the photo a valuable historical document of the consecration of the tower. But it also seems to show something else: namely, that his mother was such an integral part of the small family that it was only natural for her to come along to that crowded ceremony. I was surprised to read my grandfather's claim that a quarter of a million people gathered in the field in Diksmuide that day; most sources report 60,000 to 100,000. I imagine he was overwhelmed by the huge crowd and the ceremony, but be that as it may, what a fresh, mobilizing energy the Yser pilgrimage must have exuded in those days of the humanist Flemish Movement, with its old-fashioned belief in social uplift. And how stark the contrast with the same event in the 1980s, when it was infested with neo-Nazis, or in the years when the Flemish Block thugs showed up to spoil the atmosphere, complaining that the veterans' pacifist message was 'too left-wing' for their tastes.

The capital letter with which my grandfather wrote the personal pronoun 'Her', referring to his mother, seems somehow logical in his case. But where was his eight-year-old daughter Maria at the time? Did the child take the photograph with the old-time camera, which must have been much more complicated than the ones we use today? His stepfather Henri de Pauw was dead by then, and in September of that year, his mother too would die, still young by our standards. What I see in the photograph is a reassuringly everyday scene, ordinary people on a grassy slope, resting some twenty yards away from the crowd. There is a spot on the photo that makes it hard to see Gabrielle's expression, but it seems to me she's smiling. She looks nothing like the introverted older woman I knew as my grandmother. Her shapely legs are crossed, she is wearing heels, and she looks every inch an ordinary, well-dressed middle-class woman. She is forty-three years old. Céline turned sixty-two on 9 August, two weeks before this photograph was taken.

In any case, there is not one word about her death in his memoirs. But then again, it was in the 1930s, a decade he hardly mentions in the notes I've found. *Cilense* . . . Maybe his silence says more than enough about his life as it was then. Maybe he was thankful for the routine of everyday life, as the whole world hurtled towards new catastrophes – and he towards his first shock treatments. But knowing what I know now, I suspect that the 1930s were also when he painted the secret portrait of his forbidden dream, a portrait I would not discover until many years after I first read his notebooks.

He spent the Second World War at home, where he and his wife and daughter subsisted on his meagre pension. There are tales of the masses of fish that crowded the crystal-clear waters of the Scheldt after the first year and a half of war, there for the taking, a daily miracle of fishes, because the polluting factories had come to a standstill, and there are tales of the clean air and tranquillity after the smokestacks stopped smoking. Sure, they had to walk miles for a pound of butter, a piece of pork belly, a few pounds of potatoes, or some milk for their blossoming young daughter, but that wasn't going to kill them. In some ways, it was a reprise of the poverty of his youth. As far as I can tell from his stories, that didn't bother him. On the contrary, the stilled world put him at ease. I don't know what he thought, felt, said when he heard stories about the battle-fronts; the period is cloaked in silence. There were a few confrontations with German soldiers because he missed the evening curfew and had to show them his purchases: a pitiful haul of food-stuffs he had bought from a farmer in distant Laarne at extortionate prices. Then he would salute and say, 'First Sergeant-Major Martien, retired', and the German soldier would respond with an equally polite salute and let him go. They had ration coupons, bad bread, and a neighbour woman who, in the middle of the war, said in a broad local accent to a German soldier asking for information, 'I do recall right well, sir, that it was Friday when 'twas Saturday', and slammed the front door in the baffled German's face.

After the first year of war, there were no more supplies of paint. Paper grew scarce, and canvas even more so. For a while, he made his own paint from ingredients he'd stored in a cupboard in the back of the house, and he painted on wooden panels. When he'd used up that as well, he had to stop painting until after the war. So he started drawing in charcoal again, and refined his chiaroscuro.

A s far-fetched as it may sound, he did not notice until fairly late in life that he was wrong about certain colours. It must have been in the mid-1960s. Daltonism, or colour blindness, is a strange affliction. Because it is a variable defect in the perception of colour gradations, the number of varieties is almost as great as the number of people affected. He had a common type of partial colour blindness: typically, he would confuse shades of red and green – not the entire spectrum, just certain shades. Bright green and bright red, for example, looked mysteriously similar to him; the potent red of the ripe rowan berries showed almost no contrast with the wind-blown leaves in the treetop, especially when sunlight fell straight onto them. Dark green and black were two others he could barely tell apart, especially on new cars and other gleaming surfaces. Strangely, it was sometimes enough just to point it out to him. Then he would look more closely and say, 'Oh, yes, now I see it too.' This condition is apparently passed down the male line, but always by way of a woman who carries the recessive gene – in other words, it is handed down from grandfather to grandson through the daughter. So he must have inherited it from Mr Andries, Céline's father. His failure to observe certain nuances of colour had far-reaching consequences, since some of his hues were made out of three or four different Rembrandt oils – colours that could not be confused, because the names were on the tubes. He would screw off the tops, add a drop of linseed oil to each dab of colour, and start mixing. It was there that the trouble began; in the mixing process, he sometimes veered very far from the intermediate tones he had in mind, and because we, who lived with him, paid more attention to the sensitivity of his scenes than to the realism of his colours, some extra brown or red in certain elements of the landscape could easily be seen as a case of artistic licence or an original light effect. He never became conscious of the extent of his deficiency until the day that he and a fellow painter, Adolf Baeyens, stood side by side painting the castle gardens in Bergenkruis, a pilgrimage site not far from where he lived. They went there on foot – two elderly gentlemen strolling down the country lane in the shade of the tall beeches. Despite the hot weather, they wore tidy suits, white shirts and neckties, and had their hats on their heads. Each man had a small easel tucked under one arm and a wooden box of painting supplies slung over one shoulder. They found a comfortable spot somewhere in the great outdoors, like throwbacks to the nineteenth-century Barbizon School. Although they both painted the same rustic cottage at the edge of the woods, they returned home with two completely different paintings. Not only did Baeyens have a more angular, expressionistic style, but the house was blue in one painting and reddish-brown in the other. From that moment on, my grandfather became suspicious of his own visual faculty, and one morning while painting his umpteenth seascape with shrimpers, he noticed that – bloody hell! – the sea in the painting was not authentically greenish, but an odd shade of reddish-brown. A brown sea – Jesus Christ! I happened to witness this dramatic moment. With tears trickling from his eyes, he swore, slammed the painting to pieces on his beloved dressing table, and made a wild attempt to rip the canvas to shreds, covering his hands with wet paint in the process. He wiped them off on his smock and looked at me in dismay, without a word, hissing in helpless rage. I remember the abstract painting formed by the smears of paint on his smock; I believe I could not appreciate the full extent of the tragedy I had witnessed. This was several years after the death of his wife; I was eleven years old at the time so, counting backwards, I think it must have been around 1962. Gabrielle died in 1958. How had he gone so long without realizing?

From that moment on, there was something different about the way he painted. His style seems to have become looser, vaguer, more careless, from one day to the next, but it's also possible that his eyesight was deteriorating. He took refuge in his speciality, drawing in charcoal, which gave him the opportunity for brilliant *sfumato* effects. There are scores of half-naked girls by woodland springs, nymphlike apparitions that suggest the primeval purity of the shadowy forest, languid cloudscapes, and little-trodden paths where dappled light falls through teeming summer leaves. In these charcoal drawings, he mastered the art of evoking a melancholy, Arcadian mood. He gave away many of these drawings as gifts to family members, friends and acquaintances. I never knew him to accept a single Belgian franc for a drawing or painting; I believe the very idea was unthinkable to him, an insult to the sense of the sublime that he had sought in painting his whole life long. It might also have constituted a betrayal of his father, Franciscus the fresco painter, who had always remained poor.

He took me along to Expo 58, the world's fair in Brussels – my grandfather, who had seen the World's Fair of 1913. What I recall is white: white buildings, white avenues, bright, new, squeaky-clean architecture, large modern windows, sunlight, white sunlight, a world that dazzled me – as I remember, everything was white. To a generation still dwelling in old houses with dimly lit rooms, it was overwhelming. The Atomium looked white, the trees looked white, the world was white. Even the bread was white, white Expo bread. Why was it all white? Are they glimpses of the American pavilion, these memories of mine, or of the futuristic French pavilion? Who knows. The only thing that was black was the clothing the visitors wore, I'm sure of that. All the men wore black, the women wore black skirts (and, admittedly, white blouses), and I walked hand in hand with my black-suited grandfather, who was also wearing his black hat and black bow tie. A white-and-black world. That's all I remember. I was seven; he had lost his wife in the spring; he must have been in deep mourning at the time, missing her. I don't remember anything else about that; in my recollection, I had seen her die in her chair one early morning, with a final loud rasp. That had been in May – a long time ago for a seven-year-old child in August. Only now, a half century later, does it all sometimes seem so strangely close, that world in black and white.

Schiplaken, January 2012.
On Google Maps it looks almost as if history is still alive there, and I can imagine the woods where the fighting took place; swinging the cursor between streets named after composers and streets named after canaries, between a lingerie shop and a suburban lane, through the stone encampments of the urbanized Flemish landscape, I can explore the terrain, feel it out, as if I had a 3D military map, or as if I were flying over the places to be mapped in an army helicopter. My satellite view is toyshop quality, but it seems to bring things

closer, for the length of a distracted afternoon. The cemetery in question is on Bieststraat, fine, but when I actually arrive there in my car, it's one of those chilly, lightless days that give you the feeling this part of the world is buried under a centuries-old damp rag, while elsewhere on the planet, in more fortunate climes, the sky is filled with bright and endless blue. Everything here seems flat and bare. The new developments lack imagination, as do the ceaseless, infernal cypresses, cherry laurels and close-cropped lawns. There is no traffic on the concrete road, aside from a single delivery van, hurtling over the joints in the road with a monotonous tock-tock, tock-tock. As I take in this scene, children come pouring out of the little school next to the cemetery. A crossing guard waves a stop sign at the deserted street. Then they converge from all sides: SUVs, luxury sedans, vans and parents on foot. The children are picked up and packed into seats, doors slam, and the cars pull out of the car park one by one, disappearing from view as they head for affluent suburbs in all directions. Silence returns; you can hear the wind in the bare trees. It is bitterly cold. At the entrance to the cemetery, the flag dangles like a dead bird. I take photos of the monument – a long wall with black iron letters reading TO THE HEROES OF THE BATTLES OF SCHIPLAKEN.

The sombre sculpture in the middle, on a pedestal bearing the words PRO PATRIA and the dates of the battles (26 August–12 September 1914), is the sole testament to what must have happened in this place. The stone cross has fallen off the pedestal; what remains is a dark grey cross-shaped blotch. The bronze sculpture by Bernard Callie represents a mother bent over a dying soldier. He is wearing his capote and resting his helmeted head in her lap; she appears to be laying a palm branch on his shoulder. His knapsack still hangs from his bronze neck. One leg seems to have slid off the pedestal, a dramatic touch. The bronze is stained with moss and damp. Along the wall, behind which the roof of the little school rises up beside two formless, overgrown cypresses, are two rows of small gravestones like upward-tilted nameplates, commemorating almost a hundred fallen soldiers. I copy a few names, reflecting that my grandfather may well have known these lads: A. Van Dezande, B. De Munter, A. Vandecandelaere, J. Buffel, carabinier, D. DeBacker, artilleryman, E. De Jonghe, J. Verhaeghe, A. De Groote, L. L. Coene, J. Cravez, all soldiers of the 2nd Regiment of the Line.

There's no reason for me to be writing down these names. I do it just to keep busy, but the cold soon seeps into my fingers, and I walk on with my hands in my pockets, leaning into the wind. In a grassy field to the rear of the cemetery is a large cross on a pedestal. Over the walls, bare treetops sway in the icy wind. It happened in these woods, I think to myself. I return to the car and drive down narrow, sandy roads through desolate stretches of forest that lie strewn between clusters of houses. There is truly nothing to see, except for one smashed-up car without wheels somewhere in the middle of the woods, a kind of focal point for the surrounding desolation, the lack of anything that might indicate memory. I step out of the car for another look around; even the trees were different back then. Not one of these trees is a century old; all of them may have been planted after the Second World War. There is not a single witness here: not in the sand, not in the trees, not in the houses, not in the roads. And as I reflect on this absence in these strangely young trees, I am seized by the near-physical sense of how far removed it all is from my own time, everything that's preoccupied me for the past few years. It's almost as if the mute trees, so absurdly young, are dissemblers, conspiring with time.

I drive to Sint-Margriete-Houtem, where another horrific battle took place, pass a street named after the 22nd Line Regiment, drive by Weerde, and then past Elewijt – which he saw burning after it was shelled – from Boortmeerbeek to Kampenhout, and on to Winksele, the places where he marched, bivouacked, fought, dug, slept, and ran for his life: all sunk in the same oblivion. O peace, banal, beloved, we salute thee. A grocery, a bakery, an empty parking space, a small supermarket, an obnoxiously trendy boutique pharmacy, a rusty traffic sign, an eccentric plastic newspaper kiosk, a concrete road like a ribbon of emptiness on a wintry afternoon. Nobody outside; now and then, a speeding car. On my car radio, Stravinsky's *Symphonies of Wind Instruments*: dramatic, drifting music that perfectly complements the nameless suburbia drifting past. It's two p.m., two thirty, I can't help lingering to soak up this absolute nothingness, the nothingness called the contemporary that surrounds me like a sheltering cocoon. I return from my trip empty-handed; even a handful of the cold, polluted sand from a forest path did not seem like a form of contact with what once happened there. Speed bumps, traffic signs, an impatient idiot who flashes his headlights at me because I'm driving the speed limit and zooms past me the first chance he gets, in such a rush that he almost flies off the road at the roundabout. Flanders, 2012. Nothingness. Absolute nothingness. Safe and meaningless, thank God for that, I suppose. I take a few more photos and have another look on Google when I get home – it all seems so much more interesting there than in reality.

*

Every Friday in the summer months, he and his wife went to Bruges, and we, his daughter's family, often went with him to the Basilica of the Holy Blood, which he called the Blood Chapel, to see him carry the flambeau. Countless summer Friday afternoons, I watched him step out of the pew during the service, take up the huge candle on its golden stand, and stride solemnly towards the altar, following the officiating priest through the praying or singing crowd. The relic, which the congregation was expected to kiss during the service, filled me with a mix of revulsion and fascination. A priest sat on a small platform, holding out ahead of him the glass tube that contained the centuries-old, discoloured brown piece of cloth, stiff-armed, as if he were a little disgusted himself. As I recall, the ornamental case was edged with delicate gold trim. Every time one person kneeled and kissed it devoutly, the priest would laconically whisk a white handkerchief over the prints left by the sinful lips, so that the next worshipper could make an equally humble and sensual contribution to this age-old tradition without danger of bacterial infection from somebody else's act of faith. Outside, Bruges was buzzing with ordinary, profane life. The flags rustled, the rowing boats cleaved the muddy water of the canals, the English translation of Georges Rodenbach's famous novella *Bruges-la-Morte* was being read aloud on Rozenhoedkaai, and Rilke's poem 'Quai du Rosaire' was being recited in French. Inside, we were part of the secret ritual that had begun in the twelfth century, when Thierry of Alsace brought this bloodied scrap of cloth from the Holy Land, now part of the most explosive region of the planet (these days he would probably face a lawsuit for illegal export of national heritage, although such matters are complex in present-day Jerusalem). On Ascension Day we witnessed the Procession of the Blood, and I couldn't help thinking of that discoloured brown blood-soaked rag I kissed once a week. The older I got, the more I was troubled by thoughts of the perishability of fabric, of bloodied rags, of relics. The less likely it seemed to me that this cloth had ever been soaked in the Blood of the Saviour, the more astonished I was by the singular magic of those expressive rituals, the songs, the gestures, the centuries of dedication without any hard evidence – in short, the pure transcendent power of other people's faith. Outside was the world, and that made religion – inside, in that incense-scented gloom – alluring and profound. Abstinence always makes the world seem attractive and deep – the swans drifted over the Minnewater, the last of the Beguines were dying out as the autumn crocuses bloomed in the damp canalside courtyards that August. Japanese tourists scurried through the city without understanding the first thing about it. The Holy Blood became forever intertwined with stopping for a lavish sundae, strolling across the main square, drinking old-fashioned fizzy drinks at some pavement café, where I once stared at a pair of lovers – an older man with a piercing gaze, talking to a young blonde woman with windblown curls and goose bumps on her arms, two people in love, lost in each other's eyes, who, because they were such an odd couple and yet were so clearly sharing something intimate, filled me with a sense of the inexplicable. Religion, tourism, my first hint of the erotic, summer and high wisps of cloud, flapping banners and the smell of old churches, the slack, slow lapping of water against the prows of white boats.

'This cup is the New Covenant in my blood, which is poured out for you.' The priest's words echoed in my ears, uncomprehended. Carrying the flambeau in the weekly ritual was a way for my grand-father to carve a notch in time, a rhythm that carried the weeks all through the summer, and when I think of him, his back straight and his fragile, balding scalp glowing dully in the golden candlelight, I understand why he was so attached to it. In truth, there was some-thing medieval about him, a shade of the eternal soldier, the chivalry described in the legends of the Grail. That was why, over many years, the brown glass case in the Blood Chapel fused with the old stories of Parsifal, and I understood that my grandfather was really the Pure Fool, and always had been, the complete innocent who earned my greatest admiration because he seemed to possess no egotism, conceit or self-importance, but only an instinctive eagerness to be of service, a quality that made him both a hero and a first-class chump. And once I understood that, I travelled to Bruges again one day, after many years, and stood in the Blood Chapel watching with bated breath, and understood how little I truly understand.

Years after his death, I found in his small library a well-thumbed copy of *Bruges-la-Morte*. The main character of this tale, Hugues Viane, meets a frivolous double of his dead love and is ultimately forced to conclude that she is no more than a caricature of the woman he once adored. Some passages were underlined in faint pencil. I leafed through the yellowed pages with their endearing illustrations, the vaguely coloured etchings that evoked the Gothic hush of nineteenth-century Bruges. There were smudges of oil paint halfway through the book, and on an empty page I found the beginnings of a small sketch of a face. 'Bruges was his dead love, and his dead love was Bruges. Everything was united in a common destiny.' The ritual Procession of the Holy Blood plays a crucial role in the story. On the day of the procession, the frivolous woman is laughing at the bric-a-brac the man has accumulated over the years and naively treasured. Then she goes further, provoking him with blasphemous mockery. She takes the dead Ophelia's lock of hair and parades around the room with it. Hugues flies into a rage and strangles her, because her blasphemy has confronted him with the ironic truth hidden beneath all his sublimation. It is a story about the impossibility of repeating a great, unique love affair. But it is also a story about a modern Orpheus. Like Orpheus, Hugues descends into the land of the dead to find the spectre of his lost love, a mission doomed to catastrophe. Like Orpheus, he loses her twice, because he confuses his memory of her with her living double on earth.

How often did my grandfather read and reread this novella of

Orphic love? He underlined the sentence in which Rodenbach says that Hugues could resist suicide only thanks to his mystical recollections of Ophelia. Like the main character in the story, my grandfather secretly erected a mental mausoleum to his lost love. Like Hugues Viane, he learned that what was unique in her could not live again in her double, especially considering that the double was her timid elder sister. With that small book in my hands, I was struck by the realization that he had been a kind of married widower, mourning in secret with the same tender care as the character in the story. I then discovered something in the back of the book that surprised me, because I could not yet see the connection: a torn-out reproduction of Velázquez's Rokeby Venus, the image in front of which I had once found him weeping. A couple of pages further on was a tissue-thin piece of tracing paper painstakingly folded around a few long black hairs, once neatly wound around a fingertip to form a small, perfect spiral.

Secret passion, secret teachings that teach us nothing. Loyalty to an absence that shaped everything, giving it form and secret meaning. What mattered most to him was something he could not share with others. So he painted trees, clouds, peacocks, the Ostend beach, a poultry yard, still lifes on half-cleared tables – an immense, silent, devoted labour of grief, to put the world's weeping to rest in the most everyday things.

He never painted a single war scene. It never occurred to him to draw the things he recalled from the war, and since his death I have found no trace of the charcoal portraits of his comrades-in-arms that he mentions in his memoirs. Not one of his paintings includes a soldier, except maybe a small self-portrait, fairly academic in style, in which he is wearing his medals, probably painted before 1920 and anything but military in spirit, more like an oversized passport photo in oils. Who knows, maybe he thought it would please his ailing Maria Emelia. There is only the large, framed black-and-white portrait of him in uniform, possibly an enlargement of a photo taken just after the war. It has been touched up with charcoal, and some of the lines are so vague and blurry that I always thought it was a drawing. At the bottom of the framed photo is an inscription, 'Urbain, as he was when he came back from the war', written by my grandfather himself. The same caption is repeated on the back, but in different handwriting, possibly his mother's. That's all there is. In his countless paintings there is nothing even slightly ominous – at most a bashful, bluish cloud sliding over the evening sun, rendered with a slightly coarser sable brush – not even the harbinger of Giorgione's Tempest over a Biedermeier Arcadia.

Be that as it may, in the period when he realized he was colour-blind, he painted only a few, smaller pieces. Then, in the mid-1960s, he decided it was time for something grander. There is a fairly impressive painting by Anthony Van Dyck of St Martin cutting his cloak in two and giving half to a beggar. The iconography refers to a well-known story; it's a frequently painted theme, also depicted by an anonymous Hungarian master, Simone Martini, Jacob van Oost and El Greco. Van Dyck painted two variations on this theme, opting for a dynamic, dramatic interpretation both times. My grandfather copied the version on display in the Zaventem parish church, near Brussels, which Van Dyck painted for the Dutch chancellor of the Duchy of Brabant, Ferdinand van Boisschot, the year he was knighted.

Martin is seated high on a pale dapple-grey. His cuirass shines darkly, exuding dignity and nobility. His one visible leg is firmly in the stirrup, suggesting strength and agility. He is still young and wears a flamboyant black cap with a large plume hanging well over the brim. To Martin's left (that is, by his right hand) is a second mounted figure, dressed more plainly and riding a brown horse with a white

star. To Martin's right, we see the muscular back of the nude beggar seated on a mound of hay, painted in magnificent anatomical detail, already tugging covetously at the torn, flame-red cloak. Next to him is a second beggar with an Oriental-looking cap, thrusting his lower lip out half-sceptically as he looks up at the generous nobleman. He is crippled and on his knees, clasping a partly visible crutch that supports his shoulder, judging by the crease in the fabric under his arm. The horse's powerfully arched neck, its one raised hoof, the tensed muscles of the beggar's back – the scene radiates pure motion, energy and vivid life. Martin uses a very thin rapier, which he holds up straight in front of his chest, but because he is seated at an angle, his horizontal is our diagonal. He cuts through the upper part of his cloak at an angle of approximately ninety degrees. As he separates the lower part, it is pulled to the right and points in a new direction, towards the muscular beggar who receives it. In just a second, he will have finished cutting the cloak in two and the red cloth will fall onto the beggar in a shapeless mass. On the right, there is also a partial view of a column with an antique look; beyond it, evening clouds drift through the sky, lit by the low sun. The scene shows the hand of a master. Its vigour, bright colour and crisp lines attest not only to Van Dyck's consummate skill, but also to his youthful drive in 1621, when he painted it, soon after turning twenty-two.

It was for this scene that my grandfather spent a week putting together a large stretcher frame in the greenhouse in our backyard. He allowed six by six feet for the canvas, a surprising choice, larger than the dimensions of the original painting in Zaventem, which is only about five and a half by five. That was unexpectedly daring; to enlarge the painting successfully, he would have to lay down precise grid lines on the reproduction in his book. Decked out in his best suit, he went to De Gouden Pluim in Vrijdagmarkt and bought a piece of canvas measuring 250 × 250 cm, which he lugged home on the tram, gazing sullenly into space and attracting stares. As he walked, he balanced the large roll of canvas on one shoulder, almost slamming it into some passer-by a few times as he turned a corner. When he was just about to mount the canvas on the stretcher, he discovered it would not fit where he had planned to hang it, directly above the entrance to his room; the right outer wall of the stairwell angles slightly there, leaving no place to hang the painting. To further complicate matters, the ceiling has a slight downward slope, which forced him to bevel the top of the frame. He disassembled the stretcher and constructed something that, unbeknown to him, was very much in fashion in those days : a 'shaped canvas', with irregular dimensions. In an elaborate feat of carpentry, he modified the upper right corner, where the clouds meet a shrub growing out of a crack in the antique column. Parts of the column on the right were lost, but this was no great sacrifice. He mounted the canvas loosely, lightly wetted the back with a soft sponge, waited three days, carefully remounted it with clips, and only then hammered in the tacks. Once he was thoroughly satisfied with his work, he dragged the large canvas up the stairs, manoeuvred it into his room, beside the bed – leaving himself hardly any space to stand or worm his way into bed at night – and launched into his great work, which would take him more than six months to complete.

He drew grid lines on the reproduction and spent weeks poring over it with his magnifying glass and brass compasses, the latter a gift from the delectable Mrs Lamb of Windermere. He had no need to study the actual painting in the humble parish church of St Martin in Zaventem, where he had seen it in the autumn of 1914, during the retreat that followed the calamitous Battle of Schiplaken, and where miraculously enough, it still hangs today. He had committed every detail to memory that early Sunday afternoon when the war was still young, as he sat before his patron saint in trembling prayer, shaken by what he had been through in the weeks before, in the horror of Schiplaken and Sint-Margriete-Houtem.

Remarkably, his copy is perfectly flawless, and as far as I can tell without actually hanging the two versions side by side, all the colours are correct. Yes, his are a little brighter, as if the original painting had been cleaned. My grandfather's dedication to painting his patron saint echoed the work of his father, who had painted his own patron saint, Francis, in Liverpool. He must have been tremendously gratified to know that he had completed the circle, paying tribute to his lamented father.

In the documentation he saved with his sketches, I found a few pages torn out of the famous *Golden Legend* by Jacobus de Voragine: the story of St Martin, the Roman legionary who became a Christian. Along with all sorts of fascinating facts, de Voragine provides a list of Martin's virtues: humility, dignity in battle, righteousness and patience, devotion to prayer and skill in unmasking demons. My grandfather underlined this last one in red. Martin became the patron saint of soldiers; during battle, the kings of France carried his red cloak into battle. Anthony Van Dyck is also said to have owned such a cloak.

This theme later inspired my grandfather to make a sandstone tympanum in bas-relief, which he mounted over the front door of his small house. He was seventy-two at the time, and very energetic for his age. His great work seems to have slightly softened the pain of losing his wife, allowing him to sublimate his humble origins and family name in the picturesque light of the great Van Dyck. The finished work met with cries of admiration from all who saw it, except for his friend Adolf, who eyed the large painting, pursed his lips, and said, 'I just wouldn't have the patience for that kind of thing – for making copies, I mean.' He gave Urbain's daughter Maria Emelia a sly wink, and the friendship cooled.

When I go to Zaventem on a weekday to see the original painting, it's raining cats and dogs. Soft music is playing in the empty church. I make my way discreetly past the massive columns to the altar on the right side of the church where the painting hangs, trying to imagine him kneeling there in his muddied uniform in October 1914, on the first of the two wooden steps, with his pack, his rifle and his dented mess tin at his side, worn out from his first raw confrontations with the advance of the German armies. Because I am used to his slightly larger copy, the original painting looks a little small, and as I mentioned, the colours are slightly darker. It was painted on seven wide boards joined together and has obviously been restored: the oil paint added later shines a little too brightly, giving the masterpiece too strong a sheen. Furthermore, time and varying degrees of humidity have made the panels bulge slightly, so that you can see the six seams. The Corinthian columns of the altar where the painting hangs are decorated with gilt and faux marble. Above these Louis Quinze touches, the coat of arms of Ferdinand van Boisschot is on prominent display in a gilded half-arch. I notice the strong resemblance between this faux marble and that with which my grandfather covered the high-ceilinged corridor of his house, including the wall where he hung his copy of the painting. Marbling was one of my grandfather's strongest skills; he could decorate doors, walls and columns with wood or marble patterns like an artisan from centuries ago.

A sexton pops out of the woodwork to the right of the altar, eager to help. When he sees that I am studying the painting at length, taking notes and snapping photos, he helpfully switches on a few lights in front of the side altar. I tell him how surprised I am that a masterpiece like this one, a crucial piece of the world's artistic heritage, is hanging here, unprotected and practically anonymous, in a Flemish parish church. He folds his bony hands in a kind of devotion and tells me he was here during the Second World War, when the fragile panels were removed and hidden in a cellar to keep them out of the hands of the Nazis. He gives me a folder to take with me. I check the information about the painting, drive back to the house on the Scheldt to look at the copy that same day, and find myself startled by its bright, clear colours and vigour – the authentic glow that sometimes lies hidden in a copy.

He also made successful copies of other well-known works around that time – such as an odd portrait of a boy with two leashed hounds by Jan Erasmus Quellinus II. The child poses in a showy, girlish outfit: a frilly, shimmering blue and pink dress. It's not an especially gripping piece, but despite its anecdotal, sentimental quality, it shows the hand of a master painter. My grandfather may have chosen this typical product of the Antwerp Baroque simply because of the technical challenge involved in painting the iridescent fabric (and perhaps because of his own girlishness as a little boy, which he sometimes joked about; in the late nineteenth century, boys were often dressed as girls until they were toilet trained, because a dress saved some dirty laundry). I have not been able to figure out when he painted Velázquez's Rokeby Venus, since he did not date his paintings, but the style leads me to believe that it belongs to his early period, probably the 1930s, perhaps even earlier.

But – as if he were preparing for his final work of art – his most successful copy was after a famous portrait: *The Man with the Golden Helmet* in the Gemäldegalerie in Berlin, attributed to Rembrandt for centuries but later discovered not to have been painted by the master, a finding that sent its value plummeting from twenty million Deutschmarks to less than one million. My grandfather never had to hear that sobering news, since it was announced by experts in 1985, four years after his death. Without a doubt, this was his favourite copy. It was so successful that he made several more just like it for friends, and I do not know where all his copies might be found today (for example, I was once astonished to find, in the upstairs taproom of the Brussels restaurant Le Paon Royal, what appeared to be a copy by my grandfather of De Hondecoeter's *Poultry Yard with a White Peacock*, an allegorical painting about the dominance of evil in the world that once inspired me to write an entire book; how it found its way there is a mystery to me; it turned out to be unsigned, and was far inferior in technique to the copy in my possession).

It must have been one St Nicholas Day morning in the late 1950s when I found, among the mandarin oranges, spice biscuits and chocolate figurines on the heaped table, an ingenious little aeroplane, which the generous saint had obviously brought for me that night. It was a kind of biplane made of thin strips of wood, with its body painted blue, its wings red and its tail yellow and black. The wheels were cleverly made from two old coins, large iron twenty-five-cent pieces with holes in the middle. A thin rod ran through those holes, attaching the wheels to the body; the rod also ran through a somewhat larger hole in the body, so that the wheels could turn. Two small rivets held the rod in place. The aeroplane had been sawn with a jigsaw and then filed down, and it was only my unshakeable faith in the white-bearded saint that, for many years, kept me from figuring out that my grandfather had made it by hand for me. So I never thanked him for it, despite all the loving care with which he had constructed it. I do not know what became of the aeroplane, but I assume it was lost somewhere in the dusty pots of soil in the greenhouse, with one wheel missing or one wing broken, tangled up in a ball of string with a loose staple sticking out like a broken paw; I don't know. Decades later, with the vividness common to some dreams of childhood, the image of the aeroplane flashed before my eyes, and I could read letters and numbers on it, which were still clear in my mind when I awoke: DK100710. I wrote them down, believing he must have wanted to make the aeroplane 'realistic' by painting a code name on it. It seemed like a picturesque thought. Later that day, I recalled a few other old memories of lost childhood toys and then forgot about the whole thing.

But as I was reading his memoirs and checking a few facts, I stumbled across the date of Daniel Kinet's death. Kinet, the first pilot whose aeroplane crashed on the grounds of Port Arthur, not far from where my grandfather had seen the nude girl rise from a pool. Kinet crashed on 10 July 1910, at approximately 10 a.m. I remembered my grandfather's failed attempt to visit the clinic where Kinet would die a few days later and reflected on what a hero the man had been to him. DK100710 . . . The code on the little aeroplane turned out to have a secret but genuine meaning; it was his memorial to the hero of Belgian aviation. How many other secrets had I missed? The more I read, the more I had to learn to tolerate the awareness of my ignorance.

In the same way, other clues appeared in my memory, because his memoirs blew away the dust, and I started to understand more and more signs. The first cigarette I ever smoked was a yellowish, foul-smelling oval tube, stolen from a flat, silver cigarette box I found in the narrow drawer of my grandfather's notorious dressing table. I was fifteen and dying to finally smoke my first cigarette. I sat down with my trophy behind some bushes at the far end of the garden and smoked that strange, strong cigarette halfway down. I was immediately overcome with intense nausea, and a few minutes later I threw up. In his memoirs, I read about the silver box of cigarettes given to him by the mysterious Mrs Lamb in Windermere, and I realized that he had held onto them all those years, like a fetish, without touching them – to the best of my knowledge, he never smoked. My little sister liked to wrap herself in a long scarf in those days – doubtless the scarf he had received as a gift from the same woman when he had to return to the front, a scarf that had stretched to mythical proportions in his stories, growing a little longer with each telling. Meanwhile, he let the actual scarf fall apart in an old drawer. That too says something about how he dealt with a past that would not let him go. Clues like these turn out to have been present throughout my childhood, invisible to me, and only by drawing links between my memories and what I read could I begin work on a modest form of restitution, inadequate reparations for my unforgivable innocence in those days.

And suddenly, this image, this scene, as if it were unfolding before my eyes right now: it is a day in spring, April I think, the light is white and low, it must be late morning. He stands on the iron lid of the cistern and explains to me what it really means to be a soldier, telling me I have a lot to learn. As I stand there picking my nose and eating it, I am filled with admiration, and because of the way I blurt out, 'Can you still stand on your head?' he turns his steady gaze on me, sighs, sets down his fedora on the bench by the little wall, and ta-da, a miracle occurs: in one swift bound, a seventy-year-old man vaults into a handstand. His smock falls, partly covering his eyes, but he does not give up. Look, I hear his muffled voice say, and he raises a hand to wave at me, now supporting himself on just one hand and his nearly bald head. I see the legs of his trousers slowly sinking and his white shins poking into the air like beanpoles. His feet are turned slightly outward, away from each other. Before I can recover from my surprise, he is standing up straight in front of me again, wiping the dust from his hands, putting his hat back on his head, and saying, a little red-faced, 'You can do anything you put your mind to.' I nod in silent agreement with the words of my childhood hero and then slink shyly away. He tells me he's off to trim the bushes and makes his exit, whistling, into the garden.

All those years, something kept me from paying the mandatory visit to the endless cemeteries of white gravestones around Ypres and Diksmuide and the painstakingly recreated trenches that offer historically minded visitors the most 'realistic' experience possible. What's the point in standing next to the bridge at Tervaete, I thought, or in Stuivekenskerke, or somewhere in the fields where so many unexploded shells lie rusting in the earth, when I know that nothing can bring me closer to his experiences than the old notebooks on my desk? In the 1980s, when I was living with a girl from that part of Flanders, I would sometimes go for walks there on Sundays, visiting the Käthe Kollwitz Monument, the welcoming interior of Talbot House, Tyne Cot Cemetery, the endless burial grounds, all the things you have to have seen to join the conversation about the First World War and Flanders Fields. I read horrifying books on the Battle of the Somme and the massacre of endless ranks of charging British boys, and I wondered what anyone could add to that kind of horror today.

But it was not until a few years ago, when I visited the Citadel of Dinant with my son, that for half an hour my grandfather's world seemed frighteningly close by. The claustrophobic atmosphere of the reconstructed trenches in the war museum, the dim lighting, the naive but effective simulation of soldiers' lives in the war years – because of that bleak setting, where I had to grope my uncertain way down the slanting paths, I felt a sudden connection to my grandfather's fumbling steps in the dark. I touched the hardened sandbags, saw the scale of the battlefield, the rifles, the clumsy dummies caught like rats in a trap. It had that musty smell peculiar to historical museums. The light from the bare bulbs shone pitilessly over the motionless figures, casting shadows like gloomy stains over the artificial trenches. It was as if I were making my way back to the world of the dead, against the current, and the Eurydice of memory stood up and took me by the hand. As the finely strung philosopher with the hammer once memorably wrote in *The Antichrist*, I can no longer look at paintings without seeing gestures, because I understand that what has touched my own life is not a book of innocence, but a reading saturated with historical guilt.

Now that the end of this story is creeping up on me, I must proceed to the final paintings: to the captivating portrait of Gabrielle, and to the secret nude of her sister, which I did not discover until the last moment. I am approaching them quietly and carefully, like a man in an imaginary museum, cautiously drawing closer with his hands behind his back, removing his glasses from his near-sighted nose, leaning in towards the painting, and smiling at a detail only he can see. There is silence in the gallery of memories; a woman passes behind him, fanning herself with the folder in her hand, indifferent to the stranger with the sheepish smile on his face, staring distractedly, his nose almost touching that old canvas in the crumbling gilt frame.

The portrait of Gabrielle, based on the small black-and-white photograph on her memorial print, has an almost classical quality and rivals some of the finest women's portraits in the realist tradition. She has draped her black mantilla over her grey hair and is wearing her grey cardigan and a white lace blouse fastened with her ivory cameo. She gazes tranquilly at the viewer, utterly at peace with herself. Her eyes tell of halcyon days, days when she sat on the bench in the garden and watched the everyday things around her, which made her happy. The predominant tone of the painting is a lustrous gold, as if a kind of evening light were pouring over her face.

This nearly idealized picture expresses his love and devotion to her, and thus embodies catharsis and the final attainment of harmony. That was no mean feat, considering the manner of her death. A year before she died, she had a stroke. Her recovery was difficult: she woke up with mild dementia and had to learn how to walk and talk and eat all over again. He was caring and devoted, washing, dressing and nursing her every day – she was forced to put aside her prudery, now that it was too late for any carnal intimacy between them. Guiding her through tumble after tumble, he helped her learn to stand on her feet again, to take her first steps once more, as if she were his belated second child. Bit by bit, although her capacity to think and speak was obviously impaired, she became a fairly happy, calm and quiet old lady, drowsing away and somehow making it clear that everything was fine, that *she* was fine, the way things were. Then one morning, sitting in the chair by the window where she often sat, she had her second stroke. Her eyes flew wide open, the veins in her throat bulged menacingly, her neck and face turned purple, she grasped at her throat, gurgling, and fell sideways out of her chair. What frightened me most was the panic that struck my mother and grandfather. Rigid with horror, I looked on until my mother pushed me out of the door, saying it was time to go to school.

That image has stayed with me all my life, and was the last I saw of her; when I returned home that night she had been readmitted to the hospital, where she died a few days later. Her transcendent portrait still gazes at me, untroubled, every time I visit the house. It gives the lie to my tragic memory and yet is so perfectly rendered, so true to life, that it seems even now as if she were on the verge of speaking.

This is, without a doubt, the only great, original painting my grandfather ever produced, as if his entire life had been a preparation for that cathartic portrait. At the same time, I could not help wondering whether, as he painted Gabrielle, he had ever thought about how her younger sister Maria Emelia would have looked at that age, if she had lived. The secret image of Maria Emelia that he carried inside himself could never age, while Gabrielle grew older, as if in her sister's place, almost like the portrait of that old dandy Dorian Gray. So I have come to see my grandmother's portrait as being like one of those old-fashioned pictures from my childhood that change as you move them, which you could keep turning back and forth as long as your heart desired: two sisters, the elder still shining, apocryphally, like a light in the eyes of the younger, painted after both of them had died.

I cannot imagine that, after all this time, I will find the portrait of the other sister, carefully hidden. But a week later, I drive back to the house on the riverbank to ask my aged father about all sorts of circumstances and particulars. He has dug out a cardboard box from a half-concealed crawlspace behind a partition in the attic, where my nursery once had been. The key is missing; we carefully open the box with a thin screwdriver. It contains dozens of photographs: pictures of my grandfather's parents, for example, which give me my first glimpse of Franciscus and Céline as a young couple, posing stiffly next to a small wooden pillar and a backdrop of a mountainous landscape sometime around the turn of the century; passport photographs of my grandfather at the age of thirty; and his 'fire card' for veterans who came under enemy fire in the Great War. I learn that starting in 1938, two years after his early retirement from the Belgian Railways, this card entitled him to a modest supplemental disability pension of a few hundred old Belgian francs (and I later discover his name in the endless compendia of fire card holders, in vol. 37–38, p. 14; two lines further down was a Charles Martien of Gentbrugge, but I haven't found out whether he was any relation). Digging deeper into the cardboard box, my father and I also find a folder of postcards that my grandfather sent to his mother from Windermere in the Lake District; innumerable photos of relatives; a few memorial cards for soldiers; a beautiful wooden case containing a pair of brass compasses and a silk ribbon bookmark finely embroidered with a cross, a crown and the epigram *Bear the cross, and wear the crown*; a photograph of a pretty English nurse from Liverpool, signed, *Yours sincerely, Maud Forrester*; photographs from military school (a flat cap and blue coat with gleaming buttons); and a card providing admission to all Belgian museums, issued by the 'General Department of Fine Arts and Letters'. I also find the fragments of his father's shattered watch; next to them is a bullet with the date '1916' carved into it clumsily with a pocket knife.

But above all, again and again, I find photographs of a young woman who could not be anyone but Maria Emelia. My suspicions are confirmed when I find a photograph of her and Gabrielle together, almost like twins and yet so different in attitude and personality, each with one hand on the shoulders of their mother, who sits regally in the centre. Then I find about a dozen blurry copies of the half with Maria Emelia, most of them enlarged to a size slightly smaller than a postcard (about 5 × 3 inches). And finally, in a closed envelope at the very bottom of the box, there is a crisp, beautiful frontal portrait photograph that leaves no room for doubt: this is Maria Emelia's face. For the first time, I take in her serene features, the countenance that holds the key to my grandfather's secret passion, the young woman who could have been my grandmother, who could have passed down some part of herself to me. I take in her straight nose, her pale yet sensitive eyes, the dark hair in a severe bun, the finely pointed chin, the long neck over the opening in her simple white blouse. After a moment, I realize that this woman could never have been my grandmother; if my grandfather had married the woman of his dreams, I simply would not exist. She represents the impossibility of a different me.

The various sizes and dimensions of the many prints clearly show that they were not all made at the same time, so these decisions must not have been made casually. To obtain copies of a photo for which he had no negative, he would have had to go to the 'photographic portraitist' in the square by the Sacred Heart parish church, half an hour's walk away. Then he would have needed to wait a week for the new negative and the prints and to spend another hour going there and back. Why so many prints of the same photograph? And where is the negative? Did he always dream of painting her portrait but lack the courage? How many hundreds of times did these greyish photos pass through his hands? Why was the largest, best-quality portrait in a sealed envelope? I do not know.

Recalling the vague suspicion that came to me as I was standing in front of Velázquez's Rokeby Venus in the National Gallery in London, I ask my father if he has any idea where the copy of that painting is now. I seem to recollect seeing it somewhere in the attic as a child. We ascend the attic staircase, now rickety with age, and somewhere in a dust-covered corner we find twenty unframed paintings, which must have been stacked there for decades. The next-to-last one is the copy of the Rokeby Venus. We remove it from the stack, blow off the dust, and there she lies, nude and in quiet pride, in all her down-to-earth elegance: Velázquez's Venus.

And I'll be damned – the blood rushes to my head . . . The face that regards us in the mirror is not that of Velázquez's model but, unmistakably, the face I have just recently learned to recognize from the greyish photo in the envelope, the face with the pale, luminous eyes, the face of Maria Emelia. That explains the difference in hair colour that struck me in London . . . With a dizzying rush, I realize that this copy, however close the resemblance may be, was never a copy, but a concealed act of love; mustering all his skill as a copyist, my grandfather very discreetly altered the details so that he could briefly imagine his dead love in the nude – his greatest sin, the object of his deepest desire, which gnawed at his damaged soul his whole life long. He did not accomplish this by painting her body, which he had never seen, but by transforming the face in the reflection into hers – a face that the mirror isolates from the body. And it was this double figure that lay before us, nude and vibrant on a dusty old canvas: Velázquez's Venus with the face of the idealized Maria Emelia. In other words, what appeared to be a mere imitation concealed the original of his passion, and the charade of painting thus became the allegory of the hidden love he could never forget. For some people, no life is long enough to recover from the shock of love, not even if they live to be nearly a hundred.

Then I realize why this painting was stored in the attic for decades; the sight of it must have been unbearable to the pious Gabrielle. Who knows – perhaps this portrait of her sister as a nude Venus, this blasphemous betrayal of conjugal love, was the actual reason for her sexual denial. I will never know. After I return home, I see that the photograph in the envelope shows vague traces of a grid, drawn in faint pencil and later rubbed out.

One morning in the unseasonably cool May of 2012, I decided to go ahead and visit the Tervaete Loop, more to ease my conscience than in any real expectation of discovering what I had already learned long before from my grandfather's memoirs.

I have always been fond of the silty smell, like the memory of the vanished sea, that fills the polder landscape on some misty days – earth as flat as water, as silent and unfathomable as a sunken sea. Brackish water in the streams, silt in the air, the heavy odour of land and livestock, the deeply comforting simplicity of soil, the consolation of that self-sufficient rural life. In the midst of a landscape like this one, tens of thousands of Flemish and German, French and British lads lay in the mud, which sucked and swallowed, dried and crumbled, pulverized and cracked, and slaked its thirst in the sudden showers until it was wet and chilly and sour-smelling again – the polders, on certain days in May or in September, with lapwings darting through the air above the fields, the tart smell of poplars, the pigsties, the horizon all around. It cast a spell over the senses.

Tervaete is hardly even a hamlet. All my GPS can find is Tervaetestraat in the municipality of Diksmuide. If you drive there by way of the tiny village of Stuivekenskerke, you pass a stately country house with an archway, a broad drive and a handsome courtyard, an oasis of calm and genteel seclusion. There is now a hotel there, called Kasteelhoeve ('Castle-Farm') Viconia; in 1914, the property was known as Vicogne Farm. I walk down the paths lined with immaculate hedgerows and learn that the Germans briefly occupied the farm during the war and planned to set up headquarters there. The farm could have played a pivotal role in their plans to cross the blood-soaked loop in the Yser, just a few hundred yards away. It was blasted to rubble by the Belgian troops on 24 October 1914, shortly after the bridge over the Yser and the church of Stuivekenskerke received the same treatment. The obliteration of those three strategic points brought the German advance to a halt. Since my grandfather's memories of the Battle of the Yser date from between 17 and 24 October 1914, he must have been involved in this phase of the battle, and the farmhouse he mentions may have been Vicogne Farmstead. In the battle for this farm, the enemy troops included a soldier named Adolf Schicklgruber, later known as Hitler.

The road to the river is deserted. As soon as you reach the bank of the Yser, you can see the Tervaete bridge, which formed the boundary between two worlds: Occupied Europe and Allied Europe. There is now an information board, which informs me that 'Tervaete' is related to *vate*, a word for 'mud flat', 'a ford in the Yser Valley'.

How exposed everything is here, how flat and open, with no place to hide . . . All you could do was burrow, like rats and moles, it was your only chance: a refuge from the endless open sky. The horizon lies at about three-eighths earth and five-eighths air, the golden ratio, the ideal of landscape painters and aesthetes. Deep below the vast sky are poplars, pastures, mud flats, salt marshes, creeks, and then, straight ahead of me, the deadly S-curve in the river. A tranquil, treacherous landscape.

Just past the bridge, with the regular, delicate clucking of a few moorhens in the background, I find a small memorial. I take a picture of the inscription, so that I can type it up later:

DEDICATED TO THE FALLEN SOLDIERS
OF THE
2ND BATTALION
1ST GRENADIERS
WHO PERISHED ON 22 OCTOBER 1914
IN THE CHARGE ORDERED
BY MAJOR S.A.
COUNT HENDRIK D'OULTREMONT.

Gilt letters and a cardboard cross with a plastic rose – each time I try to set it upright, it promptly blows over in the gentle breeze. Bulls bellow in a stall across the river. In the reeds by the water, I hear a sound I have not heard for decades: the crazed rejoicing of a reed warbler. And even a cuckoo, clearly audible on the other side of the river – another bird you don't hear much any more. An old superstition claims it will be a good year if you hear the cuckoo calling in the spring.

This landscape, so fresh and unspoiled. Stillness. Peace.

These are the soft, distant sounds that he must have heard too, that all the soldiers waiting in mortal fear must have heard: an idyll in hell.

The mute landscape, indifferent nature, the charm, the oblivion of the earth, oblivion in the calm rush of the current that once divided life from death. All the birds of this misty spring morning are like the souls of strange beings, calling out something I can't understand. Mystery of time and space. What a strange planet we've grown used to living on.

A small ship called the *Doesburg* chugs past, and the high-spirited Dutch passengers wave merrily at the Belgian holding a notebook and staring into the river. Perhaps to them I am one of the charming locals. A few seagulls have come inland in search of food; something like a sleeve is bobbing in the brown water, just under the surface. A delivery van speeds down the narrow road; a dog starts up in the distance; young ash trees line the canal; the cows in the tall grass seem immersed in the green of a painting from Constable's day. With the strange loop in the river, you can't always tell the other side from this one; it must have been a treacherous business, trying to figure out what was happening where. You might see the point of a helmet and think it was sticking out of the grass on your side, when in fact the German hadn't crossed the river. Or the opposite: death could creep up unawares and seize you by the throat, roaring something in Goethe's language. Blossoming hawthorns, morning glories, buttercups, bulrushes, tansies, but no poppies anywhere, no splotches of red in the greenery. *In Flanders Fields no poppies blow.* Nature has shown a little restraint after all, with help from the farmers' chemical sprays.

Nothing rustles as peacefully as poplars by the water on a cool still day in May. Cormorants, coots and grebes drift over the water with their quirky crests. A heron on a post does not fly away as I approach, but stands and waits and seems to be pondering its own inability to ponder.

The Tervaete bridge has a bell, which jingles when the bridge opens to let boats through. You can hear the bell from hundreds of yards away; you can hear the cockerel on the farm further down the road. Everything is audible, clear and quiet. What a strange, paradisiacal trap this must have been, just before it was bombed to rubble and mud – the union of life and death in the sounds of the earth. I imagine alien beings landing on our planet at this exact moment and hearing these sounds for the first time. To brains never previously exposed to the song of the reed warbler, it must seem hallucinatory, magical, a source of ecstasy. What a miracle; how could you invent a thing like that?

I follow the deserted road along the river for a few hundred yards. There is only one place in this landscape to take cover: behind the dyke on the other side. From the Stuivekenskerke side, where the dyke is flat, this formed a major threat, because the goddamned Germans could hide behind it. You had to fire shells over it in a high arc, and then shoot blindly and hope for a good Flemish harvest. The Belgians returned fire from unpredictable places, moving quickly behind the earth wall and through the dense maze of trenches. It must have caused the Germans no end of frustration, which they took out on sentries whose attention had strayed.

The road along the dyke now seems to be little more than a favourite route for amateur cyclists. With clockwork regularity, I see them shoot by, huffing and puffing, with their plastic goggles on and their eyes on the asphalt, always wearing the uniform of the modern age: a stylish racing outfit, pricey athletic shoes, a flashy helmet, and an expensive bicycle like a whistling bird, clenched between thighs of steel. The athlete as the great-grandson of the soldier in his cumbersome fatigues. Same age, different planet.

As I walk on, I can see approximately where my grandfather must have risked his life storming the dyke. Once I have passed the loop, I start to understand how they could keep a floating platform hidden from the Germans for days, and how they could be provisioned from the other side without alerting the enemy to their presence. Literally everything comes down to that S-bend in the river. Battlefield logic, a game of chess with chance and death.

Past the bend, there is a sign: 'Anglers, show you care about our environment! Please use only the marked angling locations and do not trample the riverside plants.' Here, where not one leaf of one plant has been disturbed, the roots grow deep into the earth, which is rich and bountiful, thanks to the strange fertilizer called man, an environmentally friendly miracle substance that biodegrades easily into humus. To think that this remote, eerily silent place could become the setting for such horrors – it shows once again how any logic of war is utterly opposed to every natural fact, to ordinary time, to the usual course of things, which has no ultimate aim and retains very little of what human beings do.

Another boat approaches, this one full of schoolchildren and their teachers; to my astonishment, it's called the *Star of the Yser*. The children prattle cheerfully and wave at the figure on the bank – who even waves back. What a peaceful flatland. Just climb a tree and you could see the enemy trenches. One sole problem: there were no trees left, only pits and mounds.

A flattened kestrel is stuck to the asphalt, a cyclist whizzes over it, a few feathers drift into the air. Was it Armando who came up with the term 'guilty landscape'? Or was it Claude Lanzmann, with those insidious forests in his film *Shoah*? In any case, this landscape could be a painting by Anselm Kiefer, a landscape with the invisible scars of a submerged catastrophe. On second thoughts, that's not it, this is not Kiefer's style at all. The brushwork is too delicate, too tender; I can see every flower, each blade of grass. It's one of my grandfather's romantic paintings, of course, strange that I didn't think of it before, just the kind of thing you might expect from an old-fashioned, precise, partly colour-blind painter – gaga for green, obviously, with those marvellous verdant hues everywhere you look and no red poppy splotches to throw him off.

Past the spawning grounds for the perch, the common roach, the white bream and the gudgeon (another convenient information sign, in green), I find – at the side of the road, as if placed here for my grandfather's sake – a small shrine to the Virgin:

O MORTAL FEET
DO NOT PASS BY
WITHOUT HAILING MARY
THE MOTHER MOST HIGH

As I am wondering how a foot could hail Mary, a tractor rumbles by, with those strange, insect-like protuberances used to poison the fields. No poppies any more. It was all so long ago, a century ago; I am walking here with his DNA in my body, lonelier than alone and too late for it all. And again, the cuckoo, close now, as loud as in dreams, making me flinch.

It flies over the bushes in the cool spring air, calling as it sometimes did in my childhood. It copies the cuckoo clock in the dim middle room, and my grandfather pulls up the brass weights and says to my mother something I can't make out, something about time.

In his final years, there was one piece of music that moved him more than any other, transporting him to a far-off, imaginary place where we could not reach him until the final note had died away: the ballet music from Schubert's *Rosamunde*. I don't know exactly what he found so moving about this slightly saccharine babbling brook of a melody; I have no idea if he had particular memories of the music – if he had heard it at a concert he went to with someone, or if something had happened back in the 1950s just as it was pouring out of the brown radio relay box screwed to the wall. There were no detailed programme guides in those days, so when *Rosamunde* came on the radio, it was usually a surprise. Something like a sob would run through him, he would clap his hands to his face, we would hear his laboured panting, and then he would pull himself together, breathing slowly and deliberately, until – as wheezy as his father by this stage – he found a rhythm that reconciled his body to the shock of recognition he'd just experienced.

It begins with sprightly ballet music like a fairy dance, followed by the darker inflections of the men's response, culminating in a scrap of melody and then merging into the dancing rhythm again. But it was the Entr'acte No. 3, above all, that provoked his strange passion, an emotion that made the world around him fade away. In this andantino, melancholy mingles so naturally with a sheltered, secure feeling, casting such a veil of nostalgia and distant beauty over my childhood years, that whenever I see one of his many charcoal drawings of a female figure, cloaked in *sfumato*, fading from the yellowed paper under the dusty glass, I see *him*, seated in the middle of a landscape he drew himself, somewhere near an elusive German spring in an imaginary German forest. He has his fedora on, and I see that he is breathing heavily. But no, I hear nothing, nothing at all, until somewhere in the distance the first notes of that andantino sound, and images appear, images of a grey, silent time when secrets were a normal way of life, giving it shape, hitting it hard with the hidden softness of their unvoiced desire. The Ballet No. 2 seemed to calm him down again; this is the andantino in G major with which *Rosamunde* ends, a return to pastoral lightness after melancholy – his most fundamental mood. Maybe Schubert's personality made him the perfect kindred spirit. His gloominess, his sublimated erotic yearnings, and his penchant for turning inward, a product of his tragic life, formed a constellation of traits that spoke to my grandfather – Schubert had remained poor and underappreciated all his life, and his creative development had suffered from the threat of conscription. He bore the first name of my grandfather's father, who had also died young, and there was a blend of devil-may-care and deep feeling in his music, the grim courage to face life's reversals combined with hypersensitivity, character traits that found expression in this innocent-sounding andantino. Too many Sundays to count, he heard these strains and everything around us fell silent. Or was it just a couple of times, which my memory has clumped together into a life?

All my questions must go unanswered. But when I heard – on the very day I had taken the box with the photograph of Maria Emelia from my father's silent house and looked that young woman in the eyes for the first time – when I heard, on that day of all days, during the drive home, the andantino from *Rosamunde* playing on the car radio, it gave me such a peculiar shock that I almost drove off the road. My heart started pounding so hard that the blood thumped in my temples, and when I parked by the roadside and opened the tin box again with trembling hands and held the photograph between my fingers, something rose up inside me, as if following the lead of my dead grandfather, who seemed to possess my body like a tender demon and draw me completely into his emotions, into the world that had always been closed to me, and I'll be damned if I didn't sit there with a lump in my throat, biting my lower lip, as the voice on the radio repeated the title of the barely seven-minute andantino and moved on to Paganini, a composer whose virtuoso antics I have always abhorred. In the portrait of Schubert painted by Wilhelm August Rieder in 1875 (almost fifty years after Schubert's death, I might add, after a pastel made a half century earlier), the composer is shown with a quill in his right hand, his elbow resting on a musical score. Twenty-eight years old, he has a confident gleam in his eye, looks healthy and warm-hearted, and wears a large black bow tie over a spotless white shirt. This was around the time that he was offered the position of court composer, but rejected it to preserve his freedom, and his pose shows the same assurance my grandfather tried to project in the somewhat unsuccessful self-portrait where he clutches his easel in his left hand.

Painting grew more and more difficult for him in his final years. He was afflicted with gout, stiff joints and cramping hands, which allowed the brush to slip between his fingers, as well as glaucoma, which clouded his vision and forced him to resort to his sense of touch, sometimes spreading the paint into an impressionistic blob with his

fingers, despite all his diatribes against the modern 'daubers' and their finger-paintings – my grandfather, the minor master of devotion to painted detail, the man who had once reproduced every minuscule vein of the delicate white flower *Saxifraga urbium*, sometimes known as Painters' Sorrow. His small, frugal paintings showed odd smudges where faces should have been; he painted naive little cars with bulging tyres on the road along the Scheldt outside his window, with the clumsiness of a child who has just begun to experiment with oil paint, a strange document of fingertips gone blind, fumbling and trembling as they slid across the canvas. Another time, he tried to paint a half-nude courtier, a blotchy copy after a reproduction of Titian that turned into a kind of degenerate Degas of a blurry ghost. But he could not see the painful irony in all these little tragedies. Rigid with back pain, he would shuffle step by tiny step over the staggered, colourful tiles of the kitchen floor. Seated in his rocking chair, he would hold the newspaper up against his face, as if he wanted to sniff the news right off it. He had less appetite than a small bird and often sang softly to himself. At his advanced age, he could no longer put on or remove his socks on his own, or cut his brittle toenails. Towards the end, he could no longer wash himself. His daughter received his permission, after lengthy prodding, to put him in a bathtub once a week and take care of his grooming. Sometimes he wanted to keep his old fedora on, because he felt a draught, always and everywhere, even on warm, windless days, as if cracks had opened up in life itself; a fragile, naked old codger in a black hat, in the bath, his daughter the only one who could see or feel the scars and indentations on his back.

The doctor often had to be called out during the night, when shortness of breath threatened to asphyxiate my grandfather. Dr Rombouts, an elderly physician with impressive eyebrows and a grey Beethoven coiffure, dabbled in sculpture in his spare time, and the two old gents would sit together in the gentle glow of an old-fashioned nightlight, talking softly about the anatomy of the ideal human form, the Vitruvian man, and the mathematical proportions of the Palladian arch. Just before the first light of dawn, the doctor would return home as he had arrived: in his spotless suit, his large tie knotted loosely and with verve. As he passed through the doorway, he would turn to the aged man, who was breathing gratefully now that the cortisone injection had kicked in, and say, 'Now you be a good fellow, Sergeant-Major Martien.' And my grandfather would let out a kind of wheezy giggle and nod his head like a horse at a fence. By 7:30 a.m., he would be in his chair, waiting for his daughter to finish dressing him so that after his coffee and simple slice of bread and butter he could sit at his table, his pen clasped between his ageing fingers, and write the things I would not read until decades later, or he would try, with shaking hands and profound dedication, to sketch the contours of a medieval face, and then say, looking up from his blotted page, 'That Dürer really was a genius, don't you think?'

When I was a child, he would sometimes sing a song in English:

> *My grandfather's clock*
> *Was too large for the shelf,*
> *So it stood ninety years on the floor . . .*

He would tap out the rhythm of the closing lines on his tray:

> *But it stopped (tum tum) short (tum tum)*
> *Never to go again*
> *When the old man died (boom – boom).*

I later heard the song on a vinyl record given to him by one of his brothers, but didn't realize what it was trying to tell me, all those long years of slow-witted innocence.

*

288

There is a great deal on this planet to arouse an enduring sense of wonder, especially when seen in the light of one's impending departure. The way molecules move in water, for instance, yielding the subtlest play of shifting light as evening falls over the sea in a southern bay – say, on the rocky beach of the Italian coastal town of Rapallo, when the wind has dropped and the pink of the evening clouds performs endless variations with the deepening blue of the sky mirrored in the sea – and how living beings with eyes and consciousness, two incomprehensibly complex adaptations to this whole wondrous biosphere, can take it all for granted and go on breathing, flawlessly designed for just this sort of system.

In the last few years before his death, my grandfather, a highly trained observer, still saw much to surprise him. If anything, his surprise seems to have deepened over the years. He possessed that wondrous capacity of the very old to take an inexplicable joy in each new day simply because he was still there, and could still be part of something that far surpassed him and seemed to bear him up. I would even venture to say that in those final years, for the first time, he experienced a happiness free of care. Yet little of that can be found in the stately gloom of his self-portrait. He depicted himself hat in hand, wearing a white shirt with his signature black bow tie and a midnight-blue jacket. The look in his eyes is severe, or even glassy, and because the overall effect in no way compares to the subtle, vibrant impression made by the portrait of his wife, this self-portrait, which hangs beside it, appears somewhat vacant and soulless. While he put everything into her portrait that he had wanted to give her, he emptied himself, so to speak, and even with the help of his mirror – the same one in which he confronted his image, day after day – he proved unable to bring himself to life, however deeply he stared into his own eyes. The wordless pathos of the artist's failed attempts to paint himself is another secret that only gradually revealed itself to me over the years, and when I look at the two portraits now, I see a reprise of the silent tragedy that bound the two of them together all their lives.

Strikingly, he painted a second self-portrait a few years later, this time with his painting of Gabrielle in the background (and a still life on the other side, a faintly ironic touch). Here, too, he is bare-headed, as if he has removed his hat in front of the mirror. He looks us full in the face. In one hand is his palette, with his thumb sticking through the thumb hole. The odd thing is that he holds this palette in front of him stiffly, as if it were a heraldic shield on which he is pointing out secret symbols with his brush, a means of accounting for himself. It seems like anything but the romantic attribute of the precise painter he had always been. His attitude no longer shows the same severity; instead, he looks to me like a kind of Douanier Rousseau, the naive painter of dream animals and exotic leaves. The look in his eyes is no longer glassy, but penetrating; his pose seems artificial, but there's something so touching about it. His shoulders have become so small. At the centre of the composition are his bright blue eyes with their piercing look. The hand looks like a young man's, and the brush seems to rest in his fingers almost weightlessly, just like the feather pen in Schubert's hand.

Where he failed in his self-portraits, he triumphed in his copy of the man with the golden helmet. This austere portrait of a retired military man, the darkness around his head, the spectacular illumination that lights up the helmet with a golden glow – this is my grandfather in his final years, precisely as I remember him. And again, he has transformed the copy into a masquerade: amid the features from the original painting, the look in the eyes is unmistakably his, the way he would stare into space when he thought no one was watching, thinking about God knows what. And while he could not expel the soldier from his first self-portrait and thus failed to do himself justice, he pulls off an extraordinary victory of the painter over the soldier in his copy of this pseudo-Rembrandt – a cliché of the art world, reproduced by countless amateurs. The truth in life often lies buried in places we do not associate with authenticity. Life is more subtle, in this respect, than linear human morality. It goes to work like a painter-copyist, using illusion to depict the truth.

This paradox was the constant in his life, as he was tossed back and forth between the soldier he had to be and the artist he'd wished to become. War and turpentine. The tranquillity of his final years made it possible for him to slowly overcome his traumas. Praying to Our Lady of the Seven Sorrows, he found peace. On the eve of his death, he went to bed with the words, 'I was so happy today, Maria.' His daughter nodded and gave him a goodnight kiss. He went to his room.

There he placed his fedora on the table by the window, as he did every night. He removed his smock, untied his black silk bow tie, and hung it carefully over the arm of the chair at his bedside. He took off his white shirt, and then his undershirt, revealing the blue indentations in his back, the scars of the brutal years in the iron foundry. And when he took off his long underpants, he uncovered another bluish indentation, this one in his sagging underbelly, right next to his groin, and yet another one on his skinny thigh. The proud badges of his heroic acts, inscribed in his body. He put on his long flannel nightshirt and went to bed. In the early morning, he must have fallen ill. He threw up in the large white enamel bucket beside his bed – just a little gall, really, not even food, but the kind of fluid that seems to come straight from some bad dream. Then he lay down again, a little sulky, a little wheezy. In his dream he got stuck in a large shrub somewhere, a bush on the verge of blowing away, with very thin branches and thorns. Like a wounded beast, he hung there, with his arms and legs spread like an animal splayed open on a ladder, and stopped breathing. All the lights in his head dimmed and dissolved into a dark, unknown space. The foolhardy hero of the Yser front, who had risked his life time and again under enemy fire, died peacefully, almost seventy years later, in his sleep. His daughter found him a couple of hours later, with a perfectly calm expression on his face, his lips slightly parted as if the last thing he'd seen in his life had come as a pleasant surprise. Sunlight poured in through the east window, in the garden the irises were blooming a deep blue, and Whitsun bells were chiming all around them. My mother hesitantly touched him. He was still warm, she later said, crying.

So, only a scrap himself now in a wood of memories, he rises, lighter than a plume of smoke on the wind. At the gates of his long-awaited heaven, although itching to see his loved ones, he stands stiffly to attention and waits for admission, as if facing the army doctor in the barracks again.

Sergent-Major Marshen? St Peter finally asks, leafing through the interminable list of wounded veterans.

Non, mon commandant. Je m'appelle Mar-tien, *pas Mar*-shen, *à vos ordres.*

He salutes.

Credits

Image credits: **p. 17**: portrait of Arthur Schopenhauer, University Library Frankfurt am Main, Archives Centre; **p. 20**: *The Slaughtered Ox* by Rembrandt Harmenszoon van Rijn, 1655 © photo by Leemage/ Getty Images; **p. 28**: *The Toilet of Venus* (The Rokeby Venus) by Diego Velázquez, c.1648 © photo by M. Carrieri, De Agostini/Getty Images; **p. 48**: *The Skaters* by Emile Claus, Royal Museum for Fine Arts Antwerp, Museum of Fine Arts Ghent © photo by Hugo Maertens, Art in Flanders, www.lukasweb.be; **p.56**: portrait of Peter Benoit, Royal Museum for Fine Arts Antwerp, Museum of Fine Arts Ghent © photo by Hugo Maertens, Art in Flanders, www.lukasweb. be; **p. 67**: *Il Quarto Stato* by Giuseppe Pellizza da Volpedo, Associazione Pellizza da Volpedo; **p.243**: portrait of a young woman (La Bella) by Palma il Vecchio © photo by Heritage Images/Getty Images; **p. 263**: painting of St Martin dividing his coat by Anthony Van Dyck, c.1621, The Church of St Martin, Zaventem, Belgium; **p. 286**: portrait of Franz Schubert by Wilhelm August Rieder, 1875 © photo by Leemage/UIG/Getty Images; **p. 292**: portrait of the man with the golden helmet, attributed to the circle of Rembrandt, c. 1650 © photo by Dea Picture Library/De Agostini/Getty Images.

All other images from the author's personal collection.

Quotations: **p. vii**: from *All Quiet on the Western Front* by Erich Maria Remarque (translated by Brian Murdoch), published by Bodley Head,